Now is the Time of
~~PEACE, FREE LOVE, FLOWER POWER~~

MONSTERS

AN ABSOLUTELY GRIPPING PSYCHOLOGICAL THRILLER WITH A SHOCKING TWIST

Now is the Time of

~~PEACE, FREE LOVE, FLOWER POWER~~

MONSTERS

AN ABSOLUTELY GRIPPING PSYCHOLOGICAL THRILLER WITH A SHOCKING TWIST

from the award-winning author of The Little Woods

a.g. mock

EPOCH
THRILLERS

AGMock.com
EpochThrillers.com

First edition, Epoch Thrillers, October 2024.

Library of Congress PCN: on file with Publisher
ISBN: 978-1-7362919-7-9 | eBook
ISBN: 978-1-7362919-8-6 | paperback
ISBN: 978-1-7362919-9-3 | hardcover

Published by Epoch Thrillers in the United States
Epoch Thrillers and its raven imprint are trademarks of Epoch Thrillers

EPOCH THRILLERS
AGMock.com | EpochThrillers.com

ET 10 9 8 7 6 5 4 3 2

this one's for those who sometimes struggle
within the maze of their own convoluted minds

CONTENT WARNING

This book is for fans of the psychological thriller and/or horror genre. It may contain intense content and themes. Please note that in order to avoid spoilers, I choose not to preface my novels with specific trigger warnings. From this point on, please read at your own risk.

~ THANK YOU, AND ENJOY THE RIDE ~

"The old world is dying,

and the new world

struggles to be born:

Now is the Time of Monsters."

—paraphrased from the prison diaries
of Antonio Gramsci

) (

"He who fights with monsters
should be careful to not become one."

—Friedrich Nietzsche

Archived recording of the Gemini's actual voice,
courtesy of the Federal Bureau of Investigations
archive on kidnappings and serial killings:

TO LISTEN, SCAN THE QR CODE IN THE REEL

Case File 7 —63; Audio Document 7 —63—1

)(

The Gemini

)(

1

) (

THE POLAROID CLICKED, a flash of brilliance igniting the night. A negative afterimage swam across his blinking eyes as the camera's distinctive whir and grind spat out a thick, glossy square of paper.

Slipping through his fingers, what would soon become a photograph wafted to the floor. As it dropped through the darkness, its descent was captured when another click whitened the room; another mechanical whir filled the silence; another square dropped from the instant camera's rollers.

Already developing between their chemical sheets, the photos slowly appearing would preserve this feeling forever.

She lay unconscious upon the floor, her strawberry-blonde hair in a subtle bouffant spilling from a bright green headband. Having been carefully combed and positioned by the man just so, it framed her sculpted face and flowed gently over her shoulders.

He'd also wiped and tidied the smudged crimson of her lips before perfectly repainting their pouty contours.

Though incapable of processing what was happening to her,

the woman's eyes—those clear, bright green eyes—had remained open as her breaths came fast and shallow. He knew the Polaroids would capture that emptiness and fail to do justice to this occasion when he relived it later—

again and again

—and that just wouldn't do.

So he closed her eyes with a gentleness associated with great intimacy, careful not to disturb her smoky eyeshadow.

Or those long, enhanced lashes.

He did this despite the mascara streaks that ran down the woman's face. Traces of black lightning. These he never wiped away because, truth be known, they excited him more than just about anything else: those salty runs told a story.

There. That was better.

With her eyes closed, the woman was again perfect. Wanton. Waiting. Willing to be whatever he wanted her to be.

She was his now.

Only his.

Always and forever.

Another click. A blinding flash. The tell-tale whir.

From the rain-soaked street, the living room window of number 8213 pulsed a final time. Brilliance blanched the room.

Now darkness.

With all but one of the ten photographic squares discharged, the window was again an inconspicuous void, like so many others that lined the street like vacuous eyes. The fact that this particular one had been strobing bright white made little difference.

The residents of West Summerdale Street hadn't noticed.

One way or another.

)(

Sheila McCabe was new to the neighborhood, having moved in

only months before. Knocking on every door on the street with a smile and a batch of her famous lemon drop cookies, Sheila had made a deliberate point of introducing herself within her first month of living there. After all, as a single mom Sheila felt it was important to make new friends with whom she and her daughter could share this next chapter of their adventure.

Lord knows, life can be tough enough at the best of times. Having a caring support network can make all the difference.

It takes a village.

Now, as her brutal and methodical murder was being immortalized in instant photos by the very man who was perpetrating it, those same families were concerned with nothing but clearing away their dinner plates so they could settle down in front of their TVs. Entranced by Goldie Hawn in shiny white go-go boots and psychedelic dress, giggling to the punchline of her own jokes on *Rowan & Martin's Laugh-In,* most of the residents saw nothing.

Most.

But not all.

One woman, Gladys Noble of 8220, had caught one of the unusual flashes from the corner of her eye while calling out for Mr. Whiskers from her front stoop. But then came a rumbling of faraway thunder and Gladys gave no further thought to what surely must have been a flash of distant lightning. Swooping her wayward feline into her arms, Gladys promptly returned to the safety of her modest two-bedroom midcentury home.

Across the street and three doors down, the man in Sheila McCabe's home cared little whether the flashes of his camera were noticed or not.

Ignoring the developing squares of glossy paper now cast about his feet, he stepped softly toward Sheila and knelt before her naked body. She was bound by decorative rope tiebacks from the curtains he'd torn from the window. Her ankles were tied to one another; her wrists tethered so that her hands rested upon her abdomen as if clasped together in prayer.

Extending his finger to touch her, the man reached slowly—*oh so slowly*—savoring the exquisite anticipation with intention.

When his fingertip was all but an inch away, he paused.

Wait...

...wait...

okay—

—now.

He gasped as he made contact, the air escaping his lips in a sigh of ecstasy as his fingertip barely brushed Sheila's smooth ivory skin. Now he allowed a second finger to touch her. Then a third. He played these over her left arm, cherishing the sensation of her soft, transparent hairs beneath his fingers.

His stroke halted at the woman's wrist.

Thin and perfect, it was adorned by a petite silver wristwatch. The man delighted in the cool sensation of the watch's metal firmness; its polished crystal face.

Such a titillating contrast to the woman's warm, satin skin.

Now playing his fingertips over the slight bump of her wrist, he began to tremble as he stroked the outside of her hand. Her pinky finger was short and thin and so wonderfully delicate, and he pressed the tip of his own to it. Running his finger around it in small, sensual loops, he softly moaned in anticipation.

Now the man closed his eyes.

Moving with great forethought from the woman's pinky to her ring finger, he etched in his mind a permanent memory of the way it felt when he touched her silver wedding band. Cool and smooth, the ring was so deliciously wide that she must be very, *very* married indeed, and a grin lit upon his face as wide as that ring seemed upon Sheila's finger.

The expression twisted into something beyond joy when he again caught sight of the mascara runs down her cheeks. Oh, how those tears had poured as the woman begged. She offered him anything—*anything*—he wanted…if he would only promise not to harm her child.

Caressing the wedding ring and the woman's long, slender finger, he thought about this desperate pleading as he unzipped his trousers and touched himself until he came.

This time, he granted himself permission to ejaculate over the ring; between the woman's fingers; across the back of her hand. Despite being of a similar age, he called out to her as though she were his mommy.

He was still erect when he pulled the serrated pruning blade across the soft, supple skin of her wrist. It rasped its distinctive duotone as he pulled then pushed; pulled then pushed; the saw blade satisfying its hunger as it chewed through her bones. As it did, the woman began to stir. Her eyes fluttering. Spasming. Then the unmistakable stench rose to the man's nostrils: a smell like teeth at the mercy of a dentist's grinder as the sawblade grew hot from the friction.

After detaching the woman's left hand with the greatest of care, the man removed Sheila's gold peace sign pendant from her neck. She clearly cherished it, and it felt disrespectful to get it covered with blood when he slit the mother's throat from one ear to the other. He then went about the task of removing her head.

While ejaculating again.

) (

8:43 PM

"There's-been-a-murrr-der…" The man's voice was bright and crisp. The words were not spoken, but lilted in a singsong manner the way tattletale children sing the phrase: *I'm-gonna-tel-ell…*

Being her first week with the San Francisco Police Department, this particular switchboard operator found herself succumbing to the natural reaction anyone would have.

"*Excuse* me?"

In due time, after receiving more unnerving calls, desperate pleas for help, inarticulate screams, or just plain hoaxes, than she could count, the operator would learn to stifle such an instinctive response. Conditioning would erode any empathy until she was all but numb to the most brutal, bizarre and heartbreaking aspects of human depravity.

That day had not yet come.

"*What* did you just *say*—?"

The approaching stormfront punctuated the otherwise silent phone line with a telegraph-like series of crackles before the caller again sang the confession. His lyrical cadence then glided to a halt, emotionless as he declared:

"*There have been others. Allow me to give you a couple, so you know I am telling the truth. Are you ready to write this down?*"

With her fingers shaking as much as her voice, the operator put pen to paper. "*I*-I'm *r*-ready."

"*I took that young girl from Mount Diablo, the one they haven't found yet. And the wife from Sausalito. That one I stuffed into the trunk of her own convertible. I called it in myself. Her sexy wedding ring finger even dialed the phone for me. Make sure you pass that on to Sheriff Morris Miller over there in Contra Costa County. He'll know what it means. And if you say you coaxed it out of me, you just might get a promotion.*"

Bristling with adrenaline but with her training now kicking in, the operator steadied her voice and asked for the address from where he was calling.

"*8213 West Summerdale.*"

The switchboard operator knew that area. It was west of downtown, near Clarendon Heights. She knew this because she lived not far from there.

"*Her daughter is alone in the house. Sleeping. You might want to get there before the little darling wakes up and finds what used to be Mommy lying on the floor."*

"May I have your name, sir?"

Silence.

Interference crackled like popcorn.

"Is she still alive? Does she need an ambulance?"

"She needs a hearse..."

A gentle rumble of thunder. First over the phone line, then in the ear of the operator that wasn't covered by the mono headset.

Now she knew he'd lied about his location. The headquarters of the San Francisco police, and where the operator was currently seated, was in Mission Bay...the *east* side of the city, a good four miles from West Summerdale Street. But that thunderclap was audible over her headset and in-person simultaneously.

He was calling from somewhere close.

"And pardon me for being rude. You asked me a question which I haven't yet answered. About my name..."

"Yes, sir. What is your name?"

"...This is the Gemini speaking."

Now came the sounds of the city street: A car horn; a car splashing through standing water; the muted tones of a partial conversation as a man and woman walked past the phone booth.

More crackling.

Then a gentle hiss of static as the caller did not hang up, but instead dangled the black handset from its coiled metal cable until his dime would eventually run out. The SFPD operator continued to speak to a caller she was certain was already gone as the handset rapped against the inside glass of the phone booth. She did this because her training taught her to keep a caller on the line as long as possible, until officers arrived if she could.

Silence. Static. A light tap of the receiver against the phone booth's glass.

It was several long minutes later when the caller's voice again whispered unexpectedly in her ear, and the operator's breath caught in her throat.

"*One more thing...*" the voice offered in a gentle tone one would normally associate with a certain level of intimacy, "*...I've left another little something for your detectives.*"

"What did you leave, sir? Is it something that might harm the officers?"

"*Let's just say it will make our little game a lot more fun...*" The caller hesitated before adding: "*...For all of us.*"

In the same singsong manner by which he had begun the call, the Gemini whisper-sang goodbye.

) (

Cassie

) (

2

) (

T WASN'T GHOSTS and goblins she was afraid of, it was people. They were the real monsters. And if there was one thought that tightened Cassie Kennedy's chest, it was the growing fear that she wasn't alone in the house at night.

Like the very prowler she presaged, the idea crept uninvited into her soul each time the lights went out and the stillness and silence took over.

The mere thought of it gave her the heebie-jeebies.

On her own these days far more than she wasn't, it was everything Cassie could do to keep this thought from consuming her. If only she could share with her husband how she was feeling, she might find a way to overcome it. But she knew he'd think her unstable. Maybe even crazy. At the very least, phobic.

But weren't phobias a fear of the irrational?

This fear was anything but.

And she wasn't crazy.

Just to make sure, Cassie buried herself in research at the West Portal library where she found herself surrounded by shelves of books most afternoons. An avid reader with plenty of time to kill, the library invited her to explore a world where she could be anything she wanted to be, go anywhere she wanted to go. Certainly more than the suburban housewife and mother who, at the age of twenty-five, had already dedicated her future to everyone but herself.

The mere visit was an experience in itself, and Cassie was enamored with everything about it. From the weight of those heavy old doors with their tainted brass handles polished to a sheen by endless touches, to that cool, stale air laced with the scent of wisdom. Her senses were awakened by it the very moment she stepped inside.

And then, of course, there were the books.

So many books.

In the pages of those lovely tomes of hard-toiled creation, she found more than just words printed on paper. She found portals to a realm of infinite possibilities. And just like the building itself, Cassie's love of books stemmed from so much more than that. She adored everything about them. From the way they looked (bright and colorful modern covers or staunch classic cloth-bounds) to the way they felt in her hand (sturdy and real and worthy). Cassie especially loved the way they smelled, new or old: that alcohol scent of fresh ink or the faint hint of vanilla as the lignin slowly breaks down as the books age.

She pored over reference books. Magazines. Even this new and slightly daunting way of reading periodicals in a format called microfiche. Demanding only a fraction of the library's storage space, they were now able to carry a much greater wealth of options. For the first time ever, Cassie was able to view several newspapers from New York through the reels of film on which they were forever preserved. With their pages cast big upon a light box, she twisted and turned the machine's little knob to shift from one page to the next. More than once she turned just a shade too far to the right and the pages whizzed by in a dizzying flurry.

This she didn't care for, and after a few attempts to embrace this newfangled technology (over which her husband would no doubt marvel) she went back to her beloved books.

On the third day she found what she was looking for in a barely touched reference copy used by psychiatrists and psychologists called the *Diagnostic Statistical Manual of Mental Disorders* (*DSM* for short). Identified in 1952, scelerophobia was a disorder defined as an intense and irrational—

see, irrational!

—fear of being stalked and harmed by an intruder.

There was nothing in the *DSM* to explain a *rational* fear, however, let alone one caused by intense psychic visions.

So, with no sane comparison to help her understand why this fear was eating her up inside, Cassie suffered in silence.

She refused to even confide in her husband.

After all, how could she when doing so would be tantamount to sabotaging his dream career?

) (

It hadn't yet been three years since Bill had taken his shiny new job with International Business Machines. A growing technology firm with an office in San José, they were, amongst other things, helping NASA achieve its presidential goals in space exploration. A year prior to Bill being recruited, IBM had built a system capable of tracking the Mercury astronauts' orbital flights. Then in November 1967, just fourteen months after Bill had joined, his work became a part of history when the government launched its *Saturn V* rocket.

Amazing for Bill; bittersweet for Cassie.

When he was first offered the job, it felt like kismet. After all, the Apollo program operated from NASA's facilities on the east coast of Florida...now known as the Kennedy Space Center. It had been President Kennedy's dream that Americans would not only be the first to walk on the moon, but would do so before the end of the decade. To honor this dream, Lyndon B. Johnson dedicated this new space facility to his predecessor just one week after the president's horrifying and very public assassination.

Now, it's worth noting that Bill and Cassandra Kennedy could boast no connection to the iconic Kennedy family other than the coincidence of having the same surname. But when Bill was recruited to work at the space center that also shared their name, it felt like a sign. Overt confirmation that the Universe had conspired to gift the young couple with an opportunity impossible to decline.

And in many ways, it had.

But it made no sense for IBM to fly her husband from northern California all the way across the country to south Florida for just a day or two. So, not only was Bill immediately away from his new wife, but usually for a week at a time.

Sometimes more.

Not easy for *any* beautiful young wife and mother, let alone one with Cassie's history.

Little did she know how quickly these periods of separation were about to escalate. If she had—and this Cassie would never have admitted to her husband—she might have reconsidered their entire union. For instead of the fortuitous kismet it first seemed, it was now starting to feel like some kind of cosmic karma for Cassie's own past wrongdoings.

In this life...or another.

Bill had only been four months into his new job when everything changed. It was a date neither would forget. Nor would most Americans:

Friday, January 27th, 1967.

The date of the *Apollo I* launchpad fire.

After that tragic day, Bill's trips away from Cassie became even more frequent and lasted even longer. Which only served to fuel her fears even further. In turn, this brought on feelings of guilt and selfishness for being afraid of what most adults would dismiss as a fear of the 'boogeyman.'

But Cassie knew the truth.

She knew from experience that out here in the real world monsters like the boogeyman were far from fictional. Because terrible things really did happen. Awful things. Mortifying things.

And they most often happened to good, normal people.

You only had to look at what happened to those unsuspecting astronauts. Cassie couldn't even imagine it, those poor men being locked inside that metal cylinder right there on the launchpad as the flames grew and the heat seared and the toxic smoke choked the breath from their lungs. Yet she found herself drawn to doing exactly that: imagining it. Until it became a heavy ball in her gut, churning and tumbling and making her want to throw up.

It was little surprise that Bill returned from that trip a changed man. Always so eager to put his education and natural talents toward something more than just theory—to dedicate them to something that was real, something with meaning—Bill's entire demeanor had changed. He'd left their Twin Peaks home in mid-January brimming with anticipation and promise, only to return in early February as little more than a shell of his former self.

He didn't sleep. He hardly ate. And he'd begun drinking just that little bit more. Not enough to be a real concern at first, but certainly more than Cassie could faithfully call 'social.'

Most striking was the fact that her husband barely engaged anymore with their beautiful, sassy and curiously clever five-year-old, Isabella. It was clear the girl felt this loss as surely as her mother, perhaps more, though she couldn't quite explain why her little heart was hurting. Many was the time Cassie found herself rocking Isabella to sleep in her arms, tears drying on her daughter's soft cheeks until the gentle gurgles of sleep issued from her lips.

It was this more than anything that made it painfully clear to Cassie that even when Bill wasn't away, he wasn't here either.

Not *really* here.

A shell masquerading as the man she'd married just six years before, his withdrawal only worsened when the conclusion of the official and very public Thompson investigation was announced. This board of experts revealed that the combustion within the *Apollo I* craft was caused by a simple mistake in the choice of wire coating which, though fire-retardant, was too easily damaged. This is what caused the spark which became the fire that billowed inside the sealed capsule's oxygen-rich environment until it devoured everything that could fuel it.

The astronauts included.

As a result, NASA's entire Apollo program had come under scrutiny, only adding to Bill's worry and placing untenable amounts of duress on their marriage.

Over the months that followed, Cassie had tried to get Bill to talk about what happened. If he would only open up to her, she believed firmly that her husband might finally feel empowered enough to exorcize that terrible demon called Guilt.

Eventually, Bill did finally talk to her. Which is when Cassie learned another thing she would never forget about that day.

With a half-drained tumbler of whiskey in his hand and a soulless stare in his eyes, Bill told her with almost sangfroid poise that since she was so keen for him to open up to her, "Then how 'bout we try this one on for size…"

He then recounted in the most graphic detail how everyone on site had listened to the screams of those astronauts over the control room's comms link as all three men were essentially cremated alive.

Far from diminishing the weight of his emotional burden, Bill's admission seemed to only send him deeper into withdrawal. Soon he was in a place so dark that the young wife could not allow herself or their Isabella to follow.

It was this point when Cassie began to realize that the Florida launch center had been cursed the moment President Johnson renamed it. As bright and shiny as the world of the Kennedys seemed to most, all Cassie saw was how everything that touched that family somehow rotted and fell from the vine.

All you had to do was look at the facts.

In August of '63, the First Lady's pregnancy failed to go full-term and poor little Patrick died after less than two days on earth. Barely three months later, as Jaqueline continued to mourn this fresh and devastating loss, her husband was gunned down as he sat beside her in the back of a convertible Lincoln Continental limousine. Pieces of his brain had embedded in the nap of the First Lady's pretty pink jacket as she scrabbled to either get away, or salvage a lump of the president's brain which had skimmed across the trunk lid. Maybe both. And now, just a few short years later, public opinion had turned on Kennedy's pipedream to send Man to the moon. With social issues such as a burgeoning homeless population, mixed public opinions toward our returning Vietnam vets, and civil rights tensions at an all-time high, the people were demanding not only change, but a shift in priorities. The whole Apollo program—once the blonde-haired, blue-eyed prom king of America's future—had become the awkward, red-headed stepchild.

And these were just some of the tragedies yet to come. Still, as if it were no longer satisfied with devouring the iconic Kennedys alone, now the curse had begun to eat away at Bill and Cassie's life, too. For all intents and purposes, the man she called her husband ceased to exist after the Apollo launchpad tragedy. Consumed by the flames of failure, her sweet, loving Bill had been taken that day, as surely as those poor astronauts had been.

Now all but alone with Isabella, the once carefree five-year-old she affectionately called 'Bella Luna,' Cassandra spent most of her nights listening for the telltale sounds of an intruder she knew would one day come. Darting from one side of the room to the other, her eyes searched for signs of movement, or shadows she couldn't explain, while her daughter slept unawares in the next room. Only after Cassie would succumb to the thin and restless sleep she so vehemently resisted would her mind be permitted to escape this grainy, stress-induced reality in which she constantly resided.

But the realm of her dreams offered scant refuge.

In them, Cassie was barraged with grotesque and confusing images. Often, she saw herself in third-person, weakened and bloodied on the floor as a man in coveralls and military boots towered over her. Perhaps more frightening than anything was the fact that she was unable to see his face. Having a burlap sack pulled tight over his head, there were no eye holes for him to see; no nose or mouth holes for him to breathe.

No facial features whatsoever.

Just a blank burlap sack.

And in those dreams that blankness was as empty as the man's soul itself.

) (

FRIDAY MORNING / JULY 18

"That's terrifying, Cass."

Her friend—who was sometimes Trish, sometimes Patty, but always Patricia—grimaced through a plume of smoke as she tapped her cigarette against the brown glass ashtray. She took another slurp of coffee as Cassie cradled her own mug between both palms, savoring the warmth of the sturdy ceramic. Summer rains were threatening, and a morning mist had settled over the city. Its cold and damp seemed to infiltrate her very home to nip at her delicate fingers.

"It is."

Cassie tried to think of something more to add that would better convey the terror she felt every time this lurid dream assaulted her unconscious mind. But nothing seemed to match its darkness. Its violence.

Its intimidation.

Besides, although she and Patty had been friends for going on two years, Cassie still found herself unable to share with her that this recurring scene was borne of a fear which had shadowed her since childhood. One that, in recent months, was only getting worse.

Patricia Brewster visibly shuddered. "And you never see this guy's face?"

Cassie shook her head as she raised her mug to her lips.

"What about the location—is it here?" Patty gestured broadly about the third-floor walk-up. "In your own house?"

Cassie swallowed. Shrugged.

"I really don't know. I don't see that much of my surroundings in the vision—" She cut herself short, bristling at this particular label as if it bestowed the power to manifest the horror into reality. "I mean the *dream.* You know?"

Patricia took in the apartment slowly and shuddered. An overly dramatic shivering sound put an exclamation point on how well and truly creeped out she was by the whole thing.

"Really, Patty. It's okay. It's only a dream."

"Yeah, but is it?" Patricia lowered her empty cup and snuffed her cigarette, exhaling an impressive final billow that caught the circulation of the ceiling fan and swirled in loops until it dissolved. "I mean, c'mon, Cass. Do you really think it's *just* a dream?"

Cassie stared into her friend's eyes, a gaze as soft as it was sincere. She said nothing as her kitchen wall clock quietly ticked away the seconds, each one a thunderbolt in the electrical storm brewing in her mind.

) (

"You know, I have to admit, I kinda missed you and Bella the last few weeks," Patty said while pouring herself a second cup from the percolator. "When you stopped coming to the café, and then stopped calling, I thought maybe you'd already flown the coop or something. Pooped the scoop. Busted outta this popsicle stand. And without telling your best friend, no less." She lit another of her Virginia Slims. "I was getting a little pissed, if I'm honest."

"I know. I'm sorry. I guess the move's been just a little more than I could take. And you know me by now. If I have nothing positive to contribute, I just retreat into my little turtle shell. And take Isabella with me."

Patty took a long drag, nodding. "Speaking of nothing positive, have you heard from Bill?"

"He's still at Kennedy. So, no arguments or screaming for over a month. Which has to be a record."

Silence. A light pop like crinkling paper from the tip of Patty's cigarette which glowed bright. "You did the right thing."

Patricia could have been speaking about any number of recent decisions, but Cassie knew she meant her separation, and of course this place—her Haight-Ashbury rental. A third floor walk-up at the bottom of the Lyon Street descent, hauling groceries was a drag. But being catty-corner to the park, mere steps away, meant everything. Especially to Isabella, who simply adored taking walks there and running around the playground.

"Twin Peaks just isn't the place for you. At least for right now. I mean—" Patty pulled aside the curtain over the kitchenette's slim French door and the morning's soft diffused light filtered in from the small balcony "—just look. Even with the fog rolling in, you're so close to the Panhandle you can still see all that beautiful, delicious green. I mean, just *look*. It's life-affirming!"

The Panhandle to which Patty was referring was the long but unusually thin park abutting the eastern boundary of the much larger and far more famous Golden Gate Park. Being just one block deep but eight blocks long, on the map the park appeared to be the handle to the much larger pan of its better-known counterpart.

"Life-affirming? Sure is," Cassie said. "Hell, I get to see half-naked hippies getting stoned and shagging like rabbits. And from the comfort of my own living room, no less."

Patty's eyes lit up. "Wow, can you?"

"God, you're so easy." Cassie laughed. "No! Ewww!"

Cracking open the French door just enough to blow the smoke through, Patty took another drag. It swirled in the breeze and blended with the fog.

"Sister, I'm a whole lotta things. And 'easy' is one title I'm actually proud to admit that I've earned. There's nothing wrong with us gals getting some, too. I mean, guys get to do it. So, why not us?"

Cassie chuckled.

"Right on, babe." She held out her mug and clinked it against Patty's. "Here's to my sister from another mister." With a wink she added, "And here's to being easy."

) (

Before leaving for work Patty offered to come back and stay that night. She knew Cassie wouldn't accept the offer, but she felt she had to at least put it out there.

Living alone for Patty was no longer a big deal. In fact, she had come to relish it over the years. But this whole solo thing was going to be a new experience for her friend. Being several years Patricia's junior, it was Cassie's first time living on her own.

With any separation there's always an element of emotional turmoil. When it's a marriage or cohabitation, you also suffer the added stress of having to find a new place to live coupled with the gut-wrenching task of packing up and moving. Little else in life is more humbling than seeing your life compartmentalized into neat little cardboard boxes. Of course, as Cassie also had Isabella to think of, finding a place was even more difficult than had she been on her own. Which is why Patty couldn't have been more thrilled when Cassie revealed that she'd found this third floor walk-up. Sure, three floors of rickety old steps were a bitch, especially with bags of groceries in tow. But the price was right, and it was adjacent to the park and, frankly, was as cute as a button. Being on Lyon Street also meant it was just a few minutes' walk up the hill to the heart of Haight-Ashbury, with Patty's café being just another few blocks more. So the potential risk of seclusion and loneliness were less of a worry than if Cassie had moved to another part of the city altogether.

Her biggest concern for Cassie was the ubiquitous financial worry should Bill ever decide that he simply no longer wanted to support her. If that were to happen, Cassie could lose everything, including custody of Bella. Bill was the one who paid for her fancy private daycare, and Patty knew that Cassandra loved that little girl so much that she'd rather see her live with Bill and continue the daycare, than live with her without it.

Added to all the other inherent stressors, it made for a recipe of unease at best, soul-crushing anxiety at worst.

Lord knew it wasn't going to be easy, but that didn't mean it wasn't right. In fact, by Patty's way of thinking, being difficult and being right were often one in the same thing.

If it comes too easy, she often remarked, *it probably isn't worth keeping.*

She as good as said those very words as she kissed Cassie goodbye. She then bounded down the stairs, two at a time, and out into the morning drizzle where the mist had settled in, and now lay cold and clammy on her bare skin. Bundling her arms around herself, she began the climb toward Haight Street where her café awaited its early morning awakening. Before the trees would block her view, she stopped and turned to blow her friend a final kiss. She knew Cassie would be standing on the balcony in front of that quaint little French door, a guardian angel looking down upon her. And of course, Cassie was doing exactly that.

With a floral shawl draped over her shoulders, she craned to peer through the branches of the trees. Stretching far over the metal railing, it creaked and groaned beneath her slight weight as she waved goodbye until Patty was swallowed by the mist.

Closing the balcony door, Cassie now stood alone in the kitchen, isolated once more. Now would come the silence. So tangible you could feel it. Like a wave through an open porthole, it would saturate the apartment to hungrily fill the void Patty had only just occupied.

The kitchen chair's stainless steel legs bounce-scraped over the mustard yellow linoleum floor as she sat to finish her coffee. Amplified by the silence, their tell-tale squawk mimicked a scream almost perfectly. It was all Cassie needed for those dark, pervasive thoughts of an intruder to again wheedle their way in. Pressing upon her like great barbells atop her chest, her breaths became labored, her heart thumping faster.

She listened, holding her breath.

Waiting.

Dreading.

Almost *wishing* for the sounds—*any sound*—that would belie her inevitable attacker's covert presence.

At least then she would know that it was real.

That she wasn't crazy.

But the only sound she heard was that of her own blood as it rushed like a torrent through her ears. It was the crashing surf of anxiety in a sea of silence that battered her shoreline of sanity.

And she knew it.

After a while, with deliberation and an intense focus on her breathing, Cassie's heartrate slowed. Eventually, it mirrored the easy, reassuring tempo of the pendulum wall clock which she'd hung in the kitchen. The clock was simple. Unfussy. Dark wood and clean lines with an octagonal wood frame around its ivory face. An antique, or so she believed, she had spotted it at a flea market and fallen in love instantly. For the price tag, she simply had to have it. There was no haggling in the transaction.

Now here it was, her first official purchase as a single mom in her new place. And in this moment, it was her only companion.

It struck eight times, a rich, soft timbre.

In her mind, Cassie imagined Patty getting ready to open the doors to the café, a half-dozen blocks away. A small group of people would no doubt be keen to end their work week with a sweet treat or brisk morning coffee.

She took a final swig of her own, now tepid in her mug.

Settling into the comfortable sound of the clock's circumspect marking of time, Cassie surrendered to the fact that she too must simply keep ticking on. Regardless of what life brought.

Easier said than done.

For unlike the oblivion in which that clock existed, Cassie was all too aware of the horrors that could descend upon your life at any given moment...

)(

Janice

)(

3

)(

DON'T YOU GO too far now, Donny!" Janice Wynn shook her head, an exaggerated display of frustration as her six year old son scurried away. "I swear, that boy has no fear." Janice, perched upon the nearest bench, let out an audible sigh. "None. Whatsoever. Sometimes, I'm quite sure he'll be the death of me."

She was speaking to another young mother whose returned smile was merely the product of good manners. Offering Janice little more interest than she did the bench on which they sat, the woman resumed the task of buttoning her daughter's sweater. Wriggling as she did so was a blonde girl of similar age to Donny, with eyes as bright as turquoise.

An uncomfortable silence.

Now Janice crossed her legs, one perfectly pedicured open-toed foot tapping empty air as she twisted away from the pair...just enough to suggest her disappointment.

With a sigh as evident as it was unintended, the young mother succumbed. "I haven't seen you here before."

The observation was deadpan, spoken over her shoulder as

she instructed her daughter Lyndsey to stand still so she could fasten the final two buttons of the girl's cardigan.

Having evoked any response at all of course thrilled Janice, who twisted back to face the mother-daughter pair. "Lyndsey, what a beautiful name. And no, I mean, you haven't seen us here before because we're new, yes!"

She paused for an indication of further interest from Lyndsey's mom. When none came, Janice elaborated regardless. "Well, not exactly new here"—she gestured broadly, both hands encompassing the city skyline—"but to this park, yes!"

Lyndsey's mom gave a closed-lip grin and patted down her daughter's cardigan, smoothing it over the girl's slight paunch. She patted her on the backside and Lyndsey took off toward the playground, ponytail sailing behind her.

She turned to face her unsolicited companion. "Well, we love it here. So I think you will, too." She craned to see past Janice, eyes focused on her daughter as she entered the playground. "And frankly, Lyndsey could use the exercise. If I didn't bring her here for some playtime every day, she'd be a couch potato all summer, lying on the floor watching reruns of *Howdy Doody* and gorging herself on Pez, Swedish Fish and Pop-Tarts."

"Well, I think she's beautiful."

"She will be, after she loses about ten pounds."

"Oh, my, no," Janice remarked, genuinely surprised. "She's gorgeous. Just as she is, Mrs. ummm—" She extended her hand and the woman momentarily stared at it before offering her own.

"Veronica," she answered, contemplating Janice's impeccable manicure and surprisingly long, delicate fingers. "And my daughter is—"

"—Lyndsey. Yes, I heard. When you were buttoning up her little cardigan." She allowed her eyes to sweep over Veronica, from her toes to her nose. "And I'm Janice. Janice Wynn. It's my genuine pleasure to meet you, Veronica."

She waited for the typical response that Veronica felt likewise, but no such platitude was forthcoming.

Instead, Veronica asked about her son.

"So your boy's name is...?"

"Donny."

"Oh yes, I remember you calling after him when you first sat down." Now Veronica scooted forward on the bench, observing the playground and the handful of children playing there. "Which one is he, again? I didn't actually see him. He must have—"

not existed

"—made a beeline for the swings directly behind you so that he was out of my line of sight."

"Donny does love his swings!" Janice admitted, pointing toward the children. "He's that one, there."

Veronica spied at least three boys where Janice had indicated. "The blonde? Or that cute little boy with the dark hair, maybe?"

"Mmmmm," Janice affirmed. She pulled a mini Tootsie Roll from her purse, offering it to Veronica while enjoying one herself.

)(

Veronica and Lyndsey Roe were no longer there when Janice excused herself to the restroom a good hundred yards from where they had been sitting. Thankfully, she managed to find them on the south side of the playground. This one was sheltered beneath the trees and slightly remote from the playground.

"Yoohoo! Halloooo!" she called out as she scurried to join them, Veronica too slow to avoid being seen. "I'm so glad to see you!"

"Hello again, Janice," Veronica answered. She offered no eye contact, feigning to dig through her purse for something that must be incredibly important. "Just so you know, we won't be here much longer," she added as Janice took the liberty of seating herself at the end of their bench again. "We've been here quite a while already and—"

"No we haven't, Mommy! We only just got here! Just now!" Lyndsey decreed to her mother's embarrassment. "You're being a silly goose, Mommy!" In the most matter-of-fact manner she then said to Janice: "You look funny."

"Lyndsey! You shush now. We don't say things like that."

"Oh, it's fine my dear," Janice responded. "Out of the mouths of babes, as they say."

She unwrapped a Tootsie Roll and offered it to the girl, requesting her mother's permission with a raised eyebrow.

Veronica did not give it.

Janice duly retracted the treat just before Lyndsey's plump little hand was about to snag it. When Veronica looked away, Janice assuaged Lyndsey's dour face by silently mouthing the word 'later' and offering her a wink and a smiling nod.

"Donny's not with you?" Veronica asked, unconcerned with the biting tone that accompanied the question.

"Oh yes, he's on the swings!"

Veronica Roe saw no one on the swings.

"Oh," Janice revised. "Maybe the jungle gym, then. He does like to climb. He's a right little boy about stuff like that. Many a time he's come back with a knee full of dirt or cinders and if I make a fuss he just—"

"Aren't you bothered about where he is, Janice?"

"Oh heavens, no. Like I say, he's a right little boy and can take care of himself. He's a little man, actually, is what he is. About your age, I'd say." She held the gaze of Lyndsey who continued to study her features, clearly perplexed. "How old are you, my beautiful little girl?"

"I'm six!" Lyndsey replied with pride as she held up seven fingers. Her mother gently closed one, bending the pinkie back to her palm. "Oh yeah," the girl giggled. "This many."

"Well, that's quite a lot! And yes, my Donny is also that many!"

Veronica placed her hands on her daughter's sides and twisted her to face the playground. "Off you go, baby. We can't stay long today. Why don't you go find Donny and say hello?"

"Okay," Lyndsey complied, running off without the slightest idea who she was looking for.

"You must be proud," Janice said as she offered a Tootsie Roll to her new friend, who again declined it. "She's a delightful child."

"Thank you. I'm sure I will say the same of Donny...when I meet him."

"I do hope so!" Janice Wynn beamed. "He's truly my pride and joy. My, it is a cool one today, isn't it, dear? For summer, I mean."

"Mmm." Veronica stared off in the distance.

"I think I could do with a sweater myself, you know." Janice pantomimed shivering. "This west coast weather really is so unpredictable, don't you find? One moment it's hot, the next it's so cold and damp it's like a dead man's fingers are playing down your spine."

The simile was shocking, and Veronica twisted back to face her while also reflexively pulling back in disgust. "What an absolutely horrid way to describe it."

"But so true, no?" Veronica grinned. "I apologize, dear. I do have somewhat of a penchant for the gruesome and forget that not everybody shares my interests."

"Veronica. Not dear."

"Yes, of course dear—"she stuttered, a blush rising in her cheeks "—Veronica."

Rather than move to another bench, as was Veronica Roe's natural inclination, she chose instead to see if she could find out a little more about this person who had somehow decided it was perfectly acceptable to insert themselves into their lives.

"So...you're not from San Francisco, then?"

This renewed interest delighted Janice, and she replied with great vigor. "No, no. Pennsylvania. Western Pee Aay, as we say, to be precise."

Veronica had always found it so odd that people from Pennsylvania almost always referred to their home state by its recognized abbreviation rather than its full name. After all, it was only five syllables. Just like four other states' names. Her own beloved California, being one of them. Yet Janice and her fellow Californians didn't find the necessity to speak of their home as 'See Aay,' or any such nonsense. For the first time ever, she was unashamed to ask, caring little if she embarrassed her uninvited companion. "Why do you 'Pee Aay' guys call it that?"

"Well," Janice replied after a genuine moment of reflection. "You know, dear, I really don't know. How odd I guess we are. Although I prefer the term quirky, don't you?"

"*Hmmmm*," she mumbled, possessing no inclination to answer the question. "What brings you to the Bay area, Janice?"

"Oh, a little this, a little that. How about you, dear?"

"I've asked you to call me Veronica. Not 'dear.' And I really don't feel comfortable sharing the details of my life with a stranger. So, if you really don't mind, perhaps you can find another bench and allow my daughter and me to enjoy the rest of our morning in peace."

)(

Janice left in embarrassed silence. Veronica Roe waited until she was out of earshot before cursing her under her breath. "*Freak.*"

Young Lyndsey gasped, clapping a hand over her mouth in surprise. "Oh, Mommy. That's not very nice. You said we shouldn't talk like tha—"

"Never mind what Mommy said." As Janice disappeared from sight, Veronica scooted the six-year-old in the direction of the sand pit and swings. "Go on now. Go find your friends and leave Mommy in peace to read her book. Okay, my little plumpkin?"

She opened her book and poured coffee from a metal thermos, the oaky scent of whiskey mixing with the earthy, aromatic steam.

She filled the cup lid.

Downed it in one.

Then poured another as she opened the book and eased back into the scene she had been reading when Janice had managed to spot them a second time.

As the words flowed from the page, the sun kissed her cheeks. All around her the air was filled with sweet fragrance as a gentle summer breeze whispered through the flowerbeds encircling the bench. Thirty yards away, Lyndsey cackled and shrieked with delight, running and playing as the sounds of the children rose and fell in tranquil, inarticulate waves.

Checking the playground for her daughter once more, Veronica ensured Lyndsey was happy and occupied with all the other children...

...Then closed her eyes for a five-minute rest.

)(

"That looks like hungry work!" Janice proclaimed as she perched on the edge of a bench within the playground itself, her shoeless feet burrowing into the sand.

Lyndsey Roe nodded earnestly. "Yes! It is *very* hungry work!" Tired of playing tag, she had now set about building a sandcastle for Princess Peach to live in. "She's my best friend."

"Is she, now? Well—" Janice leaned forward "—may I join you? I do adore making sandcastles for princesses."

Lyndsey eyed her with a hint of reservation, spun to make sure her mother was still sitting on the bench, then twisted back to Janice. The sudden motion sent a cast of sand airborne, much of which found its way into the crack of Lyndsey's shorts.

Her face instantly soured. She reached behind her and

brushed at it with manic strokes that only opened the gap further and brought more sand flying.

"Oh nooooooo!" Her mouth twisted; eyes scrunching into the precursor to a blubbering cry. "It's scratchy! Momm—"

Janice knelt to be at the child's height as Lyndsey rose and prepared to run bawling back to her mother. "Shush now, dear. Your mommy is very tired and has asked me to take care of you while she naps."

Lyndsey's breath now came in hiccupping starts and stops, the tears and the howl at the precipice.

"Now, now, babygirl. Remember that yummy little chocolate treat?"

The stuttering breaths came down a notch. Lyndsey nodded. But then again, it may have been her breath catching in her throat.

"You do like candies, don't you?" Janice opened her palm, slowly as if revealing a magic trick. In it she held a wax-paper-wrapped treat. Now Lyndsey's breath diminished and softened again. She slowly reached for it.

Janice pulled it away, snapping her hand closed.

"Only good girls get sweeties. Don't you know?"

Lyndsey nodded several times, her wet eyes no longer squinty and tight but widening with anticipation to reveal irises the color of warm chocolate. Framed by her long, naturally blonde locks, they were simply stunning.

"You do know?"

Now Lyndsey began nodding fervently, her trembling lips relaxing into a hopeful smile. "Yes," she said, no longer mindful of the sand that slid down her shorts like an hourglass as she stood.

With one hand extended before her, Lyndsey took a tiny step toward Janice who still knelt in the sand.

"Hmmm. Well," the woman said as she pretended to consider her options for a moment. "I guess I *did* promise you."

Janice unfolded her fingers, this time offering no dramatic

flourish, and extended her open hand. Lyndsey Roe accepted the invitation and tentatively reached for the candy…

…paused as if it might be a trap…

…waited for Janice's single nod of approval…

…then wrapped her little fingers around the candy and clutched it to her chest, beaming with delight.

"See?" Janice assured her. "You *must* be a good girl." She winked, pointing to the chocolate flavored toffee. "And good girls don't cry. Right?"

"Right," Lyndsey said, her tone bright and prideful as she unwrapped the treat from its waxy paper.

"Now…" Janice stood, casting her gaze toward the bench where Veronica Roe appeared to still be napping, a hundred feet away. Dark sunglasses hid the mother's eyes, however, so Janice couldn't be sure. To test it, she reached for Lyndsey's hand and the child willingly gave it. "…Your mother asked me to clean you up. Whaddya say we get that nasty, scratchy, itchy ol' sand out of those drawers of yours?"

On the bench, Veronica did not move.

Janice took a small, single step forward, still surveying the bench. Lyndsey took it with her, gripping her hand with the trust of an innocent.

No movement from Lyndsey's mother.

Janice released her breath.

Lyndsey mimicked it, then carried on chomping gleefully on her sticky chocolate treat.

"I'm your Aunt Janice, by the way. I bet your mother has told you all kinds of wonderful stories about me and her. Probably a bunch about when we were growing up together?"

They began walking from the playground.

"Huh-uh," Lyndsey denied in a mutter between loud chews.

"Oh, my. Well, I guess you and I will just have to get acquainted with one another ourselves then."

To this Lyndsey nodded and they casually quickened their pace. Janice Wynn took one final opportunity to glance behind them to ensure the girl's mother wasn't charging their way.

She wasn't.

) (

When Veronica awoke, Janice Wynn was sitting beside her. She was thoroughly engrossed in the novel Veronica had been reading before she nodded off.

The mother sat bolt upright, rubbing her eyes behind her big Jackie Onassis sunglasses.

"I'm sorry, but to me she'll always be Mrs. Kennedy," Janice stated. She pointed at Veronica's glasses. "All the rage to follow her lead. A fashion icon, they say. But…marrying again, after what that saint of a husband of hers endured? And betrothed to a filthy Greek, no less. Whatever is she thinking?"

Janice read a few more lines of the book, her lips slightly moving as she formed the words in her mind. A moment later she slapped it closed with a delighted gasp. "Such a page-turner! No wonder you love it!"

Still groggy but growing tense, Veronica Roe snatched the book from the woman's lap. She lifted her glasses and scanned the playground for her daughter.

"Leave me alone Janice. I'm getting Lyndsey and we're going. I don't want to see you again. Do you hear me?"

"Well, someone's testy after her nap."

Veronica piled her things into her oversized handbag and jumped to her feet, again searching the playground.

No Lyndsey.

Now her pulse quickened, her eyes darting from the swings to the jungle gym to the sand pit.

Still no sight of her daughter.

Her breaths became shallow, a tightness coming over her chest like the skin stretched over the frame of a snare drum.

She stepped forward, covering her eyes from the glare, and scoured the park. Mothers and children were in small clusters all around, but none included her Lyndsey.

Now panic set in.

She couldn't catch her breath.

"Now, now, Mrs. Roe. No need for that." Janice tugged the bag in Veronica's grip and both handbag and woman jittered back toward her. "Lyndsey is perfectly well. Better than well, actually. She's away from you, you toxic, self-absorbed whore."

Terror widened Veronica's eyes; her pupils growing large to darken them. Coursing fiercely through her veins, adrenaline was tightening her muscles, priming her to either fight or take flight. Neither of which Veronica was doing, resulting in her hands shaking to the point of uncontrol.

"*W*-Where is *m-m*-my *d*-daughter?"

Janice stood. Faced her.

"She's quite the sweet young girl, your Lyndsey. And to be certain you understand what's happening right now—" Here she tapped Veronica on the forehead. Veronica flinched, her eyes blinking, but did not retaliate. "—To be sure you understand, I want to know that you've heard me. I called you '*Mrs. Roe*.' Did you hear that, Veronica?"

She did not respond.

"Well, I'm going to take that as a yes. You see, how could I know your last name, if not for getting it out of young Lyndsey? We had such a fine conversation, Lyndsey and I. She told me all about her best friend, Princess Peach. Just delightful."

Now Veronica began to sway, her eyes blurring. There was no way this crazy woman could know about Lyndsey's imaginary friend unless she was telling the truth.

"No, no. Don't you go fainting on me now." Janice grabbed the mother's shoulders and gently guided her back down onto the bench. "I need you to focus, Veronica. Your daughter is fine...*for now*. But there is a time limit we're working to, you see. If we dilly-dally, she's not going to be fine anymore. So I need you to listen."

Veronica absently nodded, her eyes glassy. She tried to speak. Couldn't. Her mouth dry as a desert, her lips parched and pale. She tried again, licking them. Her tongue was thick, her saliva like glue. "What do you want? Just tell me where my baby is and I'll *d-do a-a-a-a*-anything, I *p*-promise."

The words had come smooth enough...until their meaning had caught up with Veronica's own brain. Once that happened, it was all she could do to get them out.

"Well, that's good to hear, Mommy." Janice dusted herself down, straightened her skirt and began strolling down the cinder path. "I'd suggest you come, if you ever want to see her again." She paused before adding: "Alive, I mean."

4

)(

NIGHT CAME TOO quickly. No sooner had Cassie been alone in the kitchen that morning than the sun was painting Panhandle Park in an array of sunset pinks and oranges and reds. They shone through her living room window where they played across the bay window's bench seat, the feature she loved more than any other in this new home.

She couldn't tell you where the day had gone. After Patty left, she remembered waking Bella to get ready for kindergarten. Other than that, she recalled only a spattering of the morning's mundane activities.

Then nothing.

For hours.

But her body was sore and the small of her back was barking. Throughout the apartment moving boxes had been repositioned, opened, rummaged through. Several now lay flat in a tidy stack, broken down, ready for the trash. So it was all making sense. She must've been so busy unpacking and organizing, and generally making the apartment feel just that little bit more like home, that she'd simply blocked out the tedium of it all.

It wouldn't be the first time. And she would have accepted this if it hadn't been for what she noticed next:

Blood.

Hiding amongst her tiny freckles, specks of it were all up and down her arms.

At first, it elicited a sense of curiosity. After all, they were barely visible, and she felt no pain. But the more she looked, the more her anxiety throbbed in her neck. Fanning out her hands and raising her arms, she twisted and turned them as she scoured for cuts, gashes, scrapes…anything to explain the blood.

Nothing.

Now she hiked up her bell-bottoms and studied her legs closely. They, too, were covered in little red dots. With her heart now beginning to race, she rummaged in a hurry through the moving box marked BATHROOM, searching for her makeup mirror.

When she found it, she moved closer to the light and examined her face.

Nothing.

Then the realization struck.

Oh my God, Bella—

She was down the hall and at her daughter's bed before she realized that she had even told her legs to move.

"Baby? Wake up. Mama needs to have a look at you!"

Rolling over, Isabella bared her tummy from a cocoon of twisted blankets. Her eyes blinked and squinted in the shaft of hallway light that was casting a beam across her bed. "Mommy…?"

"Everything's okay baby. Mama just needs to look at something real quick."

She untangled Bella from the sheets and lifted her babygirl to eye level, scanning her body from head to toe.

But found nothing.

Thank God!

"Bella, honey, did you get any kind of boo-boo today? Maybe a little scrape playing with one of the moving boxes?"

Isabella groaned, shaking her head while pawing at her mother to let her go back to bed. Satisfied, Cassandra obliged and laid her down, untangling the blanket and tucking it all tight and snuggly around her.

Bella was asleep before her head even hit the pillow, the soft purrs of infant snores rising and falling in comforting lilts.

Inching from the room with the light-footed agility of a mouse, Cassie pulled the door all but closed.

After the incident last year at their Twin Peaks home (in which Bella had irrevocably stained the new carpet and made Bill curse up a storm) Cassie had come into the habit of leaving Bella's door slightly ajar. This way, she could find her way in the dark should she need to go potty in the night.

The light from the hallway narrowed to a thin, triangular wedge, reaching for Bella's bed but not quite touching it.

Which is when Cassie spotted it. On the floor, near Bella's side table. The can of spray paint.

Bright crimson.

In an effort to smooth over the heartbreaking transition, one of the promises Cassie made to Bella was that they'd paint her bedside cabinet once they moved into their new apartment in Haight-Ashbury. Bella had been begging for months, which Cassie of course relayed to Bill. But he wouldn't hear of it in their precious new Twin Peaks home.

"Why on earth would we do such a thing, and lay to waste a perfectly handsome nightstand," Bill replied to her question with one of his own. He ran his hand over the nightstand's yellow oak woodgrain surface. "And with such a ghastly color, at that."

Well, because it would make Bella happy, was her response.

She recalled the conversation now as clearly as if it were yesterday, again feeling the angst and frustration from having a husband who cared more about material things than he did his own daughter.

And wife, apparently.

For although Cassie never revealed to Bill the gut wrenching fear that gripped her every time he went away, she was certain he must have sensed something was wrong. He could have asked her about it; could have sat her down and taken the time to discover why she, too, had changed so dramatically since he'd taken the life-altering position with IBM.

But none of that mattered now.

She instead allowed giddy relief to wash over her. Far from ominous, the red spots on her arms were nothing but a promise fulfilled to a restive little girl in need of love and security.

Now more than ever.

See? No monsters. No boogeyman.

Just calm. And quiet.

I can do this. I am strong. I am smart. I am capable...

...I am safe.

Pulling the door just a little more closed, she quietly tiptoed down the hallway, the tension easing away as she made her way to the living room.

Overlooking Lyon street and Panhandle Park was Cassie's favorite spot in the whole apartment: the modestly upholstered bench nestled in the nook of the bay window. It was obvious that it had been fashioned by one of the owners at some point over the years as neither its quality of wood nor its craftsmanship quite matched the rest of the turn-of-the-century home's vibe. But it was cozy, perhaps more so because of this, and Cassie felt most at peace when lounging upon it.

Although money was tight, she'd splurged on the purchase of a floor lamp specifically to place next to the window seat. Its chrome dome, resembling one of the hairdryers at her stylist's salon, gave the perfect amount of shielded light by which she could read at night while ensuring the apartment remained dim enough that she didn't disturb Isabella's sleep.

Settling now onto her bench, Cassie balanced a dogeared copy of Jack Kerouac's *On The Road* in one hand, a vodka tonic in the other. Watching the fog, she then read for a bit; watched the fog some more; read again.

Two vodka tonics later, that illusive thing called sleep took her into its embrace.

) (

The voice tugged her from sleep, bluntly and without warning. In her dream it became one of those giant vaudeville hooks, while she was the performer being booed and yanked from the stage.

"There's a man in my room!"

For an instant, the actual words did not register.

"Mama…there's a *man* in my *room*."

This time, they were a douse of cold water and Cassie bolted upright in her bed, not remembering how she'd gotten here. The last thing she recalled she had been reading and watching the nighttime world from her beloved window seat.

"Baby? What?"

"There's a ma—"

"No, baby, what do you mean, there's a *man* in your room?" Though trying to conceal it from her daughter, Cassie's chest was a snare drum, her heart a series of staccato claps.

Isabella lowered her head as if ashamed, or confused, or both, and pursed her lips around her thumb.

"Oh…did you have another accident, baby?"

Isabella's response was to suck on her thumb even more aggressively.

"Come here, my little Bella Luna. It's okay."

Cassie opened her arms and Isabella shuffled into them to be engulfed by her mother's embrace. In turn, the young girl threw her arms around her mother's neck and pulled herself tight to Cassie's bosom, squeezing so hard she nearly choked her.

"Hey, it's okay. Look," Cassie patted the bed. "Why don't you come and join me the rest of the night?"

As Isabella began climbing up onto the bed, Cassie spotted the large wet patch still creeping across her daughter's PJ bottoms.

"On second thought, how about we run ourselves a nice warm bath, huh?" She took Isabella by the hand and together they walked down the hallway, flicking on every light as they went.

She dropped the rubber stopper in the bath and ran a mix of hot and cold from the taps.

"Now, how about you take off those jimjams, and I'll go make sure there are no more boogeymen in your room. Deal?"

Again devouring her thumb, Isabella nodded in agreement.

"Okay then. Deal. I'll be right back, Bella."

Smiling at her daughter as big as she'd ever smiled before, Cassie left the bathroom. The smile on her face, however, did not leave with her. Dissolving the moment she began inching down the hallway, Cassie fought the short, quick breaths that began to bubble up into her throat as the hot poker of panic took hold.

Come on, Cass. You know there's no one there. It's just the over-active imagination of a five-year-old. Her mind's way of...

Four more steps and she would be at Isabella's room.

...deflecting from the kind of accident she knows, deep down, she shouldn't be having any more. It's a figment...

Three steps.

...of her imagination. A projection of...

Two steps.

...her mourning for our old life. A remnant...

One step.

...of a bad dream.

Cassie was standing at the threshold when the light inside her daughter's bedroom clicked off. Beyond the door still slightly ajar, darkness took hold as Cassie froze on the spot.

Heart pounding, hands trembling, her breath caught in her throat and would not release.

"I told you, Mommy."

Cassie twisted around to see her daughter naked in the hallway, the girl's brow furrowed as she slid her thumb back into her mouth while slowly raising her other arm...

...and pointing behind her mother.

) (

Tears of alarm glazed Cassie's eyes as she pivoted back to her daughter's bedroom door more slowly than she thought herself capable of moving. As she did, she listened past the faraway babbling of the filling bathtub and the immediate sound of her own shallow breaths—which had not only released but were now coming rapid and harried.

There, between both of these sounds, Cassie found another:

The muted breathing of someone else.

With a scream she spun the rest of the way around and flailed at the man's face, punching and scratching as she howled for Isabella to run—

Run baby! Run!

—and get away from here; to run downstairs as fast as she could; to get help.

But Isabella did not move.

Rooted in place, the whites of her eyes grew as the boogeyman in the big dark clothes and heavy boots and scary sack over his face deflected her mother's every blow.

When he then raised a ball-peen hammer high above that featureless burlap sack, Isabella did not blink. Instead, the light in her eyes simply dimmed when he brought the hammer down upon her mother's head.

Again.

And again.

And again.

The five-year-old did not understand when her mommy's eyes—dilated black and filling with blood—locked with hers for what would be the final time. Naked and shivering in the hallway, Isabella stood motionless and silent as the boogeyman then tied Cassie's hands and feet with clothesline. It was the same plastic line Mommy had stretched from one bathroom wall to the other because they could not yet afford a fancy clothes dryer like they had when they lived with Daddy.

Isabella plucked the thumb from her mouth as the boogeyman tore the nightgown from her mother's body.

"Mommy?"

Prone on the floor, naked, bloody and bound, Cassie's mind formed the three words she wanted more than anything else to say to her daughter. Her mouth, however, could not form their sound.

"My bath is ready, Mommy."

These became the last words Cassie would hear.

Her last image was her beautiful Bella Luna, confused and stunned, standing mere feet away as the faceless man now took what Cassandra Kennedy alone had the right to give…

5

) (

YOU DON'T HAVE to worry about your mommy, my sweet little Lyndsey. She won't yell at you." The man dropped a sack of sugary treats at the girl's feet.

It hit the dirt floor with a hollow thud. The sound quietly echoed through a dark chamber beyond the tiny pen in which Lyndsey Roe was huddled in a tight ball in the corner.

"And she won't stop you from eating what you want." He bent down and opened the sack, presenting it to her. "Not anymore."

Lyndsey shrunk away, her mouth trembling. Her dirt-covered cheeks were streaked with thick lines where the tears had wiped them clean. Her shorts and pink t-shirt were encrusted with grime, the young girl tossing and turning throughout the night, only sporadically managing to sleep between fits of forlorn wails.

"*I-I*-w-want-*m-m*-my-*mommy*!"

She kicked and pressed as far into the corner as possible, her mouth twisting into a shriek.

"Hmmmmm," the man mumbled and took two steps back. "Well, Lyndsey. I'm afraid that's not possible. You see, we made sure your mommy wouldn't be awful to you anymore. You can eat as many sweeties and fun things that you want now."

Lyndsey screamed for her mother again, this time starting to her feet and turning to face the wall, howling. If she could have clawed her way inside of it, she would have.

"Now, now. There's no need for that. We're your new family now. And I know you don't know us very well, but I think we're going to love you more than you've ever been loved before. Doesn't that sound nice?"

Lyndsey's cries only intensified, growing so loud that they eventually fell mute, her little throat swollen and sore, her vocal cords strained and stretched.

) (

Janice Wynn came in after the man could do nothing to relieve the little girl's intense distress.

Kneeling in the corner next to Lyndsey, she softly caressed her long blonde hair, now sweat-soaked and knotted with grime. She offered soothing whispers of reassurance in her ear, her breath fine and warm upon the girl's neck.

It was gentle and kind and caring.

Not at all the comportment of the person who had slit the throat of Lyndsey's mother in the adjacent cell, then marveled at the life flowing from her squirming body.

6

)(

ASSIE'S SCREAM WAS a nerve-shredding echo...but only in her mind. Again Isabella repeated: "My bath is ready, Mommy." The five-year-old was pressing both hands against her mother's back, putting her whole body into it as Cassie lay asleep on the window seat. Contorted around a splayed-open paperback and a half-empty smoked glass tumbler, her mother rocked back and forth with each of Isabella's attempts to wake her.

"Get up, Mommy!"

When Cassie did wake, the scream in her head became real and Isabella recoiled with a start, tears instantly filling her eyes.

"Oh God, Bella, I'm so sorry!" Cassie half-sputtered. Confused and blinking, she took inventory of her surroundings:

...Her daughter...favorite paperback...a cocktail glass (now spilled)...window bench seat (still wet)...Lyon Street below...their beautiful park catty-corner...

It had been a dream. An awful, nerve-shredding dream. There had never been an intruder in her home. Cassie was still alive.

And there had never been an odd woman in the park called Janice, or a mother called Veronica or—

God help me

—a little Lyndsey Roe. All of it had been figments of another night terror. A product of her mind torturing herself over her decision to separate from her engineer husband.

She grabbed Isabella with gentle hands and pulled her close, giving her daughter a deep—and safe—embrace.

"Ohhh, baby, it's ok. Mommy just had a really bad dream. I'm so, *so* sorry that I scared you." Isabella's lower lip trembled, but not as dramatically as a moment ago. "But look at the time! My goodness. We have to get you to kindergarten, Bella. It's well past eight and Mrs. Munroe will be livid!"

Isabella scrunched her nose, pulling away. "What's libbid?"

This was the tension break Cassie needed and she giggled. But only a little. The day she'd found out she was pregnant with a baby girl, Cassie had sworn she'd never make her daughter feel 'less than.' Bella deserved better than to feel the way she herself had been made to feel for so much of her childhood. Or at least what she was able to recall from her limited and spotty memory. "Livid—L-I-V-I-D. It means your kindergarten teacher will be very, *very* upset with us."

What she actually meant was that Mrs. Munroe would be very upset with *her*. But she chose to omit this part of the explanation.

"But why, Mommy?"

"Well, because you're supposed to be there by now, Bella. Remember the little rhyme Mrs. Munroe taught us? *'In your seats by eight, or else you'll be late.'*"

Isabella crossed her arms, taking on the air of being stern while shaking her head. "Now you're just being silly, Mommy! We don't go to kindergarten at night!"

Cassie began to correct her, pointing out the clock in the living room which, when she hung it this week, she'd noticed was about two minutes slower than the pendulum clock in the kitchen. And in this very moment the kitchen clock was beginning to whir. That meant it was winding up in readiness to gong the half-hour.

"See, Bella. It's already eight-thir—"

Interrupted by what she glimpsed out of the corner of her eye, Cassie did not finish the sentence. As it should be this time of day, the sun was low to the horizon in Panhandle Park. But with the park being the next block north of the apartment, the sun should have been low to her right.

But it was low to her *left*.

The breath caught in Cassie's throat, and she inadvertently tightened her grip on Isabella's arm more than she realized.

"*Owww*, Mommy! You're hurting me!"

Cassie released her grip slowly in response, staring into her daughter's eyes. "Isabella, how long has Mommy been asleep?"

The five-year-old pulled away the moment her mother fully released her wrist. She backed up three steps and shook her head, not wanting to say.

"Bella, baby. *How long have I been sleeping?*"

Thinking she was in trouble, Isabella took another two slow steps backward until she was against the old green couch which had been left by the previous tenant—the couch Cassie could not turn down. For now, at least.

"Last night, Mommy," she finally whispered.

"Honey, I know I went to bed last night. Just like you." Cassie lowered her speaking volume. Softened her tone. "But baby, how long have you been awake while mommy slept?"

Isabella did not reply, evaluating in her child's mind what answer her mother would most want to hear. Unable to decide, she closed off her stance by pulling her arms tight to her chest and lowering her head. She then told her mother the truth:

"I tried to wake you, Mommy. But you've been sleepy all day."

)(

It wasn't possible.

How could it be possible?

She'd put down Isabella a little later than usual last night. Closer to nine than it was to eight-thirty. But given their mind-numbing combination of recent—*major*—life changes, Cassie figured it wouldn't hurt to let her daughter stay up just a few extra minutes.

Just this once. She'd made sure Isabella understood before handing her daughter a small bowl of cereal, no milk.

She remembered pouring herself a drink, grabbing her favorite book, and nestling up with a throw on the window bench seat. There she'd periodically read between absent periods of watching the fog roll past until she had grounded herself.

Oh, that's right

She remembered now. All of it. She had been nervous, that awful feeling again that she wasn't alone in her home.

So she'd poured a second drink. And maybe a third?

She recalled the gong of the clock, so that had to have been around ten-ish. Ten-thirty, latest. As it was now eight-thirty, that meant she had been asleep for over twenty-two hours.

It wasn't possible.

And yet the sun had already begun to set over Panhandle Park. Most of the happy families there had already begun to leave, replaced by rambunctious teens, a few older couples, and the odd jogger or two taking advantage of the cooler evening temps.

So Bella was right—she had lost an entire day.

It was unfathomable.

"I'm sorry, Mommy."

Cassie snapped back to the moment. "Oh, babe. Come here, Bella." She patted her hands together over her heart, then opened her arms. "You have no reason to be sorry, baby girl. Come over here to Mommy."

At first Isabella did not budge. But when she saw that her mommy really meant it, she grinned and ran into Cassie's arms.

"My bath is ready, Mommy."

"Awww, you ran the bath like a big girl? Who's a good girl, then?" Cassie rubbed her nose over her daughter's, what she liked to call their Eskimo kisses. "Just promise me that you'll never get *into* the bathtub without me being there, too. Okay?"

To this Isabella nodded enthusiastically and led her mother by the hand to the tub full of water which had already gone cool.

Cassie made no mention of it and simply let some of the water out and added more hot, along with her daughter's favorite bubblegum scented bubble bath. By the time Isabella changed out of her little jeans with the big flowers sewn on the back pockets, and her red, yellow and brown striped shirt, the tub was all but overflowing with soapy bubbles.

"Promise you won't ever go away like that again," Isabella demanded as she dipped her toe into the mass of foam. She settled into the water and immediately dunked her head. When she reemerged, it was crowned with a soapy beehive.

"I promise. As long as you'll always forgive Mommy when she acts like a little silly billy goat."

Isabella nodded as dramatically as the smile which had lit upon her face. She said nothing, instead kissing her mother on the lips so that they both shared a tiny taste of the bubbles—the flavor of which was everything like soap and not at all matching its sweet bubblegum scent.

"Then I guess we have a deal, Bella."

) (

Patty came over that Monday morning, as she often did before opening the café. Located just off Haight Street, Brewster's was the namesake of Patty's perfectly suited surname. (She'd once told Cassie—in much less of a joke than at first it seemed—that with a name like Brewster her career choices boiled down to running a coffee bar or a brewery...and she didn't much care for beer.) Mondays were one of her busiest days, with Patty's most regular patrons desperate for their Brewster's coffee fix after a Sunday off. But eager to finish the phone conversation she and Cassie had started the night before, Patty was standing on the stoop of Cassie's walk-up a good ten minutes earlier than usual.

"Holy Christ on the cross, Cass. I don't even know what to say."

For the first time in recent memory, Cassie actually found her longtime friend struggling to find the words. She felt the same but tried to articulate it with honesty. "I'm scared, Trish." While she didn't know why, Cassie always reverted to calling Patricia 'Trish' instead of 'Patty' when things were heavy. "I didn't just see it all. I *experienced* it. It felt *real*."

Patricia shook her head and lit a cigarette. Once she was at the café there wouldn't be another chance until she'd gotten through the early morning rush. And that could be hours from now. "I really don't know what to say, hun. I mean, it all sounds batshit crazy, right? But then again..."

"...Maybe it's not," Cassie finished for her. "I know. You've told me for a while now that you think they're more than dreams."

"Girl, I *know* they're more than dreams. There's no 'think' about it." Patty took one last puff, breathed in deep, then snuffed the glowing butt underfoot as she exhaled a long, steady plume. "But you've never seen someone else in your visions, dreams, nightmares...whatever you want to call them...before."

"Not like this, no."

"And tell me again, were you this Veronica-lady in your dream?"

Cassie shook her head. "Not really. It was me at first. The man was coming for. Like always. Only—" For a moment Cassie was no longer there, her mind drawn back to the horrifying images of being attacked, of being violated; of her apartment becoming the park, then somewhere dark and dank and saturated with low, base vibrations. Images of Veronica gasping and gulping for air like a carnival guppy in a bag as her blood pulsed from her throat.

While the man watched.

While Janice Wynn watched.

"—Only this time it was *too* real, Patty. *I believed it. I felt* it. To me, in that moment, it *was* real. Does any of this make sense…?"

Patty gently puffed out the sides of her soft pack of smokes and peeked inside. Only one left.

Fuck it, she thought. *I'll buy a pack on my break.*

She tapped the last one out and lit it as Cassie watched, envious—and not for the first time—at how nice it must be to have such immediate comfort at the tip of your fingers. And to indulge in its succor whenever you needed.

"It does make sense," Patty answered through a shroud of smoke. "And you say this happened after I left on Friday?"

"Yes. I can't exactly tell you much about that afternoon, though."

This made Patty squint, one eyebrow raised. "Meaning?"

"Meaning, I know I unpacked more boxes, but I must've been on autopilot or something. Because next thing I knew it was night, Bella was snacking on cereal before bed and I was reading in my favorite spot—"

"The window seat?"

"—The window seat, with a couple vodkas and tonic going down just a little too smooth."

"A couple?"

Cassie's cheeks flushed, her freckles more apparent against the pink. "Maybe one or two more than a couple?"

"Ahhh. Yes. Well, that'll fuck with your sense of time and memory, to be sure. What happened next?"

"Then the dream. The vision. Whatever you want to call it."

"Where the faceless man was coming for you."

"Yes. And this time, he got to me. And he was doing these terr—" Stifled by her own words, Cassie swallowed hard before attempting to speak them aloud a second time. "—He was doing these terrible things to me while Bella watched in shock. Then next thing I know it's no longer me, and we're no longer here, in my apartment."

"You were at the park then…?"

"At the park, yes. In my dream, I mean. And I was a fly on the wall, so to speak. Watching this Janice woman—"

"Janice Wynn," Patty confirmed. "Oh, I'm not gonna forget any of these names. Trust me."

"Yes, Janice Wynn. And she's harassing this lady."

"Veronica Roe."

Cassie swallowed, her eyes temporarily focusing on something far away that Patty could not see. "That's correct. But there's something not quite right about Janice. Even Lyndsey noticed."

"Oh? You didn't tell me this bit. How so?"

"I remember this so clearly. Little Lyndsey said, 'You look funny.' And she was right. Because Janice *did* look funny. By which I mean funny odd, not funny ha-ha."

"Can you tell me how she looked odd?"

Cassie shook her head. "No. I just know that I felt it. And you wanna know the weirdest thing?"

"Patty half-chuckled before taking a long drag of her Virgina Slims cigarette. "Sure. I mean, it's gotta be really weird if it stands out from all of this."

"It is. Because Janice *knew* she looked odd. She didn't deny it. And she didn't brush it off, either. She said, 'Out of the mouths of babes.' Isn't that freaky? She knew she looked not quite right."

"I wish you could somehow show me your dreams, babe. 'Cause this is some Grade-A shit right here." Patty snuffed out her cigarette underfoot and tossed the empty soft pack into a waste can ten feet away. "And that's a three-pointer!" she proclaimed, her right hand hovering in the air from its follow-through as Cassie appeared confused. "That's a basketball term, babe. Not your thing. Anyhoo—"

"Anyhow, I think maybe I need to go to the police."

Patty lowered her arm. She stood expressionless. Started to say something. Stopped. Closed her mouth. Exhaled. Opened her mouth again. It was a great impression of a fish out of water.

"Wow," she finally said, her usual sarcasm fully in check. "You really do feel serious about this one."

Cassie told her she did.

"Are you sure, Cass? I mean, what if they have no record of this woman and her daughter going missing. Or, worse yet, what if they do?"

"Then I tell them everything I know."

"And then they lock you up for having information you could not possibly have unless you had something to do with the crime."

Cassie smirked. "I told you it was a man."

"You told me it was a woman called Janice Wynn who lured them away."

"Right. And I have my I.D. on me that proves I'm Cassandra Kennedy." Cassie opened her arms and moved closer, beckoning a hug. "I love you, Patricia. I *so* do. And I know you're only looking out for me. But I'll be fine. Promise."

Patty moved in for the embrace and squeezed her friend as though both of their lives depended on it. She pulled away and looked Cassie over. "Fine. Then when do you wanna go? If you wait till Michele comes to relieve me at two, I'll go with you."

"No..." With her thumbs hooked into her jeans' belt loops, Cassie's fingers had begun unconsciously tapping her hips. Patty noticed her shifting her weight from one foot to the other. "Thank you though. I need to do this now. Before the worry drives me crazy. And besides, if it's even the slightest bit true, then that little girl needs my help. So I gotta do this, Trish."

There it was: the tell. She called her 'Trish' again.

Now Patty knew this was really happening.

Despite two customers already waiting, Patty waited outside the locked café and watched Cassie jump onto a cable car. By the time the café owner would be cashing out her first customer, Cassie would be telling the San Francisco police intimate knowledge about a child's kidnapping and a mother's murder.

Knowledge she had come about by way of a psychic vision.

God help her.

7

)(

HEY RESSLER, THERE'S a woman in the lobby who says she has info about that missing mother and daughter case from the Panhandle." The desk sergeant disappeared before Doug Ressler could voice his objection.

"Christ almighty," Ressler shouted through the door already closed. "Have Sid handle it. Hey! I said—" He watched through the frosted glass as the sergeant walked away without looking back. Ressler's only acknowledgement that he'd been heard was when the sergeant's right hand shot high above his shoulder. It looked suspiciously like his middle finger had shot up with it. Hard to tell though, through the semi-opaque window. But likely.

He whipped him the finger back. The sergeant wouldn't see it, but it made Doug Ressler feel better.

The woman was sat in the lobby, making herself small at the farthest end of an inhospitable wood bench. Hard and angled just right to be uncomfortable after mere minutes, it was a relic from the station's 1930s remodel, a good three decades earlier. She was in her mid-twenties or so, strawberry-blonde hair, pretty face. Ressler's first thought went to her having a little more meat on her bones for his taste, but there was certainly something alluring about her as she tapped her toes and studied her nails in nervous anticipation. Sid Younger, his partner for nearly seven years, abhorred the way he eyed every woman as a potential mating partner—

sexual conquest, Sid actually called it

—but to Doug Ressler, it was just part of his DNA. After all, it was the sixties now. Sexual freedom, especially among the fairer sex, was all the rage now. That whole *Leave it to Beaver* vibe of the fifties was no longer the way America looked. Young women didn't aspire to be like housewife and mother June Cleaver anymore—they aspired to be like Raquel Welch, Ann-Margret and Brigitte Bardot. It wasn't unusual now to see women in boob tubes with no bra, their nipples hard and pressing through. And, well, to Ressler's way of thinking, if you weren't hip to the scene, you were just a square.

He, for one, was going to embrace it for all it was worth.

'So go ahead,' he once told Sid, tired of the man's incessant badgering. 'Call me a feminist. 'Cause unlike you, my right-angled friend, I'm all about that Flower Power, Girl Power, Expanded Consciousness, whatever.'

'As long as it gets you laid, that is.'

To this Ressler just shrugged, a kind of 'if you can't beat 'em, join 'em' look across his face.

And besides, he wasn't married. Sure, he and Siobhan Jacobs, the head of forensics, were something of an item. But who knew how long that would last? Ironically, it was becoming increasingly clear that Siobhan saw it as much more casual than Ressler wished it to be. So, the best way Doug was able to keep himself grounded and not get too attached was to allow himself the privilege of a little look, a little flirt, a little fantasy.

Here and there.

Knowing the woman was still not aware of his presence, his eye wandered to her left hand. A simple gold band adorned her third finger.

Well, fuck a duck.

He cleared his throat and Cassie winced, her hands dropping to her lap with a slap.

"I'm Detective Douglas Ressler." He extended his hand and she politely stood. No boob tube here. And definitely not braless. *So, no loss then*, he thought to himself and cleared his mind. "I'm told you have something to share about the missing persons case from last Friday?"

Cassie Kennedy shook his hand. She was still holding it as she rose to her feet and introduced herself. She spoke loudly to be heard over three uniformed officers and one suspect who was clearly resisting. They had come charging through the lobby, doors slamming and F-bombs flying.

Doug Ressler was deaf to it.

It made Cassie Kennedy cringe. "Is there maybe somewhere we can talk that's a little quieter?"

She told him everything she'd seen: how the vision had begun as one of her usual nightmares but had felt so real that she truly believed she was being attacked at the time.

"And if I'm honest, Detective Ressler, I'd still swear, even right now, that it really happened. If I didn't know the truth about what was really taking place, that is."

He commiserated without looking up from the tablet of notes he was taking. Until she described how the dream had morphed into a vision of Veronica Roe and her daughter Lyndsey.

"Wait. Hold on a minute." He put his pen down more forcibly than necessary and slid the tablet to one side. Leaning in with his fingers interlaced, his look hardened. "Are you telling me that the information you want to share is from a *dream*?"

Cassie felt herself shrink. Just like that she was a child again, facing the wrath of her uncle for doing, or not doing, something right. *Anything* right, it sometimes felt. She wetted her lips. "A, well, a vision, I would call it. Not a dream. A psychic visi—"

"Christ on the cross, lady!" He struck the tablet of notes and it spun across the table, hit the wall, and dropped to the floor, pages fluttering like a bird falling from the sky. "Do you have any idea how busy we are around here?"

He lurched to his feet.

Now Cassie *was* that little girl about to be punished.

"Strike that. Do you know how fucking busy *I* am? I stopped what I was doing to come out here and talk to you. Now I've just wasted time that could have been spent trying to find that little girl." He moved to the door, glaring. "*You* have wasted that time."

"But I thought I was helpi—"

"Helping? By feeding me some bullshit about a psychic vision? God*damn*it. I knew I should've let Sid deal with you. You fucking nut jobs crawl out of the woodwork at times like this. It's sick, is what it is."

"But I wanted to *help*." Now Cassie stood, her legs feeling weak but determined to finish what she came here to do. "How could I know their names, if what I'm saying isn't true?"

"Ever hear of the *San Francisco Ledger*, lady?"

"You mean the newspaper?"

"No, I mean the ferry to Alcatraz." He shook his head. "Yeah, the paper, Mrs. Kennedy. It's been all over the headlines since Saturday."

Cassie was shaken. She stuttered. "I-I don't read the paper. I'm sorry. I—"

"The TV then. Channel 5 has covered it every newscast as well. You know, maybe I should charge you with wasting police time. Hell, for all I know maybe you got something to do with it."

His eyes drilled into hers, unspeaking. She was trembling. Which meant there was no way she had a damn thing to do with the disappearance. And he knew it. *But fuck.* The job was hard enough without bored housewives like this playing armchair detective. What was the name of that ludicrous Agatha Christie character that was still so popular…wasn't it Miss Maple or Mrs. Mabel, or something like that?

"Miss Marple," Sid corrected once he'd returned from finishing Cassie's witness statement after Doug had charged out of the interview room in a simmering rage. "One of the best creations of modern crime fiction, by the undisputed matriarch. Just because you're an ignoramus who doesn't read does not mean the rest of us are."

"Yea, yeah. Whatever you say. I don't know why you even bothered to spend another minute with that crackpot. If it were me, I could've slapped her as easy as looked at her after hearing the word 'psychic' come out of her mouth." He lowered his voice to a near-mutter. "Pretty mouth, though it was."

"Yeah," Sid Younger responded with a shake of the head. "You're a real feminist, Doug. I can see it clear as day."

"Alright, lose the attitude. I just don't see why you'd waste another minute with her."

"Because maybe there's something useful in there. Like, maybe she actually knows Veronica Roe and wants to keep her distance. So she comes to us with a story that what she says came from a vision. When in fact, it could be the real deal and maybe the lady's just scared of getting in the middle of a shitstorm." Sid slid his interview sheet across the table. It spun between Ressler's arms. "Ever think about that? Because that lady you just insulted and intimidated gave us a name."

"Yeah, I know it. The names anyone in San Francisco could've fathomed from the media."

"Not those names, Doug. She gave us the name of the perp. We need to dig up anything we can find on a Janice Wynn."

8

)(

YOU MUST HAVE been scared shitless." Patty was wiping down tables with fervor, a Virginia Slims cigarette slowly burning itself down in an ashtray at the small high-top table in the corner she kept for personal breaks. "I would've shat myself."

"Well, would you have been shitless, or would you have shat yourself? You can't have it both ways."

Patty chuckled, working her way toward the cigarette table. "I can if I shat myself first. Then I would've been shitless."

This made Cassie laugh out loud, the first positive expression of emotion since returning from the police interview. "The second guy was nice. Detective Younger. He apologized for the other guy and took the time to hear me out."

"Well, this other guy sounds like a real dick. I know the sort. Always checking you out. In their minds they're halfway to fucking you before they even open their mouth."

"Spoken like a true lesbian." Cassie giggled, giving her a wink.

"Takes one to know one, bitch."

"I can hardly be a lesbian when I have a husband." The words had barely left her lips before the conscious realization of her recent separation had dawned. Again. It was becoming clear that it was going to be awhile before a permanent acknowledgment of this new life would finally take hold.

"Well, more's the pity for us. That's all I can say."

Cassie tossed the rag she was using at her. "You know if I were, you'd be top of my list."

"Oh, there'd be a list now, would there?"

Cassie floated both hands along her sides, accentuating her contours. "Well, my lovely, a girl like me doesn't come along just every day. I think I'd be in high demand."

"You got that right," Patty said between puffs, leaning back in the bar chair as she smoked the cigarette down to the filter. Whether she was referring to the first part of her assertion or the second, Cassie did not know. Maybe it was both. "Speaking of you being in demand, you've just given me the perfect segue for an idea I've been tossing around in my head…"

)(

"You want me to give readings to your café patrons." Somewhere in the deadpan clarification was the hint of a question from Cassie.

"Isn't that what I just said?" Patty was now wiping down the counter, tossing Cassie her rag back in the process. "Help me get this place open, then we'll talk. Okay, sugar?"

It was quarter till ten before the rush slowed to a trickle. With nowhere else to be, Cassie stuck around and helped take orders, bussing tables in-between.

With only a handful of remaining customers sipping their coffees and reading newspapers or books in various nooks and crannies of the café, Patty settled into her special table near the back and lit the Virginia Slims she'd been jonesing to smoke for more than an hour.

"Oh. My. God." It was an expression of near climactic release, Patty's words rasping through the smoke she pulled into her lungs then held before tilting her head back to blow it up to the ceiling. "That was some morning rush, eh?"

"The crowd, or the nicotine?"

Patty snickered, a light choking cough. "Both."

"You know those are gonna kill you one day, right?"

"My customers? You got that right." She laughed again. It was real and unabashed, and so unlike Cassie's own self-conscious manner that it was one of the things she loved about Patty the most. "But seriously. These slim little things?" Patty rolled the cigarette back and forth between her fingers, examining it. "Never. After all, we're biologically superior to men. Haven't you heard?"

She was referring to the cigarette brand's prominent magazine advertisements in which a strong, beautiful brunette in blue velvet jumpsuit, purple stockings, red knee-high leather boots and flowing superhero cape appeared to be squaring off to the reader. With a Clint Eastwood squint to her steady gaze, she was as alluring as she was tough. All around her, the body copy text of the ad illustrated the dozens of ways in which Philip Morris espoused their claim—from women being more resistant to starvation and fatigue than men, to their naturally superior immunity to baldness, color blindness...and even nomadism.

"And that logic is about as solid as it is scientific."

"What can I say? We've come a long way, baby."

Cassie half-chuckled, realizing she'd teed it up perfectly for Patty to quote the cigarette's famous slogan.

"Yes, we have. But not far enough to see through the bullshit of a bunch of Fifth Avenue advertising execs whose only goal is to sell more cigarettes. Our health be damned."

Patty feigned a scowl.

"There, you ruined it." She snuffed out the cigarette, acting as though it were to appease her friend. But Cassie was fully aware that it had already been smoked down to the filter. "Okay? Happy?"

"Very," Cassie answered, equally feigning her gratitude. "Now, can we talk about your idea? Please?"

"What's to talk about? You've been reading tarot for as long as I've known you. You have visions—"

"I have dreams."

To this, Patty shot her friend a look that would give the Virginia Slims superhero gal a run for her money. Cassie raised her hands in mock surrender as Patty continued.

"That's not what you told the police yesterday. So, as I was saying before I was so rudely interrupted...you have visions. You've done readings—"

"For friends."

Patty's squint tightened. "Girl, I swear, if you don't let me finish—"

"I'm sorry!" She mimed zipping her lip, smiling. With her lips clenched it looked a bit creepy. "The floor is yours," she mumbled from the corner of her mouth, a muffled utterance between pursed lips.

"Damn right it is. Not only the floor, but the walls, the ceiling. The whole goddamn café." Crossing her arms and settling back into her chair, Patty waited for her friend to verbally respond in any way whatsoever. When she didn't, Patty continued. "You've done readings, and they've been spot on. And now you've shared information that could actually help the police in a missing person's case, whether they appreciate it or not. It's remarkable, actually. You have a gift, babe. So why not put it to good use by helping lots of other people? It would get you out of the house more. *And* give you some much-needed cash of your own. I mean, what if Bill just decides he doesn't want to help you anymore?"

"He wouldn't. Don't forget about Bella. She's not just mine."

"Yeah, but is that enough? If he really decides he just wants a break? Your're not actually married, babe. The laws don't apply to people in our situation."

Of course, Patty was right. But the separation alone was a hard enough pill to swallow. She didn't even want—couldn't *allow* herself—the emotional or mental space to even think about things getting worse.

"I could get a part-time job."

"Yes, you could. But that wouldn't bring in much. It certainly wouldn't be enough to get by if the worst were to happen. Plus, it would probably be hit-or-miss when they'd give you a shift. So how would that work when you've got Bella to consider? I'm just saying there's a way to get you some more time out of that apartment *and* get you a little more money of your own. On your own terms." Patty sighed, lowering her voice which had grown agitated. "Look, chick. I think you could do with just a little more of both of those things right about now, don't you?"

In the manner of one of Bella's classmates, Cassie raised her hand to speak, her mouth tightlipped as she her hand bobbed up and down with vigor. Patty mirrored the whimsy, instantly adopting the role of teacher pointing at her enthusiastic student above a sea of invisible classmates.

"Yes, you there. The pretty girl in the third row. I'm sorry I don't remember your name, young lady. Kathy, is it?"

Cassie mimicked unzipping her lip.

"It's Cassie, ma'am," she corrected and tittered, the bashful but exuberant young student. Clear as day, Patty could see her in pigtails and poodle skirt back in grade school. "But seriously, I don't know, Patty. Do you really think I could do it?"

"I do." The response was swift and without hesitation. "And who knows? Maybe it'll also help you come to terms with this god-awful recurring dream or vision or whatever the hell it is that you keep having. Because if you don't get a handle on what it's trying to tell you, I'm afraid it may end up driving you crazy…"

Patty considered sharing what was really on her mind—the worry that tied her stomach into knots as she lay awake at night, worrying about Cassie being all on her own. Worrying that her vision of a faceless attacker could actually be a real threat. After the vision she'd had of Veronica and Lyndsey Roe, it felt more prophetic than ever. In the end Patty simply concluded with:

"…Or worse."

)(

Cassie chose the following Monday afternoon, when the café was far less busy. It would give her a chance to ease into it. Patty had placed a RESERVED FOR PSYCHIC sign on one of the small rounds so it would be hers whenever she wanted. Tucked away in the corner, it was private enough to offer a more intimate experience while still being visible enough to generate some curiosity.

From her macrame bag, Cassie pulled out the cloth mat on which she always drew her cards. She laid it neatly over the table-top. Beautifully embroidered with a stylized galaxy that graded from royal blue to black, at its center was a five-pointed star with each tip connected to the others by a crisp white thread. Running her palms over it with sincerity, Cassie smoothed the cloth as she absorbed its energy, absorbing its vibration while also allowing her own energy to be absorbed into it.

Next came the cards. A gift from Bill when he returned from Florida on yet another trip that ended up being longer than expected, each of the seventy-eight cards was handcrafted and individually painted. So, in essence, it was a box of six-and-a-half dozen small but original paintings. That alone was enough to make it inexplicably special, but there was more to it than that. From the moment she'd unwrapped them, Cassie felt a vibrant energy from the cards. A dynamic, positive pulse as if the deck had a heartbeat of its own.

"Oh, Bill. They're just…spectacular!"

"A spectacular gift for a spectacular gal." He winked, pulling her close. "I thought of you the moment I saw them."

"Cocoa Beach? I can't even imagine them selling something like this."

Bill shook his head. "And you'd be right. The beachfront shops there are all sandcastle kits and plastic rocket ships. This is from a daytrip we took for a meeting over on the Gulf side of the state, around Tampa Bay. A quaint little artsy town called Gulfport."

"Well, I just adore them. Thank you for thinking of me." She lifted herself on her tippy-toes and gave Bill a peck on his cheek.

"I always think of you, Cass. Don't ever forget that."

Don't ever forget that.

His words now echoed in her mind and suddenly the memory, which had begun so sweetly and filled with light, had bittered, becoming dismal grey.

It weighed heavy in her gut.

This is a mistake, she warned herself as her pulse quickened. It must've been convincing, for she had already begun involuntarily sliding the cards back into their box.

"Hey, whoa, there!" Patty had returned to her table with a cup of chamomile and a pep talk. Instead, she found Cassie packing up her stuff. "Got some more urgent plans I don't know about?"

"This is a mistake, Patty. Really. I don't think I'm ready to—"

"—Ready to what…run away? Too late for that, hippie chick. Your first paying customer is already here and walking this way."

She slapped four dollars on the table and watched Cassie's expression as the realization dawned. Not only did someone want to experience her gift, but they were willing to pay good money for the privilege.

"This is for me…? But I haven't even started yet."

"Yes indeed, chickadee. The house already took its cut." Patty waggled a dollar bill in the air before stuffing it in her shirt with a wink. "So yes, you actually have started."

The girl was younger, maybe late teens. The aura surrounding her matched the long red hair that flowed in enviable waves down her back to settle somewhere below her narrow waistline. A tie-dyed earth tone mini dress was cinched round the middle with a strip of beige leather. A pair of strappy sandals, while matching her makeshift belt, did little to protect her feet from the grime and dust of the city streets.

She was smacking bubble gum as she took a seat. Bracing her elbows on the table, she rested her chin in the heel of her hands as though her head were simply too heavy for such a slender neck to hold upright of its own accord.

Her name was Paige, but apparently everyone had taken to calling her Pegs. "Because I used to be so skinny," she explained. "You know, like I had peg legs or something."

Now Cassie couldn't help but draw her gaze to the girl's legs demurely crossed and extending at an angle from her side of the small table. The left was gently bouncing up and down atop the right. Tanned and toned, they boasted calves most women—and some men—would die for.

"Anyway, sounding so similar to my name 'n all, I guess it just stuck. I kinda hate it, but also kinda like it."

She shrugged and popped her gum.

Pegs was looking for answers about a boyfriend who, in her own words, had up 'n left in the middle of the night. She hadn't heard from him in over two weeks and wanted to know where she could find him.

"Oh, uh. Well," Cassie began to clarify with apology softening her tone. "I'm afraid Tarot readings don't work like that, honey."

The young woman's unblinking eyes remained transfixed on her own. Soft and full and perfectly round, their innocence belied the natural sensuality that oozed from her like warm honey. Had they been rich chestnut instead of dazzling hazel, they could have been the same doleful Bambi eyes from the movie Cassie and Bella had watched one rainy Sunday as Bella nodded on and off in her lap.

"Please, ma'am. I need this. Like, *really* need this."

With a muted sigh Cassie took the Tarot deck into her hands. Warm to the touch, the young woman's energy had already begun flowing through the cards as Cassie began a slow, mindful shuffle.

"Okay. But sweetheart…" The instinctual dance between her hands and the cards paused. "I want you to know that we may not get anything. But I will try my best and we'll see where the Universe leads us. Do you consent?"

Pegs nodded, her gratitude manifesting as a soft smile embellished the warmth in her eyes.

"I want you to close your eyes and take a deep breath. In through your nose. Then hold it and count to three. Then, you're going to expel it from your mouth very, very slowly. Okay? We'll do this together, Pegs. Three times."

By the third, Cassie felt Pegs' aura soften. Initially fiery red, a color associated with intensity and passion, it was now closer to a soft pink. A clear indicator that she had lowered her defensive shield and was permitting her caring, more nurturing side to come forward.

"That's really good, Pegs. Now, as I said, Tarot doesn't show me things in a concrete way. There's no such thing as peering into a crystal ball and seeing the lottery numbers, or where Aunt Sally misplaced her wedding ring before she died." But it can give us some extraordinary insight to your situation if we ask a powerful question with intent. Something open-ended rather than a closed, yes-no type of question. Do you understand?"

Pegs nodded.

"Now close your eyes. Focus on your heart, and when you're ready—and take your time, okay? There's no stopwatch here—I want you to open your eyes and ask me what you most need to know. What will help you make your life all that it can be?"

Pegs did as instructed, and after one more deep breath, she slowly opened her hazel eyes. Glowing with warmth they held Cassie's gaze and, in this moment, they were the only two in the world. In reality Brewster's had become unusually busy for a Monday afternoon. But none had existed but Cassie and Pegs. The café was now a sacred space, a haven of their own devise where they were one with each other and together were one with the Universe.

"Pegs," Cassie said so softly it was all but a whisper. "What is your question?"

Releasing a gentle breath she asked, "How does the Universe see my future relationship with my boyfriend?"

"Good. Now cut the deck, sweetheart. Close your eyes once more and allow yourself to sense the cards. To *feel* them. And when you're ready, trust your intuition; trust your place in the Universe and present to me the three cards which are the only ones meant for you in this specific point in time and space."

Closing her eyes once more, Pegs raised her chin and breathed in the pink aura she could not see. The aura which Cassie not only saw but *felt*. It twirled gently into Pegs' mouth between lightly parted lips and filled her lungs with its soothing light. When she exhaled, a soft breath that was little more than a whisper, her loving light kissed Cassie's face and became one with her as Cassie took it deep into her own lungs.

Now they were ready.

As sure and silent as an egret harvesting its meal from the water, Pegs slid three cards from the deck Cassie held in her outstretched hands. Pegs' intention was clear. These were the cards that awaited an audience with their divine goddess.

Opening her eyes, she handed them one by one to Cassie who laid them on the table in the shape of a pyramid.

"This," Cassie anointed as she placed the first card face down in the pinnacle position, "is you, Pegs."

She slid the next from her palm with a gossamer touch and placed it in the lower left point of the triangle. Also face down.

"This is your boyfriend. You may now reveal to me his name. First name only, please."

"Chris," Pegs answered in a voice as soft as silk. "His name is Christopher, but he goes by Chris."

"This card represents Chris. And this one—" Cassie turned the final card over and allowed it to float to the table in the triangle's third position. It fluttered in its descent, rotated in the air, and landed face up. "This one is the construct of your future lives. Together or not, this represents your future as it appears to the Universe in this present moment in time."

Cassie released the breath she'd been unconsciously holding. Visible to those who would permit their third eye to see it, an aura of purple flowed from her lips with fine wisps of Pegs' pink. Merging into one, they dissolved in the air between them.

"Now we delve into the wisdoms of the Universe."

She smiled as her eyes widened, brightened. She beckoned Pegs to join her in rising up from their near trancelike states into a fully alert and lucid one. The Universe had spoken. All that remained was the assimilation of its divine message.

Cassie turned over the first card at the apex of the pyramid, the one representing Pegs. The eighth card of the Major Arcana, *Strength*, was presenting itself upside down.

"Ahh, yes. Wow. Validation if ever there was." She absently tapped the card three times, and the sound was rich and commanding. If a sense of safety were a sound, this was it. "Unlike its Minor Arcana counterparts which signify more temporal circumstances or events, when a card of the Major Arcana shows up it is showing us a powerful energy at play. Perhaps overshadowing, it represents the potential for a life-changing shift."

"And what does this one mean? *Strength*." Pegs wetted her lips, a nervous energy rising in her countenance. "And why is it upside down? That kinda feels to me like it's not a good thing."

"We must remember one thing, Pegs. The cards are like a snapshot: they're how the Universe sees things in this immediate moment. But how we interpret what we're seeing is the most important aspect of understanding that picture. What do you feel it says to you, this upside-down card?"

"I think it's saying that I'm not feeling very strong right now."

"See, your intuition is quite impeccable, Pegs. A reverse card, oversimplified, does essentially mean the opposite of its right-side-up interpretation. Which isn't always a negative thing. This is a perfect example. Reversed, this card indicates the current state of your inner strength, Pegs. I'm seeing self-doubt, low energy. Raw emotion. That you feel like the ground is quicksand and every time you think you've found a rock to stand on, it all shifts and you're in danger of being sucked down again."

Cassie didn't have to ask if this interpretation was correct. Pegs' bright hazel eyes had glossed over, thick wells forming in the corners. Cassie handed her a tissue and Pegs wiped the tears from her eyes before they could fall.

"Oh, sweetheart. I understand how you feel. Everyone under-stands…if they're being honest. Because we've all been there. And many will be there again. But it's what we do about it that matters. Remember, this card signifies a major shift or life-altering opportunity. So while the Universe may have exposed a vulnerability it recognizes in you right now, it also reveals that all that's about to change. You're stronger than you think. A force to be reckoned with, sister!"

Cassie winked and this brought the hint of a smile to Pegs' lips. While still wet and glassy, her eyes brightened just slightly.

"Now this card represents Chris. Interesting that it also is upside down, don't you think?"

Pegs nodded, again wiping her eyes.

"Before I tell you what it reveals, that in itself has meaning. To me, this card is saying that you're both in the same metaphorical boat right now."

Cassie waved her open palm above the card and allowed it to hover there, absorbing its energy as her eyes partially closed. Its warmth radiated into her hand and spread to her wrist. It crept up her arm until she removed her hand and the feeling dissipated.

"Mmmm, yes. Okay. So, this card of the Minor Aracanum is in the suit of Pentacles which relates to the material realm of our lives. Finances, gain and the physical manifestation of our surroundings. The ninth card depicts a wealthy individual walking through abundance with their small companion, or pet, by their side."

"But upside down it must mean a lack of abundance?"

"To a degree," Cassie affirmed. "Yes, it can mean financial hardship or loss of possessions. But it can also reveal that Chris is suffering a sense of delay or frustration in his current circumstance. He may be feeling fearful about his own ability to provide for himself and the *small pet*—a vulnerable soul—who relies upon him for its safety and well-being. As a result, Chris may be over-investing in his efforts to try and make ends meet."

Cassie went silent.

Clutching a disheveled tissue with both hands, Pegs settled back into her chair without breaking eye contact. Cassie's gaze, however, had transitioned to a thousand-yard stare as her third eye took over and she viewed only the inside of her mind.

Pegs' Self-doubt. Low energy. Raw emotion. Quicksand.

Chris's frustration, even fear. A kink in his plans. Pushing himself to provide for the vulnerable soul walking beside him.

Cassie snapped back to the moment. Pegs' eyes again welled with tears while her own had become bright and focused.

"Pegs, sweetheart. You're *pregnant*, aren't you."

)(

The café buzzed and thrummed in the background, but only Pegs and Cassie existed.

Pegs dropped the tattered tissue and wiped away her tears with the back of her hand. Her voice cracked with emotion.

"Y-You can see that? It *really s-says* that?"

Cassie answered with a nod of her head, empathy softening her features. "Is it correct?"

Now Pegs nodded weakly in return, breaking eye contact for the first time and staring at her sandals. They scraped back and forth in small lines, emitting a dry, repeating *schhwickk–schhwaa* sound beneath the table.

"Does Chris know, sweetheart?"

"He s-s-s-suspects that I a-a-am."

"And you talked about it? The day he 'up 'n left,' as you say?"

"Yes ma'am."

Cassie handed her another Kleenex and Pegs dabbed at her eyes cast down. Every so often her breath would hitch, and she'd let out a soft whimper as she fought to hold back the hysterical sobs looming just beneath that fragile surface.

"Well, I guess we've gotten to the root of the issue. So, whaddya say we move on up from here, sweetie? Because I happen to see some very good news the Universe wants you to know."

She tapped the third card—the one in the lower right corner of the pyramid—which had floated from her hand and landed face up, so it was visible the entire time. Its message now made such sense to Cassie that it couldn't be more clear if it tried.

"Here, in the final position reserved for your future—yours and Chris's—we have the three of cups. Before I share the insight this card hails, how many individuals do you see on this card, sweetheart?"

"I can see...I guess...*three*?" It wasn't a trick question. Three people were clearly depicted on the card. No more. No less. Yet Pegs' response oozed with a lack of conviction that was on the verge of debilitating; far more a question to answer her question than it was an answer in, and of, itself.

…Self doubt…Shifting ground…Quicksand…

"And what significance do you sense in that number?"

Now Pegs lifted her head and began to straighten in her chair. She dried her eyes once more, but this time fresh tears did not replenish those she wiped away.

"Chris, me…*and baby makes three*?"

It was still spoken as a question, but it was clear that it came from a place of hope, not trepidation. Indeed her very tone and cadence and the unconscious rhyming of the words were testament to Pegs' blossoming change in perspective.

"Yes. I also believe that is what it's proclaiming." Cassie reached out and lay her hand over Pegs' and now the young woman hiccupped a light laugh borne of joy. "And do you see how these merry souls are emerging from the mouth of that horrible monster? This shows them overcoming what has been a dark situation. They are happy, joyous and—"

"—Celebrating." Pegs was openly smiling now, her relief evident in the liberated laughter of the reprieved. "They're celebrating!"

'Yes! They are! And here, do you see?" Cassie brought her attention to the woman standing tallest, head and shoulders above her companions. "See how she pours her chalice over her head as the other two clink theirs together in a toast?"

"Oh, yes. I see that…"

"She's finally forgiven herself, Pegs. More than that, she has grown strong and confident. Doubt and recrimination have been replaced by assurance and kindness. The water washing over her from that divine chalice has washed away her sins. You may call them her shortcomings, some even say it is nothing more than self-imposed guilt. Whatever your perspective, she is free."

"...And she looks happy," Pegs added. "Doesn't she look happy to you?" She pulled the card closer, turning and examining it with eyes that no longer reminded Cassie of the woeful fawn in *Bambi*, but of glorious hazel windows shining with hope and joy.

"Yes, Paige. She does."

) (

Cassie read the cards for two more people that day before her energy was depleted. Both readings were as successful as the first.

That's all it took for word to spread through Haight-Ashbury of a psychic—an impressively gifted psychic—offering readings for cheap out of Brewster's Café. While Cassie had only planned on offering readings one day per week, she found herself doing them every day that first week. In return, it seemed that half of Haight-Ashbury now frequented the café, just to see if they could find themselves at the receiving end of Cassie's astonishing gift.

Now, Cassie would be the first to admit that not every reading was as powerful, or every guest as remarkable, as Cassie's first three. But no matter how commonplace or repetitive their inquiries were—

Can you commune with my dead grandmother?

(No, that's a medium, which is slightly different, and I don't have that ability.)

Is my husband cheating on me?

(Sometimes he was. Sometimes he wasn't.)

Will I get that promotion at work?

(This was a yes more often than it wasn't.)

—Cassie felt buoyed by helping people find their way. Most left with a sense of satisfaction that they'd found what they were seeking. Certainly that they'd gotten their money's worth when they dropped their crisp five-dollar-bills in Cassie's donation pail.

A few, however, were not.

More than once that week a café patron had up 'n left (to use Pegs' words) when they realized the woman at the back table was not here to drink tea and chat with her girlfriends, but was in fact a godless pagan performing witchy hocus pocus for money.

The first two times it happened, Patricia Brewster sent them packing. They probably weren't from around here anyway, so no big loss: it wasn't like they were going to become regulars or something. Because nobody she knew—certainly nobody from 'the Haight'—would act in such a rude and close-minded fashion. And Patty wanted nothing to do with their money if they were gonna skunk up the vibe with minds so small it was a miracle their heads hadn't already shrunk to the size of an egg.

While this image made Cassie laugh and yes, she agreed with Patty's take on it, she didn't much care whether they accepted her or not. As far as she was concerned, they had just as much right to enjoy a beverage and some respite from the relentless summer heat as she and her clients did. So she told Patty to not even give credence to people like that, because making a fuss over them is exactly what they wanted.

"Just nod and smile and let them stay, Patty. Don't even worry that they might be bothering me, okay? Because they don't. I'll be damned if I'll let someone's bad juju harsh my mellow." She gave Patty a hug, rubbing her concern away. "Now, boss lady, if they up 'n leave of their own accord, as Pegs would say, that's on them..."

At the opposite end of the spectrum, they met one guest who'd waited quietly for more than two hours to see Cassie while drinking nothing but complimentary glasses of water, which Patricia was more than happy to provide. When it was finally this particular guest's turn, they asked with a modesty bordering on timidity, if it were at all possible to receive their reading for free.

Though Patty's first inclination was to say yes, she understood Cassie's shaky financial situation all too well. Not only did she have herself to take care of, she also had Bella. Things with Bill were progressing downhill at a rapid pace, and if Patty were being frank, she really didn't expect them to last much longer.

And then where would she be?

Even though Cassie called herself Bill Kennedy's wife, Patty knew that wasn't completely true.

In Cassie's heart? No question about it.

In the eyes of the law? Not even close. Cohabiting partners or a domestic relationship at best. And neither could shine a light on an actual marriage if legal push came to legal shove. Of course they had Isabella, but Patty didn't think that would make one damn bit of difference if Bill were to decide he just didn't feel like supporting his 'wife' who no longer wanted to support him.

Or even live with him.

Without some money of her own coming in, things could spiral downward for Cassie. *And fast.* As it were, some of Bill's weekly checks—the ones he'd promised Cassie she could always count on—had begun arriving just that little bit later than before.

The most recent hadn't arrived yet at all.

So, Patty declined the guest's request. Not without some considerable guilt. And a tinge of embarrassment for them both.

When Cassie discovered what happened, she made a pledge to Patty right there on the spot. From that moment forward, she would read for anyone. Whether they believed in the Tarot or Cassie's ability, or whether they thought it was all a big joke and something to do for entertainment. Whether they could donate the five bucks, or whether they couldn't. Regardless, they would all get a reading if they wanted one.

After all, this was Patty's café. She was the one who'd put her neck on the line, trusting enough in Cassie to believe she wouldn't make her—or her establishment—out to be a laughingstock. And Cassie wanted to pay that back to her by never making Patty feel she had to turn somebody away. Certainly not on her account, her own finances be damned. To Cassie Kennedy, the money wasn't nearly as important as her peace of mind.

And surely, didn't Patty feel the same?

Which of course she did.

So that was the last time they turned anyone away.

Little did they know how quickly this altruistic policy would become one they would never forget.

Not because of someone who didn't believe, but from someone who very much did. And not because of someone who was unable to pay, but from someone who very much could.

) (

Her name was Meredith Harper, and she wasn't looking for a 'will I find love' reading. Although a dedicated wife and doting mother, Meredith wasn't seeking insight from our guides beyond as to whether or not she might become a grandmother soon, or if her husband would get that final promotion he always wanted.

Because unbeknown to Meredith Harper, she was about to become the innocent harbinger of a truth so dark—and forged from a secret buried so deep—that even Cassie Kennedy herself had long forgotten it.

And that memory was about to change everything...

9

) (

THE READINGS HAD been going on for weeks, virtually every day, and for the first time in ages, a gaggle of customers were waiting on the café's sidewalk when Patty unlocked the door. Filtering in amidst a buzz of enthusiastic chatter, they chose their tables and proceeded to lay out books or newspapers before ordering a coffee, tea, or their favorite morning pastry.

One guest did none of these things.

Instead, she made a beeline for Patricia Brewster.

Well-dressed and in her mid-forties, she crowded the counter as Patty read the names of guests here to see Cassie.

"I'm well aware that a few of your patrons arrived before I managed to do so," the woman explained. "Equally, from our sidewalk small talk prior to you opening, I understand that at least two are preparing to sit for a reading with Cassie as we speak. Nonetheless, it's crucial I see her straight away."

Despite the woman's best efforts to remain dispassionate, a grave urgency had crept into her voice.

A pregnant pause.

With the self-assured confidence of someone who doesn't feel the need to micromanage their bank account, the woman then procured a hundred-dollar bill from her purse and slid it across the counter.

Pristine without a fold, dogear, wrinkle or crinkle in sight, the bill looked freshly minted. Patty imagined it being extracted from a currency strap of ninety-nine equally impressive others by a white-gloved bank teller with the nimble precision of a surgeon.

Inwardly bursting with giddiness but maintaining an air of detachment, Patty plucked the hundred from the counter, thereby furnishing the bill its first crinkle. As she examined it, she also noticed from the corner of her eye that the woman was unconsciously squeezing her hands together. So hard that it must be painful.

Realizing Patty had caught this nervous tick—the product of a restrained anxiety she was doing her best to keep from spilling over—the woman's aloof attitude softened.

Her eyes pleaded silently.

Folding the hundred in half, Patty slid it beneath the register's drawer and changed it out for tens. Given previous conversations about helping those in need, coupled with this woman's state of distress she was trying so hard to contain, Patty had already made the decision to move her to the front of the queue.

The official government-issued portrait of Benjamin Franklin didn't exactly hurt the woman's cause, though.

"Okay, hun. Wait here a mo' and I'll see what I can do."

With a sheepish smile Patty approached the two patrons who were booked to see Cassie first. Implicating herself in a fictional scheduling error, she offered both ladies their breakfasts on the house. Both being older women, and Brewster's regulars, each appeased her with assurances that they've made many such mistakes of their own in the past.

And of course we'd be happy to help, my dear.

Tucking one of the tens into the pocket of her apron, Patty crept over to Cassie and pressed a tight little fold comprised of nine others just like it into her unexpecting hand.

"For a single reading!" Boasting a self-satisfied grin and an '*I told you so*' look on her face, Patty winked as Cassie stared at the cash, her mouth agape.

"A hundred dollars? Patty, that can't be right. That's a fortune."

"A fortune given for a fortune told," Patty teased.

"Trish, be serious now. That's more than most people I know earn in a week. Are you sure?"

Patty nodded with the exuberance of a child. When she answered, she found herself all but whisper-squealing. "*Hell yes, I'm sure!*" She thumbed over her shoulder, pointing out the well-heeled woman at the counter. "See, hippie chick? That intense-looking lady? *Thar she blows.* Your first whale."

Suddenly Cassie felt oddly and uncomfortably self-conscious.

"You're on a roll, babe. And you deserve it." Patty waved at the woman preening herself at the counter, gesturing for her to come on over. "This gift of yours is really something. And it's starting to make a real difference. Now, the two of you gals go have a chat with the universe, or whatever. And have yourselves some fun!"

)(

Fashionably dressed in a rib knit A-line skimmer and matching coral jacket, the woman appeared every bit the confident, independent career woman who not only had her ducks in a row, but probably had them labeled and lined up in alphabetical order. Which meant she was probably also the kind of person for whom the cost of living posed absolutely no concern.

In short, she was everything Cassie aspired to be.

Why would such a woman feel compelled to pay twenty times the going rate—more than a week's wages for most—just to jump to the front of the line? She couldn't begin to imagine that her guidance would help this woman achieve, well, *anything* in life. Quite the contrary, Cassie wondered if she wouldn't do well to turn the tables, in this case literally, and pay *her* to learn how she could model her own life after this this woman's.

She was about to say that very thing and return the money when the woman cut her short.

"Meredith. Meredith Harper." The woman extended a perfectly manicured hand whose nails were now bitten down to the nub. Her smile was thin and closed, refusing to yield to what Cassie imagined were probably the whitest and most perfectly aligned teeth she'd ever seen.

"Cassandra Kennedy," she reciprocated, shaking the woman's hand, and Meredith's head tilted just enough to reveal her piqued curiosity. Leaning ever-so-slightly closer, she looked Cassie up and down as if she were weighing whether she though Cassie could actually be a member of that dynasty. Before she could ask the question which always came next, Cassie put pay to it. "Sorry. No relation."

Meredith straightened her shoulders and eased back into her chair, a silent *ahhh* issuing from her mouth. And Cassie knew in that instant that for one fleeting moment, this smart, confident, affluent woman had actually wanted to be more like *her*.

"It's a pleasure to meet you, Meredith," Cassie said.

"Likewise…*Cassandra*, was it?"

"Cassie is just fine," she offered, setting the tone for a more intimate informality which would be more conducive to the session. "How may I help you today, Meredith? Is there something in particular you're seeking? Perhaps I can help you find the answer…with the Universe's blessing upon the cards, of course."

The woman's austerity melted away. Lowering her head, she fought to choke back the emotions. Cassie spied a tear on her cheek before the woman self-consciously wiped it away.

"M-My...*daughter*..." Meredith spoke the words as if doing so would manifest a reality she was not yet willing to accept. "...Please, I'm begging you. Help me find my daughter!"

10

) (

MEREDITH HARPER'S EYES were glassy as she raised her head. She now spoke with the slow and measured deliberation of the forlorn. "She—*Hannah*—disappeared last week. At first, you think they've just lost track of time, you know? Went shopping and didn't realize how late it had gotten. But her husband, Jerry, was beside himself. 'I just know something's happened,' he kept saying over and over, and it was everything we could do to keep that boy calm. Getting all riled up wasn't going to help anyone. And besides, Hannah was going to come rolling into that driveway any moment. But then—"

Meredith swallowed hard, looking off into the distance. Cassie knew she was seeing nothing in the café, her mind taking her to that evening with her son-in-law and the moment she was about to share next.

"But then we saw the blood. Well, *I saw* it. First, it was just a drop. In the kitchen. Small and hardly noticeable. Barely even red. It was more of a rust color, like a stain."

Meredith began pointing, a weak and incomplete motion that

reminded Cassie of the way a dog's leg will twitch as it runs in its sleep. In her mind, Meredith Harper was no longer sitting in the café on a bright summer afternoon, but standing in her daughter Hannah's home as the August sun began to set and the summer storm clouds rolled in.

"There was another…in the breakfast nook. I didn't say anything right off. Lord knows I've cut myself peeling potatoes or slicing carrots more times than I could ever count. But I began to see a pattern—a trail of sorts—and I followed it. The drops were bigger and closer together as I made my way down the corridor to the bathroom. They were dark, like I said. Pretty much dry. But a few of the bigger ones were still claggy and when I pressed my finger against one, the dark film over it gave way and the tip of my finger came up sticky and deep red. That's when we went to the police. And, well, they…they…"

Now the fatigue was apparent in the woman's features; the weight of worry recognizable in her darkened eyes.

"Oh, Meredith…I'm so sorry."

Cassie took her by the hands.

A wave of energy swept through her like a current and Cassie was forced back in her chair.

Except that chair was no longer in the café.

It was in Hannah Wilson's house.

A week earlier.

The same day Meredith had just been describing.

There the mother stood, examining her reddened fingertips in the hallway. She was not aware of Cassie in this fractal of space and time because Cassie, of course, had never been there. Now there merely as a ghost of sorts, she was an invisible spectator; both present and not present at once.

Cassie barely registered what was happening before time slowed so dramatically that for a moment—if it could be called that—it stopped completely.

Impossible though it was, Cassie watched in amazement as the second hand of the Wilsons' pea green plastic wall clock ceased ticking. Then began moving backwards.

The pause between each ticking second no longer remained steady, each becoming half as long as its predecessor. In what would have been less than three seconds of actual time, the clock hand had spun a full cycle in reverse. In that backward minute, Cassie now saw firsthand what Meredith Harper had been describing. Rubbing her thumb and index finger together, but now doing so in reverse, the drop of blood did not smear across her fingertips but reshaped into a well-defined spot. Bending down, Meredith dabbed it onto the beige carpet and it reformed with the rest to become slightly larger again. When Meredith lifted her finger, the blot turned from bright red back to dark, almost brown, the film of its bubble again dry and rust colored.

Now Meredith was rising from her knees, striding in curious backward steps. Pausing in two separate places as she went—the second so briefly it barely counted as a pause—she continued to scurry backward into the living room where she spun in wild reverse circles around Hannah's husband Jerry. Frenzied hand gestures centered around the bathtub soon became so fast that they were all but visible. Meredith Harper herself then became a blur as she and Hannah's father disappeared in reverse through the front door and were gone, having never been there.

Whirling backwards around the home in a flurry, Jerry Wilson ducked in and out of various doors until he, too, was little more than a streak of color sucked out through that same front door.

Now came a moment of stillness, the scene mildly trembling like a time lapse recording from a camera poised upon an unsteady tripod.

Then Hannah appeared.

The door flew open to reveal the young wife cocooned in a translucent shower curtain. Printed with a pattern of blue bubbles, great pools of blood flowed slowly within its folds. Crawling before her like a thousand animated cilia, Hannah's long blonde hair pulled her lifeless body through the doorway. Behind her, grimacing and leaning back as he resisted the pull of Hannah's slinking hair, a man with no face gripped Hannah's ankles like the handles of a wheelbarrow. Unable to stop her hair from tugging them both into the house, he blindly reached behind and slammed the door shut.

No longer trying to resist, the man released Hannah's legs, guiding them slowly to the floor.

After a few reverse laps around her body entombed in plastic, he grabbed Hannah by her ankles. Once more he leaned back, resisting with great effort as Hannah's long blonde hair again pulled them both through the living room and down the corridor. As they passed the pea green wall clock, Cassie saw its hands rotating counterclockwise at a furious pace:

3:42

3:41

3:37

3:26

Now in the bathroom, the man unwrapped Hannah's lifeless body amidst a flurry of choppy, unnatural motion. As he began to roll her corpse from the shower curtain, the smears of her blood flowed together to become rivulets.

Clamping his right hand over Hannah's unmoving lips, he plunged the hunting knife gripped in his left into one of the many blood-soaked slits in Hannah's chest. Sucked from the plastic sheet, a plume of blood arced through the air, following the motion of the blade before squeezing into the gash in Hannah's body with surgical precision. The man did this again and again, miraculously stitching Hannah back together until all but three of the incisions were gone.

With the next retraction of the knife Hannah's back arched in a violent spasm, her panic growing with each of the next two plunges of the knife that inserted more blood into her body. After the last, once the man had healed all the slits in her soft, young skin, the rivers of blood had returned to her body, the shower curtain once again clean.

She became still.

Only her chest rose and fell, shallow breaths as the faceless man clenched the shower curtain beneath her and magically pressed it out from beneath Hannah's unconscious body.

With the reverse flourish of a magician pulling a tablecloth from beneath a place setting, he then cast the sheet from his hands. Flying up to the metal rail over the tub, the plastic curtain threaded itself upon a dozen hooks until it had hung itself neatly back where it belonged.

Straddling her unawares, the man now kissed her—long and slow—upon lips that were bloodied and swollen. He then dealt Hannah Wilson three brutal punches to the face. Each one cleared some of the blood from Hannah's mouth and chin as her head rocked to the side. By the third blow, all of it had been cleaned away and Hannah's lips were no longer puffy.

Her eyes shot open.

Reanimated, Hannah sucked in a scream as she lay upon the bathroom floor, kicking and grabbing fruitlessly at the sink basin, the tub, the hamper. Finding no grip, she clasped her fingers around the man's forearms as he now spun her around and pushed her out of the bathroom: again the wheelbarrow with her long blonde locks acting as the wheel.

Once in the corridor, the man knelt. He wrestled with the young woman on the floor until they leapt together to their feet, clinging to one another in an unnatural embrace. The man set a finger to her lips, mouthing *shuussh*, and in an instant, Hannah's fear and confusion melted away to a natural smile as the man released her.

Over her shoulder, the frenetically spinning hands of the pea green wall clock began to slow.

3:16............3:15.........

Side-by-side, Hannah and the man now walked backwards into the living room. There they paused, chatting, but speaking so quickly it was impossible for Cassie to know what was being said. Though somewhat stilted, she felt the interaction to be cordial, a modest smile upon Hannah's face.

It remained as she escorted the man to the door, both of them walking in reverse, opened the front door and saw him out.

Alone, Hannah danced a bright backstep through the living room to the record player. Lifting the needle, she removed a vinyl album from the turntable. Her hitching, jerking movements slowed and in a few moments, they resembled normality.

Here the scene halted.

Time reset.

Hannah now moved naturally, both in direction and speed. She again pulled the record from the paper sleeve she'd only just placed it in. Palming it onto the turntable while taking great care not to tarnish its grooves with the oil of her fingers, she lowered the needle to the wide outside track.

A week later, in a café forty minutes away, Cassie Kennedy heard the faraway sounds of wolves crying. This was followed by four powerful, orchestrated chords that were the unmistakable intro to Deep Purple's new single, 'Hush.'

The song wasn't even through its first verse before Hannah's doorbell rang. With a smile as genuine as the young woman herself, and filled with nervous anticipation, Hannah Wilson danced across the living room to answer it...

)(

Cassie gasped, releasing the breath that had been balled in her throat. She unclasped Meredith's hands, mere seconds after taking them into her own, and Meredith reeled back in her chair.

Brewster's Café went quiet.

Twisting in their seats, a few mid-afternoon patrons craned to see what had rent the gentle, almost hypnotic murmur of coffee cups and casual conversation. Behind the counter, Patricia cut the steam from a frothing wand and its hissing gurgle bubbled to silence in a pitcher of lukewarm milk.

Only the soft jazz being broadcast from local a.m. radio KFRC was immune to the outburst as it lilted away in the background, none the wiser.

At their table in the corner, Meredith Harper's face had gone ashen. Cassie's wore the panic of a little girl lost.

The entire vision had taken place in the blink of an eye. Now Cassie was left to face Hannah's mother.

A woman who would give anything to know where her daughter was; a woman who had come to her for help.

"You've seen something," Meredith stated with rising emotion once the lightning bolt of surprise had dimmed. Finding herself able to think with greater clarity, the mother repeated, "You've *seen* something!"

This time, that overwhelming sense of yearning had returned to Meredith's voice…along with a subtle inflection that rang of hope. Deep within eyes which had been dulled by unbearable loss, Cassie saw a spark of promise attempting to ignite them.

Still, she had no reply.

How could she? What could she possibly say?

A flurry of thoughts spun through her mind, not one substantive enough to provide a foothold as Cassie clung to the crumbling vertical rock face that was a new reality.

"You know where she is—" Rising from her chair, Meredith's voice had also risen. She either didn't notice or didn't care that her chair had toppled in the process. "—You know, don't you?

Where my daughter is!"

) (

Meredith Harper's chair slapped the floor with a snare drum clap.

"I don't." Cassie's answer came without hesitation, almost a reflex. Now she found herself also rising from her seat, gesturing for Meredith to settle down. "I did...*experience*...something, but please, Mrs. Harper. You must calm down. *Pleas—*"

Too late.

With a damp coffee-stained dish towel over her shoulder and fists firmly balled into her hips, Patricia was already at their table.

"Everything groovy over here, ladies?"

It wasn't really a question.

Meredith Harper showed no interest in the café owner, if she even noticed Patricia at all. Standing before a toppled chair with her palms hard and flat to the table's surface, Meredith leaned aggressively forward toward Cassie.

To Patricia Brewster, who'd been entirely unaware of what was really going down, this was unacceptable. For all her fancy clothes and crisp hundred-dollar bills, in Patty's mind, Meredith Harper was no different than any other client. And any one of them had the potential to be less than thrilled about the outcome of a reading.

...No, she was not going to become a famous actress. And no, there wasn't a million dollars on its way from some mysterious and long-lost relative...

Patty Brewster reached for Meredith's forearm.

She was a heartbeat away from escorting her through the front door when Cassie stopped her with a silent plea that conveyed an apology as much as it did a commitment to handle the situation.

Patty released her arm, and as if stirring from a sleepwalk, Meredith was back in the present moment. Becoming aware of

Patricia's presence and the steely gaze of the majority of the café's patrons, she sat without a word. Shrinking in her seat, she smoothed her skirt across her thighs and avoided contact with anyone.

With an audible and very deliberate *harrumph*, Patty returned to the espresso counter where a beatnik who was surely a writer of sorts was impatiently waving his check.

"Look, Mrs. Harper," Cassie broke the awkward silence, reaching for Meredith's hand. "I can only imagine where your mind is at. I have a daughter too. Isabella—I call her Bella, sometimes Bella Luna because her eyes are as big and bright and beautiful as the moon—is five years old. She's my absolute everything. I couldn't even begin to imagine how I'd be if something ever happened to her."

A tear formed in Meredith's eye as she again wrung her hands together so tightly that her fingers began to whiten.

"But yes, I did see something. And I'd like to share that with you. If…" Cassie unclenched Meredith's hands and took them into her own. This time, she did not spiral into a vision. She did not see the woman's daughter overcome in her hallway, then stabbed in her own bathroom to be wrapped in a shower curtain and dragged unceremoniously out of the house, her long blonde hair trailing behind her. What Cassie saw was only Meredith Harper: Terrified Mother. "…If you'll please just take a breath, we can talk. For a start, I need you to validate that what I saw was a legitimate vision, and not just a product of my own imagination. Okay?"

Without looking at her, Meredith nodded. The tear which had welled in her eye reached critical mass. It slowly breached her eyelid before rolling fat and wet down the mother's cheek.

"Okay then. Meredith, does your daughter listen to music?"

As if a marionette on a string, Mrs. Harper's head snapped up. Her eyes glistened. "Oh my God, yes. Hannah *adores* her music."

"Good. Okay. What kind of music does Hannah like?"

"Oh my. Well, she enjoys all kinds of music. Always has. Hannah wanted to be a dancer when she grew up. Had the body for it, too. But then she married Jerry and all that changed." Meredith's spirit became warmer, brighter, as though she were capable of shining her light directly into her Cassie's soul. And for one intense moment Cassie found herself wondering which of them had the real spiritual power here. "But you know how that goes. We all know. Don't we, sweetheart?"

Cassie did not reply.

Now her light extinguished as quickly as Cassie had sensed it. Meredith Harper scrunched her nose, the way you do when you suddenly smell something unpleasant.

"Hannah's really been into that awful rock music recently. Jerry, her husband, has been digging it, too. In fact, I wouldn't be a bit surprised if Jerry was the one that got Hannah into it. I mean, we love Jerry. He's a good son-in-law, I suppose. But I've always felt that he's a bit of a bad influence upon Hannah."

A faraway look clouded her eyes and Cassie could tell the mother was again back in her daughter's home on the day Hannah went missing.

"So, you don't care for today's music?"

Mrs. Harper's eyes refocused. "You know, dear, I just don't get it. Neither does Hannah's father. This new music—it's all just a bunch of noise if you ask me. Just awful. Truly terrible."

Cassie ignored the editorializing that reminded her too much of her own estranged husband, and proceeded to the question that would be the first real test of her vision's credibility:

"Do you know if Hannah owns an album by the band Deep Purple, Mrs. Harper?"

) (

Meredith Harper broke into tears.

)(

Holden

)(

11

)(

HANNAH AND JERRY had been high school sweethearts. He was on the track team; she, the marching band. It was the drumline she craved to be part of, but her parents—her father in particular—wouldn't hear of it.

Not nearly ladylike, he'd reasoned.

So, she settled for the clarinet. It was hardly the same. While the drummers were pounding out a beat, their sticks fast and furious, she was breathing into a reed with her dainty fingers pressing lever keys and tone holes to produce what was at best an irksome sound. Of course, a good player could really make a clarinet sing—just look at jazz greats like Jimmy Giuffre and Art Pepper. But Hannah Harper was not a great player.

Given their respective choices in extracurricular activity, Jerry and Hannah's paths rarely crossed. It's not often you'll see a marching band at a track and field meet, after all. But their late summer practices sometimes overlapped. Hannah and the marching band would be in the school's parking lot, the crumbling blacktop lined off in orange cones to signify the hash marks on a football field; Jerry and his fellow runners would be on the adjacent practice track. On these occasions they might run into one another, both beading in sweat as the Pacific Coast sun scorched Jerry's infinite cinder loop, and the heat rose from Hannah's treeless rectangle of blacktop in visible thermal waves.

It was after one such occurrence that Jerry Wilson, soaked to his bones with sweat that glimmered upon his skin as if he were coated in baby oil, overcame his dread and asked Hannah on a date. It was little more than a burger and a Coke float at the local diner on the southern outskirts of Sausalito, but to Hannah Harper, it might as well have been the Ritz.

All she saw was Jerry.

They dated throughout the rest of his senior year and vowed to keep their relationship alive while Jerry attended U.C. Berkeley and Hannah finished her final two years at South Sausalito High.

Though the distance between them was less than thirty miles, for Hannah to visit using public transport meant taking no less than three buses and one trolley ride. A grand total of a good hour-and-a-half's journey each way. But with the high school's football team so often playing on a Saturday afternoon—which meant Hannah was marching on that turf and puffing pained notes into her clarinet during halftimes—any possible visit was limited to a Sunday. She would wake at six to catch the first bus just before eight, getting to Jerry's dorm around nine-forty-five. The latest she could return was the three-thirty-five bus from downtown Berkeley which, after the numerous changes, got her home sometime close to five-thirty. Just in time for Sunday dinner with her parents.

Then it was dishes, homework, and an hour of TV with her folks. This was followed by a reasonable bedtime so Hannah could be up bright and early and ready for school the next day.

And so the cycle repeated.

It didn't take more than four or five of these Sunday visits for the luster to wear off for Jerry. The first, he was awake and waiting, flowers in hand. The second was after a late-night drinking session with his new friends and he had been hung over and listless most of the day. He did little other than lie around his dorm room drinking more beer between naps while Hannah took walks alone around the beautiful campus. The third and fourth were nondescript. For the fifth, Jerry did not make an appearance until Hannah had been waiting outside his dorm for three hours. They had lunch together in the local campus café, then it was right back on the bus for Hannah and another soul-destroying series of rides home.

Still, she loved Jerry and understood that college was a time for him to not only learn, but to make new friends and grow into the man she so wanted to marry. In the absence of being able to see one another in person, they made do with letters every few days and a long-distance phone call on the weekend. This was limited to ten minutes by order of Hannah's father…*because they weren't made of money and that boy could make a little more effort too, y'know. Get a part-time job or something. After all, it wouldn't hurt for the kid to understand the cost of being an adult and actually paying to call YOU every now and then.*

After graduation, Hannah worked as a waitress at the very diner where she and Jerry went on their first date. She'd had plans of studying performing arts, dance in particular, and dreamt of being a star one day. But parcel to those plans was her attending the Los Angeles campus of the University of California, four hundred miles away.

Jerry wouldn't permit it.

"We already barely see one another. If you're even farther away, we'll never get together," he explained on one of the few days he spent with Hannah when he was back home for his three week Christmas break. "And I gotta tell you, Han, college boys can't be trusted. They'll be on you like flies on shit. And then we'll be through." He swiped his palms together as if he were wiping filth from his hands. "You just gotta trust me on this."

And she did trust him.

Because he had said more than that. He also said she could start at UCLA once he'd graduated and they were finally married. He'd find a job in the city so she could go to school while he went to work.

After all, Los Angeles was a bustling place.

"Heck," he added, "living in a city like that you could run into some big time director who would want to make you a star. Look out world! The next Ginger Rogers is here!" He squeezed her tight and spun Hannah round and round until she was giddy.

"Gee, wouldn't that be neat!" she agreed once she'd caught her breath.

"*Wouldn't?*" Jerry half-asked, half-reprimanded. "I think you mean *won't* that be neat, don't you, baby? 'Cause there's no 'maybe, shoulda, coulda or woulda' about it. It'll happen!"

So, Hannah waited.

Besides, the diner wasn't so bad. She met lots of nice people there and after six years, the owners had become like her second family; the other waitresses, her adopted sisters.

Because she'd never left.

Sure, they'd gotten married right after Jerry graduated from Berkeley, just like he said they would. But the L.A. part of the plan just never happened. It wasn't Jerry's fault. He was offered a position he couldn't refuse with a happenin' new company on San Francisco's North Beach which offered Jerry more money in his first year of employment than Hannah's father had earned in any of his. That meant a nice house—a new two-story near the water in Sausalito—nice things, including not one but two TVs.

And the most gorgeous cars Hannah had ever seen.

"To make up for UCLA..." Jerry said as he handed her the keys to a brand new 1966 Ford Galaxie convertible. "If my baby's going to keep working at that crummy little diner every day, then my baby's gonna get there in style."

It was the most beautiful thing Hannah had ever seen. Pearl white, with a matching soft top. Red leather seats. Chrome wheels inside a set of whitewalls that still smelled like rubber. Those sexy fins that ran alongside each long, slender barrel that eventually ended in those groovy round taillights.

And that trunk.

That sleek, massive trunk.

"Just think of the shopping you could put in there, baby doll."

And Jerry was right. She went shopping almost every weekend, either before or after her shift at the diner, and boasted a dreamy wardrobe her mother could only imagine having. The irony of this did not escape her as Hannah was required to wear a uniform at work—the same pink skirt and button-down blouse that all the waitresses wore. She just wore hers with more of the buttons buttoned.

Over the years, she'd earned a few promotions. Rising to the level of dayshift manager over the wait staff, she'd occupied the role for about eighteen months now. And Hannah loved the additional responsibility. But most of all, she loved that she was still able to interact with all the neat people (and a few not so neat—but that came with the territory) who she felt privileged to meet every single day. People from all walks of life. She especially loved the conversations.

Oh, those conversations!

She had them with business owners and executives, actors and directors, writers, singers, musicians and just about every other kind of famous person you could imagine. But the conversations she enjoyed most were those she had with the other regular folks, folks just like her: the secretaries and school nurses, the accountants and clerks; salesmen, garbagemen and servicemen.

A young man from the latter category was her most recent

acquaintance. He was twenty-something years old, just like her. Went by the name of Holden. And was freshly home from Vietnam.

To look at him, you wouldn't think Holden a soldier, let alone a combat infantryman on the front lines of a war being fought in an exotic land on the other side of the globe.

For a start, he was built differently than most men she knew. Something about his appearance struck Hannah as being less American G.I. and more European male model. Slight in stature. High sculpted cheekbones. Skin that was smooth, hair that was shiny, and hands that weren't thick and calloused, but on the cusp of being delicate...the way Hannah imagined an artist's or a pianist's might be. It wasn't a stretch for her to picture Holden's long, slender fingers tipped with a set of immaculately manicured and painted nails. Pondering this more than once, she wondered if they would be even prettier than hers.

Then there was the fact that Holden was softly spoken with impeccable manners, possessing a natural, easy charm that made you just want to be around him.

It's not difficult to understand why Hannah found him so relatable. For a man, Holden exuded remarkable balance between his inherent masculine and feminine traits. He didn't seem to share that same predisposition for toxic masculinity that most men in Hannah's life—her husband Jerry included—were so concerned with projecting. And yet Holden—*unlike Jerry*—had waded through rice paddies, crawled through jungles, burnt leaches from his body and shot M14 rifles. And Holden knew what it was like to kill a person. There was no doubt whatsoever in Hannah's mind that he'd put his share of commies in their graves before their comrades were able to return the favor.

Oh, and there was one more thing. A big thing.

Holden liked music. *Loved it.* In one of several moments of vulnerability he even admitted to Hannah that it was one of the few things that helped get him through that twelve month tour of duty. Which, along with everything else, made Holden just about the most intriguing person Hannah could ever want to meet.

Their platonic friendship started with the usual casual mundane chitchat, remarking on the weather, what cool things they had done over the weekend, or what they were planning to do next. But it wasn't long before those conversations took on the heft of actual substance:

WHO WAS THE BIGGER INFLUENCE ON THEM GROWING UP, THEIR MOTHER OR THEIR FATHER? Holden said neither. His mother had been killed in a car crash when he was only young. His father had been a Methodist preacher prior to serving in World War II but had come back a different man. A broken man. One day, not long after Holden's mother had died, Holden's dad left and never came back. Holden, his brothers and one sister then spent a brief time with their aunt and uncle. But something happened there— something bad—and they were then bounced around the foster system for years. Until Holden reached eighteen and was drafted to serve his twelve month tour of duty in Vietnam.

After hearing this, Hannah felt unexpectedly guilty for having grown up with such a vanilla, run-of-the-mill childhood in such a normal, middle class family. The exuberance with which she was going to speak about her mother—her best friend—now seemed selfish and perhaps even childish, so she simply said, 'my mother,' and asked the next question that came to mind:

HAD HE EVER INDULGED IN PSYCHOTROPIC DRUGS?

Yes, Holden admitted without compunction. They definitely had helped him expand his consciousness. But he also felt they were somewhat overrated, especially given the side effects and a lingering anxiety he experienced more times than he didn't.

Hannah, on the other hand, had never, ever even thought about taking them. The mere idea that everything could be entirely out of her control just filled her with dread...though she was now becoming more curious than ever before.

WHAT DID THEY THINK ABOUT THE LOVE-INS AND THE SUMMER OF LOVE TWO YEARS AGO, AND DID THEY PARTICIPATE?

Holden did, twice in July and once in August. He hung out with tens of thousands of strangers who'd flocked to Haight-Ashbury and adjacent Golden Gate Park from seemingly every place on earth. All three times he'd planned on just taking in the vibe and chilling to some killer live music from local Haight residents the Grateful Dead, Janis Joplin, Jefferson Airplane and more. But when Timothy Leary exhorted the crowd to *'turn on, tune in and drop out,'* Holden found a single day morphing into a mind-blurring, week-long marathon of music, sex and limitless possibilities.

Was he glad he'd taken part?

Absolutely.

But in the moment, it hadn't felt so much about societal change as it did an excuse for a throng of disenfranchised but hopeful young people to get high and fuck. It certainly didn't seem to match all the hype about social justice, equality and creating a better future. But then again, maybe that was how the winds of change blew. Perhaps they began as a whisper. Because underneath the music and the noise and the drugs and the sex, the point was being made that just because certain things had been accepted, not accepted, or always done a particular way, didn't mean that that was how things had to go on.

Maybe that's all the Summer of Love was really about.

Hannah had no idea.

That summer had been the second year of her marriage to Jerry, and he had expressly forbidden her from going anywhere near Haight-Ashbury or Golden Gate Park that summer. *For your own safety, baby doll*, Jerry assured her, sealing it with a passionless kiss on the cheek.

But, with a coquettish grin, she now admitted to Holden that she had been propositioned despite staying away from those places. At the grocery store, no less. By two men draped in beads and a beautiful brunette with flowers spilling from her hair. Apparently, Hannah was just far-out-gorgeous. Especially in the eyes of the brunette. So they began coaxing her to drop out with them and make it a foursome.

Hannah was tempted.

So tempted.

After marrying Jerry, the contemplation of throwing all her physical, emotional and sexual inhibitions to the wind would have been terrifying and foreign. It would also have been the last thing to ever cross her mind. But in that moment, it felt like total freedom. Here was the chance to emancipate the vibrant, dynamic girl she once had been, but had locked away in a place so deep and dark that she'd almost forgotten that girl ever existed.

Would it hurt to let her out again, just this once? Just for the afternoon? Because, and let's be honest here, Jerry would never in a million years suspect her of doing such a thing. So, would he ever really find out?

But with a dozen eggs, four sirloins, two cartons of milk and several bags of frozen vegetables in the trunk of her Ford Galaxie convertible, Hannah chose to do the responsible thing. The expected thing. She chose to go back home to Sausalito.

Maybe I'll meet you guys there?

Before the last syllable had passed her lips, she knew it was a lie. She fidgeted with her car keys, timorous but bristling with a nervous energy she hadn't experienced for a very long time. She just couldn't do that to Jerry. Neither could she relinquish control of her polished, enviable new life to that girl she had once been…the girl who would have envied this opportunity the most.

Right on. Catch ya there.

The trio responded with smiles that felt sincere despite the blindingly obvious charade. They flashed her the peace sign and wished her love and light and the best life she could live.

Peace out, sister Hannah.

) (

Neither of them planned for it to become an affair. But Holden now frequented the diner more often…only when he knew Hannah was working. Hannah knew this because she had asked Tina, who had become one of her best friends over the years. Funny how working at a place will do that. Because if it weren't for the diner, Hannah and Tina's paths would likely never have crossed. Not only was Tina a fair bit older, she was also nothing like the friends Hannah had in school. Tina Mercer was brash. Opinionated. The antithesis of well-read and couldn't tell you a beat poet from a beetroot. But she was fun. And also the most genuine person Hannah had ever met. Life may not have handed Tina much in the way of brains or beauty, but her account surely had been stocked to overflowing with blind optimism. And, more importantly, a proclivity to want to spread it.

"Oh yes, indeedy," Tina chided, digging a finger into Hannah's side as they snuck a quick cigarette near the dump bins behind the diner. "Only when you're on shift, girlie-girl. Never see that handsome young buck anywhere near this grease pit elsewise."

After several minutes without speaking, Hannah snuffed her cigarette against the wall and tossed it into a half-filled bucket. She fingered her wedding ring, twisting the wide band round and round as her friend watched out of the corner of her eye.

"It's a tough call, hun," Tina admitted as she too contemplated the options while smoking her cigarette down to the filter. To make sure it was out, she squeezed and rolled its ashen tip between fingertips permanently stained by nicotine. A dry, sandpapery sound scored the awkward silence. "I can hear them gears whirring away from all the way over here. What's going on inside that pretty little head of yours?"

Hannah shrugged, still looking within. Her eyes had lost their shimmer, locked in a thousand yard stare.

"Okay then," Tina responded. "What's going on in that great big, beautiful heart?"

"Gosh, Tina, I wish I knew. I really do." An unconscious sigh escaped Hannah's lips as she emerged from her kaleidoscope of ethereal, colliding thoughts. A shiver like the sensation of soft trailing fingertips tingled between her shoulder blades.

"Oh, I think you know plenty good enough what's in your heart. Your head just doesn't think you should dance to the rhythm that drum is beating."

She was right, of course. Hannah had known for a while now that she had romantic feelings for Holden sparking in the furnace of her emotions. Now that the pilot light had been lit, all it would take would be for her to turn on the valve. If she did, that gas would ignite, and she just knew its flame would burn hotter and brighter than it ever had for Jerry.

She'd experienced a similarly intense moment of passion when the three exotic hippies had propositioned her last summer. Returning to an empty house, Hannah had been bristling with such an intense sense of lust that she'd dropped the bags of groceries on the counter and rushed to the bathroom. There she stripped to her bra and panties in front of the mirror and masturbated. It was the first time she'd done such a thing so brazen, and the orgasm that came as she watched herself was more fierce than any she'd ever had.

Now, she had that same urge to drop everything for Holden. Except there was something much deeper about this desire. Something that felt like love. *Real, actual love.* Not safety. Not security. But somehow, the opposite of those things. With Holden, she felt her life was impatiently waiting for her. Scary, uncertain, wonderful life. It was a blockbuster movie she couldn't wait to see; a bestseller she was restless to read. And every second that ticked by without doing so was another second she wasn't experiencing what was hers for the taking.

"Phew. Well—" Tina responded once Hannah had finished speaking her thoughts aloud "—sounds like that heart of yours is gonna have you dancing to the beat *no matter what* your pretty little head has to say about it."

Hannah sucked in her lips, nodding.

Then, after a pregnant pause worthy of the timing of Carol Burnett, and in a voice uncommonly similar, Tina clarified:

"So…in front of the mirror, you say?"

Hannah gasped. She shrieked. "Oh my God, I can't believe I actually told you that." The heat in her cheeks rose as she shrank against the wall. "What was I thinking?"

Tina did not immediately reply. Giving Hannah the side eye as she bounced all ten fingertips together, she was an evil mastermind pondering her next move. "Well, well, well. Guess which girl's just got herself some new after-work plans…?"

She drew both thumbs toward herself with a slow and steady certainty, her eyes and her smile widening.

Another pregnant pause.

This girl, she mouthed, a single eyebrow raised.

And the way a summer thunderstorm sweeps away the mugginess of a sweltering day, Hannah's rolling laughter dissipated the fear of the decision that, in truth, she had already made…

12

) (

I T ALL CAME to a head on Hannah's twenty-fifth birthday. Jerry forgot. If he didn't, he showed no indication of such before heading off to work as usual. She would have given anything to hear, 'I can't wait to give you your gift later' or, 'I won't be late— we're going out!'

Instead, Jerry gave her the customary peck on the cheek.

And a task.

"I'll see you tonight, Hann. Oh, and don't forget to collect my dry cleaning, will ya? That new place on Stafford I like."

Hannah stood in silence in the living room, listening to the throaty hum of Jerry's Corvette fading into the distance as her enthusiasm trailed away with it. Her profound disappointment had nothing to do with the lack of a gift, or even the categorical absence of any ceremony. At just twenty-five, she already had pretty much everything she needed. And she never really did enjoy birthday parties—or any occasion—where she was made the center of attention.

All those people staring at you? Waiting for something clever to come out of your mouth? Pretending to be on your side, but really, they're silently judging you? No thank you, very much.

She preferred being on the periphery. Not the spotlight.

So, it was none of the above that hurt. What pained her heart more than anything was the simple fact that they'd been married just three years and already Jerry was so indifferent that he couldn't remember even one special day.

Was he a busy man?

Of course.

But did that make it alright?

With the advent of her budding friendship with Holden, Hannah had been second-guessing her emotions more and more these days. And more often than not, in these little internal cross-examinations, she found herself coming to the same conclusion. Not only did Jerry no longer put in the effort, he didn't even *pretend* to anymore. Just three years in, and already he cared so little that he couldn't even bother to have his secretary schedule a reminder.

So no, it wasn't the presents or the pomp that would have made Hannah's morning perfect. But a kiss—a real kiss—coupled with a simple, 'Happy birthday, my love!'

Both effortless.

Both costing nothing.

Both priceless, to Hannah at least.

Both might also have kept her alive.

)(

The diner where Hannah worked was the antithesis to the otherwise mundane start of her twenty-sixth year. Arriving as she did on any other day, Hannah was greeted *this* day by a sea of pink and blue helium balloons bouncing along the ceiling, and a rousing cheer from everyone in the restaurant. Staff and customers alike.

Behind the counter, with a smile threatening to break free of the confines of her face, Tina kicked off a round of applause.

Mortified, Hannah lowered her gaze and shielded her burning cheeks with her hands. She skirted awkwardly between tables of clapping customers and made a beeline to Tina.

"You're awful, Tee!" she whispered. "You know that? I told you how much I hate this stuff."

Tina replied by wrapping her arms around Hannah's waist. Kissing her, she laughed with genuine mirth while squeezing her tight. "I know. I'm such a little dickens."

"Such a little dick, more like."

To this Tina feigned outrage and disbelief, covering her mouth wide with surprise. Taking a step back, she fanned herself with an invisible hand fan, now the demure southern belle whose sensibilities had just been injured. "I dare say, child. The *mouth* you have on you. And in mixed company, no less. *Tsk tsk tsk.*"

"God, some days I just really hate you."

"I know. Hate you too, babe." Tina kissed the soft part of her cheek, just in front of her ear, and Hannah shivered.

Wasn't Jerry supposed to be the one giving her the feel-good goosebumps?

"Thank you, Tee. So much. Seriously. You have no idea how much you've turned my whole day around."

"Oh, I think I have some idea."

"*Uh-hem.*" From behind, a man cleared his throat.

Jerry.

It had to be.

It all made sense now, the way he'd acted so normal. Like he didn't even know it was her birthday. No good wishes. No kiss. Certainly, no gift. Even going so far as to give her a chore.

See! He didn't forget. He organized... all of this. A surprise party. My first ever.

With any lingering bashfulness gone, the many eyes upon her became invisible and Hannah saw only her husband.

"Jerry! Thank you so mu—"

She swung around to find herself facing Holden, hands behind his back, his eyes glimmering clearest cerulean. "Any chance a cat like me can get in on this action?"

She hadn't even noticed Holden in the crowd. But then again, had she really been aware of *anyone*? Battling every impulse to just turn tail and skedaddle the moment the place had erupted into cheers, it was all she could do to pick her way through the crowd of swimming faces.

Thank God they hadn't burst into song—that godawful song—or she might've legged it.

From behind Holden's back, a decorated cake magically appeared. Ablaze with burning candles, wisps of smoke rose from a few that sizzled and popped. Their radiant heat became a gossamer veil before Holden's face, causing it to waver the way the road ahead appears malleable, almost liquid, on a blazing summer day. And for just a moment, Hannah saw someone else in Holden's features. Someone she didn't know.

Someone—some*thing*—frightening.

The effect was fleeting. Just like that road, which was always solid as a rock, the face was again unmistakably Holden's: handsome, warm and unerringly steadfast. He cleared his throat...

...and began to sing.

Supporting him, the entire diner became his backup singers: "*Happy birthday, to you. Happy birth—*"

Heat flushed Hannah's face and she cringed, smiled, laughed, cringed some more until the last note had been sung. She clapped, hands high in the air, applauding every one of them for making her feel so special...and awkward. The perfect combination for any birthday. "Aw, thank you. Thank you so much. Everybody!

This really means so much to me. I love all of ya!"

Choruses of, '*Love you too, Hannah!*' erupted from various pockets around the restaurant until the clamor of conversations and cutlery against ceramic plates slowly returned.

Hannah twisted back to Tina and Holden. "Oh, you two...!" She palmed her cheeks, still warm and rosy. "Thank you for doing this. Both of you. So sweet!"

"Don't blame me, kid." Tina shrugged; pointed toward Holden. "Your friend here is the culprit."

"Holden? How incredibly thoughtful." She lifted up on her toes and gave him an innocent peck, anyone watching be damned. Holden was now a friend, and a good one at that. And Hannah wasn't about to let idle gossip stop her from thanking a friend. "How did you even know?"

He winked at Tina. "Let's just say a little bird told me."

"Well, thank you again. And thank you too, little bird."

"Oh, and this is for you." Again something seemed to magically appear from behind his back. "That same little bird may have said something about you being into this scene."

He handed Hannah a flat, square gift wrapped in silver paper with black satin lace tied beautifully around it, a bow sitting proud at its center.

"Oh, Holden. You shouldn't have! Seems like that little bird's been rather chatty..." Carefully preserving the ribbon and bow, she stripped the paper away to reveal the record album, *Shades of Deep Purple*. "Oh my God. I love it! Thank you! Don't you just dig their single, 'Hush'?"

"It's the best. That howling wolf at the beginning? So cool."

"Then you should drop by sometime. We could listen to it together—" She'd presented the invitation before she realized it. Delayed apprehension now swept across her face. "Oh. Holden, look I'm sorry. I wasn't thinking. You know I can't—"

"Sure, I'd like that," he cut in, not allowing her the opportunity to retract the invitation. "I think that'd be a real gas, y'know?"

Hannah cast her eyes down. She stared at her feet, noting how one pointed inward toward the other when she was nervous.

"You know I'm married, Holden. I can't just have men around..." She paused, weighing if she should add the rest which was already on the tip of her tongue. She decided she would. "...No matter how handsome and, well, just far out perfect they are."

"Hmmmm."

"I mean, what would Jerry say?"

"Why would he say anything?"

"About me inviting a man over to listen to music? I really don't think that would be his cup of tea. Jerry's not into music like you and me are." Hannah swallowed, the taste of her next words bitter and thick. "And he just wouldn't be, well, *happy* about me inviting you over, that's all. He can be the jealous type, and I'd be afraid he'd ruin our friendship."

"Well, who said your husband has to be there? Doesn't Jerry—" Holden hated saying that name. He vowed there and then to never speak it again. "Doesn't...*he*...go to work? All the way across the bridge, in the city somewhere?"

)(

It was one week later when the doorbell tolled the beginning of Hannah's brutal and barbaric end. She had just pulled the album from its paper sleeve, taking great care not to taint the vinyl's grooves with the oil from her hands. Holding it between her palms, she threaded the record onto the turntable's spindle and lowered the needle to the wide outside groove.

First came the faraway sounds of wolves crying. Then four powerful, orchestrated chords that were the unmistakable intro to the single, 'Hush.' Deep Purple weren't yet through their first verse before Hannah's doorbell rang.

With a smile as natural and genuine as the young woman herself, Hannah Wilson danced a bright step across the living room to answer it.

) (

It wasn't who she expected...

13

)(

JESUS, CASSIE, YOU really saw all of that?" Patty was slack-jawed, an unlit Virginia Slims clinging to her bottom lip. Cassie replied by only nodding. "Please tell me you did not tell Meredith Harper you saw her daughter attacked like that? Good God, Cass, you can't have told her mother that."

Cassie barely shook her head no.

"Christ, girl. Thank God. I mean, what if you're wrong?"

"I'm not wrong."

She almost considered reminding Patty that it was *she* who always claimed Cassie had a gift; *she* who insisted her dreams were psychic visions; *she* who had persuaded her to do readings here at Brewster's.

"Well, what do we do now?"

"We don't do anything, Trish."

Once again, and quite unconsciously, she'd truncated the last part of Patricia's name instead of the first. The only person to ever call her Trish, and only when she was under duress, they'd often joked that if she were ever kidnapped, Patty would know it was her if the abductors were to put her on the phone and she called her Trish. The fact that she was addressing her that way now told Patty that she was taking this harder than she might be letting on.

Stepping away to pull another espresso, she lit her third cigarette in ten minutes. As the burr grinder turned rich Kona Arabica beans into sand-like grains, the habitually pleasant fragrance of the café warmed and brightened further. "Did you see his face?"

Cassie indicated that she hadn't. "Just a blur. Sorta fuzzy. I mean, he had a face. But to me it was devoid of any features. Same as the man who comes for me in my own dreams."

At the counter, Patty forced steaming hot water through the portafilter, and the machine gurgled and spluttered until two dark and broken streams of espresso solidified into caramel-colored ribbons. It was almost hypnotic until the phone rang, its jangling peel amplified as it rebounded from the breezeblock walls of the empty café.

Cassie jolted in her chair, while Patty seemed to not hear it at all. Focused only upon the details of her friend's vision, she was lost in thought.

"Like one of those clothes mannequins, Cass? You know, like the creepy ones over at the Emporium that only have bright white material for a face, almost like a bleached football...?"

"Yes!" Cassie snapped her fingers and touched the tip of her nose as if they were playing charades and Patty just guessed the first word correctly. "Exactly like that. Only dark instead of light like that. See? How can I possibly go to the police again? What on earth would I tell them this time?"

The phone kept ringing.

"Without cementing your identity as a whack-job, you mean?" The question was genuine, Patty refraining from the sarcasm she would typically employ right about now.

"Yes."

"Nothing, babe. You can't say a damned thing. You stay far away from there and that Detective Douchebag."

Cassie laughed, a sharp little snort. "You mean Detective Ressler, I think."

"Isn't that what I said?' Anyway, the last thing you need is to insert yourself into a second investigation. Seriously."

Persistent, the caller hung up but then immediately called back. The phone rang twice as Patty's edict hung in the air. A third time. A fourth, as Patty walked back to the table, latte in hand. A fifth. Then nothing but the fading echoes of someone's query left unattended.

) (

Patty turned the sign on the door to read CLOSED a good two hours earlier than usual. She and Cassie sat alone at a table at one of the two bay windows. After the jarring bell of the telephone, the silence lay heavy.

Cassie was the first to break it.

"I can't, can I?" she finally responded, "Say anything, I mean."

"No babe. You can't. They'll either commit you or incarcerate you this time. No joke. Can you imagine how that convo would go? 'Remember me? Great! This time I'd like to share some very specific info about a sadistic murder I happened to witness.'" Here Patty paused, nodding as she played out listening to the response from an imaginary phone comprised of her thumb and pinky fingers outstretched as if they were the receiver's ear and mouth pieces. "'Yes, I was sitting in a café, miles away from where it happened. Oh, and this was a week later. Uh-huhm. Oh, well let me explain: I saw the whole event in another psychic vision. Like the last one I reported. Only this one ran backwards through time.'" She paused again, nodding as a grin started to creep onto her face. "'Yes. Uh-huh…Well, you see, I was about to give a tarot reading—'" She nodded again, "'Of course I can come right on down there, Detective Douchebag. And bring a change of clothes for the next ten-to-twenty, you say? Right-oh.'"

"Okay, Patty. I get it. And I agree with you. But you don't hafta be such a C-U-Next-Tuesday about it."

Patty laughed hard and sudden and real, a coffee mist spraying from her lips. Cassie found herself chuckling right along.

Until reality set right back in moments later.

"Oh, Patty. What do I do? That girl's mother believes her daughter is still alive and out there somewhere. How do I tell her that she'll never see Hannah again?"

What a strange thing to contemplate, wanting to actually remove someone's hope instead of bolstering it. But hope, that wonderful thing that buoys us in times of hardship, can also be the most cruel thing. Sometimes it prevents us from finding the truth. From accepting. From—*eventually*—moving on.

"What did you say to her before she left?"

"I certainly didn't tell her what I saw. I told her she should go to the police again.

"And what did Mrs. Harper—Meredith—say to that?"

"She said she already did. Of course. The very next morning. As soon as Jerry told them Hannah still hadn't come home." Though speaking to Patty, Cassie's gaze was to the side and far away. "She said a couple of deputies came within the hour. Asked Hannah's husband, Jerry, some basic questions. Looked around. Checked out the drops and dried splotches of blood."

"And?"

"Insisted it was nothing more than you might find in any house if you looked hard enough. Especially if the person did a lot of cooking, or maybe worked on fixing the place up. You know, using knives or saws, that kind of stuff."

"So, now they think she's Julia Child?" Patty asked.

"Or Ms. Ace Hardware."

Patty drew on her cigarette, the tip glowing as the sound of the burning tobacco quietly crackled and hissed. "You gonna see her again?"

"I said she should check for a Deep Purple album on Hannah's record player. If there is one, it would validate a few things I was seeing. You know, basically ensuring that I'm not wrong…"

"But you're not wrong."

"No, I'm not." Cassie took a deep breath. "I'm sure of it, Trish. Like, *really* sure. Just like I was—still am—about Lyndsey Roe and her mother Veronica."

"Have there been any updates on that poor little girl, by the way?" She watched Cassie squirm. "Oh, come on, girl. I know you checked in about it. You wouldn't be you if you didn't."

"I called and asked to speak to Detective Younger, the nice one."

"And did anything you tell them help their case?"

Cassie lowered her eyes, barely shaking her head. She spoke in a whisper. "He said they found no record of a Janice Wynn in the San Francisco tax registry."

"Okay, so maybe she's not from here."

"That's what I said, too. Of course they already thought of that. I mean, this is what they do. Hey, can I get a drag of a cig?"

Patty's eyes widened. "Really?"

Cassie nodded. "Just a little puff. I really need it."

She accepted the filtered end of the freshly lit Virgina Slim and pinched it between her lips, inhaling hard. The heat of the smoke hit her lungs and came right back out in a hacking plume.

Patty chuckled and took the burning cigarette from her fingers as Cassie intermittently gasped and coughed. It was a minute before she got it under control, the tears gathered in her red eyes.

"Better?" Patty asked and blew a smoke ring toward the ceiling.

"God, how do you handle those things without hawking up a lung?" She downed half a glass of water, clearing her throat one more time. "Mr. Younger said they checked the records of every county in California. No Janice Wynn. Anywhere. Which was at least nice of him to tell me, because he probably shouldn't have. I think it was his way of saying, as sweetly as possible, that I'm a little bit far out, so to speak, and should maybe keep my distance from here on out."

Patty stubbed out the cigarette. Its bent carcass sizzled and continued to ooze wisps of smoke as she talked, focusing only on Janice Wynn. "So, she doesn't exist? Or she's not from Cali."

"Right. And yet I know what I saw, Patty. I know what I *felt*. How else would I know her name, not to mention the names of Lyndsey and Veronica?"

Patty picked up a copy of that day's San Francisco Ledger. "Maybe from this?"

"Are you saying I made it up?" Cassie stiffened, sitting upright and crossing her arms.

"No babe. I'm just playing Devil's advocate here. What if you saw a headline about them being missing and didn't realize it? Or maybe heard a news report and it just didn't register until your vision that night. Is that possible?"

Cassie frowned. She shook her head slowly once, and Patty tossed the broadsheet paper back down on the adjacent table.

"Look, Cass. I believe you, hun. I'm just trying to help you figure out what to do here. Because if it's real—and I *do* believe you're really seeing these things—then we have to find a way to use it to help these people…without the cops having you committed or something."

"That's why I need to have this vision validated. If that Deep Purple record is on the turntable in Hannah's home, then I know I'm right."

"And if it's not?"

"I don't know how to answer that, Patty. If there's no album like I said, then I got it all wrong. Which means Hannah wasn't attacked. And that would mean there really is no Janice Wynn, either." Cassie considered this for a minute. "But it would also mean that I'm crazy."

Patricia said nothing more, crushing the smoldering cigarette butt against the inside of her demitasse cup. The embers sizzled in the loam of the dark Arabica.

) (

It wasn't the next day or so that Meredith Harper returned to Brewster's Café.

It was right now.

Yanking on the handle, the door shuddered in its frame but did not open. She did this twice before scurrying to the window and cupping her hands either side of her face. Peering in, she scanned the unlit room. It was only a moment before she spotted Cassie and Patricia at a table in the other window and she ran there now, knocking fervently on the glass which flexed with each blow. She then took a step back and raised a cloth tote bag as if it were her most prized possession being displayed to her classmates in a grade school 'Show and Tell' report.

She then returned to the front door and waited.

"Meredith," Patty greeted as she unlocked the bolt. "Are you here to see Cas—" The words weren't out of her mouth before the mother brushed past her, a missile locked on target.

Barely capable of restraining her enthusiasm, she trembled visibly as she stood before Cassandra Kennedy, *Tarot Card Reader and Psychic Extraordinaire.*

"You were r-right," she stuttered, pulling a purple square of cardboard from her tote bag. On it, five oddly colored men's faces stared back at Cassie, their looks ranging from shy to guileful. Above them, emblazoned in funky block capitals, were the words: SHADES OF DEEP PURPLE. Meredith tilted the album cover and the record in its sleeve came sliding out, almost pitching to the floor.

It was only saved by Cassie plucking it out of the air before it bounced off the table's edge. "Look at it…go ahead. Just look…!"

Brimming with an odd mix of validation and trepidation, Cassie removed the album from its paper sleeve. She pinched it by its edge as Patty gawked over Meredith's shoulder. The vinyl was covered with a fine dust, its rich black color now a spotty patchwork of grey. "What is this, Meredith? What am I looking at?"

"Turn it over!" The woman was barely able to contain the feelings bounding through her like an emotional calliope. "But be careful…" She pantomimed using her palms to hold and rotate it.

Cassie followed her lead and slowly wheeled the record so that SIDE A was facing up. There, clearly visible in a heavier coating of dust, was a single, perfectly defined fingerprint.

A right thumb, to be precise.

Cassie gasped and nearly dropped the record.

Patty drew in a breath, then let it out as a single, run-together exclamation. "Holy-shit-on-a-stick."

Meredith trembled as she spoke. "You were right, Cassie. You were right! This rock album was on her record player. In the living room. Just like you said it would be." Seeing Cassie's blossoming confusion, she explained: "I went straight over there after I left you this morning. Jerry knew nothing about this album. Said he'd never even seen it before, let alone bought it for her. So I took it straight to the Marin County Sheriff's office, just like you said I should do."

Cassie was mute, astonished as Meredith Harper spelled it out for her: "That's *not* Jerry's fingerprint. They took his prints last week when Hannah first went missing. Just a matter of protocol, you see. So they were able to compare it and rule it out. This one," she reached down and drew an invisible lasso around it, "is too small to be his thumb print. But it's also too big to be my baby's."

She held her thumb close to the record, just above the powder, but ensuring not to touch it.

"See? Hannah has dainty fingers, just like her mama. Our hands are almost identical in size."

If that's true, Cassie contemplated, *then she's right.*

By the very nature of perspective, Meredith's own thumb held inches away from the album should have eclipsed the dusty print if it was even similar in size. Instead, Cassie could still see ridges and sweeping whorls of it peeking out from behind Meredith's thumb. Yet it appeared smaller than she expected. Bill, Cassie's own husband, was hardly a bruiser, but she imagined his print being quite bigger than this one.

"So if it's not Jerry's, and it's not your daughter's…then whose thumbprint is this?" Cassie puzzled over the album, perhaps unaware of speaking the thought aloud.

Meredith nodded, a swift and certain gesture. "Exactly. Don't you see? It was my baby's twenty-fifth birthday last week. And Jerry certainly didn't buy her this record. In fact, when I popped by with my own gift, Hannah admitted to me that Jerry didn't even remember it was her birthday."

"When exactly was Hannah's birthday, Mrs. Harper?"

"Tuesday, the twelfth of this month."

Ten days ago, Cassie calculated. "And what day last week did Cassie go missing?"

Meredith's expression clouded, her optimism bordering on sanguine excitement instantly dissipated. "A week ago. Thursday, the fourteenth."

Just two days after her birthday.

"Do you know if Hannah had any guests over for her birthday, Meredith? Or maybe the day after…like last Wednesday?"

"None. At least not that I know of." Meredith Harper lowered her gaze as if what she was about to reveal was her fault. "Jerry, Hannah's husband, is a very—well, let's just say—a very *strict* man. He isn't the type to throw a party…or even allow her to have friends around very often."

"Not even on her birthday, for God's sake?" This was Patty's question, posed as she took a seat next to Cassie and indicated for Mrs. Harper to do the same. "Not even if she was home alone?"

"*Especially* if Jerry's not home," Meredith replied. She'd begun wringing her hands so tightly that the ends of her fingers were losing all color. "And like I said, I *was* with my daughter briefly on her birthday, after she got back from work, that is...but before Jerry got home. I like to leave before he gets home. That way there's less chance of upset, you understand." She sought concourse from the other two women before continuing. "And I know she chose to work a double the next day—Wednesday—so no one could have been at the house that day either."

"Which leaves only Thursday." Cassie was already following the logic to its natural conclusion. "That means this fingerprint either belongs to the person who gave Hannah the record...or to whoever—"

"—Whoever was with my baby the day she went missing," Meredith finished for her. Rather than fill her with trepidation, this notion seemed to spark a renewal of Meredith's hope, for a glimmer returned to her eyes. "And if it helps the police find the person, maybe they can tell us where Hannah has gone."

Forcing a thin smile, Patty acknowledged Meredith's summation without pointing out the obvious. Politely excusing herself, she disappeared through a beaded curtain to a small office where Cassie knew a flask of Scotch awaited the café owner in the bottom left drawer of her desk.

Cassie, now alone with Meredith, also had nothing to say. Instead, she bowed her head and gently closed her eyes, taking one long, deep breath after another and releasing each more slowly than the previous.

Both bolstered and terrified by knowing her vision was real, she took Meredith by the hand.

Meredith did not interrupt. Despite an impulse greater than

any she'd ever had, she did not speak. She did not demand to know what else Cassie had seen that had led her to ask about the record album. She did not insist upon the answers to questions that had to be swallowed like a fistful of horse pills forced down her throat.

Instead, the mother clasped Cassie's hands, squeezing them so tightly that her fingernails had begun to pierce the skin. On the back of Cassie's right hand, minuscule beads of blood appeared like sundrenched freckles.

Cassie did not notice.

What she did notice was the electric charge that ran through her upon Meredith's touch; the heady feeling like she'd had one too many drinks. Her focus on the café was growing blurry, the colors and the sounds becoming faint.

In their place was the bright, crisp yellows and whites of a living room, one she'd seen before.

A doorbell.

And the driving beat as Deep Purple's 'Hush' began to fill her ears, feeling the sound in her chest as —

)(

—Hannah lowered the turntable's clear acrylic dustcover. Cassie watched as Meredith's daughter danced brightly across the sunken living room, brimming with giddy anticipation. This brought a smile to Cassie's own face as the young wife reached for the doorknob. Also like Hannah's, Cassie's smile darkened when the door opened.

Standing on the stoop was not the man Hannah had so desperately wished it would be. And yet, it seemed that she somehow knew him. Although inviting him in, uneasy concern was etched upon her face as she stepped to one side, her hands clenching and wringing one another as the faceless man strode into the living room.

Now Cassie was no longer watching the scene play out in third person but had become one with Hannah. She saw the scene through Hannah's eyes; felt the air of the ceiling fan across Hannah's skin; smelled the mix of cologne and sweat through Hannah's nose.

Held the scream beginning to form in Hannah's lungs.

"You have a beautiful home here, Mrs. Wilson." *That voice. Cassie was certain she'd heard it before.* "I'm assuming your husband is not with us at the present moment?"

To be clearly heard above the music, the man was speaking more loudly than was necessary. For dramatic effect, he cupped his hands around his mouth like a megaphone to further project his voice.

Hannah did not volunteer an answer. Her downcast eyes— *now Cassie's eyes*—scanned the pile carpet as if studying the very fiber of its composition.

"Might I turn this down, Mrs. Wilson?" the faceless man bayed, a preemption more than a question as he was already halfway to the turntable. "And do you mind if we drop the formalities and I call you Hannah? After all, you already know me too...in a roundabout sort of way."

Gripped in her right hand, Hannah Wilson's left visibly trembled. Her nervous energy immediately coiled its way into Cassie Kennedy, who now found herself staring down at the hand she had never before seen: the wrist more slender than her own; nails painted a garish pink she would never choose to wear.

The wedding ring she did not recognize.

Meanwhile, the faceless man had turned away to carefully raise the clear acrylic cover of the record player using only the indecorously long, filth-encrusted nail of his pinky finger. Lifting the needle without care, the music fractured with a crackle and pop through the stereo's two large speakers.

Spotting Hannah sidling toward the door in his periphery, he spun back toward Hannah without warning. In his haste, his left foot caught on the carpet's thick pile and for the briefest moment, he faltered. Bracing against the stereo cabinet, he shook his head in a humorless and unhurried fashion while issuing a *tsk tsk tsk* between gritted teeth and a grotesque, facsimile smile.

Hannah-cum-Cassie gasped.

And there the scene froze.

Like a film projector forced to hold on a single frame, the image of the faceless man quivered and twitched. Cassie focused hard, mentally zooming in to the partially obstructed hand he'd thrust behind him. Slowly releasing another breath and then holding it, she honed in on her target the way a sniper might.

The vacillating, film-like image steadied.

And there it was, clear as day: in the act of catching his balance, the man's greasy thumb had pressed upon the black vinyl record. It was unmistakable. What's more, its location near the edge of the album matched the spot where the Marin County Sheriff's Department had preserved his error in white aluminum powder before duly photographing and cataloguing it.

This elicited a fierce tremor of excitement in Cassie that surged through her. It was because of her prompting that the killer's fingerprint had not only been discovered, but had been preserved before it could be contaminated.

How easily it might not have been, Cassie thought.

All it would have taken was for Jerry to find that record sometime later and simply put it away. Not only would doing so have tainted the evidence, but the album itself would have vanished amongst hundreds of others in the Wilsons' sizeable collection, never to be noticed again.

Without Cassie's vision, the evidence wouldn't exist.

The terrifying reality of such transience didn't bear thinking about. Because not only were visions like these exhausting, they also felt largely out of her control.

Uncertain that she'd be able to drop into this moment again, and not knowing how long she might be able to remain here now, Cassie fought the exhausting pull of reality and took note of as much as she could. Above all else, she wanted to see the killer's face, once and for all, before this opportunity was gone.

Concentrating more mental energy than she thought possible, Cassie focused only upon the man's empty mannequin head. And little by little, sporadic portions of his features began to materialize. But none appeared simultaneously with any other:

Part of a nose.

A glimpse of a chin.

The unexpected glimmer in the wavering hint of an eye so blue it surely had been fashioned from the sky itself.

Her stomach tightened, a knot the size of a softball growing as her energy plummeted and the captive scene began to quiver more violently and blur. Pushing with every ounce of energy she had left, Cassie held fast despite the searing pain that now scraped her from the inside out until she had barely the strength left to govern her body's own functions.

A mouth appeared. Lips so full and hot that Cassie felt the tingle of blood coursing through them as if they were her own.

Then all at once, in a moment not unlike a flash of lightning, the features came together and formed a distinct, cohesive face. It was a psychic sucker punch to the stomach, and the air vacuumed from her lungs as the scene unfroze.

Speeding up so fast that the motion became blurs of color, the center of the image melted into brilliant light and Cassie was ejected from the vision.

She burst into reality the way a person having held their breath for too long bursts through the water's surface. The vision's colors were now the café's colors, and they whirled together in a cyclone of haze and blur. And just like that, the killer's face was gone.

It made no difference, for Cassie had already seen it: a face she would never—could never—forget.

Because it was the face of someone she knew.

14

)(

WHAT STARTED AS a soundless shriek was now a hissing, sucking gasp for air as Cassie came out of the vision and pushed away from the table. Cups and condiments tumbled to the floor. Startled, Meredith Harper nearly tumbled from her seat as well, but managed to lurch to her feet instead.

"Listen, I—I'm so sorry, ladies. I don't…honestly…I don't know what happened," Cassie lied. Even at a whisper, her voice cracked with emotion. "I saw—"

the face of someone I know

"—nothing else." Real torment added a layer of natural credibility to the lie that Cassie couldn't have fabricated if she'd tried. "I think maybe I just pushed myself too hard to see something that might help you, Meredith. God, I'm so sorry."

The light in Meredith Harper's eyes dimmed and she lowered her head, avoiding eye contact. To say she was beyond tired was an understatement. She was tired of being fearful. Tired of feeling weak and fragile. Most of all, Meredith Harper was tired of not knowing. But how could she not worry when her only child was missing? Was she to simply ignore the weight of mourning and desperation that came from such a loss?

Cassie gave her a thin, consolatory smile.

"I wish I could tell you something else, Mrs. Harper." Cassie took the mother's hands in hers and they felt cold and somehow insubstantial, like the woman herself was beginning to fade away. "I truly do. But I just haven't seen or felt anything beyond a feeling that I was meant to ask if Hannah owned a Deep Purple record. I don't even know why—or how—I knew to ask you that. It's not like I saw anything...it was more of a feeling."

Meredith nodded, still unable to make eye contact.

"But because of that, you were able to find a fingerprint. And the police are working on it, right? Going through their database for a match?" Cassie softened her voice, moving closer. "When you came to see me this morning, I'm sure you thought, 'Maybe this girl can tell me what happened to my daughter.' Or perhaps you believed I'd get some kind of image that would show us where Hannah actually is right now. But I've given you everything, Meredith. And I know you'll find your daughter soon. Alive and well. I'm sure all of this will prove to be just some terrible misunderstanding."

The lie was acid in her mouth. But she saw no other way. How could she possibly expose Meredith to the brutality she now knew had taken place in Hannah Wilson's Sausalito home?

More importantly, how could she admit that the vision not only revealed to her the man's face, but that it was a face of someone she knew?

) (

The vision couldn't have been right about that, Cassie insisted to her spinning mind. *No, this time I was wrong. Period.*

She began running through a list of reasons why it had to be wrong. For a start, she was hardly experienced at this. She'd only been offering 'intentional' readings for a matter of days. Up to now, they were just a fun thing to do for friends or herself. Truth be known, all she expected was to lay down a few tarot cards for people, tell them what they wanted to hear, and make a few bucks in the process. It was a chance to spend more time around living, breathing people for a change, instead of hiding away between stacks of books at the library. And if it helped give Patty's café a little extra something to draw more customers, then all the better. Her friend deserved that success.

She never expected to receive *real* visions: things like Lyndsey Roe's abduction or savage attacks on young wives in their own home. Her only consolation was that if her 'gift' was wrong about the identity of the man, then maybe it was wrong about a lot of things. Maybe Lyndsey Roe and her mom were just fine. Perhaps they had taken off from an abusive man. And envisioning Hannah's attack was only more evidence that Cassie's own subconscious fear—

scelerophobia…see, irrational!

—was rearing its ugly head. More intensely than ever before. Except now it was projecting itself onto other poor unsuspecting victims.

Just like the curse of the Kennedys, she reminded herself. *Never satisfied, it keeps eating in concentric circles outward until it devours everything and everyone in its radius.*

And in an odd way, this made Cassie feel better.

Because maybe—just maybe—telling Meredith she would soon find Hannah alive and well somewhere wasn't as far-fetched as it first felt.

Pulling a tissue from her purse, Meredith wiped away the tears clinging heavy to the corners of her eyes. She thanked Cassie for everything she had done and apologized for any pressure she might have placed on her, feeling a sense of responsibility for that terrible seizure. "Are you sure you're alright now?

Cassie nodded, reassuring her with a hug before walking arm-in-arm to the door.

"Keep praying, Meredith. And make sure you keep your hope alive." *Now, why in God's name would you tell her that? Is it Meredith you're trying to convince...or yourself?* "You be sure to let me know when you hear something."

She couldn't stop herself. The need to dismiss the vision was so strong she would've said anything if it would have helped corroborate what she wanted to be true. It was like some rare verbal disease beyond her control. The words just kept spilling out until she closed the door and locked it.

Evading the silent judgment in Patty's glare, Cassie skirted around her friend to banish herself to a booth at the farthest end of the café. Sliding onto a cracked vinyl bench with her knees tucked up to her chest, she pulled herself into a tight ball. Resonating from a place she could not reach, the face of that man—

a man she recognized

—glared at her—

directly at her

—as he stood with his back to Hannah's record player. Its wrongness was a low, humming drone running through her, like the ominous thrum of a subwoofer you can feel but not hear.

Yet it just wasn't possible.

He... wasn't possible.

She wept as that face was all she could see in her mind's eye.

A face she had known most of her life.

) (

"Now," Patty said with a tinge of rancor as she rifled through a drawer for the pack of Virginia Slims every cell in her body was aching for her to find. "You wanna tell me what you *really* saw?"

The cigarette popped and crackled, its gently glowing tip becoming poker red as Patty took a long, fulfilling drag. Not only was this first hit the most satisfying to her yearning lungs, it was also the most intense. In a split-second the draw was rushing a magical little chemical called nicotine through her bloodstream to the adrenal glands that would welcome it with a spectacular release of adrenaline.

And just like that, everything was a little bit more manageable as a wave of chemical bliss quenched a thirst in Patty's body, mind and soul in a way nothing else ever had.

Or, she was starting to believe, *probably ever could.*

Easing into Cassie's booth with a slow exhale that felt as close to the ebullience of salvation as she believed she'd ever get, Patty seated herself opposite her friend. Cassie's head was buried in her knees as she rocked back and forth, arms cradling her legs, her tidy little Mary Janes planted firmly on the vinyl seat.

If a vision of a brutal attack hadn't brought such a response, Patty couldn't even begin to imagine what could. She began to ask once more…but immediately decided against it. She cut herself short, and her words issued as a tiny wisp of air as she chose silence over answers.

As unsettling as that may be.

After smoking two more cigarettes down to their filters, a measurement of time as precise as any clock in her book, Patty could no longer stomach it.

"*Eh-hemmmmm.*"

No response.

"You alive down there, sister?"

Cassie's reply was a sideways shake of her head.

"Oh babe. You gotta tell me what happened."

Another little head shake. This one even smaller.

"Cass. Hun…" Patty squeezed her more substantial frame into

the booth next to Cassie until she was tight up against her. Still, half a butt cheek hung over the edge. "Hey, how 'bout you scooch over just a smidge and let a sister rest *all* her ass?"

This stopped Cassie from rocking, and though she hadn't lifted her head from the tight human ball she'd created of herself, Patty was sure she heard the lightest breath of a laugh. It may have been mixed with the sniffles of a nose in desperate need of being blown, but it was there.

Patty tugged a handful of cheap paper napkins from a tabletop dispenser and slid them through a gap formed by the crook of Cassie's right elbow. Cassie blindly grabbed them, and when their fingers lingered upon one another's, she did not pull hers away. Quite the opposite, she entangled them into Patty's even more. When Patty then gripped and held her hand tight, the warmth was like a soothing mitt in winter and Cassie unwound herself from the protective ball she had created.

Clinging to her friend, she exploded into tears.

They embraced in this way until the well had run dry. When Cassie finally pried herself away, she sat upright, her eyes as bloodshot as her beet red face. A clear runnel had formed from her nose to her upper lip, and Patty thrust another wad of napkins her way, unable to resist the opportunity for a snarky comment. "Nice boogers, bitch."

To this Cassie more than sniggered, at last taking her first real breath since Meredith Harper had left them.

"God help me, Trish." As if these four words were the limit of her emotional reach, she stifled another choking sob.

"Huh-*uh*," Patty countered before this new cry could take hold. "No, ma'am. We've had enough tears for the day. *Christ*, enough for the whole goddamn *year*, I think…and it's only August!"

To this Cassie half-laughed, half-wept, a gulping hiccup cut short only because she couldn't catch her breath.

"Do you want to tell me?" Patricia's voice was unusually sedate, the words slow and soft. They enveloped Cassie like a blanket. "After what you witnessed in this morning's vision, I can't even begin to imagine what you saw this second time around that would cause such an intense reaction in you." She tugged Cassie close, wrapping her in a side embrace that felt like safety itself.

Cassie took a long breath. Rubbed her eyes with the heels of her hands. Started to reveal what she saw—then didn't. Instead, shaking her head again and again and muttering, "I can't tell you, Trish…I just can't. I just can't. I can't!"

"Hey, it's okay, chick. I get it." Patty caressed her back in small, soothing circles."

"But do you, though?" Cassie jumped to her feet. "Trust me, Patty, I wish you did. I wish I could tell you. Christ!" Stretching her arms high above her head, she screamed, pacing in small circles. "Patty, I love you. I want to tell you. So bad! But I can't. Can you understand that? Please tell me you can understand."

"I do. Some things you just have to work out for yourself. Remember, you haven't always known me. I've had my share— *more than my share*—of shit shows in my life. Some you can only get through with the help of your friends. You make them buy tickets and sit through it with you. After all, misery loves company. And you know as well as I that a gaggle of miserable bitches can be a force of nature!"

She lit another cigarette and pulled on it hard.

"But then there are the other kind…" She tilted her head back and puffed out a ring of smoke that wafted to the ceiling. It walked along it for a short distance before separating into wisps that clung to the stained popcorn plaster like clouds. "…The kind of shit shows you gotta sit through on your own. The whole god-damned, godawful show. And you pray to Christ that the ending ends up being worth it."

The fact that this was one of *those* shit shows for Cassie was written all over her face. "But I still need you, Trish."

"Oh, babe," Patricia assured her through a fog of bittersweet smoke. "You're always gonna need me."

"Always," Cassie agreed, wafting away the smoke drifting between them and then embracing her. After a minute she added: "Do you mind if I ask you for something?"

Patty was nodding. "Of course, chick. Anything. Name it."

"There's something I have to find the answer to, then I'll know without a doubt that what I've seen is real. If that's the case, I'll go to the police and tell them whatever I can if it will help Hannah."

"Makes sense, chick. What can I do to help?"

"Can you look after Bella for me? Just for the evening? Maybe overnight at the latest?"

She would need to feed Bella her supper, she explained. And of course stay with her for the evening. If Patty was willing to do that, Cassie might be able to find a way to get through this terrifying, inexplicable shit show, to use Patty's metaphor.

"Is that all? *Sheesh*. I thought you were gonna ask me for a kidney or something." Patty stubbed out her cigarette. She lifted Cassie's chin with a gentle nudge of her finger. "You know I will, chick. I love that little girl. Bella and me? We're gonna have ourselves a girls' night in!"

"Really? You'll do that for me?"

"Hell to the yes! Do you need me to bring my sleepover bag?"

Cassie shrugged. A sheepish gesture that meant maybe.

"Oooh, yay! A slumber party it is then. What time, hun?"

"Can you come over with me right now?" Cassie looked around the shop, at the broken cups and shards of ceramic saucer scattered where she had been sitting with Meredith Harper. She looked at the clock on the wall. It edged ever closer to Isabella's arrival from kindergarten. "If I clean this up while you grab your things real quick, I think we can make it over to my place just in time."

)(

They did just that.

In the kitchen of Cassie's third floor walk-up, Bella jumped into 'Aunt Patty's' waiting embrace and they smothered each other with kisses. Cassie, satisfied that her daughter was more than comfortable with this arrangement, said her goodbyes and assured them both that she wouldn't be *too* long. She preempted what she knew would be Patty's inevitable plea of caution by adding that *yes, she would be safe*.

"You damn well better be," Patricia warned as she lowered Bella to the floor and scooted her toward the living room where the TV beckoned.

"You know I will, Trish. But thank you. You know I love you."

"Well, I can't stand you," Patty replied, and Cassie laughed.

"Fine. Unrequited love it is, then."

"Hmm." Patricia leaned back and gave Cassie a theatrical once-over, her finger tapping her lip. "I guess you're not too bad looking, babes. I suppose I could be convinced to do ya'…at a pinch." After a pause and squinty nod that encapsulated everything sleezy she could muster in a look, Patty added, "I've had worse."

"Oh my God," Cassie exclaimed in mock astonishment. "I didn't mean it *that* way!"

Of course, Patty knew that. Still, it didn't stop her from teasing Cassie about it whenever the opportunity arose. After all, she'd been candid about her own sexuality from the first day—virtually the first moment—they'd met.

Patty had been a regular at Twin Peaks Tavern, her tried-and-true Saturday night hangout on Castro; Cassie had been a pretty young thing who'd decided to pop in for a drink based on nothing more than the bar bearing the same name as the neighborhood where she lived. It must have been sometime during Bill's busy period with his fancy new job with IBM, because he was in Florida.

"Has been for ten days already," Cassie had declared in a rather less than astute response to Patty's attempt to pick her up. She also told her new friend that she'd been suffering a pretty bad case of the doldrums for a while now, being as how she was essentially on her own for so much of the time. Which she hated. Because it kind of freaked her out, truth be told. "But no worries," she assured. "Nothing a lively drink and matching conversation won't cure—with anyone other than Isabella, that is!"

So there she was, in one of San Francisco's oldest and most iconic gay bars. And Patty remembered just how seamlessly Cassie had fit in. Like she'd always belonged there. Except for the whole 'not being attracted to other women' part.

What a shame, Patty thought.

Almost two years later, she still found herself echoing that sentiment every now and then. Especially on those rare occasions when Cassie was no longer the meek, squirrelly girl next door but had transformed into a take-charge, badass bitch.

Occasions like right now.

"So listen," Cassie said, drawing Patty back to the present moment in time. "I don't know how long this is going to take. But I should be back tonight. Late, but sometime tonight. I know you have to open the café in the morning, so at the very worst, it'll be before you have to head up the hill to Haight. Either way, I'll find a payphone so I can call you with an update, or let you know I'm on my way back. I promise."

"I wish you would just tell me where you were going, Cass. Or at least what you're up to. I'd worry a whole lot less."

"I'm sorry. I know I'm coming across somewhat clandestine. But I'll be fine. Promise. And when I come home, I'll have made this right, or as right as I can make it. And then I can tell you everything."

"You sure you don't need a heavy along for the ride, someone to have your six?" Patty clenched her hands together in a makeshift pistol. With a fierce squint she made a *pew pew* sound as she swung her outstretched arms in an arc across the room.

Cassie grinned. "I think you mean *bang bang*. Unless that's a kid's pellet gun you've got there. In which case, I think I'll roll the dice." She shouted goodbye to Bella who was lying in front of the TV, beguiled by the *Linkletter Show's* most popular new segment, 'Kids Say the Darndest Things.'

She then pecked Patty on the cheek, grabbed her handbag.

And was gone.

) (

Cassie did not call home that night.

Curled up on the couch with Bella nestled up against her, Patty tuned the TV to *This is Tom Jones* and pretended she wasn't the least bit worried. During one of the commercial breaks she treated them both to ice creams, even though she knew Cassie wouldn't approve.

"Huh-uh. Nope. Not gonna happen," Cassie had once scolded her when Patty offered a then three-year-old Bella a scoop. "That stuff will rot her little teeth."

Having to pull the spoon away just as she was about to devour it had felt to Patty like something akin to abuse. When Bella's big, beautiful eyes instantly saddened, it *definitely* felt that way.

But hey, she was the sitter now. So it was her call tonight.

Right?

Besides, as the clock ticked and the moon swept past the treetops and still no call had come from Cassie, she was prepared to do anything to keep her concern from spiraling into anxiety.

After getting Bella off to sleep, Patty waited diligently by the phone. Bundled up on the couch, she pulled the rotary base as close as its cord would stretch, every now and then lifting the handset to make sure it still had a dial tone.

Which of course, it always did.

Eventually, Patty finally drifted off to a restless and uneasy sleep, contorted on the couch with the phone next to her head. But even in sleep, panic pressed upon her chest like a fifty-pound weight and she was besieged with dark and surreal dreams. One was a nightmare so intense that she started from sleep with her pulse throbbing in her left wrist. She then spent the next hours pacing laps around the apartment and periodically checking on Bella in between testing the phone.

Always three minutes late, the pendulum clock in the kitchen chimed once to mark the half-hour.

3:33am.

And Cassie Kennedy still hadn't called.

) (

SATURDAY MORNING / AUGUST 23

She still wasn't home when Patty and Bella shared a plate of eggs with a side of freshly griddled bacon.

Patty felt scraped from the inside out.

Bella was blissfully unaware.

She not only devoured her own breakfast, but the remainder of 'Aunt Patty's,' which had barely been touched.

"Oh, Bella. What are we gonna do?"

Briefly ignoring her breakfast, Isabella regarded Patty with those big, beautiful eyes that never ceased to melt her heart. Now, if Bella could only reveal where her mother might have gone last night, that heart might finally stop attempting a jailbreak from Patty's ribcage.

Then again, what difference would it make, she argued with herself, *even if they knew where Cassie had gone?*

Cassie was a capable adult. She was smart. And she was

strong—a lot stronger than she looked. What was Patty supposed to do, just come swooping in like a coffee-brewing Wonder Woman or something?

Cassie was just fine. She could feel it. So, it was just plain rude that she hadn't bothered to call with an update. Hell, for all Patty knew, Cassie could even be with Bill right now, playing house and fucking his fool brains out while she was stuck here with Bella, worried out of her damn mind.

As mounting frustration edged past her concern, Patty sprang from the table. "Right, sunshine. Eat up. You'll have to come to the café, I'm afraid. And hopefully Mommy will meet us there soon."

It was her only option. And her only hope was that Bella would quietly occupy herself, or perhaps nap in the back room, while she herself prepared for a bustling Saturday at Brewster's.

15

) (

THEY FOUND A woman's body that night. Exactly where the anonymous caller told them it would be.

"*Look for a newish Ford Galaxie convertible. White. Red interior. Headlights on. The engine will probably still be running.*"

It wasn't difficult to find.

After a young woman by the name of Rosalie Sherwood had disappeared from Mount Diablo just a few months earlier (and still hadn't been located) the park no longer attracted the volume of visitors it once had. In fact, it had become a running joke among locals that the only visitors who still came fell into one of three categories: cheap armchair detectives, macabre rubber-neckers, or your run-of-the-mill dropouts getting high on pot and smacking tambourines as they 'found' themselves in Diablo's dramatic and ancient landscape.

With so little traffic these days, it wasn't exactly rocket science for the authorities to locate a brand new convertible idling and filling with rainwater on the side of a desolate mountain road.

Not once you knew where to look, at least.

Contra Costa County itself is sizeable enough. Add to that a sprawling, unyielding topography of more than twenty-thousand acres, and Mount Diablo becomes a big headache for a small Sheriff's Department already stretched to its limit. Which is why the caller had provided the most precise directions they could:

Quarry Road.

Above the serpentine.

But before the final bend to Round Top.

At first, Sheriff Morris Miller believed the anonymous caller was a concerned but perhaps wary citizen uncomfortable giving their name. That changed when he pulled up next to the abandoned car and his own headlights glared back at him from the shattered panes of a PT&T payphone booth. The broken glass refracting their light in all directions, the booth lit up like a rectangular roadside beacon in the driving rain. The glow was made all the more eerie with the pulsing blood red reflection of the rooftop cherry spinning on Miller's patrol car.

The sheriff unclasped his holster. Though he did not draw his Colt .38, his palm was firmly against the rosewood grip as he stepped from the cruiser.

The convertible was a white Ford Galaxie, just as the caller had said. Its headlights were shining bright, and in the moonless night their high beams intensified the dagger-like appearance of the slanting rain.

Miller edged around the car, ready to pull his revolver.

No one was there.

He pitched back half a step when a crack of static exploded from the radio. Turned up to full volume, a mix of interference, silence, then sudden bouts of music ebbed and flowed, fighting for attention against the screaming wind. The engine was still running, also as stated by the caller, and had been idling long enough for the cold night rain to sizzle and turn to mist as it struck the car's hood.

The soft-top roof was down, and rainwater had pooled in the footwells and over the soft red leather seats. Something about that seemed to make Sheriff Morris Miller the most uneasy of all. Somehow, it just felt unnatural to see. If it hadn't been for the fact that this was a crime scene, Miller, a car enthusiast at heart, would have thought this sacrilege beyond acceptable. As it was, a missing woman's body had been reported somewhere around here, and ruined leather sports seats were the last thing on his mind as he took out his flashlight and panned its beam in a wide arc around the car.

A man screamed and Miller wheeled around, his chest tight as his fingers stiffened on his revolver.

—*Matty told Hatty... about a thing she saw*—

He released his held breath, loosening his grip on the rosewood handle as Sam The Sham & The Pharaohs belted out 'Wooly Bully' in a sudden spark of reception from the radio station in San Francisco. The heart-stopping blast lasted only a second before the radio's reception once more fell to crackling interference and faded to an echo in the night. Miller exhaled, swearing under his breath that the moment Deputy Rankin arrived with the camera and evidence kit, he was turning that goddamned radio off.

It sizzled and cracked quietly in the background, white noise as the wind picked up. Building to a low howl, it buffeted the car and tugged at the sheriff's hat. He held it fast with his revolver hand as he swung the flashlight over the pay phone booth where broken panes rattled in their metal frames.

Inside the booth, the phone's black Bakelite handset dangled from a braided metal cord. It twisted and banged against the glass as more rain-soaked gusts whistled through the busted panes. It had been at least thirty minutes since the call to the operator had come through. Maybe longer, given the drive and horrendous conditions. But the operator had stayed on the line after the caller had left, and she was still on the open line now.

With an involuntary groan that betrayed his age, Sheriff Miller crouched down at an uncomely angle to speak into the dangling handset without having to touch it. In a voice loud enough to be heard over the gusts of wind and rain, he thanked the operator for a job well-done and assured her that yes, it was absolutely okay for her to disconnect the call now.

The receiver clicked. It beeped a fast, pitchy rhythm.

Morris Miller was deaf to it.

Clenching his lower back as he rose to stand, he sucked in his breath. Not in response to the lower back pain which had plaguing him for days, but at the sight of the phone's rotary dial.

A woman's severed finger was wedged in it.

Tottering in the wind, the tip of the long, neatly painted nail had been jammed under the dial in the hole reserved solely for the number zero. It gave the finger the appearance of levitating, as if it were a being unto itself preparing to call the operator of its own accord. Below the finger's second knuckle, just above the hacked tendons and cleaved bone, a woman's wide platinum wedding band gleamed in the beam of Miller's flashlight.

) (

Hurrying toward the booth, Deputy Rankin clutched a camera and bag of tools to his chest, curling himself into them in his best effort to keep them dry. Miller stopped him short of entering the booth and the rookie stared through soaking wet bangs as his sheriff gave him instruction.

"You can dust the handset, the top of the phone case itself, the coin slot and maybe the inside handle of that glass door," Miller shouted over the rain while keeping his broad-brimmed hat from flying away. "But don't waste your time trying to lift a print from the phone dial itself. You won't find anything."

Rankin smirked. Surely the sheriff was joking. Or testing him. He apologized when the sheriff's countenance did not change.

"Son, there will be no need to dust it—" Miller stepped to one side to afford Rankin a view inside of the booth "—because our killer used the victim's own severed finger to make that call. Besides, we're turning off that fucking radio before we do anything else."

) (

The woman's handbag was still on the passenger seat. Beside it, unclasped and gaping open, a change purse sat heavy with nickels, dimes, and just a few quarters. Some of the coins had tumbled from it and were now submerged in the water which had pooled in the well of the red leather seat.

Miller blocked out the deafening mix of music and interference blaring from the dashboard speakers and picked up both bags.

Her killer used her own fucking dime to call us.

He repeated this deduction aloud to Deputy Rankin who stood near, but slightly behind, the sheriff, observing intently.

In the handbag, among a mix of the usual personal items and makeup, was the woman's pocketbook. Like the change purse, it was swollen with cash.

Carefully emptying it, Sheriff Miller laid its contents on a mat to be photographed.

Seventeen ones; three fives; a ten and one twenty.

Sixty-two dollars...

Along with the coins, the total had to be nearly a week's wages for most people. Despite it being visible, it was all left untouched.

...So robbery was not the motive.

The pit of Sheriff Morris Miller's stomach came heavy, the realization dawning that this horror had been perpetrated for no other reason than simply because it could.

Lifting the wallet to his line of sight, he studied the driver's license housed in its clear pocket, undisturbed.

He spoke the woman's name aloud.

Swallowing hard, he dissolved the knot which had formed in his throat. He rebuffed the tears that would come later as he would sit alone in his living room and repeat the young woman's details over and over in his head. This he would do until the wee early hours, and was a side of Sheriff Morris Miller his deputies would never see, or ever even know about their relentlessly strict superior. Because in this moment, all that mattered to Morris was that they did the job they were entrusted by the community to do. And that they did those jobs to the best of their abilities.

The mourning and sorrow would come later.

Which is why, though the cacophony of static and splintered songs blasting from the car's stereo had birthed an ache in Miller's head like no other, he was unwilling to introduce Rankin to cutting corners by asking him to just shut the damnable thing off. He knew the rain-soaked interior would yield no fingerprint evidence. The incessant downpour had put pay to that. Still, he patiently waited as young Deputy Rankin meticulously examined its entirety, taking photos of every square inch first.

Massaging his throbbing temple, Miller separated himself from the process...and the noise. He lit a cigarette behind the phone booth where the wind was least bothersome. Despite its pragmatism, something about loitering here out of view, sucking warm, round smoke deep into his chilled lungs, felt oddly taboo. Like those cold Friday nights behind the school bleachers of Clayton Valley High as the 'Ugly Eagles' got their asses handed to them on the football field. And just like those nights, Miller quickly snuffed the cigarette under foot when one of the teachers wandered his way. Only now, that teacher was a Channel 5 news van pulling up to Jim Alcorn and Mike Christian, two of his veteran deputies, who were directing it to the soft shoulder of

Quarry Road. A safe enough distance to keep the reporters from contaminating the scene.

Miller eyed them with his usual disdain. While he was far from trusting of any of the media, he did at least have a professional respect for them.

Most of them.

There were a notable few for whom this principle did not apply. One of them was a reporter for Channel 5 News.

Please God, don't be Mike Driffield, he implored a deity he once believed in. ('Once' being the operative word.) After years of witnessing firsthand the atrocities Man perpetrated upon Man, Morris Miller was no longer sure if he were capable of continuing down that arduous and horror-stricken path of blind faith.

He signaled to Deputy Rankin that he'd done enough, and to please silence that fucking racket by turning the radio off.

) (

If the rain had put pay to any evidence they might have found 'inside' the convertible, it did even worse to the outside.

Though it had now slowed to an annoying drizzle, it had already come down in sheets had all but destroyed any marks which on any other day would have been an evidential windfall. Forget trace evidence, the tokens here were big and brash and smacked of a killer who was either too stupid to understand what he was doing, or understood all too clearly.

Miller was certain it was the latter.

Not only was this perp aware of exactly what he was doing, how he was doing it, where he was doing it and when, he clearly also felt invincible. To the point that he relished this opportunity to play a little game with Morris, taunting the sheriff with clues that could so easily tie him to this crime but had instead been rendered moot by the storm.

Miller shook his head, the anger rising as he stared at four congealed fingerprints plainly visible on the trunk's left edge where the killer had raised the lid with a hand coated in blood. There they were, plain as day. Yet like a watercolor painting held under the spray of a lawn sprinkler, the rain had rendered them utterly unusable.

This metaphor of a painting could not have been more apt, for the same was true of two long, parallel and slightly curved lines the killer had traced diagonally across the trunk's lid. As if the woman's blood had been a pot of paint and the killer's finger a brush, he had drawn them across the trunk's vast white lid as if it were his canvas. To Miller they looked like two parentheses back-to-back but in reverse order. And despite the blood having dried gummy and hard, they too had run in the torrential rain with no possibility of capturing a print.

Miller stared, silently pondering.

As frustrated as he was intrigued.

He ensured Rankin had taken a dozen or more photos of each bloodstained mark before donning his leather gloves. With the keen new deputy peering over his shoulder, Miller unlatched the trunk's catch with a click. In the fresh silence it made a snapping sound like a twig underfoot. The trunk lid bobbed open.

The stench was a two-by-four strike to the face.

Miller reeled, twisting away and shielding his nose and mouth with a scowl, the color of his face draining away.

Beside him, Deputy Rankin fell to his knees, heaving until his supper painted the gravel. Apparently, seeing the rookie vomit was a hoot to Deputies Jim Alcorn and Mike Christian who, at the crime scene's perimeter, bent over laughing and mimicked the spectacle.

They didn't notice Sheriff Miller advancing on them.

Before he knew what was happening, Jim Alcorn (merely the nearest of the two) had been seized by the collar and was being uncermoniously escorted to the rear of the convertible.

Clenching the scruff of Alcorn's shirt in a fist the size of a catcher's mitt, Sheriff Morris Miller thrust the deputy's head inside the trunk. "You do *not* make light of one of my crime scenes. Do you understand me?"

Inches from Alcorn's face lay a contorted and bloated corpse. What only days before had been a vibrant and beautiful young woman, a wife, and perhaps even a mother, was now lying in the juices of her own decomposition. Her body had been twisted and bent unnaturally so that she fit in the trunk of her own car.

She was missing the ring finger of her left hand.

And she had been decapitated.

In the clotted wound of her open neck was a squirming mass of maggots. They wriggled in endless fluid-filled blisters now bubbling over the dissolving skin.

"You arrogant, soulless piece of shit," Miller castigated. "I said, *do you understand me,* Jimmy?"

Nodding furiously while wrestling from the sheriff's grip, Deputy Jim Alcorn dropped to all fours at the Sheriff's feet and deposited a partially digested TV dinner for one onto the gravel shoulder of Quarry Road.

Tying off the last section of crime scene tape, Deputy Mike Christian did not laugh this time.

But the Channel 5 News guys did as they continued to set up for their live shot—a scoop guaranteed to secure them the six o'clock lead story.

)(

Mike Driffield was anything but retiring about how stoked he was that they were the first TV crew on the scene.

"So fucking wild, man!" Driffield beamed. His cameraman nodded, silently closing his fingers one-by-one in a five second countdown until they were live. "We're gonna be the ones who get to name this killer," Driffield declared. Before the cameraman closed his last finger, the reporter couldn't resist adding: "Seriously, how groovy is that!"

What Driffield found so groovy was the fact that when they arrived, the convertible's radio happened to be momentarily blaring British pop star Donovan's latest hit, *Hurdy Gurdy Man*. Dark and moody, the song was an eerily appropriate soundtrack to the harrowing scene as it unfolded.

And so the killer's moniker was born.

"...drawn in blood by a crazed killer." Feigning solemnity, Mike Driffield shared the gruesome details of the scene with his viewers while his cameraman panned away from the reporter and zoomed the live shot in to the Ford Galaxie's trunk. Offscreen, Driffield continue to narrate. *"Looks like this sadistic murderer, who this reporter is dubbing the Hurdy Gurdy Man, has targeted yet another young female victim in this dark and foreboding landscape, suitably known as Mount Diab—"*

Live on air, Sheriff Morris Miller plucked the microphone from Driffield's hand and hurled it across Quarry Road.

Sailing over the guardrails, its audio cable unspooled. Like a cartoon dog reaching the end of its leash, the mic then snapped violently backward and slammed into the ground with an explosive boom as feedback resounded through TV speakers across the San Francisco Bay area.

Shrieking, the cameraman tore the headphones from his ears.

Stupefied, Mike Driffield stood agape.

"How groovy was *that*," Sheriff Miller asked as the producers back in the studio cut the remote feed and the live shot fizzled and went black.

16

)(

"WELL, WE SEEM to have lost our live feed," the news anchor stated with some incredulity, visibly shaking his head without realizing it. Or perhaps he did. *"I apologize for that. But to recap: responding to a report from an anonymous caller, the Sheriff's Department of Costa Contra County has discovered the body of a woman, yet to be identified, in an abandoned vehicle in Mount Diablo Park. We will release more info the mo—"*

A jarring bolt of electric panic shot through Patricia Brewster, making the living room of Cassie's walk-up swim before her eyes.

"Oh Christ. Oh Christ. Oh Christ, *oh Christ*—!"

"—er news, Los Angeles police now believe there may be a connection between the Hollywood murder of pregnant actress Sharon Tate-Polanski and four others in the early hours of August ninth, and grocery store magnate, Leno LaBianca in—"

Playing on in the background, the voice of the news anchor continued to announce (with some considerable verve) his story about death and destruction in Hollywood. He might have been reporting that aliens from another galaxy had landed and were now setting up shop in the White House. It would have made no difference: Patty heard nothing after 'yet to be identified.'

Her eyes wide with disbelief, she clutched her chest as it rose and fell with her exaggerated breaths; her other hand clutched the armrest of the couch so tightly her knuckles were white.

"Please don't be Cassie, please don't be Cassie—"

Overcome by a sense of vulnerability and unable to stay in one place, she leapt from the sofa and began pacing the throw rug in the center of the living room.

"—Please don't be Cassie!"

Tears began to well in her eyes as she struggled to process what she'd just heard.

"Okay, you gotta calm your ass down," she chastised herself. "We don't even know that's Cassie."

But you can feel it, can't you?

The voice in her head was as immutable as it was cruel. And in her mind, it was coming from the newscaster on the TV.

Your best friend's dead, and you could have stopped it.

"But how?" she cried out, and in Bella's room she heard something stir.

You could have said no to watching Bella, that's how. Cruel to be kind, isn't that what they say? Then she couldn't have gone. She'd be pissed, sure. But she'd be alive...

"Get out of my head!"

Now Isabella inched out of her room with small, halting steps. Bleary-eyed, she hesitantly approached the living room while nervously surveying Patty.

"Oh, Bella. You poor little thing. I'm so sorry." Patricia bent down and made herself small, less threatening. She opened her arms wide, inviting Bella in. "Come here, baby. It's okay. Aunt Patty's okay. Everything's okay."

Bella lingered in place, briefly swayed as if she were going to fall back to sleep right there and then. She allowed Patty to take her into her arms, and they returned to the couch. Holding Bella tight to her bosom, the two rocked slowly back and forth until Bella's sleepy eyes could stay open no longer.

It turned out to be exactly what Patty needed as well. Consciously slowing her breathing to a calm, restful rhythm, she soothed her own nerves and assured herself that Cassie was fine. That Cassie was not that poor woman they found.

That Cassie would be home any minute.

As the broadcaster's voice continued in the background, a calm, hypnotic drone, the clock in the kitchen gently ticked away. Seconds became minutes, and by the time the clock gently chimed half-past-eleven, Patty, too was sound asleep with Bella snoring sweetly in her lap.

)(

SUNDAY MORNING / AUGUST 24

With the dawning day came the promise of another glorious, carefree summer Sunday for all who would soon make their way to adjacent Panhandle Park.

That wasn't the case for Patricia Brewster and Bella Kennedy.

Cassie was still not home. And with no call to let her know she was safe, a panic-ridden Patty reluctantly picked up the phone.

She hesitated.

Placed her fingertip in the hole reserved for zero.

Paused again.

Then slowly spun the dial until her finger reached the little metal dial stop.

Let go, Patty, she told herself. *Stop hesitating and just call them. What can it hurt?*

She lifted her finger and the clear plastic disk rotated back again, clacking ten times.

"Bell Pacific Operator," a voice announced.

In nervous, faltering words, Patty asked the woman to please connect her call to the San Francisco police.

"Putting you through now."

The line clicked and hummed before a second operator, this one running the switchboard at police headquarters, answered.

"I need to report a missing person," Patty muttered, her nervousness impossible to hide and concern etching every word. One hand unconsciously wrapped the phone's spiral cord around her index finger as her other held the receiver so tight her fingertips had begun to pale.

"I'll put you through to the staff sergeant on duty. Please hold."

Staff Sergeant Reagan came on the line moments later and graciously listened to Patty's concern.

"It's no trouble at all, ma'am. We're happy to send a car over and have an officer take your statement?"

Again Patty teetered over an answer.

This is all becoming so formal. What if Cassie is just fine and I'm blowing this out of all proportion?

"Ma'am? Would you like an officer to come by?"

In the end Patty agreed and gave the address to Cassie's Lyon Street apartment. "Third floor. Ring the bell and I'll come down."

)(

Patty nervously peered through parted curtains, watching for the police car to arrive. Bella quietly amused herself by playing with a stuffed animal. Sitting in the rectangle of sunshine streaming through those same curtains, she was blissfully unaware of the possibilities that lay ahead. And for that, Patty was endlessly thankful.

Still, she found herself half-whispering under her breath: "Oh,

Bella. I hope Aunt Patty's doing the right thing."

Of course she didn't expect Isabella to stop playing or actually answer her. But it would've been nice to have at least one other person understand how she was feeling right now. Though she also lived alone, Patty was constantly surrounded by people coming and going at the café. Being cooped up in this apartment with only Bella as companion somehow smacked of claustrophobia. As beautiful as Cassie's place was, right next to the park, and as amazing and sweet as Bella was, there was just something solemn and isolated about the vibe here. For the first real time, Patty was experiencing a glimmer of Cassie's actual life.

A tense thirty minutes crawled by and still no officers had arrived. Out of her mind with worry, Patty settled on the floor and was distracting herself by playing with Bella...when the front door to Cassie's apartment creaked open—

) (

Disheveled and pale with her face drawn with exhaustion, Cassie stumbled through. Patty's relief washed over her in a cool wave as she rushed to greet her. It became an unsettling mix of gratitude and trepidation when she embraced Cassie and felt her friend's trembling body against her own, saw the dirt and shoes worn thin.

"Cassie, my God, I've been so worried! What happened to you, babe? Where have you been?"

Clinging to her friend but not speaking, Cassie nodded repeatedly. The faraway look of someone in shock had stolen the focus from her bright blue eyes.

"Cass, can you hear me?"

More nodding. A tighter squeeze.

Patty gingerly walked her to the bedroom before Bella could see her. "I've called the police already, they should be here any minute, babe."

"No police," Cassie mumbled, but in the quietness of the bedroom it was as loud as it was unexpected. "Please. Patty. Call them back and say it was a mistake."

"God, Cass. Look at the state of you. How can I do th—"

"It looks worse than it is. Just do it, Trish." The focus had returned to Cassie's eyes. "For me?"

The officer was already en route, but Patty caught him circling the block, searching for a parking spot. She explained that her friend was back, and that it had all been a big misunderstanding.

To which he replied, "Of course it was. It always is."

She apologized for wasting his time, and he grunted but was more than happy to head on his way. One less stack of paperwork to fill out before he could head home for Sunday lunch.

"He's gone," Patty proclaimed as she mounted the last step slightly out of breath, pushing the door which had been left ajar.

No one heard her.

"Cass?"

She was nowhere to be found. Neither was Isabella.

"Cass! Where are you?"

Patty searched the apartment's five rooms before rushing to the balcony. There, crossing the street to Panhandle Park, were Cassie and Isabella.

What the serious fuck?

Patty tackled the three-story stairs a third time and managed to catch up to the pair near the playground. Cassie had all but collapsed on a park bench. Bella was already engrossed in a game with several children she often saw there.

Standing in front of the bench, hands on hips, Patty deliberately blocked the view of the lawns where Bella was playing. Cassie strained to see around her, but Patty only moved whichever way her friend did.

Eventually, they ceased the charade and Patty raised her hands in surrender, shrugging her shoulders.

"I give up. Seriously. Like, what the hell, Cass? I look after Bella for three days. Have to take her to work with me, by the way. And sit by the phone with my nerves shot, waiting for you to call—the call you promised so I would know you were okay. Then you just show up three days later and take Bella to the park without saying a word, like nothing happened?"

Embarrassed or uncomfortable, Patty wasn't sure, but Cassie refused eye contact. She stared intently at her hands and the dark stains in the creases of her cuticles.

"I'm serious here, Cass!"

"I know, Trish."

"That's all?"

"And I'm sorry, okay?"

"No. Not okay. I need more than that this time, Cassie." Patty mock-pulled at her own hair in frustration. "You've been *so* withdrawn. And, well, just plain AWOL. *So much* these past few months. Christ, girl, it was only last week that we were sitting in your kitchen having coffee and I was telling you how much I missed you when you'd disappeared for—what, was it like, three weeks?—before that. *Again.* And now you not only do it, but abandon Bella? What is *happening*, babe?"

She crossed her arms and let out an exasperated huff before settling on the bench next to Cassie.

Neither spoke, the tension between them so thick it was palpable. Their mutual silence all the more evident by the bright staccato tones of sporadic laughter from the playground and the occasional bark of passing dogs where Bella and her friends were playing chase.

This time, Patricia wasn't going to be the one that caved. So they sat there until Bella broke from the pack of children and began to amble brightly in their direction.

"Okay," Cassie said and turned to face Patty. "I want to share this before Bella gets here. So please just listen."

Patty agreed, her expression softening.

"I can't tell you where I was or what happened," Cassie explained, "because I don't know myself, Trish."

Her words trailed off until they were barely audible.

Only Patty, sitting close and leaning in, would have been able to hear them. She began to respond; faltered; closed her mouth, almost comically resolute. Tried once more, this time extending her hand to Cassie who took it without hesitation. "I'm being careful about how I respond because I know I have a tendency to come across as a smartass in these situations. To cut the tension. But I'm not right now, I just want to make sure I'm understanding you, alright?"

"Yes, of course."

Reticent to say what she wanted—*needed*—to say, Patty continued to tee it up softly: "I'm not trying to argue here. Or, as you would say, be a real C-U...what's the rest, again?"

"A real C-U-Next-Tuesday," Cassie meekly offered. The smallest smile—so small it must surely be the smallest a smile could be and still be called one—lit upon her face.

It was gone as quickly as it had come.

Patty did chuckle, though. No vibe, no matter how bad or serious, would prevent her from laughing at that phrase. It just tickled the absolute shit out of her. Every time.

"Yeah, that's the one. I'm not trying to be a real cu—well, one of those—I'm just trying to understand. So, here goes, I might as well just say it: did you have, like, a three-day bender? Were you tripping out on something?"

Cassie shook her head fiercely, her response vehement and unquestionable. "No! Nothing like that." She looked across the expanse of lawn to see Bella slowing to a walk but still headed their way. She waved and Bella quickened her pace. "You think I'd do that shit when I have *her* to think about?"

Patty wanted to believe that Cassie wouldn't. But after this weekend, she was starting to think anything was possible.

Bella was now ten yards away.

"I get blackouts, Trish. I just—I don't know—kind of *disappear* for a bit. I can't explain it. I left here Friday feeling this inexplicable but undeniable pull to check out the Presidio for some reason. I remember getting there…and the next thing I know I'm hiking through Oakland toward the bridge."

"Oakland? Christ, Cassie. That's across the bay. What were you doing in Oakland? And where's your car?"

Cassie shrugged, displaying little concern. "I'll report it gone, stolen, whatever. I'm sure it will turn up." Then to Bella, who was speeding toward her lap: "Hey my gorgeous little babygirl! Are you having fun?"

Bella was all smiles as she decided not to leap into her mom's lap but onto the bench between them instead. Cassie grabbed her face with both hands and gave her a kiss.

"Okay now, go play some more while Aunt Patty and I talk." She swatted her gently on her backside and Bella was off and running toward her friends who were now playing tag. One of the girls tapped Isabella as she trotted past, and cheerfully shouted, 'tag, you're it!' When Bella managed to turn on a dime and almost tagged her right back, the girl shrieked with delight, twisting away just in time.

"Wait," Patty said after a moment's reflection. "Are you telling me you *walked* home? From *Oakland*?"

Cassie didn't answer but felt every one of those twelve miles in her feet which burned and ached as if their soles had been beaten with a board.

"But there's something else, Trish. Something I need to share with you about that vision I had of Hannah."

Patty steeled herself, shuffling on the bench and placing her hands together in her lap as she gave her full attention. "Alright."

"I didn't tell you Friday at the café. But that episode I had? It was because I did see something else, the second time Meredith came, when she brought that rock album. Something important that could actually help Meredith get some closure." She paused, visibly poring through the repercussions of what she was about to say. "Something that w-would *really* h-help the police."

Her voice had begun to tremble. Patty saw her throat tighten, could see the reflexive swallows as though Cassie was trying to keep the words from coming out. She placed her hand over Cassie's, and despite the morning's burgeoning August heat, her fingers were cold. She nudged herself a little closer, pulling her legs onto the bench and tucking hem beneath her so she could nestle into her friend.

"I'm here babe. And I'm listening, okay? Whatever you have to say, it's okay. You can tell me. And we'll get through it, together. You, me and Bella. The Three Musketeers."

Cassie was again staring at her hands, now enveloped by Patty's. The warmth felt like safety. She waggled her fingers and winced at the sight of her ragged nails and the stains around them, so evident when in such close proximity to Patty's perfectly manicured nails with their immaculate French polish.

She nodded.

"I just want you to know you're the best friend I could ever ask for, and—"

"Whoa, hey." Patty squeezed her hands gently, rubbing her fingers. "This is starting to sound like a goodbye speech or something."

"No, not a goodbye speech, Trish. But it might end up being, after I tell you what I saw. And I mean you leaving. Not me."

Patty chuckled and patted Cassie's hands. "Not me, sister. I'm afraid you're stuck with me for life." Across the great lawn, Bella was rolling on the ground, squirming with joy and scratching her back in the scent of the freshly cut grass, mimicking two of her friends. "Just tell me what you want to say, Cass. It's gonna be alright. I promise."

Cassie took a deep breath, brought her eyes to meet Patty's. "I saw that man's face, Trish. The one who attacked Hannah in my vision."

For a split second, Patty was gormless, her mouth agape. "My God, babe. Can you describe it? Like, would you recognize him if you saw him again?"

Cassie's eyes started to moisten, her lips parting. She nodded her head just once. It would have been imperceptible to anyone but Patricia.

"Yes." Now the tears welled over her bottom lid and ran freely down her face. "I would. Because he's my brother."

17

) (

ATTY INSISTED CASSIE soak in the tub for as long as she needed. *Just get yourself right. I'll hang with Bella and keep her occupied. Then we'll figure this out.*

As Isabella napped, they sat on the wrought iron balcony at a small round high top Patty had given her friend as a moving-in present. It was a used one from the café, part of the inventory she was changing out, but it was solid and comfortable and looked perfect in the bohemian chic vibe of the home.

"His name is Solomon." Cassie settled back and focused on the sound of her own breathing. How it mingled with the chatter of the birds in the tree canopy at their same height, or the whisper of the gentle summer breeze that brought the scent of the cut grass from the park and the lavender blooms in the small courtyard below. It moved her hair like fingers playing lovingly through it. "I haven't seen him for a very long time."

"I didn't know you had a brother."

"Three, actually." Cassie said and leaned forward, a chamomile tea cupped in her hands. "Well, officially two now, I guess. Joey died when we were just kids."

"Oh my God, babe. I'm so sorry." Though finding this all rather hard to wrap her head around, Patty didn't let it show. "You've never talked to me about them."

Cassie shook her head, deep in thought as she stirred her tea.

"What happened to Joey, babe, was he sick? Or some kind of accident?"

Cassie stopped stirring her tea and the spoon jangled lightly against the cup as it swirled a full rotation then stopped. "Kinda, yeah."

"You sure you're ready to talk about this? I feel like maybe you need some more time."

"No, Patty. I'm ready."

To Patricia Brewster, this was the best indicator of all that she really *was* ready: the fact that she'd just called her Patty…instead of Trish. "I know I probably sound like I'm talking in circles. But this is all a bit much. Y'know? That's just one cut in a very deep wound that's never fully healed. Not really. There's always a nagging ache. But sometimes, if I'm lucky, I can ignore it and it goes away."

She looked deep into Patty's eyes and the pain Patty saw in them was as evident as it was old. It explained a lot about who her friend was: all the little idiosyncrasies that made Cassie Kennedy the amazing, complex, kind and fierce woman she loved.

"We were orphaned at a very young age: me, Joey, Solomon and our youngest brother, who we always called Catcher because of *Catcher in the Rye*. Joey was the oldest. Me and Solomon were in the middle. Anyway, for a short while we were in a public home with other kids."

"God, Cass. I knew none of this."

Patty began to lean over the table to give her a hug, but Cassie laced her fingers around her wrist and politely coaxed her back down into her seat. A soft smile played on her lips.

"No more tears, Pat. If I start again—" *Now that was a new one. Patty had never heard Cassie call her Pat. Not once in all their years.* "—I think I might never stop."

"Sure. I understand." Patty placed her hands upon the tabletop, one atop the other. "I didn't mean to interrupt. This is all just, uh…"

"Just a bit much. I know. But it's high time I tell you."

"Speaking of high time," Patty said as she slid her hand into the purse hung over her chair and pulled out a prim metal case. "I think I might need something a little stronger than a chamomile tea for this." She clicked open the case and extracted a tightly rolled joint. "Do you mind?"

"Of course not!"

Now, for the first time in days, Patty basked in a smile from her friend that was full and real. Because not only had she toked up in front of Cassie plenty of times before, but Cassie had joined in herself more than once.

Now was one of those times. Cassie snatched the joint from her hands and lit it herself. She inhaled, held it as long as she could, then coughed it out in a skunk-scented haze, her entire body rocking.

Patty grabbed the spliff before it might fall from her hands. "Been awhile, I guess."

Still barking, Cassie nodded rapidly. Patty chuckled and sucked the smoke into her lungs. To her it felt warm and comforting…and like home. After a few seconds she raised her head and blew it high above while Cassie caught her breath.

"It has…" Cassie beckoned for the joint and this time took a modest hit, allowed it to roll around inside her, then blew a thin stream from her pursed lips. "Mmmm. That's better. She reveled in the sensation, staring up at the sky and blindly passing it back to Patty. "As I was saying, we were in a children's home for a short while. But not long after, our aunt and uncle from Pennsylvania came to claim us."

"Oh, thank God, babe."

Cassie's face soured, vehemently shaking her head. "That's what we thought, too. But no, Pat. God wasn't the one to thank for that. If ever the Devil had a hand in something, it was bringing our aunt and uncle into our lives…"

18

)(

THE BOY WASN'T sure how many days it had been. Solomon was the one who'd kept track. Of the four of them, he was the most organized, so it made sense that he was the one who'd gouged lines into the doorjamb until his thumbnail had bled. He did this every morning, or at least whenever they all agreed it was morning.

Because not only was it quiet in the closet,

(so quiet)

it was also dark,

(so dark)

the way the boy imagined a grave must be.

So, who really knew?

He could still hear that sound as the old paint cracked and flaked away beneath his brother's ragged nail. Even though he could never see it, the boy always knew when Solomon's skin had rubbed raw and the blood had come, because the sound wasn't dry anymore. And there would be a sharp metallic scent that sliced through the round, stifling stench of their own B.O.

This way we won't give up hope, Solomon assured them.

The boy, whose name was Joey Albrighton, now ran his fingers up the wood. He began at the cold cement floor and counted the lines upward in the dark. He would've sworn he could see them but knew that was impossible.

There was simply no light.

He thought his eyes would get used to it by now and he'd at least be able to see shapes or something. His teacher, Mrs. Billings, said that's how evolution worked: how the fish grew legs so they could leave the water. But Joey thought she was full of you-know-what, because he'd been locked in the darkness for a very long time now and still couldn't make his eyes see anything.

Twenty-seven.

That's how many lines Joey counted that Solomon had scraped into the doorjamb. But his brother had been gone for a while now and Joey was the only one left, so he no longer knew exactly how many days had passed.

Joey didn't feel sorry for himself. He'd volunteered to stay so the others could go. With Cassie being a girl 'n all, Joey figured she shouldn't have to suffer through any of this. Besides, she'd been crying, shaking and throwing up all the time in the beginning. And who could blame her? But Catcher, their youngest brother, was only eight. So they all agreed, even Cassie, that he should be the first one to get out. She would then be next. Followed by Solomon. Because not only was Solomon the most organized, he was also the smartest and would know what to do.

Joey would be the last to go. And even though Solomon didn't want to leave him behind—which Joey knew was the truth—they all agreed that Joey would stay in the hopes the Monster might not notice the others were missing. Being the eldest, he'd inherited the role of stalwart, ad hoc guardian, and he was going to do whatever it took to live up to that responsibility.

But now that he was alone, Joey shivered with cold. His

fingertips were starting to go numb. He was even more skinny than he had been when Solomon was still here. And he was so thirsty his tongue had begun to swell and he could barely swallow.

While he never would have admitted it to the others, Joey now felt the weight of his fear as he waited, listening for the sound of those footsteps pounding slow and steady down those rickety old stairs...which he knew they soon would.

But Joey also knew this: when that sound did eventually come, he'd find it in himself to do whatever he had to. He was willing to protect the others—especially his sister—at any cost.

That was Joey's purpose.

Though, if he were honest, he was no longer sure he'd survive even one more time.

But he had to try.

)(

It might sound odd, but he didn't blame the Monster. Not really. After all, that's the nature of monsters. They just can't help it. Monsters hurt people. But his aunt? She's the one they hated. Because she should have known better.

She did know better.

Still, she let the Monster come.

Sometimes, she even held them down and read from her bible while the Monster did the awful things Monsters do. Her favorite was Ecclesiastes 3:1.

To everything there is a season, and a time to every purpose under Heaven...

It was one of those times—one of those terrible, nightmare times—that Joey discovered a way to escape. As she'd held him down and her words poured over him like a mantra, Joey focused only upon his aunt's hands. Her long, slender fingers; nails that were always so perfectly manicured; that wedding band that was wide and plain and glimmered in the light of that single, naked overhead bulb. Even though it was not very bright in the cellar, after the blackness of the closet, that shimmer was as bright as the beach sun reflecting off the water when you've forgotten your sunglasses.

So that's where he went while it happened.

To the beach.

"Shhhhh, now baby," his aunt would coax between bible verses as her left hand lovingly covered his mouth. So close to his face, Joey could hear the gentle ticking of her wristwatch as its tiny second hand marked every excruciating moment. "Be still and it will all be over soon. Go to your special place, my handsome little boy. After all, you're hungry, aren't you?"

And so Joey blocked out the pain and the sickening sounds by allowing the ticking of that watch to take him to his shimmering water. He permitted himself to be swept away by the shrieks of a lone seagull and the rhythmic pounding of the surf washing up against the beach. Instead of the real sounds.

If he were a good boy and didn't thrash or fight or cry *too* much, Joey would be allowed something to eat when it was all over. If he weren't, he'd receive a *correction*, which Joey quickly learned was just his aunt's fancy word for a beating. It was never the Monster that dished out the corrections, only his aunt. And she did this any time Joey made the Monster's visit, well, less than it could be.

At first, he went hungry for days. But he knew he had to eat if he was to have a chance of getting out of here. Once he learned how to go to his beach, his aunt would bring him a sandwich and some water. Sometimes, if he were especially good, she might even bring him a few potato chips before locking him away in the closet again. And if he could make himself go to sleep, he wouldn't notice that he was still hungry.

In that sleep Joey would again be with Cassie, Solomon, and Catcher, whom Joey missed most of all. He knew they would all be together again one day. But for now they were safe, and to Joey that's all that mattered.

So maybe now you understand why Joey let the others get away first. And once you get to know Solomon, you'll realize why Joey being the one to stay behind was the only real option.

)(

If you were wondering where their parents were while all this was taking place, don't.

Their mother was gone.

Three years earlier she'd drank herself to death. Which is to say, she was found at the bottom of a hill in the mangled remains of the brand new 1951 Roadmaster their father had custom ordered from Buick just the year before. He made certain his children knew that a bottle of Tequila was found sloshing around in there with their mother's dead body, runnels of the clear liquor flowing down her bloodied face and into her twisted mouth as its distinct aroma blended with the pungent scent of her warm blood.

Stupid bitch. Same in death as she was in life, he proclaimed as he cursed the woman for destroying the only thing he ever loved.

(And in case there's any doubt, the object of the man's deepest, most heartfelt affection had four wheels, not four limbs.)

The children had no idea where their father was now.

After their mother's accident, he was often absent and would be gone longer and longer each successive time. When he did eventually come back, he'd be cursing and screaming about how the stupid cow had screwed him over yet again, leaving him with these fucking parasites. That he never wanted to be a father in the first place. And how he should've just punched her in the stomach when he'd returned from active duty, only to discover what the whore had done while he was fighting for his country and his life.

These violent fits were when Joey's youngest brother first started to hide and beg his brothers to protect him. Solomon was big for his age. But in reality, he wasn't that much older than their baby brother. So, even though Joey was barely a few years their senior, it was he who would willingly step in front of the belt as their father was swinging it with the intensity of another alcohol-fueled rage.

Again. And again.

And again.

The final time they were left on their own was the longest. After eating the last of the Spam and resorting to expired tins of dog food, a man appeared on their doorstep. It was not their father, but a man in a suit accompanied by other men in suits. And a handful of police. A nice lady called Maureen was with them as well, and once Joey believed she was really on their side, he told Maureen where she could find Cassie and Solomon...and even his youngest brother, Catcher. That way they could all go together to a safe place with the nice lady; a place where a bunch of other kids—kids just like them—lived too.

They were at the county home for only a matter of weeks before their aunt and uncle claimed them. The family wasn't supposed to leave the state and take the children back to Pennsylvania until the official hearing, but the adults didn't care.

The children were their rightful kin, they said, *and that's all there was to it.*

The next thing Joey remembered was the clean pine scent of their car as he and the others all squeezed onto a long bench seat between his uncle at the wheel and his aunt next to the window. With his belongings stuffed into a paper shopping bag on his lap, the children's home grew smaller in the rearview mirror and Joey felt Catcher take his first real breath in as long as he could remember. At last, they were with people who really cared.

)(

Life couldn't have been more perfect. They went to school with the other kids in the neighborhood, came home and did their homework. They ate dinner together as a family—real meals on real plates at a real dining table—almost the moment their uncle got home from the office.

After chores and cleaning up were done, once they'd brushed their teeth and gotten into their jimjams, they'd gather together in the living room where they'd listen to the nightly radio serials.

They were captivated by shows like *Mystery Theater*, *Tarzan*, and the personal favorite of Joey's youngest brother, *The Shadow*. For once, life was so good that Joey wondered if Mama had died on purpose and her ghost had gotten rid of Daddy so they could be with Mama's sister. She must've known that was where they truly belonged.

Everything was just that good.

But then Catcher started getting the visits, always late at night. He told Joey he would wake up being tickled by the Monster. Sometimes he didn't have to tell Joey this, because Joey could hear him giggling in the bedroom next to his. But then the tickling changed. Became something else. And their youngest brother became something else with it.

Just like that, the warm joy of their shiny new life was snuffed out as quickly as its flame had been lit.

The nighttime visits and the awful sounds lasted longer than any of them could count. And if Catcher screamed or kicked or did anything to make a fuss, the Monster would make their aunt come to keep the boy calm and still, holding him while she read from Ecclesiastes. Until, that is, the night Joey could no longer bear it.

Sprinting into Catcher's bedroom, Joey threw himself on the Monster, scratching and punching and biting.

The next morning their aunt separated them, locking them in different parts of the house. But deciding that windows made this too risky, she locked them in the basement instead.

She didn't have to worry about windows down there.

Despite being a bright summer morning, it was cold and damp and dark. But Joey found the switch for an old yellow bulb that dangled from a frayed wire in the ceiling. Solomon found a dusty old lamp. Although both were faint and sometimes sizzled and flickered, together they kept the cellar from being *too* dark.

With nothing else to do, the four found themselves scouring the basement. What they were looking for, none of them knew. The only way out was the door at the top of those creaky old stairs, and their aunt had locked that behind her with a resounding bang. So they made a game of it to pass the time.

And that's when they found them:

Toys.

They had been hidden away, carefully tucked out of sight in different parts of the cellar. And they had been played with to the point of being worn and tattered.

Joey's youngest brother found one behind a stack of old lawn chairs whose aluminum frames had dulled with age, the weave of their plastic mesh seats dry-rotted away. Two more were secreted away behind the furnace. One was inside a box of faded newspapers. And the last, Joey's sister found in the back of the closet, behind a box of little white mothballs that stunk like nothing else they'd ever smelled.

With a little imagination, despite their faded colors and broken pieces and one that reeked like old ladies and chemical death, these five broken-down toys helped occupy their time...

Until their aunt came and took them away.

Then unscrewed the bulb from Solomon's lamp.

Then gathered Joey and his siblings and locked all four of them up in what had once been a coat closet. Doing this made it easier for their aunt to manage them and their unruliness. And in his own way, Joey understood that.

From the other side of the door they could hear the deadbolt scrape and click. Then the sound as she climbed the old wooden stairs that creaked and groaned with every footstep. When she then flicked the switch and that last dangling bulb in the middle of the basement fizzled out, even the glow beneath the closet door went away. Leaving them in blindness.

This first time was just a few hours.

Other times, and if she had been especially unhappy with their unruly behavior, they might be in the dark so long that they'd miss out on lunch or supper.

The thing was, Joey never exactly knew what it was that they had done wrong. But he figured it must've been something very terrible for their aunt to punish them so.

It was Solomon who soon figured out that instead of pathetic sobs or wails or whining, they would do better to revert to pleas of remorse instead.

Apologizing for what, they did not know.

But that didn't really matter. If their aunt believed them, then eventually she would let them out.

Eventually.

Then everything would go back to being normal again for a while. Even wonderful, some of the time.

But the trips to the cellar closet started happening more frequently, and each time they lasted a little longer. Afternoon would bleed into night. All night would become the next day. The next day would blend into several. Several, into an entire week.

And of course, you never knew when the Monster might come.

) (

This latest trip to the closet was the longest.

Which is when Solomon came up with the plan. They managed to get their youngest brother out first. Then their sister. And eventually Solomon, too, had left.

Now Joey was all alone.

He had just run his fingers up the doorjamb, again counting the twenty-seven lines, when he heard those terrible footsteps and the telltale squeaking of the basement stairs.

Shaking and going weak in his arms and legs, Joey's heart pounded as if he'd just run a hundred yards. His only solace, thin as it may be, was that this time would be his last.

It had to be, one way or the other.

There was just nothing left in him.

He pressed away in the darkness, shrinking beneath a shelf as the bolt on the other side unlatched with a clang. When the door creaked open, blinding light poured in. Within it, a stark and towering silhouette filled the doorway, an image which had prefaced Joey's beach visits so many times before. Clenching his eyes closed, the boy thrust a defensive but trembling hand before him as the Monster took one slow, deliberate step nearer.

What happened next happened fast.

Hidden behind the boy's back was a wire coat hanger. He'd meticulously bent and unbent it until it snapped, then untwisted and reshaped it until it had become a skewer. With its looped handle now gripped tightly in his fist, his muscles tensed as hot adrenaline coursed through him.

Except it was no longer Joey cowering in the corner.

It was Solomon.

And when the monster reached in, the boy struck—

19

)(

SUNDAY EVENING / AUGUST 24
Cassie's Haight-Ashbury apartment

CASSIE KENNEDY LEANED back in her chair, feeling as though her insides had been scraped out. Nothing was left of the joint they were sharing but a smelly roach in the ashtray, and Patty had reverted back to her Virginia Slims while rummaging through Cassie's cabinets.

She found a bottle of vodka in the tiny cabinet above the fridge, the one you have to stand on a chair to access.

"Jesus, Patty. Don't fall. I can't afford the hospital bill."

Patty groaned, a sound like *aeerggghhh*, as the top of the fridge creased her diaphragm. With one final push she stretched toward the back of the cabinet and snagged the bottle by its thin neck, dragging it out. "Why the fuck do you keep it so high up and so goddamned far back?"

"Honestly?"

"No, I want you to lie about it. I haven't had enough drama for the day, so figured maybe you'd make something up that would whet my whistle."

"My, we are a snarky bitch, aren't we?"

"Not *we*," Patty insisted. "Just *me*. And I'm damn proud of it." She spun off the cap, a generous pour half-filling her tumbler of ice. She presented the glass to Cassie across the room and Cassie nodded. She poured a second.

"I'm afraid this particular story is rather boring. You see, I keep a new bottle all the way up there, and at the back of the cabinet, because if I can't manage to get to it, then I know I've already had enough. My version of portion control."

Patty's mouth turned down at the corners as she nodded. "Hmmm, very clever. Maybe I should try that. Then again, I'd probably fall on my ass in a drunken stupor and break my tail bone or something." She took a sip of the ice cold vodka. "Mmmm, good stuff."

They sat in silence, staring into their own thoughts, until Patty had all but sucked the liquor from her ice cubes.

"Joey died that night," Cassie said, her expression morphing from somber to empty. A blank slate Patty couldn't read.

"Christ, Cass."

"I know." She took a big gulp, finished the drink and thumped the glass on the table upside down. "I hate going back there. But I'm glad you know now."

Patty hurried to the kitchen to pour another, relieved that her back was turned when her eyes glossed over, her lips and hands beginning to lightly tremble. At least the weight of the full tumbler steadied her shaking hands. She hid the trail of a tear creeping down her cheek by bracing herself against the kitchen counter and speaking over her shoulder. "What—" She cleared her throat, composing herself. "—What happened to Solomon?"

"When my aunt heard the screams, she came running down to the basement. Solomon was standing over my uncle, the twisted coat hanger in his left hand. Shrieking and flailing and trying to scuttle away, my uncle was holding his right eye in his."

Patty swiped away a tear with the back of her hand before

turning around. "I can't believe what you guys went through. And I'm sorry, but your uncle deserved that. I only wish that coat hanger had skewered the piece o' shit's brain." She slammed half of the drink in one gulp.

"I used to wish that too. Every damn day. For years. Trust me." Cassie considered turning her glass over and having another. Patty saw and gave her a nod, but Cassie again declined. "No, I better not. I've got Isabella."

Now Patty laughed, which felt a lot better than anything she'd been feeling since Cassie got home. "I don't think she'll mind if you have a second drink."

"On top of the weed? I better not. But I'm fine, really."

"It's your funeral." It was a poor choice of phrase, and Patty almost withdrew it. Instead, she immediately spoke over it. "You were saying you *used* to wish that? So, you don't anymore?"

"Cassie shook her head, settling back in the sofa, sliding her legs up and under herself. "Not really. You have to eventually let that shit go or it will eat you alive. From what I understand, my uncle was permanently blinded in that eye, and it affected him for the rest of his life. Which wasn't long. He died of an acute brain aneurism about three years later, apparently."

"And Solomon?"

"Solomon was committed to juvenile detention. Basically a prison for kids. He was far too young to be tried as an adult. Instead, he spent the rest of his childhood in a semi-drugged haze, locked in a grey concrete building behind barbed wire fences, watching his back and appeasing psychiatrists."

"Poor kid. That's awful. That had to be hard, especially for him."

Cassie tilted her head. "It was. It was fucking awful. Soul-destroying. But why do you say 'especially' for him?"

"Well, he's a lefty. Like yours truly." She reminded Cassie that she'd revealed that Solomon was found with the coat hanger in his left hand. "And we lefties are typically more creative. A little wilder. Free-spirited horses that can't be tamed." Patty fluttered her eyelashes, trying to ease the tension. When Cassie did not respond, she assumed her serious voice again. "It had to be excruciating for him to be locked away, twenty-four-seven."

Cassie smirked. Or at least it seemed like that to Patty. Her tone bordered on the verge of caustic. "Very clever girl, aren't you? Or observant, at the very least. You know, I've always admired you Pat. The café, your courageous lifestyle. In fact, I've always loved you, in a way. And you know? All this time, I've never given you enough credit for being as sharp as your really are." Now her expression had warmed. "So, I'm sorry for that."

Perplexed, and a little uncomfortable, Patty dismissed it with her usual irreverence. "Sharp? Moi?" She fanned her fingers over her chest and assumed a French accent. "But *madame*, I am—how you *Ameeeehricans* say—dumb as *ze* box of *ze* rocks."

"I'm serious, Patty. I never give you enough credit. For who you are and all you've done for me. I love you, girl."

"Awww, I love you too, Cassie." She plopped herself on the sofa and leaned into her friend. "And I'm proud of you. Not only for living through such hell and coming out the other side, but becoming the beautiful and strong person you are. *And*...I'm proud of you for sharing the truth about it with me. I know it has to be super hard to talk about. I just want you to know I'm here for you if you want to talk more."

"I know, babe. That's why I wanted to tell you now. 'Cause I'm really freaked about seeing Solomon's face in that vision."

"Well, let's think about this logically. It might not be literal, you know? Like, maybe it's a subliminal thing. Hell, we don't even know for certain yet that what you saw even happened."

Cassie *was* certain, and said so.

"Okay, I know you are," Patty assured her as she sat up and slid her legs under her so that she and Cassie were facing one another on the couch. "But just humor me, alright?"

"Sure. Hell, Pat. If it helps me get a grip on what the fuck is happening, I'll do more than humor you!" Cassie winked, the comment meant to be overtly suggestive.

A flush spread across Patty's face, its warmth spreading down to her belly. "Oh, my. I do say!" Now Patty was a demure Southern belle, fanning herself.

Cassie play-punched her on the shoulder and they both laughed.

In her normal voice, Patty continued to share her theory. "But listen, seriously. When was the last time you saw Solomon?"

Now Cassie's expression fell, again solemn. In all but a whisper she admitted it had been that very night: when Solomon had attacked their uncle and Joey had died.

"I think Joey thought we had all gotten away. That's why he stayed behind and took the abuse for the rest of us. To protect us, y'know? But we didn't, Patty. We were in the house the whole time." Her face screwed into a mix of a scowl and a sob. She cleared her throat. She untucked her legs and placed her feet on the floor, her head now in her hands. "God help me, we were in the house the whole time. He died for nothing. Joey, my big brother, died for no fucking reason at all!"

Patty had nothing to say that would add any value, so she chose instead to only listen, to be the empathetic ear she'd just promised her friend she'd always be.

"We were separated that night, Patty. I never saw any of my brothers again." Cassie was on the verge of breaking down in tears all over again, which Patty knew was the last thing her friend wanted. So she curtailed them by swiftly jumping to what had been on her mind since Cassie claimed to have seen her brother in that awful, awful vision about Hannah Wilson.

"Okay, babe. Well maybe that's it. I think you're missing your brothers, so badly, that you just want to see them again. I mean, Christ, Cass, that was what—" She began counting on the fingers of both hands. "—Sixteen years ago?"

Cassie nodded without looking up.

"And maybe this guilt you've carried all your life about Joey's death and Solomon's commitment to that awful institution—guilt that isn't deserved, by the way—is rearing its ugly head again because of Meredith Harper. Can that be something you'll at least consider?"

Cassie made brief eye contact, barely nodding.

"Okay then." Now Patty felt as though a weight had been lifted and she leapt to her feet. "I think that's exactly what's happening here, babe. I think the whole Hannah Wilson thing wheedled its way into your subconscious and plucked at all these feelings you had buried deep down for way too long. And they came out in this awful, insidious imagery of Meredith's daughter being killed."

Patty's relief was so strong she was almost giddy. It all made sense now. And the feeling of wholeness was almost better than the pot she'd just smoked.

"See? It doesn't mean you're crazy. It also doesn't mean you're a fraud, or that your gift is a fluke. Because none of those things are true. You are *so* gifted, and I have no doubt that you *did* tap into some supernatural insight when you saw that Paige—*Pegs*—was pregnant, even though she was skinny as a board. But that doesn't mean that what you saw happen to Lyndsey Roe or Hannah Wilson has to be real." She took a breath. "Thank God you didn't tell Meredith Harper what your vision had shown you about Hannah. My God, can you imagine?"

"So you don't think that what I saw was real? Then how do you explain me knowing about the Deep Purple album on Hannah's record player, the one she took to the police?"

"I think," Patty admitted as she poured a third vodka and lit yet another cigarette, "that Hannah Wilson is a young woman like you. And I think young women these days are more open about digging things that girls like me weren't allowed to dig when I was your age. Rock music, for a start."

"So you think it was coincidence. A good guess—"

"—I think the odds were in your favor. Or maybe you genuinely saw it, just like Pegs' pregnancy. But that doesn't mean the rest of your horrific visions have to be real. Think about it: you're seeing the face of your long-lost brother as the killer. I mean, what would be the odds?"

Cassie conceded to her point. "Pretty long, I guess. I can appreciate that much, at least."

"And besides, chick. If you haven't seen Solomon since you were, what, nine years old, then how would you even know what his face would look like today?"

It was a valid point.

"You're right, Pat. See? A smart cookie. Just like I said."

"You know it, bitch." Patty opened the gleaming cigarette case and without warning tossed Cassie a joint. Like a viper, Cassie's right hand snatched it tumbling from the air.

"Just a few hits. Then I really need to get Bella up and give her some dinner."

"So, you're a righty. *Interesting…*"

Cassie was perplexed.

After a moment, the penny dropped.

"Oh, because Solomon is a lefty. Yeah, he's the only one. The rest of us were…*normal.*" Given how grave the conversation had been, Cassie emphasized the last word and shot Patty a cheeky grin, just to make sure her friend knew she was joking.

"Thank God for that," Patty retorted. "Not sure there's enough room around here for any more awesomeness the likes of me."

) (

A few hits ended up being the whole joint as an uplifting sense of relief washed over them both. For the first time in as long as she could remember, Cassie felt truly free of the nagging fragments of angst and fear and worry that lacerated her sense of peace and calm on a daily basis.

Maybe it was the first time ever that she'd felt this way.

They watched reruns of *The Andy Griffith Show* and *Bewitched* and *Batman* until the news came. That was a bit of a buzzkill, so Patty gathered her things and prepared to head home. They were in the middle of their goodbyes when the news anchor's voice caught their attention as he teed up a supplement to a story they'd run in the previous night's broadcast:

"...As some of our regular viewers may know, a remote broadcast last night was interrupted before we were able to bring you the full details. I am now able to share the rest of that information. We would like to caution parents that some of these details and images we're about to share may be too graphic for our younger viewers or the faint of heart.

"Reported missing approximately seven days ago, twenty-five-year-old Hannah Wilson of Sausalito was found yesterday evening after an anonymous tip was received by the Contra Costa County Sheriff's Department. Deputies discovered Hannah Wilson's body in the trunk of her Ford Galaxie convertible, abandoned in Mount Diablo park. Her head had been removed from her body..."

They stood in stunned silence as the television filled the room with its uneasy hum, making a mockery of their deduction that Cassie's visions had been nothing but figments of a traumatized subconscious. Flickering across their faces, the screen flashed between images of the convertible, a glimpse of a body (as brief as the blink of an eye), and the odd markings scrawled across the trunk in what appeared to be blood, a symbol like two backwards parentheses.

Heavy tears of guilt and frustration blurred Cassie's vision, her hands trembling as the news anchor continued to share details of the brutal attack Cassie had seen so vividly in her vision. This included morbid details about the number of knife wounds, as well as Sheriff Miller's belief that Hannah Wilson was killed elsewhere and her body driven to Mount Diablo postmortem.

Patty's face drained of color, her bloodshot eyes saucers of disbelief and alarm.

"...*According to Sheriff Miller, the victim's husband has now been brought in for official questioning. It is our understanding that no charges have yet been filed at the time of this broadcast.*"

"I-I knew it." Weak, strained and cracking, Cassie forced her voice from a throat constricted with dread. "Patty, I sh-sh-should have *d-done* s-something."

Patty gripped Cassie's arm tightly, her own words barely audible as she tried to offer comfort in the face of a shared horror.

"You tried to, Cass. What else could you do?"

Though she meant it, the consolation fell flat, lying there like roadkill. Cassie had followed what Patty believed to be genuinely logical deductions. They had finally dismissed Cassie's visions, both women convincing themselves that the images were too horrific to be real. But now the weight of that mistake pressed heavy upon them, leaving them to grapple with a paralyzing sense of dread and responsibility.

"*In other news, NASA is busy preparing for its second mission to land astronauts on the Moon with Apollo 12—*"

Cold disquiet fell upon them as the newscaster's voice trailed away. Cassie stared unblinking at the flickering television, the light playing grotesquely across her features.

"Is it possible *you* were the one who made that anonymous call?" Patty whispered as she reached for Cassie's hand. It felt as frail and bloodless as hers had become

"No. Um...I mean, I don't think...No!" Cassie lurched away, pulling back her hand. Still, she did not take her eyes off the screen. The broadcast was now showing B-roll images of Cape Canaveral. Bill would be there at this very minute.

At least, he should be.

"I told you, Pat. I don't remember anything after I left here Friday. Whoever called the sheriff's department, it wasn't me. *It can't have been me.* I had no idea where Hannah was. I saw the attack in her home. I saw the man—who I thought was Solomon—dragging her away. Nothing after that. How could I possibly know she was in the trunk of a car on a remote mountainside, an hour away from here?"

"So, you're back to the Solomon story? God, Cass. I thought we explained at least that part away. But now—" Patty rubbed her temples, her face ashen. "—Now, I don't know what to think. Fuck!"

"Listen, I'm not changing lanes here, Pat. I agree with the things you said. About Solomon, I mean. Yes, in my mind when that man looked up at me—you know, standing at Hannah's record player—I truly believed it was my brother's face. But the things you said about all that past trauma bubbling away under the surface makes me wonder now."

She stepped across the living room and picked up the phone receiver.

"Wait, Cass. Who are you calling? I think we really need to think before you tell the police anything. Especially now that—"

Cassie *shushed* her as the operator picked up. "I'd like to be put through to Kennedy Space Center, please."

Patty heard a murmur from the other end of the line, something indiscernible.

"Yes, ma'am." Cassie said. "I understand it is a long distance call. I accept those charges."

Patty heard the faraway drone of mechanical ringing, then came the lower timbre of a man's voice, stiff and official.

"This is Mrs. William Kennedy speaking," Cassie told him. "My husband is an engineer working with you as part of the team assigned by IBM."

Now the man's voice lightened, rising in pitch. Patty made out something about him knowing Bill, but little else. Rather than patch her through, however, he was sharing some information Patty could barely make out.

Whatever it was, Cassie tensed up and pressed the phone receiver firmly to her ear, muffling his voice so that Patty was no longer able to hear him. A moment later she thanked the man and hung up, her hand trembling so palpably that the receiver nearly missed the phone's cradle.

"He's n-not there," she relayed to Patty, her voice teetering. "That gentleman said he w-was h-home."

"Bill's here? In San Francisco? Right now? But aren't they supposed to be gearing up for a second moon landing—why would they send him home at a time like this? It doesn't make sense."

Cassie agreed, calming herself with a breath and pouring another vodka, this one neat. "I know. But he just told me that Bill's been back almost two weeks now…"

20

)(

WHAT ARE YOU saying, Cass? 'Cause it kinda sounds like now you think maybe Bill is somehow mixed up with all of this."

Cassie hung up the phone and unconsciously bit at her lip. "I don't know what I'm saying, Trish. But I just can't shake what you said."

"About?"

"About why I might have thought it was my brother's face I saw in that awful vision about Hannah. What if you're right? What if the face I thought I knew was someone else's?"

"Like Bill's?"

Cassie nodded.

"Oh, Cass. You can't possibly think Bill has anything to do with this. I think you're beyond exhausted…and maybe a little bit stoned…and just need to meditate on this and find your center again." They were words of wisdom that Patty decided she would do well to heed herself. From the moment she'd heard the newscaster utter the words, '*broadcast last night was interrupted.*

I am now able to share the rest of that information,' Patty's own pulse had skyrocketed, her head beginning to ache in a slow, rhythmic thump. "And I'm going to go home and do the same. It's been a long, stressful weekend and frankly, I need to sleep."

Cassie half-heard, still staring at the screen as if it were communicating only to her. "Poor Meredith," she said to no one in particular.

"Poor Meredith," Patty echoed. "And poor Hannah. I can't believe it's true."

"Mmmmm…" Cassie murmured before snapping back to the moment, her attention fully upon Patricia. "What's that you said?"

"I said, 'and poor Hannah.'"

"Yes, of course. It's so, so sad. And scary."

"And poor you, Cass. You saw it happen. I can't even begin to imagine what you're feeling right now."

More stunned now than anything, Cassie attempted a smile and assured Patty that she'd be fine.

"You know, I always knew you had something special, girl. But I didn't expect it to be so strong. If I'm honest, I kinda expected it to be at the lost-heirlooms-found level. Not the caliber of this."

"Tell me about it."

"The Universe has bestowed a special gift upon you, Cassandra Kennedy. I think the important thing now is understanding it. And learning how to use it."

"Yeah, some gift. Thanks, Universe. I would've preferred some nice earrings. Or maybe a new watch." Cassie's voice was deadpan despite the obvious joke, everything about her as numb as her tone. "I don't know about the whole *understanding* thing, though. I think I'm going to hang up my cards for a bit. No more readings at the café. I love you, and I know it helped business, Patty, but I hope you'll understand."

"Of course! I wouldn't think twice about it." Patty made her way to the door, grabbing her pack of smokes and lighter. "I kind of regret persuading you to start giving readings in the first place now. I just thought it would be good for you. Y'know?"

"I know."

"You sure you'll be alright? If not, I'll sta—"

"Go," Cassie insisted and playfully turned her friend toward the door, ushering her out. "Go home. Get some sleep. You need it. We'll be fine."

Patty began the climb to Haight Street, a cigarette already between her lips. She turned to wave before the trees obstructed her view of the balcony. She knew Cassie would be watching over her until she was gone from view, just as she always did.

But this time the balcony was empty, the house already in darkness.

)(

SEPTEMBER 1969

They did not see each other for weeks. Neither one had made a conscious decision to maintain the absence, it just felt a natural progression for both of them, given all that had happened. Time was needed to process it all. And space was a good thing.

For now, at least.

In Cassie's mind, however, everything had changed. *She* had changed. Feeling less and less like Cassandra Kennedy and more and more like Cassie Albrighton, the girl she had once been, the idea of seeing Patty, or coming to the café at all, felt like a part of her life that was either off limits, irrelevant, or both. The very thought that she might bump into Meredith Harper sent shivers down her spine.

So she physically sequestered herself from the world in the same way as that dark, oppressive cloud over her thoughts had isolated her from it emotionally. Why she felt this way, she couldn't say. Though she debated it with herself more times than she could count, she just couldn't explain these feelings to herself, let alone to anyone else.

Least of all, Patty.

She took to distracting her burdened mind by dedicating time with Isabella. They went for long evening walks as Cassie cleared her head and Bella frolicked in the less intense heat and easy breezes that heralded the first hints of the coming fall.

During the days when Bella was at kindergarten, Cassie again immersed herself in the library. Steadfast and reliable, she cherished the safety and solace she'd always found in books. Unlike real life, which was plagued by clutter and confusion.

Her life, at least.

Knowing beyond a shadow of a doubt that her lingering fear of violence and violation was the furthest thing from irrational, she was no longer concerned with the trappings of scelerophobia, or any other such psychobabble nonsense.

Far from avoiding her gift, Cassie now committed herself to the task of learning more about psychic abilities. She scoured books on documented cases of extrasensory perception in other people's lives, in the hopes of removing some of the chaos and uncertainty from her own. It was time to fully accept the person she really was—that bright, promising and powerful girl called Cassie Albrighton who had been overshadowed by the woman Cassandra Kennedy for as long as she could remember.

Even before that person had willingly taken Bill's last name.

The first step in that process was to acquire an understanding of which spiritual gifts she naturally possessed, which she did not, and which she might be capable of further harnessing.

The cases she focused on the most shared detailed records about peoples' abilities to perceive distant events and locations; past events of which the viewer was not consciously aware; or the power to gain information about a person or object through touch. These were respectively known as clairvoyance, remote viewing, retrocognition and psychometry, and Cassie memorized their names and indicators until they became part of the person she now believed herself to be. Which was also the person she had once been—a long time ago and a world away.

At last she had found an explanation for all the feelings she'd had but never quite understood. Of her discoveries, perhaps the two most salient were known as astral projection and bilocation. Both explained the process and ability for one's consciousness to separate from one's physical body. Instances of the former—astral projection, also known as an out-of-body experience—had been documented as far back as the late 1600s in a Chinese handbook on alchemy called *The Secret of the Golden Flower*. She found references to the latter—bilocation, or the means to be in two places at once—in belief sets that ranged from Hinduism and Buddhism to witchcraft and the occult. But perhaps the most startling examples were found in what is arguably the most mainstream or widely accepted doctrine of all: Christianity. Exhaustive research uncovered several documented occurrences of bilocation over the last two millennia, each one attributed to a saint. Cassie found what she felt was the most notable in A.D. 40: eyewitness accounts of this ability in the beloved Virgin Mary herself.

Hail Mary, full of grace, the Lord is with thee...

Cassie's mind immediately jumped to the recital, a throwback to her aunt chanting from the other side of the closet door. She could hear the woman's velvety voice as surely as if she were with her now; still smell the perfume her nose would forever recognize—a heady mix of lavender and vanilla with a soft musky undertone—mingling with the clinging tang of cigarette smoke. This latter component of her aunt's scent was not so dissimilar to the one she now associated with Patty. Unlike her best friend, however, the presence of Cassie's aunt had almost always been accompanied by a subtle change in the electric charge of the air: a lightning storm no bigger than a molecule, but as tangible to Cassie as the nose on her own face.

These sensations, and so many more, Cassie had experienced every time her aunt knelt before the locked closet door, praying for the wayward souls of Cassie and her brothers. While behind it, huddled together in the pitch black and biting cold—or slowly dehydrating in the stifling heat—the children's tummies rumbled and their muscles atrophied as their eyes weakened from prolonged periods in the dark.

"I'm glad we stabbed your sicko husband," Cassie exclaimed out loud without realizing she had done so. "I only wish it had been you, you nasty bitch."

Two of her fellow bookworms shushed her.

Another had a look of genuine shock that twisted the woman's features almost comically.

"*I'm so sorry*," Cassie whispered in a hushed apology. She raised her book to display it to their hard, squinty eyes. "A crime thriller. The husband is the baddie. I guess I got swept up in it."

The shocked woman nodded, her face untwisting with a silent *ahhhh*. But the other bookworm shushed her again. Two others, a man and a woman sitting together in the corner, each reading a copy of the same book, cast her understanding smiles before burrowing back into their own pages.

Only one older gentleman felt determined to cling to his aggravation, shooting her the evil eye for a good thirty seconds. He was clearly convinced that by doing so he was serving up justice. A kind of Bookworm Batman, if you will.

Far from keeping her quiet, imagining the man in a bat cowl and leotards only caused her to break out in a fit of the giggles she couldn't stop.

Bundling up her stack of books, Cassie quickly checked out. She was still laughing out loud, much to the curiosity of many passersby, when she caught the streetcar to Haight-Ashbury. If she hurried, she'd be home just before Bella got back from kindergarten.

) (

"See? Mama's not crazy after all, my beautiful little Bella Luna!" Cassie wiggled her fingers maniacally in the air (she was an iconic baddie, after all—at least according to the old man in the library) and pounced on Isabella with a bout of tickles. This made her daughter squirm and howl with delight.

"There are no scelerophobics in this house, babygirl. Just us hippie witchies and our ability to bilocate. And if mama can do it, you'll be able to do it too, when you grow up." She picked Bella up and spun her around, dancing to music only she could hear, humming badly without care. "There shall be no more Kennedys in this house, no Ma'am. The curse of that name stops here. Right now. From here on out, it's Cassie and Isabella *Albrighton*. You and me against the world, little one."

She had loved Bill. And was fond of the woman she had become. But even more than the life they created together, Cassie missed the strong, fearless person she had once been.

Cassie Kennedy must go, her fears and phobias and unsolicited, uncontrolled visions gone with her.

It was time to bring Cassie Albrighton back into the light.

) (

So their weeks passed, with Bella flourishing at kindergarten and Cassie buried in the exploration of her newly discovered gifts.

She read. She slept. She daydreamed and listened to music. As days became weeks, she returned to consulting her Tarot cards, divining insight into the future and what it might hold if she were to remain on this current path. And most importantly of all, she began meditating, allowing her consciousness to free itself from her body and travel where it may.

At first, she only saw the inside of her own head, a place she didn't much care to visit for all the traumas and concerns that still hid in its darkest corners. But after a few weeks she found herself able to float away, if only a few feet, to look down upon her body as it sat on the living room rug in the lotus position. She was able to do this most easily when she had just a puff of one of the joints Patty left behind. There were only three in the shiny metal cigarette case she'd forgotten to take with her, so Cassie smoked them sparingly. Just enough to relax her agitated soul.

Once she'd attained this level of projection, the next came much more quickly. Within days, Cassie found herself soaring over Panhandle Park, able to drop into any situation and watch it from the perspective of a fly on the wall. All the while meditating on the floor of her walk-up's living room.

At last she'd achieved the same level of astral projection as she had when she'd experienced the remote viewing of Lyndsey Roe's abduction from the park and her mother's subsequent murder in a dark and dreadful place. Cassie now believed that she had seen both occur in real time, though she had no idea how or why this had happened.

The difference between then and now was that Cassie was the one controlling it. The situations she dropped into were not only of her own choosing, but were much more innocuous: A young couple's plans regarding their upcoming wedding as they strolled hand-in-hand through Panhandle Park. An older man jogging. A young boy playing chase with his dog.

But sometimes when she dropped in, those conversations would stutter, the people briefly faltering or even stopping what they were doing as if they sensed Cassie was there. Practicing to the point of obsession, she soon became adept enough to achieve this state almost at will...and without the subjects of her astral projection sensing her presence at all.

She floated unnoticed about a family's picnic celebration of the eightieth birthday of their patriarch. She hovered invisible over two hippies making love in a secluded copse of trees—

Patty would love this, she thought

—daring to move so close that she could smell their sex. She took up residence on a bench, becoming party to conversations both inspired and banal. In an odd manner, Cassie felt a growing emotional closeness with the regulars she saw in the park. A kind of extended family or circle of friends of which she had become an honorary member, though none of them knew it.

For the first time since sequestering herself and Bella from the outside world, Cassie felt the pangs of longing and loneliness from her self-imposed isolation. She missed seeing people in the flesh; feeling the air brush across her skin as they walked by. She longed to have a conversation with anyone but Bella Luna. And while it might seem odd, she pined for the pleasing scent of shampoo in freshly washed hair or the subtle sweet aroma of perfume on skin. She craved the smiles that lit up a friend's face when they met you and yearned for that human touch: the feel of their skin—warm, and soft—as they hugged you.

But most of all, she longed to be with her friend again.

The desire for all of these things was more than emotional. Just as you physically ache for that intense moment of release when you've gone too long without truly fulfilling sex, so Cassie again felt what her brother had once called '*little zapples*' bubbling up from within her. Like teasing prickles of sensation that came from somewhere deep inside, once she felt them they would not stop until they were satisfied.

Mrs. William Kennedy would have ignored them. Suppressed them. Shoved them down even deeper to a place where they would fester and rot until they ultimately destroyed her.

Not Cassie Albrighton. That girl would welcome them. Submit to them. Fulfill their needs as they shaped her into the powerful and shiny creature of this world she was always meant to be.

The very idea of it was an opiate.

At last the time had come to go and see her friend again. It was time she finally introduced Patty to the real Cassie Albrighton.

) (

The anticipation of it made her giddy with relief. In this heightened state, Cassie was a whirlwind of ideas and action, blissfully and frenetically tackling every and any chore she could think of. All the while, her new future became that tropical island that's finally in sight of the shipwrecked man who is weak and mere seconds moments from drowning.

The idea of it finally being within her reach was still impelling her forward when the first knock came on Cassie's door.

Hard.

Loud.

It yanked her back to the here and now with a crash. Her apartment, which had been filled with warm color and light as she tidied and cleaned and organized and straightened, now dissolved to cold, hard shade.

The second knock was a thud.

The third, a reverberating bang.

In its frame, the door shuddered. From her room, Isabella peeked out and Cassie waved her away, yelling.

"Hide, Bella! Now!" She frantically scanned for something in the apartment she could use as a weapon. "Go! Hide! And don't you come out until I say so!"

One final, thunderous crack and the door flew in.

Silhouetted in its busted frame was the figure of Solomon Albrighton...

21

)(

I T HAD BEEN nearly three months since little Lyndsey Roe had been abducted from Panhandle Park. Still the authorities had no knowledge of the whereabouts of either the girl or her mother Veronica. Two months had passed since Hannah Wilson's brutal slaying, and the sheriff of Costa Contra County was as much at a loss as his brethren at the San Francisco Police Department.

The initial buzz about each had been everywhere at first. But as the weeks progressed, concern receded into idle chatter, which in turn devolved into unfounded speculation. In the case of Lyndsey Roe, this included a not-so-whispered rumor that the six-year-old's mother had to have had something to do with the little girl's disappearance.

As information waned and speculation grew rife, the *Ledger* resorted to publishing sporadic editorials about both cases in a bid to keep eyeballs on their paper's column-inches. It didn't matter if the basis for such were factual or not. After all, the young wife from Sausalito was deceased, and the mother-daughter pair who disappeared into thin air from Panhandle Park in broad daylight were still at large. So who was to say otherwise?

Internally, the editor defended his stance on the matter by insisting that any ongoing interest the newspaper was capable of drumming up was better than the cases falling from the public eye altogether. The authorities in both matters had precious little to go on as it was. If the public stopped caring, which he assured his team was largely down to the paper's ongoing coverage—or not, as the case may be—then the cops might as well kiss goodbye to any more leads, cry uncle and chalk up two more 'Ws' on the perp's side of the scoreboard.

"If you think you're going to tell me how to run my newspaper, then we're moving on," he told the chief of police while treating him to a filet mignon at the editor's favorite Nob Hill restaurant. "If that happens, your leads dry up. No public interest equals no more leads. It's that simple and you know it." He threw back a whiskey sour and signaled for another. "You've got nothing else to go on right now, Herb. So here's the bottom line: if we give in to your demands and stop editorializing on those cases, in a matter of days the public won't even remember their names, never mind you catching the sick fuck who killed Hannah Wilson." He plucked a piece of gristle from his teeth with his steak knife. "And you can kiss goodbye to any hopes of ever finding that poor little girl and her mother, to boot."

The catalyst for this impromptu meeting was a small piece the *Ledger* had run in the last few days. In it, an ambitious new journalist by the name of Bobby Sutherland revealed that a psychic had been spotted coming to police headquarters in Mission Bay shortly after Lyndsey Roe's disappearance.

Where Sutherland had gotten his information, no one knew for certain. Patty's guess was Chinese whispers: someone had told someone else about a surprisingly gifted psychic causing quite a stir in the Haight-Ashbury district—a psychic who had appeared around the same time Lyndsey and her mother had gone missing. One person would have told another, and so it would have gone, *ad infinitum*, until the whisper found ears in this eager young reporter. Fashioning this weak hypothesis into an even weaker story, Sutherland's only goal was to fill a few more column-inches toward his weekly quota.

Edited back to a meager two-hundred words, and consigned to page twenty-eight below the fold, the article was birthed into relative obscurity. Further hindered by an ardent denial from SFPD Detective Douglas Ressler, the allegation passed from the collective consciousness as quickly as it had been born, being perceived as printed gossip far more than investigative insight.

Just as attention upon the Roes had tapered off, so public interest in the case of Hannah Wilson's murder also dwindled once Contra Costa County officials admitted they had little to no promising leads.

While Jerry Wilson, Hannah's husband, remained a person of interest, word on the street was that he was no longer viewed as a credible suspect. On the other hand, they were actively seeking information from any member of the public who might know the whereabouts of a man they identified only as Holden. In the weeks leading up to Hannah's disappearance and murder, the man had been a frequent customer at the Sausalito diner where Hannah worked. To help jog memories, there was an unstated suggestion that the two might have become rather close friends immediately before Hannah's murder.

According to Tina Mercer, a colleague and friend of Hannah's, Holden was a veteran recently home from his tour of duty in Vietnam. She did not recall seeing him at the diner previously and did admit that he and Hannah had gotten pretty close, pretty fast. There was no suggestion of impropriety of any sort from the waitress, however.

"Though a big part of me really hopes there was," she said in an interview with a reporter from the *San Francisco Ledger*. "Holden was a very handsome young man. Polite. Quiet. He had that air of respect about him that you only seem to find in military guys, y'know what I mean? And sure, the police are right when they say he seemed to care a lot about Hannah. Because he did. It was like they just hit it off, straight away. He was sweet and even helped me organize a surprise birthday party for her when that *REDACTED* husband of hers couldn't even bother to remember. So yeah, I don't mind sayin', I really kinda hope now that she *was* getting some of that Holden sugar before she died."

When asked if she thought Holden might have anything to do with Hannah's murder, Tina replied that there was a better chance of us putting men on Mars.

And that was the last the people of San Francisco heard of Hannah. No sooner had Channel 5's Mike Driffield dubbed her killer the Hurdy Gurdy Man, than public interest had already latched itself onto the next sensational headline.

Not one to throw in the towel, in a late September broadcast the TV reporter fought to reignite the public's interest by doubling-down on his theory that the Hurdy Gurdy Man was not only still active, but was operating all across the San Francisco Bay area. He reiterated his claim that Hannah Wilson's August murder was perpetrated by the same sadistic predator who had abducted Rosalie Sherwood from Mount Diablo in June.

Nothing new there. Driffield first made the allegation in his remote live broadcast from Mount Diablo the night Hannah was discovered in the trunk of her convertible. Driffield was in possession of no information to corroborate the claim, merely laying it at the feet of Hannah's unknown boogeyman despite Rosalie's disappearance remaining a mystery that could just as easily be a runaway situation as it could an abduction.

The big kicker to Driffield's latest broadcast was his claim that the Hurdy Gurdy Man was also responsible for the disappearance of Veronica Roe and her daughter Lyndsey in July.

Like Rosalie Sherwood, he argued, the mother-daughter pair were still at large. He also noted that Veronica Roe and Hannah Wilson were both married females in their mid-to-late twenties.

But that was the extent of any similarities between the three cases. As such, Mike Driffield's last desperate effort soon fizzled out, effectively erasing any more mention of the Hurdy Gurdy Man from casual conversations. And when the clever moniker Driffield assigned the killer faded away, so did Driffield's dreams of becoming the first San Francisco TV journalist to be awarded an Emmy.

)(

That all changed a week later, when the following arrived on the desks of both Bobby Sutherland at the *San Francisco Ledger*, and Mike Driffield at *Channel 5 News*:

FOLLOWING PAGES:
the famous Gemini wordsearch,
courtesy of the evidence archives
department of the San Francisco Police.

[Federal Bureau of Investigations
Case File 10-63; Document 10-63-2]

ive killed befoe- publ
  or I
will
agaoin

you Have
until oct 13
to find ME
first

```
J  G  Y  B  8  I  Z
D  P  L  R  E  N  N
F  W  I  Q  S  B  S
I  8  G  H  K  E  W
C  2  H  O  R  D  M
O  1  T  G  B  S  I
O  3  H  W  7  X  N
K  R  A  P  B  H  E
I  A  A  N  N  E  A
E  S  M  X  A  N  1
S  E  O  H  G  P  T
5  M  M  L  H  U  M
T  O  J  H  R  E  H
F  N  C  E  B  L  L
W  S  T  Y  R  S  O
L  F  A  S  A  S  R
1  I  C  W  I  Z  G
2  N  O  V  V  R  E
2  Y  Q  N  A  R  E
3  M  T  U  C  X  S
```

the Legder and Tv

```
T  C  P  U  Z  A  L  T  E  R  O
Y  C  U  A  S  Z  H  D  S  H  B
P  M  D  P  E  3  L  O  L  F  S
H  P  E  C  J  R  V  6  U  Q  I
E  L  P  I  T  L  U  M  S  S  B
R  E  W  O  L  F  K  Z  E  S  E
Y  H  Y  O  U  S  T  F  Q  B  X
N  I  3  E  G  Z  I  L  S  H  M
S  M  A  S  V  W  Q  V  P  M  B
F  B  I  S  O  E  I  K  L  D  S
N  Y  L  I  R  L  W  F  X  S  I
M  G  P  D  K  A  E  N  D  U  T
V  E  E  G  B  D  E  O  Y  O  E
V  E  L  T  K  R  W  O  X  O  N
R  Z  D  X  H  E  O  H  U  N  L
B  P  N  B  A  M  V  L  N  J  S
E  Y  A  G  X  M  L  I  Q  S  U
O  T  H  S  T  U  A  D  B  O  I
S  L  N  V  E  S  H  O  J  H  L
H  V  A  A  T  W  E  R  C  O  Z
```

22

)(

AFFECTIONATELY KNOWN TO locals as the 'Cop Shop' due to the number of uniformed officers and detectives who frequented the bar after their shifts, O'Malley's Tavern on Pier 40 was virtually an extension of the station itself.

Unlike other bars or cafés where conversations about rapes, shootings, stabbings, kidnappings or any number of other heinous acts might only be muttered under one's breath, at the Cop Shop, those topics comprised half the conversations.

In all honesty, it was where a good number of their cases were cracked, the files able to be closed. You'd be amazed how your mind opens up when you're no longer staring eye-to-eye at your problem but permitting yourself to place it to one side…for a bit, at least. It's also why Detective Doug Ressler, after a lifetime of chronic alcohol consumption, would one day be saddled with a half-dozen unpleasant symptoms of hepatic steatosis. But when that day did eventually arrive, if you were to ask him whether he would do things differently—whether he would go back in time and exchange his health for the peace of mind the closure of those solved cases provided a hundred and twenty-seven families of murder victims—he would tell you he wouldn't change a thing. Every time. Unequivocally.

"I can't believe we're actually sitting here, dicking around with a crossword puzzle, acting like it'll make a damn bit of difference to any of our cases." Ressler waved down one of the barmaids and asked for two pints of beer.

"A stout for me," his partner Sid Younger amended, offering the waitress his best smile and mouthing 'thanks' before correcting Ressler a second time. "And it's a wordsearch."

"What do I give a shit, Sid?"

"You said it's a crossword. It's not. That's where you're given clues and empty boxes where you write your answers. With a wordsearch, the answers are right in front of us."

"Okay Poindexter, whatever floats your boat."

"What floats my boat is the possibility of uncovering some real clues about who sent this. I think it's our guy from the Roe disappearance."

"Why would he do that, help us to catch him? I don't buy it."

"Because he's bored. We're not even close and he wants to play. To be challenged. He's the type of sicko that gets off on it when we're getting closer. The thrill of the chase, and all that. Either that, or he's an egotistical S.O.B. who wants us to know just how much smarter he is than us."

Ressler rolled his eyes. "Maybe it's all just a goddamn hoax and we're wasting our fucking time—"

"—You're not." The voice that cut across Doug Ressler's was feminine. Foreign. A lilting cadence filled with an easy confidence. "Detective Younger is right." (She pronounced this as *roight.*) "Violent psychopaths are inherently narcissistic. They're selfish. Vain. Attention-seekers. And they place a high value upon their own intrinsic cleverness."

Although Siobhan Jacobs had relocated to the San Francisco

Bay area a full dozen years earlier, the time had done little to dull her bold Belfast brogue.

As if she weren't difficult enough to understand already, Ressler remembered thinking in the first moments of meeting her. A licensed psychiatrist from Northern Ireland, Jacobs was a specialist in profiling homicide cases and was also the county's head of Forensics. *It's like listening to a leprechaun spouting off a bunch of psychobabble gobbledygook.*

Though to be fair, in the spirit of full transparency, that wasn't the *first* thought that had come to Ressler's mind when they met. The first was something much more akin to how boss the leggy, strawberry blonde doc would look sprawled out across his bed. And he'd made it his mission to find out. A mission that took nearly three years to achieve, only to be gone in a puff of smoke in a matter of months.

Biggest mistake ever: don't shit where you eat.

"Thanks for that." Ressler chimed. "Feel free to go into all sorts of boring detail about it with whoever you're here to meet."

Jacobs leaned in, propping her hands against the booth's tabletop. "Oh, don't you worry. It's not you."

"Thank God for that." Ressler crossed his arms and leaned back into the bench seat as Jacobs grabbed the 8x10 photo of the wordsearch puzzle and spun it toward her. But Doug slapped his hand down, loud and fast, pinning it beneath his palm.

"Jesus Christ, Doug." Always more pronounced when she was irritated, surprised or drunk—and she certainly wasn't the latter—Jacobs' Irish brogue enunciated it as *Jayyy–zis Christ, Dooog.* "Do you want me to study it now, or don'tcha?"

Sid sighed, shaking his head. A *here we go again* look drawing his face long. "Listen, kids. Can we just play nice in the sandbox together for once? I asked her to take a look, Doug. Unless you're digging the idea of scouring this thing for endless hours?"

Refusing to honor Jacobs with eye contact, Ressler released

the photo of the puzzle while his eyes bore into Sid's, which his partner duly ignored. Sid snatched up the photo and politely handed it to Jacobs. "We appreciate it, Siobhan. Well, I do, at least."

"I know *you* do, Sid. But I d'know how you do it, day-in, day-out, with this one here." Jacobs side-nodded in Ressler's direction, equally refusing to make eye contact with him. "Really, I don't."

"He's not so bad, deep down. You should know—you guys were all but inseparable when you were together."

"Ten weeks," Siobhan confirmed, making it apparent that she had counted each and every painstaking one of them. "Nothing compared to you, Sid. So, how long did you say you've been saddled with this tosser, again?"

The coming month would mark seven years since Ressler had asked his captain to assign Sidney Lee Younger as his partner.

Asked? More like a mandated, their captain was wont to tell any who had ears.

San Francisco's first black officer promoted to detective, Sid Younger was an idealist determined to change the system from the inside-out. Having worked closely with the city's urban youth for half a decade, he came to realize, at least by his way of thinking, that the best way to change the direction he saw things heading was to sleep with the enemy.

He'd earned a bachelor's in criminal justice with a minor in psychology from Stanford. Combine this with his familiarity of the workings and vibe of the inner city, and Younger was a shoo-in for detective from the outset.

The lieutenant at the time, an old boy with ancestral connections to Mississippi's lingering antebellum south, didn't see it that way.

Which left Sid two options.

He could go back to social work and continue to treat the symptoms. Or he could at least begin to affect some kind of cure by accepting the only position on offer to him: beat cop. (Which, according to the kids he worked with, now lumped him in with a group they scornfully called flatfoots, pigs, blues, the fuzz, heat, or five-ohs.)

The beat he was first assigned relegated Sid to overnight 11-7 shifts in the Tenderloin district. Nestled so innocuously between Market Street and Van Ness Avenue, the Tenderloin was one of the most deceptively dangerous districts in the city.

It was six long and arduous years before the old boy boy lieutenant—who relished every opportunity to remind Sid that he was his superior—hung up his badge for good. Dogged by allegations ranging from accepting bribes to racketeering connections in organized crime, the lieutenant decided that retiring to another bay all the way across the country in Tampa, Florida, might be a pretty good idea.

Not only did this get Sid off one of the worst beats in the city, it also enabled him to finally make detective.

Now reporting for duty on the third floor instead of the first, Sid became a lone, optimistic black face in a sea of tired white ones which ranged from the diffident to the distrustful.

On his first day, Sid Younger came dressed for success in a cashmere blazer he'd saved a month to buy.

On his second day, he came back from lunch to find the blazer draped over his chair with the word RAISIN scrawled across the width of its back in black marker.

A hackneyed reference to that year's controversial and equally lauded film, *A Raisin in the Sun*, it didn't help that Sidney shared the same first name as the movie's award-winning lead actor, Sidney Poitier. Or, to make matters worse, that Sid's last name was the same as the character Poitier played.

With his colleagues laughing as he took his desk, Sid refused to honor them with the response they hoped to get. Instead, he studied the blazer, dusted it off, and went straight back to work on the pile of papers before him.

They called it a traditional rookie indoctrination. Lighthearted antics, and Sid's non-response only served to infuriate them more. So the constant vitriol and mutterings grew.

'...Black-as-coal piece of shit thinks he's better than us...'

'...Chip on his shoulder big as dog shit...'

'...Not one of us, and never will be...'

The worst was the most menacing for its lack of censure:

'...He'll learn, by God...'

Though it tore him up inside, the incessant attacks were anything but unexpected. In his previous work with some of the city's most disenfranchised youths, Sid had witnessed instances of police brutalities that would haunt your dreams...and perpetrated for no other reason than the color of their skin.

And because the cops could.

By comparison, a ruined jacket was nothing.

To make a point of how he felt, at the end of that second workday Sid proudly donned the vandalized jacket and took the roundabout way to the stairwell, parading through the maze of desks with his head held high.

If it had all stopped there, perhaps things would have turned out differently. Perhaps Sid Younger and Doug Ressler would never have become intrinsically entwined in one another's lives. But one affront escalated to another until that Friday night Sid was jumped on the way to his car by three guys with pillowcases over their heads. As he lay bleeding in the parking lot, barely conscious and unable to move or speak, they tore open his shirt and poured a pint of bleach over his chest.

Just for fun, they emptied a box of raisins over him.

Doug Ressler wasn't one of them.

He'd heard the rumblings, though. He just thought it was the usual chest-beating and spineless bravado from a clan of cowards.

But that same weekend, as Sidney Lee Younger recuperated in

the hospital with a broken jaw and chemical burns to his chest, three of Ressler's colleagues mysteriously found themselves respectively with a fractured cheekbone, two broken ribs, and a cracked orbital bone that nearly blinded one.

For some reason, Douglas Ressler's right hand was wrapped in bandages when he came to work that Monday, the sweet tang of bourbon oozing from his pores. Unable to draw his weapon, he was relegated to desk duty the rest of the week.

Then the following week as well, even though his hand had healed.

Six weeks later, Sid returned to the station.

Little did he know that long before he'd set foot through the door, the captain had already assigned him to be Ressler's partner.

Doug made clear to all and sundry that he had no idea why the captain had done such a thing.

"But," he added as he lit a Marlboro without breaking eye contact with any of them, "I guess it's alright by me, anyway. Seeing as this young negro fella here seems to have more grit than all the rest of you assclowns combined."

"Jesus, Sid, Seven years with Ressler? I'd kill myse—" She cut herself short and clamped her lips tight, but it was already out there. Now she did look at Ressler and refused to look away until he met her gaze. It took a good minute, which is a long time during awkward, uncomfortable silence. "I'm sorry, Doug. It's just a stupid, heartless expression. You know I didn't mean it that way."

Ressler softened.

He breathed out.

Uncrossed his arms.

"Don't worry about it. You wanna make it up to me? Take that fucking puzzle home, see what you can find out. If it's legit, we've got three days." He downed the rest of his beer and left before the waitress had brought his second. "I'm going to bed."

It wasn't yet seven in the evening.

)(

FRIDAY / OCT 10

As enthusiastic as she was exhausted, Siobhan Jacobs met Ressler and Younger at the station the following morning, brimming with nervous energy.

"God, Jacobs. You look like you were up all night."

"Gee, thanks, Sid."

"You know I don't mean it like that. You so look drawn though. Were you *really* up all night with that puzzle?"

Jacobs nodded. "I was, yes. And I'm spent, to be sure. But I have a lot to share with you two!" She pulled the 8x10 photograph of the wordsearch from a prim leather attaché case, along with a lined notepad covered in scribbles and notes, along with a traditional silver fountain pen. "Where do you want to start?"

This she addressed to Doug, gracing it with a consolatory thin-lipped smile, and he silently mouthed 'don't worry about it.' Then he offered her a coffee. Not from one of the bean-burners (what they called the percolator pots that sat half-empty on hotplates all day until the coffee resembled lukewarm sludge) but fresh from the new café down the road.

It was still steaming, the milk foam the perfect amount of frothy. She placed her hand on Ressler's shoulder, giving it a gentle squeeze. Sid noticed how she lingered just that little bit longer than she normally would have, had the shoulder been anyone else's but Doug Ressler's.

"How about you just start wherever you want," Sid suggested as Jacobs caught him eyeing her hand and immediately withdrew it, a flush rising to her cheeks.

"Right. So here's the helicopter view. Then we can take a

deeper dive on any points you'd like. Sound good?"

"Absolutely," Ressler agreed quietly with great forethought. "Thank you for ruining your whole night to do this. Personally, I'd rather chew my own arm off than look at that thing for longer than a minute or two. I don't know how you do it."

Jacobs smiled, almost bashful. "Well, thank *you* for saying so, Doug. I appreciate that." She dragged a worn, steel-legged chair up to the two desks pushed together and laid out the 8x10 of the puzzle and her notes. "Now, like I said, let's look at the overview. For a start, I believe without a doubt this puzzle was sent to the newspaper and TV station by someone who has either killed before or has, at the very least, acted in some kind of predatory fashion."

"So you believe it's legit," Sid Younger confirmed more than asked.

"Yes, I do. And there is a lot to unpack here. I found over thirty viable references I believe are a mixture of validations that the sender of this puzzle is not only someone to take seriously but that it may also be a confession of sorts."

"Well, before we go there, I have one big, stupid question." Doug Ressler raised his hand while leaning back in his chair, tipping it onto its two rear legs. When Siobhan addressed him, he slid his raised hand behind his head and balanced there, teetering. "Why a puzzle? Isn't it fucking childish?"

"That's actually a really good question."

Ressler snorted. "Well, maybe don't act so goddamn surprised, about it."

Sid Younger almost choked on his coffee.

Jacobs ignored them both, barreling into a response. "It is a rather juvenile way for him to communicate to us, I agree. But there's good reason for that. We develop our social coping skills very early in life. It's how we learn to interact with our peers and the world around us. But if a child is exposed to prolonged or intense abuse or neglect, that process is interrupted. It may even cease to evolve altogether. The result can be a minimized or even non-existent social coping mechanism."

"Meaning?" Though Ressler knew better than to say it, once again all he heard was that leprechaun and that gobbledygook.

"Meaning, Doug, that their emotional development is stunted. In essence, a part of their personality remains forever at the age at which the person experienced said extreme trauma."

"So," Sid qualified, "if, say, a nine-year-old is beaten by his father. Hard and often. You're saying his development can be stuck at the level of a nine-year-old's."

"Psychologically, yes. Partially."

"Does that mean he's intellectually retarded?" Ressler brought his chair back down to rest on all four legs. He was spread across the desk, now intent on finding out where this line of thought was going to take them.

"Not at all," Jacobs answered. "In fact, many psychopaths are of above-average intelligence. Their social awkwardness is sometimes attributed to having near-genius level IQs."

"So, you think we have a psycho on our hands." This was from Doug as he sipped his own coffee from the same café.

Siobhan Jacobs thought about her answer before offering it. "I think we have an unknown perpetrator with an above-average I.Q., who was hurt as a child and has now hurt others as an adult. I think this is a cry for help before he does so again."

"So, he's smart but socially inept? Like, book smart, street stupid?" Sid asked.

"That might be the case," Siobhan conceded. "But he may also be very good at picking up on weakness and opportunity. So if that's what you define as 'street smart,' then I'd say we're looking for a man who is both book smart and street smart. What he's lacking is the empathy gene."

"*Empathy gene—*" both Ressler and Younger said in unison,

and Siobhan Jacobs grinned, glancing from one to the other. "See, that's how I can tell you guys have been together a long, *long* time. You even act like an old married couple. Next, you'll be finishing each other's sentences. How adorable."

"Yeah," Ressler quipped. "We're fucking precious. What's an empathy gene?"

"It's not a real gene, *per se*," Jacobs explained. "It means that the part of development where a child learns empathy by receiving it and watching it applied to others—be it other people, animals, pets, etcetera—is stunted. They themselves have not been treated with empathy, so they don't understand it. It's a key piece of their personality that will not evolve the way it does with emotionally healthy individuals."

"So what you're saying is that hurt people hurt people," Sid exclaimed. "You know, people who've been hurt end up hurting other people."

"No, no, we get it," Ressler mumbled, unimpressed. But to Siobhan Jacobs, this was perhaps the most sublime and poignant thing to ever come from Sid's lips. She adored him, that much was true. He was kind and generous and forthright. But Sid was hardly known for having a reputation for profundity.

Now, if only Doug Resler could take a page from his book, maybe there would still be a chance at their reconciliation.

As though he sensed her thoughts, Ressler rolled his eyes.

Okay then, Siobhan reconsidered. *Or pigs might learn to fly.*

She cast the unwelcome negativity from her mind and repeated, "Hurt people hurt people. And I think this poor guy has been very badly hurt in his time."

"Poor guy?" Ressler sat upright, becoming rigid. "You're about to tell us where this guy fits into our caseload, based upon what you found in this stupid fucking puzzle, and you're feeling bad for him? Because let me tell you, if he fits into any of *our* cases, nothing about him deserves sympathy."

Siobhan retracted. "Of course, you're right. He doesn't deserve our sympathy. But he does deserve our empathy. If not, then how do we differ?"

It was a good point, and Sid nodded, pulling his mouth into a pensive pout.

"In fact," Jacobs added. "I'd go so far as to say that finding him demands our empathy. If you canna' put yourself in his shoes—" her Irish lilt had become more prevalent as Siobhan's emotions ran deep "—I'd be willing to bet that you might never catch this bloke. And honestly? I think he wants you to."

"Well, how 'bout we find out what we're pinning on him before we jump ahead of ourselves here." Sid recommended they delve into the puzzle. "What did you find? Let's zoom in from that helicopter view and get down 'n dirty with some specifics."

This lit a spark in Siobhan Jacob's eyes and she cracked her knuckles before flipping through pages of notes and scrawled facsimiles of various grids of the puzzle.

"I wish I'd had a few of these photographs so I could've marked them up separately. It would've made the whole discovery process go faster, to be sure. But I made do with scribbling sections of it out until connections like words and phrases became apparent. So, pardon if it looks a bit of a mess, yeah? I promise, it all makes sense. So, here goes.

"Like I said, I found a good thirty words or numbers hidden in here with varying degrees of relevance. That part will be up to you to decide. Some of them might very well be dead ends—ruses added to the puzzle to confuse or distract us. But I believe most of them are legitimate clues. The first I want to show you is this one that he's circled himself." She turned the photo of the puzzle for them to see. At the top, the sender had circled the words **STOP ME**. "That tells me a lot about him. For one, you'll notice that the standard wordsearch convention of connecting complete words up, down, left, right, or diagonally do not apply. He is applying the standard convention to letters, not to whole words. So the letters must be adjacent to one another, in any direction, but the word or phrase itself might make this snake-like pattern. This tells me he's a rule-breaker. Or maybe you'd call him a trailblazer. Take your pick. Secondly, he does possess a certain sense of equity: he gave us this first clue to forewarn us that he isn't following the typical rules here."

"So he's giving us a heads-up," Ressler noted. "But at the same time, he's taunting us. 'Stop me.' Sounds like a cocky asshole."

"Or maybe," Siobhan countered, "it's a plea. As in, 'please stop me.' Because, on a subconscious level, he wants us to stop him before the thirteenth of October."

"Depends on how you wanna look at it," Sid said and tossed his paper cup into the garbage.

"I think the next clue provides the lens through which we can determine what he means." In the lower left quadrant of the grid Siobhan ran her finger around the diagonal phrase, **HELP ME**. "I also found the word 'help' two more times, interlaced with one another up here."

She traced her finger over them both in the top right quadrant. They shared the same **L** and **P**.

Sid absently nodded.

Surprisingly, so did Doug Ressler. "Okay, but you said you had evidence he's killed, or at least preyed upon others, before?"

"Maybe. I wouldn't call it evidence, but an indicator. His way of telling us. Which is why I'm even more certain he *wants* us to stop him. She ran her finger in a snakelike pattern starting on the bottom line, four letters in. They watched her do this twice to no avail. The third time she tapped each letter and spoke it: "R-O-B-I-N-H-O-O-D. Robin Hood."

"Jesus Christ," Ressler said. "Is he really making himself out to be some kind of populous hero?"

"No, I don't believe so," Jacobs challenged. "It's more mind games. He's testing us to see if we're as smart as he is. Do you remember the story about that girl who went missing from Mount Diablo in June?"

"I remember she had a flower's name, or a color, I think," Sid replied. "Scarlett? Violet?"

"Rose." Ressler snapped his fingers. "That's right. I remember now. Her face was on a missing persons poster in our lobby, guys. Twenty year-old, I think. Pretty girl. I passed by that fucking poster every day and thought nothing of it."

The gravity of the admission weighed heavy on them all, for they had each done the same.

For weeks.

"I'm afraid you're right," Jacobs confirmed. "Her name was Rosalie—*Rose*—Sherwood. I've already verified it."

Sid pulled a small leatherbound journal from his blazer's inside pocket and scribbled a notation as she spoke. "So you think whoever sent this had something to do with Rose's disappearance? If so, first thing I do tomorrow is speak to Morris Miller and see if he has any updates. For all we know, she's already been found and is home watching *The Carol Burnett Show* right now."

Ressler doubted it. Jacobs was certain of it.

"Robin Hood was from Nottingham," she explained. "England. He and his merry band of robbers were infamous for having a hideout in the wilds of Sherwood Forest."

"And...?"

"*Sherwood*, Doug." Siobhan leaned in, lowering her voice. "The name of the girl who went missing in June was Rosalie *Sherwood*."

You could hear a pin drop.

"God-*damn*-it." Doug Ressler slid the 8x10 of the puzzle his way and stared at the serpentine of letters. It was suddenly clear as day: **ROBIN HOOD**. "Christ, Siobhan. Do you agree with Sid? Has he got it right, that whoever sent this is claiming responsibility for abducting Rose Sherwood?"

"Yes."

Ressler again tilted back on his chair, wavering to the verge of imbalance as the thoughts raced through his mind. "Okay then, you know what I'm gonna ask you next…"

"You're going to ask me if there's any link in this puzzle to Veronica Roe and her daughter Lyndsey who went missing from Panhandle Park in July."

Without shifting the photo from Ressler's line of sight, Siobhan showed them two words on the left third of the puzzle. **PAN** went up at a reverse diagonal. Immediately above the **N** was another **P**. The word **PARK** ran backwards from there, ending with the **K** on the outer left edge of the grid. The word **HANDLE** was right of center near the bottom, running in reverse up the page.

"Coincidence?" Sid asked, though he already suspected not.

"Perhaps," Siobhan agreed, "if I hadn't also found this."

Five letters in from the bottom left was a **C** with a letter **A** above it. Then a **V**, **I**, **A** and **R** rising upward from there.

"Caviar?" Sid asked, confused.

Awareness dawned in Doug Ressler's eyes and the front legs of his chair slapped the floor with a clap as he hunched over the puzzle. "Fuck me."

"Alright, someone wanna let me in on the joke?" Sid threw up his hands in surrender. "What am I missing?"

"Caviar is fish eggs," Ressler explained. "The unfertilized eggs of sturgeon, to be precise."

"And…?"

"Fish eggs are also known as fish *roe*, Sid. Roe, as in Veronica and Lyndsey Roe."

"But we're still not done yet. I need you to look at this." The head of forensics ran her finger backwards near the top of the puzzle.

RENNIDYCUAS

Sid and Ressler both shrugged, and Jacobs presented them

with her notebook where she'd handwritten the letters backwards. They now spelled:

SAUCY DINNER

"Tell me where Hannah Wilson worked. That's the name of the young wife Sheriff Miller found in the trunk of her convertible, right? And wasn't she from Sausalito?"

"She was," Ressler confirmed. "Morris—the sheriff—he and I talk from time to time."

"They go way back," Sid elaborated, and Siobhan Jacobs seemed surprised.

"Even longer than he's known you?" She failed to hide her apparent amazement. "Hell, Doug. I didn't know you could hold a relationship for longer than a couple months. Now I've got two examples that prove me wrong. So I guess it was just me, then…"

She appeared crestfallen and had to clear her throat. Ressler did his best to ignore it, though a cloud like something close to regret had settled over his expression.

"Anyway, you two. As I was saying, Morris called me that night. Late. Was pretty shaken by it all and needed to vent. Which just isn't like him. So I let him, and he gave me the skinny on Hannah Wilson. And you're right: she worked for years at a local diner there. A Sausalito diner."

"Saucy dinner," Sid repeated beneath his breath. "God almighty." Ressler was on his feet.

"Mother*fucker*. Are you going to tell me that piece of shit Mike Driffield from Channel 5 was right all along? I swear, Siobhan, if you tell me the perp who Driffield was trying to name the Hurdy Gurdy Man is a multiple murderer…"

"A *serial* murderer is what I hear the FBI is starting to call them," she corrected. "They've just launched a new section of the Bureau called the Behavioral Science Unit. It'll explore the behavioral connections between unusual and bizarre murder cases. Or as you would call it, Ressler, they've formed a witches' coven."

"Warlocks," Sid corrected her. "The FBI is all men. Male witches are called warlocks."

Both Ressler and Jacobs smiled in wide-eyed surprise that Sid would even know such a thing. They shared a cheeky smile between them before Siobhan carried on.

"At my conference last month, word was going around that this new unit's going to start interviewing killers in prisons across the country who meet certain criteria to build a profile of what a serial killer looks like."

"Looks like?" Ressler asked.

"Behaviorally, not physically. They want to find commonalities that link them. And one of the biggest factors they're looking for is a childhood filled with extreme and unrelenting abuse."

They allowed this to sink in as they huddled around the puzzle and silently comparing it to Jacobs' notes. When Siobhan spoke again, it was a list of some of the other words she'd found, many that were innocuous everyday words or phrases without any obvious connection. Words like **LION** and **WOLF**. **FLOWER**, **HOUSE**, **WIFE**, **RING**, and **COOKIES**. The word **LIGHT** was there, as was **MULTIPLE** and **ALTER**.

(This one Sid questioned, wondering if it was a misspelling of the word 'altar,' as in a place of worship, but Jacobs wasn't sure.)

Then more ominous words like **MINE**, **HALLOWEEN**, **MONSTER** and **SLAVES**. There were numbers typed among the letters, also breaking from wordsearch convention. But in these Siobhan Jacobs could find no obvious meaning.

Until Sid and Ressler both lit up over the numbers **6**, **7** (twice), **8** and **10**, that is.

"What's the connection?" she asked but realized the answer as soon the words had passed her lips. "Six is June, Seven is July—and there's two of them—eight is August. And ten is October. Whoever sent this letter is telling us he took Rosalie Sherwood from Mount Diablo in June. In July he moved an hour west to San

Francsico and abducted Veronica Roe and her daughter Lyndsey Roe from the Panhandle in broad daylight. Hence the number seven appearing twice. In August, he took Hannah Wilson from her home in Sausalito—

"Which is Marin County," Sid interjected.

"Right. A third jurisdiction. He stuffed her body in the trunk of her convertible and dumped it at Mount Diablo in Contra Costa County. No wonder we haven't connected the dots before now: this guy's operating in multiple jurisdictions where each agency is concentrating on their own case and not catching the link with open cases outside their boundaries."

"Street smart," Sid accepted. "Very street smart." In a way, he was almost impressed.

"But the number ten," Ressler questioned. "October. He's threatening to kill by the thirteenth. Did you find any clues that can tell us who? Or where? What about all these other numbers?" He pointed to **31** and **1223** and **8213**. "Don't they look like addresses to you? Maybe house numbers?"

They all agreed that they did.

Their perp had given them the address of the woman he was planning on preying upon next. But with over a million homes in San Francisco, not to mention those in neighboring Marin and Costa Contra counties, the question wasn't *if* they were house numbers, but *on which street?*

With hundreds of possible combinations (you could add three zeros to the end of that figure if any of the numbers were transposed) the likelihood of them finding the right one was little better than random chance. Unless there were more clues in the puzzle to narrow it down.

Which is exactly what Siobhan Jacobs dedicated herself to do over the next three days.

If she didn't fine one, come Monday they were going to have the blood of another victim on their hands...

23

)(

AFTER TWO MONTHS, Cassie showed up at Brewster's Café just as Patty was saying goodbye to her last customer of the day. She was already turning the key in the lock when she spotted her prodigal friend.

Her first instinct was to continue locking the door anyway.

After a moment's hesitation, she swung it back open and held it as Cassie ducked under her arm and scurried in.

Patty finished locking up and turned off the OPEN sign. Without saying a word she faced Cassie with her arms crossed, a stained table rag reeking of sanitizer gripped in her left hand.

Cassie pivoted on her toes, a sprightly double-footed pirouette, and flashed Patty her best and brightest smile. As contagious as a sneeze in an elevator during flu season, Patty instinctively returned the smile despite not wanting to.

"So, I guess this is where I say something inane like 'long time, no see.'" Patty's delivery was deadpan. "Instead, I'll just say that you look...different. Happier, I think.... *Better*."

"This is the new old me!" Cassie spun again, her skirt twirling and rising like a fabric hula hoop. She swept her hands from her head to her waist, a gameshow assistant showing off the prize package. "Patty, meet Cassie Albrighton." To herself she said, "Cassie, meet your best friend, Patty."

She curtsied, genuflecting.

Patty scoffed and went back to clearing tables, her attention no longer reserved fully for her friend. "Did you ever decide about talking to the police again?"

The question was cordial, but direct and impersonal. Spoken in the manner of a polite but busy waitress asking if you've had time to look over the menu yet.

"Okay, so that's how you're going to play it?" Cassie rose from her playful bow and backed up to the counter, elbows firmly planted on its surface and her hands hanging over its edge. A James Dean vibe if ever there was one.

"Play what?"

"Like I'm just another one of your guests."

Patty twisted to the side, sweeping her hands through the air as if showcasing the café to a first-time visitor. "Mine. Yes? Which makes *you* the guest."

"Umm, I'm your friend, Patty. Your *best* friend."

"Best friends don't just disappear for weeks on end the way you do, Cass." She made herself busy wiping down the same high top table she'd already cleaned twice in the last thirty seconds. "You completely blanked me. Do you know how many times I called? Showed up on your doorstep and rang your buzzer? Hell, once I even stood beneath your balcony and sang-shouted for you to let down your hair, *a la* Rapunzel. 'That I may climb thy golden stair...'"

"That's awfully literary of you."

"Well, I'm more than a pretty face, you know."

"Yes, you very much are. And I'm sorry." Cassie revealed the hand she'd been casually concealing behind her back. In her palm was a small blue box tied with a magenta ribbon. She presented it to Patty and the act succeeded in breaking the café owner from her cycle of absentmindedly cleaning the same table over and over again.

Patty gave the gift a fleeting glance. But with Cassie she locked eyes. "I was worried, Cass." Her monotone had softened into her natural inflection. "Shit. I was more than worried."

Cassie said nothing by reply, only jiggling the gift in her extended arm. "It's from Bella and me. She misses her Aunt Patty...almost as much as I do."

Patty shook her head and casually plucked the present from Cassie's open palm. "Thank you."

"Bella Luna helped choose it. I wrapped it."

"Of course."

"Of course," Cassie echoed.

"It's very pretty. I almost don't want to open it." But she was already sliding her finger beneath the magenta ribbon as she raised the small box to her ear, lightly shaking it. "I can't begin to imagine what it is. Something from Tiffany's?" she chided.

"It doesn't make up for me going AWOL since August—"

"That's right, it doesn't," Patty was quick to agree. But a gentle smile unclenched her lips as she referred to the gift: "Still, you shouldn't have. Really. You need to watch your dollars. Now as much as ever, Cass. Unless you've discovered in these last two months that you're the sole heir to a recently deceased and very wealthy uncle you didn't know you had?"

"I found a dollar bill on the sidewalk the other week. Does that count?"

Patty couldn't maintain her stalwart diffidence after that, and laughed out loud, hard and real. She wrapped her arms around Cassie, the gift still cradled in her left hand. "God, I've missed you, Cass. And Bella, that precocious little girl. How is she?"

"She's been keeping herself busy. You know, she loves seeing all her friends at daycare. Which has given me time to reflect and learn about my gift, the visions, all of it. Then there have been long walks in the park. We've now explored all of Panhandle and on through most of Golden Gate Park as well."

Patty scrunched her lips together, eyebrows raising high. A Stan Laurel grin if ever there was one. "Must be nice. Some of us have been stuck in the same old routine here. Day after day."

"Yeah, yeah. Thriving business. Surrounded by friends and adoring customers all day. Sucks to be you. Open your damn gift already, will ya?"

Patty chuckled and tore the paper from the box, tossing it aside with the heedlessness of a child on Christmas morning. She raised the small, unadorned box to her ear and shook it one more time. Something like a spritz of water dashed the side of her face. "Uh oh. Is this fragile? Here I am shaking the hell out of it and—"

"It's not fragile," Cassie assured her. "Just open it."

Skeptical, Patty swiped her hand over her cheek. It came away with a fine red film across her palm. "What the hell?" She turned over her hands, inspecting them. Gave a scoffing chuckle. "I think I must've given myself a papercut or something. Look at this—"

"You haven't. Just open it."

Circumspect and quizzical, she opened the box with measured movements until the flaps released.

Along with the stench.

Patty gagged, the back of her hand shooting up to cover her nose. "Oh, Cass. What the hell is this?" Her question was muffled, uttered between coughing spasms.

Cassie grinned, a smile that did not reach her eyes. "*Look.*"

And Patty did.

Lying in a bed of pale blue tissue paper was a severed finger.

Cassie Kennedy's wedding ring finger, to be precise.

On it, her wedding band gleamed as if freshly polished, a shiny gold ring encircling a long, ivory finger stained red. It shifted in the box from side to side as Patty's hands began to quiver.

Still, she brought the box closer for a better look. Surely, she wasn't seeing what she thought she was seeing.

"Oh it's real alright," Cassie Albrighton assured her and displayed her left hand.

A cyclical jet of blood pulsated from the stub where Cassie's third finger had been. It arced high into the air and painted the high top table Patty had been repeatedly cleaning. Laughing maniacally, Cassie swung her arm round and round and the red spray pinwheeled through the air as its foul, ferrous stench coiled deep into a place within Patty where she would smell it forever.

She dropped the box and fell to her knees, screaming.

)(

She was still screaming when she woke.

Snatching her hands from beneath the duvet as though they had been trapped in an oven, she turned them over and over before her eyes.

No red film was smeared across her palm.

She wiped her cheek and looked again.

Clean.

Then once more.

Nothing.

Still only half-conscious, she expected to find the immaculately wrapped gift of her friend's finger neatly tucked away under the sheets alongside her.

She threw off the covers and they billowed to the floor.

No box.

Between heavy gasps she cursed her morbid imagination, forcing herself to sit upright. She pressed the small of her back against the headboard and its cool, reassuring firmness was both physically and emotionally grounding.

Christ help me, she muttered beneath her breath as she openly broke down and wept. Her hands blindly searched the bedside table for her pack of Virginia Slims as hot tears blurred her vision and stung her eyes.

)(

As the first rays of light crept through her bedroom window over the café's awning, Patty wriggled into a brown and yellow paisley dress and boots that stopped just below her knee.

The signature hustle and bustle of Haight-Ashbury's diverse marketplace had yet to commence, and Patty found its silence almost unnerving as she fast-walked to 122 Lyon Street.

She rang the buzzer to apartment #3. Then again. Once more, this time holding it obnoxiously long.

When no one answered, she stepped back and called up to the balcony, cupping her hands around her mouth like a megaphone.

"Cassie!"

The French door to the tiny balcony was slightly ajar. Not like Cassie at all. The Cassie she knew was terrified of a potential intruder. She'd never leave a door unlocked, let alone open. And especially not at night when Isabella could wander out there unsupervised.

She called out again.

A curtain from the second-floor unit rustled. A man by the name of Joe lived there. His first name was all she knew about him, but they'd exchanged hellos on the stairs enough times to recognize one another. Patty gave the covered window a cursory wave, a reflex of social covenant more than a greeting.

From inside the third floor walk-up: a weak, solitary cry.

...Isabella...

Patty formed her hand megaphone a final time and shouted as loud as she was able. The strain was like acid rising in her throat as the words burst from the depths of her lungs. "Cassie Kennedy! Open the front door!"

The bottom pane of the second-floor window shot up with a bang. From between the curtains Joe's face peered out, his eyes squinting in the morning light. "Come in already! Christ! We're trying to sleep here!"

He withdrew into the cool darkness and pulled the curtains tight as the front door buzzed, barely long enough for Patty to race up the three outside steps. She snagged the handle and pulled just as the sound stopped.

Thanks, Joe.

She took the stairs two at a time. Panting, she pounded on Cassie's door.

It was met by another whimper coming from inside.

"Cassie, it's Patty."

A deliberate pause.

"Cass, open the door…"

Another wail, this time louder.

"Cassie, open the goddamn door!"

She slammed both fists into it…and the door creaked open. Where the strike plate should be recessed in the jamb was only a cavity edged by fresh splinters. The latch of the lock was still extended.

There's no way I struck it that hard. She nudged it the rest of the way open. The strike plate was lying a good ten feet inside the room, bent and twisted. *Now I know I definitely didn't strike it that hard.*

"Hello…?" She crept in, holding her breath as she lingered just inside the doorway. "Cass?"

She waited for a response.

When none came, she called out for Isabella.

From somewhere near the kitchen came a tiny response.

"Bella? Are you here, babygirl?"

Again, she received a barely audible keening by way of reply.

She shouted for Cassie one more time and when her friend still did not answer, Patty let herself fully in.

If she wasn't already on high alert, the ammonia smell did the trick. Like a floundering boxer who has a vial of smelling salts snapped beneath his nostril's, she twisted her head away with a gasp. She covered her nose with the back of her hand as she navigated past a pool of dried and crystallizing urine.

Oh, God.

She bolted down the corridor toward the two bedrooms.

"Cassie? Bella?"

Both rooms were empty. In Cassie's, the bed was still neatly made, no one having slept in it.

"Hello...anyone?"

In the living room a bag of potato chips had been picked clean, the waxed paper bag itself shredded. Not a crumb remained.

Picking her way through small, congealed puddles of lime yellow bile, Patty eased her way into the kitchen. She pulled a knife from the wood block and brandished it before her. "If there's anybody here, I want you to know I have a knife!"

She caught the faint sound of a cry once more.

"Hello...? Bella...?"

The figure came at her faster than she could react.

With a shriek, Patty stabbed at the air but missed, striking a nearby cabinet instead. As the tip embedded in the painted wood, her hand slipped from the handle. She released it just before her palm had slid down the length of the razor-sharp blade.

The figure ran into her open arms—*Isabella!*—and Patty never been so relieved that she had the aim of a blind person.

She wrapped Bella into her embrace as her breaths raced and her body shuddered, and Isabella pressed so close that for a moment they appeared to be one.

"Oh my poor baby, what happened? Where's your mama?" But Isabella did not respond, only pressing her shape deeper into Patty's bosom. "You look like you're starving, babygirl! Oh Christ, what happened here?"

As Isabella burrowed into her, Patty scanned the room with fresh eyes. The signs of Bella's abandonment were everywhere. When whatever happened here went down, Bella must have peed herself in the living room. Alone and terrified, whatever potato chips had been left in that discarded bag appeared to be all Bella had eaten...for who knows how long. No other packages were lying around; no cupboard doors open, even though Isabella could easily reach the lower cabinets.

Gently loosening Bella's grip, Patty prised her from her bosom. Weak and scared, Bella shook like a leaf as Patty looked her over at arm's length. The little girl's lips had dried to flakes, and she was visibly thinner than she had already been.

"Bella, where's your mama, babe?"

She filled a wide-mouthed glass with water, which Bella all but inhaled. A moment later, she was spraying watery bile across the kitchen floor.

Stroking her back as Bella retched over and again, Patty twisted away to hide the tears.

God, help me. How fucking long has she been gone?

Once Bella's vomiting became a bout of dry heaves, Patty gave her another water—this time allowing her to take only the tiniest sip. When she was certain Bella was able to keep it down, she gave her another. This they did for several minutes until the glass that was full had been completely emptied.

Bundled into Patty's arms, Isabella wept. Her own eyes streamed with tears of fear and outrage as she carried the five-year-old across town to her modest flat above the café.

)(

Once Bella had soft food in her tummy and enough sips of water to soften her lips, Patty laid her down in her bed and closed the curtains. Her first instinct was to call the police—she already had the phone in her hands.

Then she remembered the last time Cassie had gone missing: how Patty had to wait on the street to call them off because Cassie had shown up out of the blue after three days.

This time, it would also be calling the police *on* her.

Not *for* her.

She dropped the receiver back in its cradle.

Oh, Cass...where are you, this time? I should never have let us be apart this long. Why did I not try harder?

Patty clamped one hand over her mouth.

Then the other.

Standing alone in the silence, she shrieked until the muffled wail faded into a muted cry laden with tears.

Then she picked up the phone...

24

)(

C ASSIE AWOKE IN a room she didn't know, sprawled across a dirt floor in the dead of night. Pressing heavy upon her, the weight of the stagnant air was oppressive as wet wool. Her head throbbed. Though enveloped by darkness, she knew her bare, sweat-soaked arms, legs and face were caked with dirt where she'd been lying in the filth.

How long she'd been here, she had no way of knowing.

Nor could she recall how she'd gotten here.

Or where 'here' even was.

None of this mattered when the odor struck. Thick and putrid, it attacked her waking senses with a fetid sweetness that not only clung to the inside of her nostrils but filled her mouth and coated her tongue with a taste like grease.

She recognized it immediately.

Bill had once treated them to a week in the mountains of Oregon to escape San Francisco's blistering summer heat. When they returned home, the house was in darkness. The few lights they'd left on were off. The ceiling fans were motionless. But worst of all, no hum came from the Frigidaire which Cassie had only recently stocked.

When she'd swung open its robin's-egg-blue door, no little light came on. Instead, she was met by the stomach-heaving fragrance of rancid meat, eggs, curdled milk and rotten fruit. In the semi-opaque compartment marked VEGETABLES, a wonderful new feature designed to keep her fresh produce crisp, she spied the silhouette of something large and wet. Then she remembered the full head of cabbage she'd bought the week prior to their vacation. Having every intention of trying out a new homemade coleslaw recipe, time had run away from her and she'd never gotten around to it.

After this, she never would.

Covering her nose and mouth with the crook of her elbow, Cassie yanked open the drawer. Actively decaying in a slurry of its own algae-brown juices, the cabbage skated forward. Displacing the liquid as it came to a sudden stop, putrid brown sludge sloshed the fridge's interior and front of Cassie's new ivory slacks. Wanting to curse but retching instead, she wrested the drawer from its slides and emptied it into the kitchen sink. The base of the cabbage had compressed with rot so that it was no longer round, but a gelatinous dome of furrows and convolutions that looked every bit like an embalmed human brain. Repulsed but unable to look away, Cassie watched as it drifted slowly toward the drain upon a film of slime.

Now that same vile image and those carious stenches were again roiling her gut. But this time they were accompanied by a smell that galvanized them until they were as palpable as the phlegm-like aftertaste of a bad oyster.

It was an odor she knew from—

that cramped and lightless coat closet in the basement of her aunt's Pennsylvania farmhouse

—a lifetime ago, and one she would never forget: the slick,

petroleum stench of mothballs.

Crouching on all-fours, Cassie threw up in the darkness.

) (

"It gets better." The disembodied voice came from somewhere in the darkness. It was faint. Weak. A very young woman's. Or maybe an older child's. "The smell, I mean."

Cassie heaved and coughed, a dry painful bark. Had she been a character in one of Bella's Saturday morning cartoons, it would have been accompanied by puffs like desert sand billowing from her mouth.

"Well, it sorta goes away," the voice said. "Or maybe I'm just used to it by now."

Cassie swiped the back of her hand across her chin. Panting to catch her breath, sinewy strands of mucous came away. "Who are you?" Her words were thin. Strained. Painful croaks from a throat lined with sandpaper. "*Where*—are you?"

"Try not to talk," the voice answered. "You're dehydrated. I've barely heard a sound from you since you showed up three days ago—"

Three days? It wasn't possible. She'd only just left Isabella. Hours ago, tops. So, that couldn't possibly be right.

"—and haven't had much water. Only what he managed to get into you while you were out. Just enough to keep you alive, I'm guessing."

In the dark and the silence, Cassie sat stunned.

Her head throbbed.

"And I'm Rose Sherwood. Rosie to my friends. Rosalie when I'm being formal. Not that it matters. You'll never be able to tell anyone I'm here. That I didn't run away. That I'm still alive…"

As Rose audibly swallowed, Cassie's second sight anticipated six more words yet to be spoken. No sooner had they formed in

Cassie's mind than Rosalie Sherwood did indeed speak them:

"…Because none of us ever leaves."

Cassie said nothing. Absorbing.

Trying to understand…*any of this.*

Somehow, she'd stepped out of her apartment and into one of those childhood puzzles made up of hundreds of numbered dots. If you have the patience to draw a line through them all, and in the correct order, they'll reveal a hidden picture.

Except a fog had settled over her brain, making it impossible to connect any of them. The result was a baffling melee of neurons firing at random to create a surreal and terrifying dream.

Until her mind chose to simply flick the OFF switch.

) (

"Are you still there?"

A pause.

"Hey, you."

Another interval, this one longer.

"Hey. Lady. C'mon. What's your name…?"

Now a sense of rising panic:

"Hey, tell me you're still alive over there!"

How many times had Cassie herself used some variation of that same decree when addressing Isabella, the five-year-old staring out the window, lost in a world of her own?

It was hyperbole, intended as humor.

But coming from Rosalie's detached voice in this dark, fetid place, it felt terrifyingly literal.

"I'm alive," Cassie barely whispered to herself. "I'm here."

Had she blanked again?

She cleared her throat, swollen and hot with pain. Forcing the words out loud enough to be heard made each a red hot ember. "*You said…your name…is…Rosalie Sherwood?*"

Rose brooded in silence before deigning to reply.

"Don't do that again, okay? You scared me. I don't wanna be alone in here anymore."

"*Yeah*—sure." The dryness in Cassie's throat still continued to fight her. "I Promise."

"Thank you."

"How...*old are you*...Rosalie?" The words were coming more easily now, the pain being relegated behind Cassie's desperation to understand what the hell was happening.

"I'm twenty-one now. At least I am if I've been keeping track of time right. It's finally legal for me to drink."

—*Costa Contra County Sheriff's department say that twenty-year-old Rosalie Sherwood, wife of Robert Sherwood, daughter of Miles and Leona Layton, went missing last week in*—

In her mind, Cassie heard the news report as vividly as the day she'd stumbled upon it, turning the radio's dial in search of the Beach Boys or the Beatles to match the mood of that early summer day in June.

It was October now.

"Wait, you're telling me that you're 'Rosalie-Sherwood-from-the-news' Rosalie-Sherwood?" Cassie's throat again fought her insistence to speak, and by the second 'Rosalie' her question had trailed off to little more than a husky wheeze. In much different circumstances it might have sounded sexy.

"Uh huh, I guess so." Rosie contemplated the idea that she had been all over the news. "Have they been looking for me?"

Cassie nodded in the dark, a sibilating *yessss* hissing from her protesting vocal cords. Her tongue felt thick and sluggish, her larynx as if it had been serrated by razor blades.

"Maybe you can just knock once for yes, twice for no," Rosie suggested. "You really shouldn't speak. You still need water."

Cassie knocked once.

"Okay, good. So, they were looking for me?"

Again, a single knock.

Rosalie exhaled with a relief that was audible. "Did they know I was at the park…over at Mount Diablo?"

One knock.

"And they're still looking for me, right?"

Uncertain how to respond, Cassie hesitated. She chose to knock three times.

"Wait. Was that three knocks?"

One knock.

"So not a yes, and not a no?"

One knock.

"Does that mean you don't know? If they're still looking for me, I mean."

Though she didn't want to, Cassie knocked once.

"Oh."

) (

You promised you wouldn't do that.

The voice floated dreamlike in Cassie's head: Bella's voice.

You said you wouldn't go away like that again, she mewled.

"Oh, baby," Cassie's own voice sounded distant to her own ears as if it could be someone else's. "I'm so sorry. Mommy's just very sleepy today."

Shunning a patch of morning light which had lit upon her face, Cassie twisted away, squeezing her eyes tight. She felt the pain rising in her head. "Bella, honey. Will you close the curtains, please? For Mommy?"

A faraway reply.

A foul odor.

Cassie sucked in her breath, trying not to cough.

"Bella? What's that smell, baby?" She opened her eyes to a room she didn't recognize. "Baby? What's that smell—"

Thick and humid, the air reeked of the unimaginable and Cassie covered her nose with both hands to keep from retching. Her fingers slid across cheeks that were slick with sweat.

"Don't ask," the voice answered, no longer distant or dreamlike. And no longer her daughter's. "I don't wanna tell you, and you don't wanna know."

Cassie bolted upright. Not from her couch, but from a dirt floor. The spear of light which had blazed hot over her face was gone, leaving her effectively blind until her eyes might adapt. She reeled backward, stumbling against a wall concealed by darkness. It felt rough and cool on her skin in contrast to the wet, dense air.

"Who *are* you! What's *happening* to me?"

"I told you." A muted moment. Then a response that no longer shielded the young woman's exasperation. "I'm Rosalie. Rosie. Remember? You must've passed out again—"

Rosie?

"—but maybe that's a good thing. Because he came back. I could hear him giving you water. From a sponge or wet cloth or something. At least, that's what I hope those sounds were."

Cassie gagged, dry-heaves that tore at her empty gut.

"You don't remember him being here?"

Cassie did not remember.

"Rose—? Where *am I*...?"

"You're two to my right, I think. There's one between us—the bad one. I'm in number three. Are you in number one?"

That was far from what she meant, but Cassie found herself squinting, sharpening her vision in an attempt to answer the question anyway. Inching on all-fours, her outstretched hand arced back and forth through the empty air, grasping nothing but darkness. She hadn't crawled more than two or three feet when her hand came upon something solid.

Something heavy.

Something immovable.

Blindly running her fingertips over the object's contours, it felt like some kind of timber gate or slatted wood door. The type you see in spaghetti westerns where the hero gets himself tossed into a makeshift jail in some rinky-dink little one-horse town. It's a cliffhanger that ends the show with a close-up shot of the guy grabbing those bars and peering out with a steely gaze as the camera tracks closer and closer. And that's where he'll stay…at least until next week's episode.

Except Cassie knew she was no hero. And if she couldn't figure out what was happening, there would be no episode next week.

A surge of panic jolted through her chest, a physical sensation that choked out her breath like drowning. Her heart was beating too fast; her skin cold and clammy despite the oppressive heat.

Cassie Kennedy screamed.

But no sound came out.

Help. Please! Though loud and clear in her mind, the cry was soundless. *I don't know where I am! I think there's some kind of door? But I can't see anything—*

"Well, you'll know soon enough," Rose muttered. Though it could have been a direct response to Cassie's inaudible appeal, Rose was in fact answering her own question which Cassie hadn't. "That light that came through the bars a moment ago? That's the sun coming up. Think it's hot in here now? Just you wait."

No sooner had Rosie said it than fleeting patches of amber slowly filtered through the bars. Shifting and coming together into a single shaft of light, swirling dust gave it the shimmering appearance of a material thing. It could have been one of those transporter beams that so delighted Bella when they watched the latest episode of *Star Trek* together on a Friday night. All it needed was a futuristic sound effect.

Mesmerized by the memory, Cassie Kennedy was no longer on all-fours over a pile of her own vomit. She was not suffering the acid smell of her own bile as it mingled with the fetid stench of rot coming in waves from somewhere beyond the door. She was not being schooled by a disembodied voice called Rosie. And with eyes slowly adapting to the changing light, she was not staring at a makeshift jailer's door.

Instead, Cassie was in her living room. Safe and sound. On the couch with five-year-old Isabella who howled with unbridled giddiness as those sparkling beams of light and magical sounds transported the show's characters to another place or time.

The delusion abandoned her as swiftly as it came when the dawning sun began to expose her new space in patches of shadow and light. No longer concealed, Cassie clearly saw four crude walls constructed from a haphazard mix of brick and cinderblock. They defined a room so small it was barely larger than she was. If she were to stretch, she was certain she could touch all four while standing in one place.

Not a room, Cassie corrected herself. *Not even a cell.*

With no toilet or sink, no bed or chair, this empty four-by-six dirt floor enclosure was nothing more than an animal's stall.

A slaughterhouse pen.

"See? I told you."

There was a sudden weight to Rose's voice. A sense of knowing while wishing more than anything that she didn't.

Cassie forced herself to her feet and took two small, hitching steps forward on legs that threatened to buckle. Tingling with pins and needles and lacking even the most basic coordination, she immediately collapsed against the door with an outcry of pain. The heavy timber bulwark shuddered in its frame and together with her shriek, the sounds merged to echo like a gunshot through a vast chamber Cassie could not see.

"God*damn*it! What is this fucking place!"

...place...

...ace...

...ce...

Her words boomeranged back in chilling echoes.

"*Hey!*" Rose whisper-shouted. "*You have to keep quiet.*"

Cassie did not heed her warning. Gripping the door's thick vertical bars, she shook them and screamed.

Again her cry returned to her, a diminishing wraith-like wail.

With all her weight leaning into it, Cassie gave the door a shove. It drove outward.

But only an inch before catching on a hasp latch with a metallic *clang*. Rebounding back into its frame, the door issued a report like a small explosion.

"Stop it!" Rosie openly shouted this time. "You gotta *cut that shit out!*"

...ut...

...t...

"If he hears you, he'll *get mad.* At *both of us!*"

...us...

...s...

Cassie didn't care. She'd be damned if she were gonna just sit here and wait for this guy—*whoever the fuck he was*—to come back and do whatever sadistic shit he planned, just because some good little obedient victim like Rosie Sherwood said so.

She pounded on the door once more and crumpled to the floor as the merging echoes faded to the sound of silence.

) (

"Tell me," Cassie said as she hid in a corner where the sun's direct heat couldn't reach.

It was a while before Rosie's voice replied to her through the walls. When it did, there was a sense of despair to it that hadn't been there before. "Tell you what?"

"What happened to the woman. The one whose smell I know that is. I know he did something awful here..."

25

)(

MAYBE NOTHING'S GOING TO happen tonight after all," Sid Younger posed aloud as he shared a drink with Siobhan Jacobs at the Cop Shop. "Maybe that puzzle was just a sick hoax. A desperate play for attention."

Jacobs believed otherwise.

A desperate plea?

Yes.

A hoax?

She genuinely doubted it.

"Why isn't Ressler waiting with us?" The psychiatric head of forensics was unconsciously circling her fingertip around the lip of her wine glass. "Does *he* think it's just a hoax?"

"No. He trusts your insight. Implicitly. He always has."

Jacobs nodded with an accompanying *Mmmmm.*

Sid finished his glass, wanting another but knowing it was a bad idea, on the off-chance that the did get a call yet tonight. "He still thinks very highly of you, Siobhan. Perhaps—" He cut himself short and simply offered her a pensive smile.

"Perhaps too much?" Jacobs pressed. "Do you feel he thinks too highly of me, Sid?"

"I think you deserve the highest possible respect from *everyone*, certainly more than you get around here."

"Well thank you, Sid. That's very kind. But what about Doug?"

"I think Doug still loves you. As much as he ever did. Maybe more, now that he knows he blew it."

Siobhan Jacobs allowed this to process before responding. She mentally changed her reply three times before reverting to the first, her initial instinct. "And yet he never could say it."

Sid shrugged, grinning. "C'mon. You know Doug. He's barely told me that he even likes me. And it's been seven years." He chuckled to himself, his thoughts drawing inward. "Did I ever tell you about my first days as a detective? And how Ressler got two weeks' desk duty?"

Siobhan smiled, also drawn to the memory.

"So, I know he cares. I've always known it. How could I not, after what he did?"

"But you didn't need a hero to come swooping in, Sid. You're a smart and capable man. You could've taken care of it yourself."

"Yes, I could've. But I was in the hospital with a broken jaw wired up. Could I have taken care of it when I got out? You know it. Maybe not the way Ressler did, but in my own way."

"See? So you didn't need a hero."

"No, I didn't. But I did need a friend. Which is what he gave me. And that's better than a hero in my book. Any day."

"Mmmmm."

Jacobs finished her wine as her memories of the months she and Ressler had spent together ran through her mind like a movie on 10x speed. "'Just don't fall in love with me,' he said. What's that even supposed to mean? I felt like I was being used."

"Of course you did. I would, too. But you're the head shrink here, Doc. Do you really think he was talking to you? Or was he maybe trying to convince himself...?"

) (

8:43 PM

"There's–been–a–murrr–der..."

The call came in to the police switchboard operator just as the residents of West Summerdale Street, along with much of America, were watching musical guests Sonny and Cher walk onstage to enthusiastic applause on *Rowan & Martin's Laugh-in*.

Glued to their TV sets, none of them noticed anything out of the ordinary happening on their street. Not even Gladys Noble of 8220, whose modest mid-century home was diagonally opposite 8213. As Sheila's killer fastidiously arranged the hair, makeup, arms and legs of the recently separated wife and mother, much as a child might arrange their prized doll, the dazzling flashes of his Polaroid camera were mistaken by Gladys as reflections of approaching lightning.

It wasn't until a flurry of strobing red lights started dancing across curtained windows all up and down the street that the residents of West Summerdale finally sat up and took notice. Sporting long dressing gowns or tattered tank tops and boxers, Sheila's neighbors wandered out onto their porches and stoops, dumbstruck. Others peered through curtains tossed wide, craning their necks behind rain-speckled picture windows to catch a glimpse of the hubbub.

Desperate for a closer look, a diehard dozen or so braved the thunderstorm to crowd a police perimeter cordoning off number 8213. With hats pulled low and collars yanked high, these spectators thrust their hands deep into trouser pockets and scrunched their shoulders up to their ears as they made themselves small against the driving rain. Each seemed patently unaware of anyone else around him. But together they watched in mesmerized silence as a San Francisco Coroner's gurney was wheeled through the front door. Folded neatly atop it was a heavy black zipper bag.

There was only one bystander in this group who'd never had occasion to taste Sheila McCabe's lemon drop cookies. Slight of build and unassuming in every way, Solomon Albrighton was Everyman, just home from his eight-hour shift. Had you noticed him, you'd be forgiven for thinking his rain-soaked grey mechanic's coveralls were the color of his black boots. In the sheeting rain, you might also have mistaken the runnels of diluted red leaching out of those coveralls. Or the rust-colored whorls from the thick, compacted clots still in the treads of his wing-walkers. Both of which drifted away from the man in a lazy current toward a storm drain that struggled to keep up with the downpour.

(Surely these were nothing but the dirt of a hard day's manual labor washing away in the rain.)

You probably wouldn't have thought twice about the five-gallon workman's bucket suspended from his left hand. And you most certainly would not have expected that in it, casually covered by a hand towel which appeared to be soaked with some kind of fresh oil the color of oxblood—

probably brake fluid or engine oil

—was Sheila McCabe's head.

It wouldn't have mattered, one way or the other. With all attention rapt upon the exposed living room window of 8213, not a single resident of West Summerdale Street had even noticed the man who was not one of their own, let alone their neighbor's blood swirling down the curbside gulley.

Even Gladys Noble was oblivious, caught up in the spectacle of busyness and light while comforting a jittery Mr. Whiskers.

So it transpired that nearly every family who had enjoyed

Sheila's famous lemon drop cookies (most of whom had kept her Tupperware for themselves, despite Sheila's courteous presage for its return) gawked in communal awe. Though none would ever admit to it being true, what they eagerly awaited—as much as they dreaded the idea of it—was the moment the coroner would zipper what remained of Sheila McCabe into a bag, to be carted away in the back of a dull grey government-issued station wagon.

) (

Despite the lingering chill from the storm, the air inside the home was thick and heavy. Already on the scene, directing uniformed officers while assisting the forensics team in the collection of samples, was Detective Sid Younger.

Standing at the threshold was Detective Douglas Ressler.

As he'd found himself needing to do more and more these days, Ressler gave himself one last moment in the life he currently had before it was adulterated yet further by the horrors he knew were waiting inside: just one more set of stains to the fabric of his life that would never wash away.

For years, he'd denied this exposure had any effect on him whatsoever. By the time its impact was unmistakable, his callous and obdurate demeanor had already become his identity: something he couldn't change if he tried. The person Douglas Ressler had slowly morphed into was now so far gone that it was too late to admit it had all been a fragile façade. So he confided not in friends but in Jim and Jack—and any other bottle that would listen. He came to work in a permanent haze (which few had noticed for it occurring so slowly) and went home alone to repeat the cycle all over.

Ressler's path to self-destruction had to veer in a different direction after Sid Younger had become his partner. It wasn't something he considered, but something that simply had to be done. Nothing makes you more responsible for your own life than being responsible for someone else's.

That isn't to say Ressler felt any less jaded. If anything, the vileness of human depravity seemed to be getting only deeper and darker by the day. Neither can it be said that Douglas Ressler never touched a drop of alcohol again. Nothing was further from the truth. But he found himself coming to work that little bit sharper; caring that little bit more. And although he would never share his feelings outright, Ressler had found in Sid at least an empathetic sounding board that somehow deflected some of life's detritus. Just a little less of it now stuck.

And that was enough for Ressler.

"Hey, Sid." He snuffed his cigarette and tossed it into the mist and drizzle. "What we got—?"

"It's a bad one," Sid Younger hollered from the corridor as Ressler appeared in the doorway. There was little emotion in Younger's delivery, certainly less than was expressed in the groan he uttered as he forced himself up from one knee. A small sound like a bad billiards break accompanied it. "Damn weather. Does a number on my joints anymore. And these ribs. Can you believe? All these years later."

Doug Ressler squeezed his fist into a tight ball. The knuckle of each finger cracked in succession.

"It's the hands for me. And yes, the rain. Take anything for that today?"

"Aspirin's about it. Have a bottle in my kitchen cabinet. I down a pair the moment I see those clouds roll in. You?" Sid already knew his partner's pain reliever of choice, but figured he'd ask anyway. It was met with an eye roll. "Uh huh. Thought so, Doug. That why you're late?"

"Late? How exactly am I late? I should be getting ridden by some sweet little blonde with daddy issues right now. Not by *you*.

And especially not for showing up ten minutes later than you'd like at yet another goddamn house of fucking horrors."

Stepping into the hallway, Siobhan Jacobs had the misfortune of also stepping into the middle of their conversation. A humorless expression dulled her crisp green eyes.

"Ya know, Doug. You really can be a right—" (pronounced as *roight*) "—arsehole."

"Well, I don't know what an *arrrrse*-hole is. Sounds a bit piratey to me. You know, shiver me timbers and all that. But I've been called an *ass*-hole plenty, if that's what you mean…" For a split second, Ressler considered stopping there. But his mouth chose to just keep on going. "…My little Irish wench."

Siobhan whipped him the finger.

"Alright you two. Jesus Lord, I swear. It's like dealing with a couple children." Sidney Younger handed a sealed bag containing strands of long ginger hair to one of the uniforms. "Speaking of which, did you see that girl out front when you came in, Ressler?"

In the arms of Officer Julie Chen a young girl rocked back and forth, staring at a distant point, unblinking, far beyond the flurry of activity taking place around her. Officer Chen was strolling in small, repeating circles. Though the rain had stopped, the ground was sodden and the grass had worn down to a ring of mud.

Ressler wondered if Chen were aware she was doing this. Siobhan Jacobs chose not to look at all, having little confidence she could stave off the feelings this time.

"That's why we're here," said Sid. "So, whaddya two say we go ahead and just put this little lovers' spat, or whatever the hell this is, aside and get to doing what we came here to do."

)(

"There *is* no body," Sid shouted at Ressler, interrupting his partner's tirade against Siobhan Jacobs for allowing the victim's remains to be moved before he could observe them.

Jacobs refused to respond. Shaking her head as she walked away, she held her hands high in mock surrender.

"Doug, man. You gotta chill, brother. She's on our side."

Ressler told Sid he could give a steaming shit. "She missed the clue, brother. It was right there in that fucking wordsearch puzzle the whole time. 8213 W. Summerdale. If she'd caught it, this woman would still be alive."

"We all missed it, Doug. Christ. You're gonna blame Siobhan for that? I didn't see you offering to take that puzzle home and scour it all damn weekend."

Ressler's jaw clenched, his frustration apparent. But now wasn't the time. Or the place. "So, what the fuck do you mean there's no body?"

Sidney Younger ushered him into the living room of Sheila McCabe. "Go ahead, smart guy. Have a look. Then you tell me."

Even from the hallway the metallic scent of the mother's blood was unmistakable. It was everywhere. Absorbing into the carpet were puddles of it deep enough to still be tacky. Sprays of it speckled two walls. But most disturbing were the two overlapping patches on the popcorn ceiling which had dripped in places until the blood had congealed into a half-dozen reddish-black stalactites. It was more than enough to leave a lingering smell in your nose, a bitter tang like a penny upon your tongue.

Ressler didn't flinch.

"Okay, I'll play along. Where is she, then?"

"She...?" Sid noted, a little impressed. "Wow. I think that's the first time in seven years I haven't heard you call a victim '*it*.'"

Through the curtainless window, Julie Chen continued to wear away the grass with Sheila McCabe's daughter in her arms. Ressler's throat tightened. He swallowed hard, forcing down the emotion. The effort was small but noticeable—a quick bob of his Adam's apple. He hid it by pretending to clear his throat. "Okay, *it.*

Where is *it* then?"

"*She* wasn't here when uniforms arrived."

From the volume of blood it was evident Sheila McCabe hadn't just gotten up and walked away from her injuries.

Ressler studied the corridor.

There were no obvious blood smears on the floor.

Unconsciously biting his bottom lip, he began humming the same five notes he always did when deep in thought.

"—Hmmm. So, he carried her out?"

He looked closer, scanning the hallway to the front door. Then the opposite direction, toward the kitchen. From where he stood, Ressler could clearly see the door leading to the back yard.

There were also no drip marks. In fact, no visible sign of blood in the corridor at all. In either direction.

"She was already dead," he murmured to himself, still absently humming. "So, she had to have been drained of most of her blood when he took her out of here."

Ressler studied the living room once more.

"That's not just a lot of blood. That's *all* her blood, isn't it?"

Siobhan Jacobs hadn't heard Ressler's process of deduction, but she knew him well enough to realize what he'd just figured out. From the far end of the living room she caught his eyes and her own softened before she cast them down.

"He took off her fucking head, didn't he? The sick piece of shit decapitated this woman. In her own living room. Drained her blood right here on the carpet while her daughter slept in the next room."

"Possibly." Siobhan rejoined Ressler in the hall. She had been wearing a pair of disposable latex gloves and was now removing them to be placed in a separate evidence bag of their own. "Based upon the spray on the ceiling, its pattern, and its horizontal position relative to the hair strands we found in the carpet from the victim's scalp. I can't say that he fully beheaded this poor woman, but he certainly cut both carotid arteries. He did so with a single incision in one very fast, powerful stroke."

"You can tell all that, just from the blood?"

Siobhan nodded.

"Even though it's all over the damn place?"

"Yes, Ressler." There was no pride in the affirmation. "As I've said, I can't be sure he actually removed her head in full but—"

"—I can." Sidney Younger approached them with something that looked like a greetings card. He was holding it at arm's length and desperate to pass it off. Still, he waited until Ressler donned gloves of his own before he did so.

With a dry heave Sid made his way out the door. If he were lucky, the fresh air and remnants of rain might wash away what he'd seen.

26

FROM TWO CELLS to her left, Rosalie Sherwood's muted sobs were the only reply Cassie received.

"Rosie?" she asked again, this time limping to the door so she could speak through the makeshift bars with a voice that was dangerously close to giving out. With legs that were weak and hands that were bruised and sore, it took everything she had to tug herself upright.

As she peered through the wood slat bars, a dazzling ribbon of sunlight cut across her face. Its heat was instant and sweltering upon her cheek; its light temporarily blinding. She blinked hard and jerked to one side, already on the verge of heat stroke and dehydration. Only a little while longer and it would be sunset and the cells would again begin to cool.

"Rose, hun?" Her voice was barely audible now, a frail facsimile that was foreign even to her own ears. "I-I'm gonna... make sure we get out of here."

A painful swallow. A breath of stale and putrid air.

"But I'm gonna need you to help me make that happen, okay?"

Rosie's soft whimper lessened to a quiet, broken lament. She sniffled, inhaled, swiped her forearm across her nose. Then came the sounds of the girl shuffling to the front of her enclosure.

"I-I-I'm here."

"I know you're scared. And I am *so* proud of you, Rose. I can't imagine being in here all by myself for months."

Between stuttering breaths, Rosie mumbled something that sounded to Cassie like a combination of 'yeah' and 'mmhmm.'

"You're so brave. I just need you to stay brave for me a little while longer. Okay?" Cassie heard no discernible response. "I know it's hard, hun. But to get us out of here I need to know what I'm dealing with. So, I want you to just focus on my voice and try to answer my questions without emotion."

After a slight pause Rosalie agreed.

Cassie rubbed her throat. Inside it were a dozen razors, each slicing her larynx with every word. "R-Rosie? I need…you…to tell me…what he—" She had to pause, the pain on the brink of unbearable. She was beginning to feel lightheaded, the cell slowly moving. "W-What he does in h-here."

) (

"I don't know how many others there have been," Rose told her as both women clung to the bars in their doors. Cassie's face was pressed to hers, craning to see if she could lay eyes on her fellow captive. But all she saw were four more cells opposite, each the same constricted, hemmed-in space no larger than an animal pen. These were separated from what she presumed were four more on her side of a tight corridor barely wide enough for a person to fit. Like her cell, the floor of this tiny hallway was rough stone layered with dirt. Along its center was a swath where the dirt had been swept aside: a trail from something sizeable being dragged along the floor.

Something human-sized.

Along the wall opposite, she saw a series of ragged, horizontal lines scored into the paint of the brick and cinderblock. Running parallel to the floor, dozens of them overlapped one another. Some were deep. Some shallow. All were at the height where the fingernails of a person being dragged would have etched their last resistance.

Cassie squeezed her eyes shut, trying her best to evade the mortifying thoughts of so many screaming, terrified and injured women. Each was someone's daughter, very likely someone's wife. Possibly someone's mother.

She swallowed back her own tears and the razorblades that had once been her vocal cords tore at the inside of her throat until her words were little more than a wheezing series of syllables. "How many since you've been here?"

"There was a woman and her daughter. The girl was so scared. They killed her mother, right in front of her."

"*They?*"

"There's a lady who sometimes comes when the guy isn't here."

"What was the little girl's name? Did she tell you?"

Rose had to choke back her tears before she could answer. "Her name was L-Lyndsey. I don't k-k-know what her mother's name was…"

But Cassie did.

Veronica. Veronica Roe.

"What can you tell me about the other lady—

Janice Wynn

—the one who sometimes comes instead of him?"

"I only saw her face once. When she put little Lyndsey in my cell. But I'll never forget it, because she kind of looks like him."

"Then what happened?"

"She left and came back about an hour later with Lyndsey's mom." Rosalie hesitated as the moment played out in her mind.

"Then I heard *him*. And—oh God—the mother was screaming. She was just screaming. So loud! It was awful, Cassie. I just wanted her to stop... God help me, *I just wanted her to stop!*" In the corner of her cell, Rosie tucked herself into a tight ball. "And then she did."

Like that day, the silence was instant and deafening.

"Tell me what they did, Rose. Please. It could help me figure a way out of this."

The next minute passed as slowly as an hour with Rosalie Sherwood not replying. Somewhere in the distance, a muffled sound like a faint and faraway horn.

"I think they cut her throat. She was begging them not to hurt little Lyndsey when her words suddenly cut off mid-sentence. For a moment, there was no sound at all. Then I heard a kind of gurgling, and scuffling sounds. And I could tell she was flailing around in her cell. And then came the sound of her blood hitting the walls, God help me, I could hear it—"

Cassie covered her mouth and turned from the bars, her hands and legs trembling as she fought to stay on her feet.

"I'm so sorry, Rose." It would be so easy to just crumble right now; to drop to the floor and wait for dehydration to take her from this hell. If only she didn't have Isabella, she might have done exactly that. "What happened to Lyndsey?"

"He took her that night. I haven't seen her since. I don't know what happened to her. Maybe she got away...?"

The stench of putrefaction and rot emanating from the empty cell between them told Cassie that she probably didn't.

"What about any others? Where there more?"

"Another woman, maybe a month after that. She was still alive when he brought her here. I watched him drag her between the cells and drop her in the one between you and me."

"Are you sure she was still alive?"

Rose nodded though no one would see it. "She was breathing like she was drowning. Its sound was all wet and choked off. A couple times she cried out like she was trying to tell me her name, but I couldn't make it out. Han or Han-something?"

"Hannah?"

"I think so. Is there a Hannah that's gone missing, too?"

It had to be Hannah, Cassie thought.

"Yes. A young woman by the name of Hannah Wilson."

Rosie reflected upon this, putting a name to the horror her memory had visibly built around the sounds she'd witnessed. "She—Hannah—kept trying to tell me something that sounded like, 'Hold on.' Over and over, she kept saying it. 'Hold on, hold on, hold on.' Until she just couldn't speak anymore."

The nightmare vision of Hanah being overpowered in her own home replayed in Cassie's mind. Wincing, she watched as the man overpowered the young wife, beat and stabbed her, then dragged her away in a shower curtain, unconscious and bleeding.

It was beyond comprehension that she had somehow still been alive when he brought her here. And the thought that she spent her last breaths coaxing Rose to hold on while she herself was riddled with knife wounds and dying like an animal in the dirt, just shows what an amazing person Meredith Harper's daughter truly was.

More than a loss to the mother, Hannah's murder would leave another void in a world that was already too barren. No wonder Meredith was so impassioned to garner Cassie's help. After all, wouldn't Cassie do the very same if it were Bella Luna who had gone missing?

It was too much to bear, and Cassie slumped to the floor and sobbed until the welcoming void of unconsciousness took her.

) (

As night fell and their bank of eight cells descended into darkness, the clanging sound of a metal gate ricocheted through the vast antechamber beyond.

Rosalie Sherwood started from an uneasy sleep.

"*Cassie?*" she whispered. "*If you're awake, please, just stay quiet.*"

If Cassie had roused from passing out, she made no sound to indicate it. She was either still out cold, or finally trusting Rosie's advice. Either way was good. Silence and doing as she was told is what Rosie put down to the fact that she was still alive.

Now came the footsteps.

His footsteps.

And a familiar *skffffffd* sound that came in cycles between each labored step, a sound that Rosie had heard before.

The telltale indicator of a body being dragged behind him.

With a thump, Solomon dropped the woman's legs. From her cell, Rosie listened for a grunt as the woman's shins clapped the stone floor with a sharp sound like a ballpeen hammer tapping ceramic.

Nothing.

Now came the metallic rattle as the man unlocked the padlock and flipped the hasp from the staple loop. With a grinding creak the door to the cell between Rosie and Cassie swung outward, followed by the *skffffffd* sound of the body being dragged inside.

Knowing he was pulling it behind him and would be in the cell first, Rosie leapt silently to her feet to peer through the bars of her door.

The woman's decapitated head was resting on her chest, the face white as ash and stained with mascara runs. Her eyes, though open, were vacant and glazed over.

As the man turned her body to maneuver around the partially-open door, the woman's head rolled from her body. Her mouth sagged open. Slinking over the bottom lip like a pale pink sea slug, her tongue lolled out and dragged through the dirt.

Her neck had been sliced with almost surgical precision, her throat cleaved open from one ear to the other. Gaping flaps of skin revealed muscle and tendons and a cylindrical column that could only be her vertebrae.

Rosie covered her mouth to keep herself from gagging, averting her eyes. Instead of a swath of red, Rosie saw only more of the stone floor where the woman's corpse had swept away another layer of dirt down the narrow corridor's centerline.

Also detached from her body and resting upon her breast as if this were perfectly normal, was the woman's left hand. When her body passed through a bright blade of sunlight swirling with dust, her wedding ring glimmered like a star.

Outstretched behind her was her right arm, and when the man pulled her through the doorway, her elbow kinked at a funny angle and caught on the jamb.

Rose could tell he was tugging on her legs, as her body lurched once, twice…a third time. The fourth was a sharp and violent tug accompanied by the man's strained groan. It was followed by a pop as the woman's radius bone snapped, the ulna dislocated, and her arm twisted into a morbid, impossible angle.

Dragged into the adjacent pen, the woman disappeared from sight as Rosalie, in hers, began to dry heave.

All other sound stopped, and Rosie stifled her retching by biting down on the meat of her hand.

Had he heard her? Was he listening?

Seconds passed like hours as she held her breath, fearing the sound of those footsteps. Rising into her esophagus with the taste of a car battery, Rosalie swallowed her bile back down as the acid burned and her stomach churned until the sound of the man's movements resumed only in the adjacent cell.

First came a rummaging noise. Then a clattering of metal and the soft thumps of wood upon leather.

He was pulling tools from his bag.

Rosie had seen it just once before. Although it was probably a workman's tool bag, there was something ominous and creepy about it that reminded her of an old medical bag: the type you see in black-and-white period dramas where an old grey-whiskered doctor makes a house call with his bag of potions and tinctures and sharp, morbid tools.

Either that, or the type of bag Jack the Ripper carried.

Perhaps they were one in the same.

Now came the grating to-and-fro rasps of a sawblade.

Methodically, and with great attention to detail, the man began to saw through the woman's ribcage until the final pull of the blade fully separated the cartilage from bone. With a violent tug of both hands he spread open Sheila McCabe's chest, a sound like the staccato crack of a snare drum echoing through the cells and dark chamber beyond.

Holding her breath and trying not to throw up, Rose's world began to waver and blur at the edges as she listened to the man in the adjacent cell neatly arranging Sheila's severed limbs inside her chest cavity.

By God's grace, Rose passed out before there was nothing left but a bulging torso beside a detached head. Neither she nor Cassie had to endure the sounds which came next as the man humiliated the lifeless head of Sheila McCabe: mother, former wife, and considerate neighbor.

For the third time that night, the man climaxed.

27

)(

THE PIECE OF card stock Sid discovered in Sheila McCabe's living room had been folded and decorated by hand to resemble a Halloween card. The front was dyed black by watercolor paint. A paper skeleton and orange pumpkin cutout were glued to it. Far from scary, the skeleton was whimsical and appeared to be wearing the pumpkin to cover its private parts.

At the top right, handwritten in white ink or paint was:

FROM YOUR SECRET PAL

In the hand of the skeleton, **E3:1** had been handwritten in red pen. At the bottom left of the card, in the same white paint as the message at the top, was the beginning of a handwritten rhyme:

I FEEL IT IN MY BONES,
YOU ACHE TO KNOW HER NAME,
AND SO DIRECT FROM ME...

Carefully, Doug Ressler opened the card as Siobhan Jacobs watched attentively over his shoulder.

A Polaroid photograph slid from the crease and wafted to the floor. Landing upside down, only a black square and two white borders were visible. Siobhan bent over to pick it up but stopped when she remembered that she'd already removed her gloves.

"I'll get it." Careful not to bend the card in his hand, Ressler plucked the photo from the carpet. "Ready to see what this sicko wants to show us? Given Sid's reaction, it can't be pretty."

He flipped it over.

Staring at them from eyes forever frozen in horror was the decapitated head of Sheila McCabe. Beneath it was the pool of blood Ressler could still see from where he was standing in the corridor. Only in the photo, the blood was bright red. In the living room it was dark. Thick. An almost rust-like sludge.

"He took this photo within seconds of severing her head," Jacobs revealed. "Look. See the way that blood is so bright? In our bodies, blood is constantly circulated so it can be cleaned and oxygenated. It has an iron rating of Fe^{2+} and carries oxygen well. Once outside the body, the hemoglobin begins to break down and convert to methemoglobin with a rating of Fe^{3+} or thereabouts. It's why old bloodstains look so dark and have a smell like metal."

Ressler understood up to the point when she started rambling on about Fe2-something-or-other.

"But that's not the worst of it," Jacobs proceeded to share. "See the fear in her eyes? Not only is Sheila McCabe still alive in this photo, but it's also very possible that she's still conscious and aware."

Impossible, Ressler determined. The woman's head had been completely detached. Jacobs was full of shit. And he was happy to let her know it.

"Not at all," she refuted "Brain ischemia, or brain death, occurs when the cells don't receive enough oxygen. But it doesn't occur instantaneously. It takes at least three minutes for brain cells to begin to die."

"You can't be serious." Ressler's revulsion was apparent, from his tone of voice to his body language which had immediately become closed and tight—

protective

—his unconscious mind making himself small against an invisible threat. "You're actually telling me right now that people who are decapitated can remain alive for minutes?"

"Alive, yes. Conscious, no. Not for that long, anyway."

"But they're still aware. So they know what's happening…"

"Nobody can have one-hundred percent certainty on the matter, Ressler. But it's my scientific belief that they are, yes."

"Jesus Christ on the cross." The detective was actually beginning to pale. Over the years, Jacobs had witnessed the man in just about every awful situation conceivable. But this was a first.

"You okay, Doug?"

"Fuck you. How long?"

"How long what?"

"How long are people still able to think and feel? After…"

"Not long, babe. They—" It took a beat for her own thought processes to catch up with the term of endearment. When they did, Siobhan reflexively stiffened. All the time they had spent together was still proving a hard habit for her to break. "I'm so sorry. I didn't mean to call you that."

Ressler waved it off. "How long?"

Jacobs gave herself a second before answering, staring intently at her feet. Her hands fumbled with one another. Quick to gather herself, she raised her head and flashed a businesslike smile that felt forced as much as it did awkward.

"Higher cognitive functions like thought and emotion are likely still being processed for approximately four or five seconds after a full, clean decapitation."

"Clean." Doug Ressler couldn't imagine a word more unsuited to what he was seeing in this horror photograph.

"Medically clean, is what I mean." Jacobs took a breath to clear away the cobwebs of emotion and return to the logical, objective medical professional she was trained to be. "Precise. *Fast*. Which, in its way, is merciful, Doug. If it were you, would you rather he hack away at your neck? Or would you prefer a clean cut with a single, very fast, very powerful stroke?"

Ressler grunted.

"So, as much as it comes across like some sick scene in a horror movie, the truth is, Doug, that it's very likely Sheila McCabe was alive when he took this picture." Siobhan allowed a beat for this to sink in before she continued. It was important, for his own well-being as well as that of the investigation's, that he grasp the rest of what she had to say. "I can only hope that she was drugged." And of course, we'd run tests for that...if we had a body."

) (

After this, even Ressler needed a moment before he was prepared to examine the rest of the card. "God knows what other sadistic torments this sick fuck has in mind," he told Jacobs before marching out of the horror house to join Sid on the front lawn.

He lit another Marlboro, sucked the smoke into his lungs and waited for that moment when he could feel it cleanse away his angst. Using his thumb to slide another from the soft pack, he offered it to his partner with a shit-eating grin.

"Jacobs is right, you know," Sid revealed as he folded a stick of gum in half before popping it in his mouth. After quitting smoking some months earlier, he'd taken to chomping packs and packs of the stuff as a substitute: Doctor's orders.

Though, for the life of him, Sid couldn't figure the slightest correlation with his other health issues. Hell, it was only a few years ago that the radio and magazine ads were spouting off about how good smoking was for you. Now, the doctors seemed to be on the fence about cigarettes. Many were starting to cover their asses by preaching moderation, or unofficially prescribing cigars or pipes as a healthier alternative...as they sat in their mahogany-clad offices and lit up cigarettes of their own between patient visits.

In the most stressful of times, Sid would be seen meticulously smoothing the silver waxed paper the gum had been wrapped in. Pressed between thumb and fingers, he'd rub it warm and iron it until it was smooth and polished like a tiny rectangular mirror.

He was doing this when Ressler offered him the Marlboro.

"You really are an *arse*hole, Doug."

Ressler shrugged, a shit-eating grin replacing the temporary vulnerability which had overcome him—a vibe he was loathe to maintain. And of course, it had been Siobhan Jacobs who had made him feel that way.

Shocker. What else was new?

"Better than an asshole, I guess," Ressler said.

"Is it?"

"I'd say so." He snubbed out his cigarette, rolling it between his thumb and forefinger. After all, what was one more nicotine stain added to the burn callous which had been forming for years. "You coming back in to look over this card?"

Sid pursed his lips, shaking his head. "Huh-uh. Already read that fucking card. Once was enough for me."

) (

Holding it so he and Jacobs could both study it, Ressler splayed it wide open. Just as the front had been, its interior was saturated with black or dark grey watercolor. On the far lefthand side there appeared to be a primitively drawn tree trunk running from top to bottom. In it were lines and various markings apparently meant to represent knots and grain in the wood. The most prominent of these could easily be misconstrued for a vagina.

Or maybe not so coincidental, Ressler suspected.

A cartoon-style cobweb adorned the top righthand corner. And painted randomly across both pages were eleven eyeballs—each with exaggerated feminine lashes—again drawn in such a rudimentary manner that the whole thing looked like a child had done it. Handwritten in big capital letters across the middle was:

BOO!

Again, a cutout of a paper skeleton had been glued to the card, but this one had either been poorly positioned or had shifted before the glue had set so that it partially covered the greeting:

HAPPY HALLOWEEN!

Below this was a hand painted 'signature' in white. It Read:

GEMINI

But most importantly of all, the punchline of the rhyme was handwritten across the inside crease. Like the greeting, this too was partially obscured by the skeleton. What was visible was:

...IT IS CASS** KE**ED*

Ressler squinted as if confused, turning the card over to view the front once more. Then the inside again. This time he read it aloud, for himself as much as Siobhan Jacobs who continued to study it over his shoulder. "I feel it in my bones, you ache to know her name, so direct from me…"

He opened the card.

"…it is Cass-L-or-I-something. K-E-something-D-something. Is that last letter there a Y?"

He thrust the card at Siobhan so she could take a closer look.

"Uggh, too close, Ressler."

She pulled back, refocused her eyes. Moved in closer again. Slowly and unblinking.

"Yes, that definitely looks like a Y to me, there at the end. And that one—" she poked a finger at the middle of the name and Ressler melodramatically yanked the card from her reach. "Jesus Christ, Doug! I'm the head of forensics, for God's sake. I know not to touch evidence without gloves…which, by the way, my office provided for everyone here."

Without apologizing, he raised the card to Siobhan's line of sight while he himself chose to stare into a distant void. He shook his head. It was subtle, but Jacobs picked up on it.

"Anyway," she circled her index finger around the cartoon skeleton's torso. "Look here. That's an N, is it not? After the E?"

Ressler lost interest in the distant void and pulled the card close to examine it further. "If it is, then there's definitely space next to it for another. So that makes it Cass-*something*—"

"—Kennedy," Siobhan declared. "Cassie Kennedy."

"But our victim, the woman in that Polaroid photo; the woman who lives here—" Ressler glanced out the window, but Officer Julie Chen had already left in her squad car with the daughter of the victim. "—The name of that baby girl's mother is Sheila McCabe. Not Cassie Kennedy."

Siobhan Jacobs had no answer for him.

)(

"You sure you don't wanna join us?" In a rare attempt at genuine cordiality, Doug Ressler coaxed Siobhan into joining them at the Cop Shop for a drink. Or two. Maybe some food.

"Yeah, I'm gonna give that a pass. If you remember, that's how we got ourselves into this in the first place."

"Well, then maybe it's the best way to get ourselves out of it."

And there it was, that natural, relaxed charm that somehow oozed from one of the most irascible men she'd ever met. Of course, in time, Siobhan had come to learn why. As is so often the truth, underneath that short-tempered and combative shell was also one of the most sensitive and caring human beings she would ever have the privilege of knowing. *Little Boy Lost*, is how she'd come to think of him back then, and also how she described Doug to the few girlfriends with whom she felt she could safely speak about him and the relationship that so many people just wouldn't understand. This vulnerable underbelly, and the wit conceived of it, is why Ressler had so easily torn down the wall Siobhan had not only built around her, but also tended meticulously for years. A wall from which not a living soul had removed even a single brick. Yet Ressler had razed it to the ground with the perfunctory ease of a wrecking ball.

But since then, she had again begun to lay the bricks.

"You know, Doug…you're probably right. But I still think I'll take a raincheck. Maybe next time, okay?"

Of course, Ressler knew there was no next time in Siobhan Jacobs' mind. And if there were, it was such a nebulous, intangible concept—so far in the future and so far removed from who they had once been—that anticipating it was no longer worth its cost.

"Well, if you change your mind…"

He knew she wouldn't.

"I won't."

She knew he'd ask one more time.

"Then I guess we'll catch you tomorrow." He and Sid turned left. She turned right. Over his shoulder, Ressler craned to get just one more peek as Jacobs sauntered away. "I hate to see you go—"

"—But you love to watch me leave," Siobhan finished while waving goodbye without breaking stride or even looking back. "I know you do, Ressler. Goodnight."

FOLLOWING PAGES:
the Gemini Halloween card,
courtesy of the evidence archives
locker of the San Francisco Police.

[Federal Bureau of Investigations
Case File 10-63; Document 10-63-3]

FROM YOUR
SECRET
PAL

I feel it in
my bones,
You ache
to know
her name,
And so
Direct
From me...

"So here's the obvious," Ressler declared as he plopped himself down in their usual booth with an ale while plunking a pint of stout in front of Sid. "But humor me, alright? Let me just run it by you, if only to make sure I'm understanding it myself."

This was, in so many words, how Ressler began every one of these conversations, and Sid Younger feigned a moan of despair, leaning back in the booth and crossing his arms.

"Christ, Doug. You wanna talk about that damn card, don'tcha?"

Ressler chugged a third of his glass, wiped the foam from his lips with an exaggerated backhand, then issued his customary sigh of euphoric pleasure. "*Ahhhh*, hits the spot. And yes. I do."

"Fine, then the dogs are on you. I thought we were coming here just to blow off some steam."

Of course Sid didn't think this at all. He knew full well Ressler would want to discuss the case. And he came because he knew he could finagle a free meal out of him.

"Sure, I'll buy," Ressler said. "I think a couple chili dogs and a beer or two are a small price to pay for catching a multiple murderer."

Ressler didn't think this at all. *Cheap as a two-dollar whore*, is how Sid so often described him. But he would get the tab this time because he knew Sid would get it the next. It's just how it worked: the dance they played. And they'd been dancing for seven years, so why stop now?

"Alright, Doug," Sid complied. "Hit me. Whatcha cookin' up in that big ol' head o' yours? Shit, I can see the steam comin' out your ears as we speak."

Ressler laughed without knowing why. After all, wasn't this exactly how Sidney Younger jumped into these conversations every time they had them? By the two-hundredth or so, you'd think it would lose its sparkle. But maybe that's why he still found it so amusing: because Sid still did.

"Okay, so here's the thing. We know our victim's name is—*was*—Sheila McCabe. Yes?"

Sid nodded as he sipped his pint more conservatively than Ressler who would be on his second before their food arrived.

"But the dude gives us a different name in the Halloween card he made just for us. Siobhan thinks that name is Cassie Kennedy."

Sid shrugged. "I could see that. You fill in the blanks we can't see, and it works."

"So, is she a victim we're not aware of? Or does he plan to kill again, and for some fucked up reason he's giving us a warning about who his next victim will be?"

Sid treated the question as rhetorical. "I'm with you so far, brother. Just keep running with it and I'll let you know when you're jogging ahead too fast."

"He puts a number three and a number one in the skeleton's hand on the front of the card. Separated by two little dots."

"That's called a colon, Doug."

"Okay, a colon. Sorry I'm not a Shakespearian scholar like you."

"It's basic grammar, dude."

Ressler dropped his hands to the table. "You gonna let me get this out, or what? Anyway, those numbers are written in a hand that's making the OK sign, for whatever reason."

Sid waggled his finger round in forward circles, the gesture like a roll of spooling film. "Keep rolling."

"Then there's those eleven weird eyes drawn all over the place. Fuck, what is it with those? They look straight outta those old black-and-white cartoons they'd play at the start of the drive-in movies when we were kids. Remember?" He waited for Sid to respond, but his partner only wanted him to keep on chugging down whatever track this train of his was heading. "Anyway, so there's eleven of those eyes. And they seem to get bigger as they get closer to that paper skeleton he stuck in there."

"Could be some kind of meaning in that," Sid reasoned, "or it could be a fake clue so we spend days, maybe weeks, barking up the wrong motherfuckin' tree."

"Mm-hmmm."

"If this even is the same guy that sent that wordsearch. I mean, *we* believe it is. But what does Siobhan think? She's the expert on deviant behavior and patterns."

"We haven't discussed it yet, other than a quick glance at the scene," Ressler admitted. "But you know she's gonna corroborate it. I mean, the wordsearch threatened he would kill on the thirteenth…and here we are. The victim type, the scene, the M.O., the jacked-up games he's playing…all the same."

"Okay, but let me play devil's advocate that this is a copycat—"

"—Copycat my ass, Sid. You know it's the same guy. There's too much in common. Here, look at this a sec', will ya?" He pulled a Polaroid from the inside breast pocket of his grey sportscoat and pushed across the table.

"Jesus, Doug. Is that the pic fro—"

"Fuck's sake. Think I'd just pull evidence like that? How long you know me?"

"Long enough to know it wouldn't be the first time." Previously relaxed with his chin resting in his hand, Sid shot bolt upright. Pressed hard to the booth's backrest, his eyes were wide as a cat on a hot tin roof. "Don't go showing me that pic if it's the one I think it is. I don't wanna see it again."

"Alright, settle it down there, Nancy."

"Nancy?"

"Yeah, what are you, a little schoolgirl? It's not the lady's head. It's a photo of that fucking card he left us. Before we bagged it, I had one of Siobhan's techs snap a few with that instamatic of theirs."

With a side-eye and incoherent mutter, something that included Ressler's name, Sid leaned forward and spun the photo around to examine it. He sucked in air through pursed lips and his face visibly soured, the taste of depravity coating his tongue like burnt oil. "This is one messed up cat."

Ressler didn't disagree. Although his skin was crawling as much as Sid's, the only one who would know it was himself.

He pushed Sid to give him his thoughts.

"Okay. Okay. I'm getting there. Yeah, so what's with the vagina tree?" He scoured more closely, looking for patterns; logic. "And you're right about those eyes. This whole thing is so—so— *sophomoric*. My kids drew better than this when they were in grade school."

Speaking about his children while holding the photo of the killer's calling card churned Sid's stomach. He washed the feeling away with a stiff swig of stout.

"And, like you said, none of it makes a whole lot of sense." He tossed the Polaroid with disgust, and it spun across the table to rebound off Ressler's glass of ale. "Or, like I said, this is a copycat killing. Just think how many people in the Bay area would've seen that wordsearch. I mean, it was on Channel 5 and in the *Ledger*. All it takes is for one psycho to take the idea and run with it."

"I don't think so, Sid. I really don't. This is the same guy."

Rising above sporadic pockets of laughter and the smoky, static thrum of male voices, a woman's voice chimed in. It was crisp and clear; lilting.

"I agree."

Siobhan Jacobs appeared at their booth.

"May I?" She squeezed onto the bench seat next to Sid. "And what's more, I have the proof..."

28

WAS HALFWAY home when it hit me. So I turned around and went back to the station." Siobhan Jacobs moved Doug Ressler's beer aside and plopped her handbag and a file folder on the table. "Reagan, the staff sergeant, was about to go home but I caught him just in time. Bless his heart, he has a kid down with the flu and a wife who's about to go postal if he's late one more time. But he stayed behind to pull the file on the call that came in."

"Imagine that," Ressler chided. "A guy with a snot-spouting kid at home and a wife the size of a dump truck, going out of his way to do a favor for a stone-fox strawberry-blonde with outta sight green eyes."

Sid shot Ressler a look while Jacobs gave him the one-finger salute and started to stand. Gently placing his hand over hers as Siobhan pressed up from the table, Sid asked her to please stay.

"You're a good man, Sid. I don't know what kind of shit you've done in your life to get this kind of karma." She gestured toward Ressler. "But I can't imagine you deserve it." She turned to Ressler.

"Do you want to hear this, Doug? If not, I have a good book, a nice glass of wine and a comfy bed all calling my name."

Ressler remembered that bed.

What he wanted to say was that he would give anything to be in it again, merely lying there, staring at the ceiling and taking in the wonder of it all in as the one woman he ever actually cared for lay next to him. It wouldn't be the first time. But sadly, the last had already come and gone.

"It was meant as a compliment. I'm sorry. I'm a dick. Pleas—"

"—Compliment? I get more flattering remarks walking past a construction site."

Ressler had no response.

"Alright…" Siobhan sat back down, patting the back of Sid's hand. "Any chance a girl could get a drink, then?"

Younger caught the attention of J.B. behind the bar and mouthed 'wine' with a side-nod toward his companion. J.B.'s face brightened with recognition: he knew which Chardonnay to pour.

Choosing his tone more carefully, Ressler's words were awkward; faltering. Unlike his own. But at least they weren't abrasive. "You…were saying…you saw the sergeant's notes?"

"I was," Siobhan said as J.B. made his way from behind the bar and placed a generously poured glass before her.

"Oaky, not buttery."

'Thank you, J.B."

The bartender began making his way to three new customers leaning against the bar and searching for his whereabouts. Two steps in, he turned to add:

"And can I say, it's a pleasure to see you back here, Miss Jacobs. If there's anything else you need, just let me know."

He nodded at Sid, offering a professional smile. It faded when his eyes rolled past Ressler before heading back to his station. Along the way he waved at the waiting customers he clearly knew.

"Looks like you make friends wherever you go, Doug." Jacobs

couldn't help the little giggle that came out as she took a sip of wine and leaned in toward Ressler with a satisfied sigh. And something that felt to him like the tiniest glimmer of the way she had once looked at him.

Not that long ago.

"Yeah, I'm the life of the party. Anyway, your notes—?"

"Okay, the notes. You're not going to believe this." She took another drink, this one much more robust. "The call that came in to report the murder? It came from the killer himself."

If the rest of the patrons in the bar were still there, neither Sid nor Ressler would have been able to tell you.

"I know," Jacobs said, "That's how I felt when he told me. And, are you ready for this? He outright confessed to the switchboard operator that he was responsible for two of the crimes we pegged him for based upon clues he left in the wordsearch."

She pulled a small notepad from her handbag and rifled through its pages of scrawled shorthand that looked to both of her companions like some kind of Egyptian hieroglyphics. She found the one she was looking for, about halfway through.

"Shorthand, gentlemen. See, it pays to be a girl and get that mandatory secretarial training while you fellas get together and learn how to polish your wood, or steel rods, or whatever."

"I think you mean woodshop and metal shop," Sid corrected with a chuckle. But engrossed in her notes, he assumed Siobhan hadn't caught the double entendre, let alone intended it.

Ressler wasn't so sure.

"Whatever. Same thing. So, here it is." She gave herself a moment to decipher the symbols scrawled across the tiny, lined page. "He told the switchboard operator, and I quote, 'I took that girl from Mount Diablo in June. And the pretty young wife from Sausalito.' Now, let me see. This next bit—"

A clap like thunder made her entre body flinch and the notebook dropped from her hands.

"I knew it!" Ressler proclaimed, slapping his hands together a second time. "I damn well motherfuckin' knew it."

"But wait, there's a lot more." Jacobs rescued the notebook from a tiny puddle of spilled ale and carefully separated the wet pages. "This next bit is important, so I'm going to tell it to you exactly the way the operator wrote it down. Okay, here it is. He said to her, '...That young wife's sexy wedding ring finger dialed the phone for me.' Then he told the switchboard girl to pass that on to the Contra Costa County sheriff, because he'd know what that meant. Oh, and something about her possibly getting a pay rise if she made out like she'd coaxed that out of him." Siobhan tipped down her eyeglasses and peered over them. "Who's the Contra Costa sheriff, again?"

"Miller," Sid answered. "Morris. An old boy with a reputation for not playing nice with others. A lot like Ressler."

This made Siobhan laugh and a bubble rose from her wine as she took another sip.

"Don't listen to him. Miller's on old friend of mine. We go way back. He called me from home the night Hannah Wilson was dumped in her trunk at Diablo. He was pretty shaken up about it. But here's the thing, he never released any information about her finger being cut off. So that corroborates our guy's claim." Ressler stroked his chin, his focus drawing inward.

Sid agreed, addressing Siobhan. "The M.O. of Sheila McCabe's killer definitely matches the Mount Diablo killing, wouldn't you agree? If you're not too familiar with it, both victims were young, pretty...and married. The scenes of each show signs of dismemberment of the victim's left hand—their wedding ring hand—or the ring finger itself. And both were decapitated."

"I don't recall anything being released about decapitation in the Mount Diablo case?"

"Another detail Morris left out," Ressler pointed out to Jacobs. "Didn't feel the necessity to broadcast that particularly gruesome info all around town."

"Ahh," Jacobs replied. "What was the moniker that jackass from Channel 5, Mike Driffield, gave the killer, again?"

"The Hurdy Gurdy Man," Sid replied. "Like the Donovan song."

Siobhan shivered. "Yeah. It's creepy. And that *song* is creepy. I don't know if it's meant to be, but it gives me goosebumps. And not the good kind."

"But that leads me to ask," Sid interjected, "why our guy signed this card as the Gemini if he's the same perp, this Hurdy Gurdy Man?"

"Well," Siobhan explained, "I may have the answer for you. The Hurdy Gurdy Man is a *nom de guerre* that was assigned—"

"—A nom de-what?" Ressler cut her off, smirking.

"*Nom de guerre*, Ressler. In other words, an alias. In French, its literal translation is 'war name.' But as I was saying, Hurdy Gurdy was assigned to the perp by Mike Driffield. Not sure why. But my explanation, Sid, would be that our guy doesn't much care for it. So he gave you the name by which he wants you to know him: the Gemini. And to further corroborate that the person who called in Sheila's murder and the person who left us this card are, in fact, one in the same, he told our switchboard operator, and I quote: 'This is the Gemini speaking.'"

"Christ. What is it with these sickos and their aliases?" Sid's question was only half-rhetorical. "You know, there's one of them down in Santa Cruz who picks up girls hitchhiking, goes by the name the Co-ed Killer. And do you guys remember hearing about that case out in Wisconsin about ten years ago? Gein, I think his name was."

"Ed Gein," Siobhan confirmed. "A.K.A. The Plainfield Ghoul. He was arrested a little over a decade ago in '57 after abducting and killing a woman who owned a hardware store. Her son was a sheriff's deputy who was in the store with her, probably still in uniform, the evening *prior to* his mother going missing. I'm assuming that's the reason Gein left empty-handed that night."

"Yep," Ressler chimed in. "I'm guessing that would do it. Except the son heard Gein say he'd be back the next morning for some antifreeze. So, when the old gal went missing the next day, the son—a deputy, remember—was a smart cookie and immediately checked her receipt book."

"Let me guess," Sid said. "Gein's was the last receipt she'd written."

Ressler placed his index finger to the tip of his nose and tapped it. "You got it, big boy. And when they went to Gein's farm they not only found the deputy's mother—she'd been decapitated and was strung up in a barn, hung upside down like a deer being dressed—they also found women's faces removed and stored in paper bags, a corset made from a woman's torso, a lampshade and wastebasket made out of human skin, and full-face masks made from the skin of female heads."

Sid squirmed in his seat, raising the back of his hand to his mouth as though her were fending off the impulse to throw up. "Christ, Ressler. Why do you know so much about this?"

"Because it has an impact on our cases. Right here. Right now. The real question is, why do you *not* know so much about it?"

Sid shook his head. Still looked like he needed to vomit. Took a swig of his stout.

"Ressler's got a point," Siobhan attested. "There's real value in studying the patterns and quirks of—"

"Quirks?" Sid interrupted. "Human face trashcans? Fuck, that's a sickness, is what it is. Not a quirk. I don't like eating my corn on the cob straight from the cob—I always cut the kernels away in nice satisfying strips and then eat them. Now *that's* a quirk. Please don't put me in the same category as some psycho who wears girl masks made from real girls!"

"No, of course not, Sid." Siobhan reassured him, her eyes held upon his until Sid's softened. "There's no comparison. What Gein was doing was anthropodermia, or the displaying of artifacts made from human skins. The Nazis were renowned for it. When Allied troops liberated Auschwitz Buchenwald and discovered the horrors that had been perpetrated there, they also found numerous artifacts made from the skin of Jewish prisoners, some with the tattooed numbers clearly visible."

"I've heard that," Ressler admitted. "My old man was in the European theatre in the war. News of just how depraved the Nazis actually were traveled fast after Auschwitz."

"And how does any of this help us with our cases? We have women being killed right here in the Bay area. How 'bout we keep our focus on that." Sid crossed his arms, shaking his head.

"In a way," Siobhan reassured him, "that's what we're doing. If we understand the quir—sorry, the *pathological deviances*—of barbarous murderers like the Nazis, and Ed Gein, and the Co-ed Killer, then we might be able to understand our perp better."

"And if we understand him, maybe we can catch him. I get it," Sid confided. "I just wish it wasn't so Goddamn gruesome."

"I'll go one better than that," Siobhan countered. "If we understand him, maybe we can learn how to stop others from killing in the first place."

"That's all well and good," Ressler chirped. "But I'm with Sid as much as I am with you on this one. Sure, I see the real benefit of knowing what other sickos have done so we can use it against our guy. But curing society? That's above my pay grade. I'll leave that task to you and your gimmicky new 'forensic psychology' pals. Something to talk about at your next coven, perhaps."

"That's right, make a joke of it. We don't understand it, so we'll throw sticks and rocks and kill it and then see what it was." Siobhan Jacobs was starting to fume. "You know, Doug, it's dickheads like you who sat in Salem with smug self-satisfied smiles as the 'witches' burned. I'll have you know that far from gimmicky, or new, or a fad, forensic psychology dates back to the 1800s when Wilhelm Wundt founded the first psychological laboratory. His work was not only employed in legal cases as early as the 1890s, but also blazed the trail for behaviorism."

Her eyes had been half-closed, distantly focused as she tore him a new one. When she opened them, she saw that Ressler had formed his hand into a puppet and was moving its 'mouth' nonstop while silently mouthing *blah blah blah*.

She picked up his pint of ale and poured what remained of it in his lap. "Fuck you, Ressler. Grow the hell up, will you? This is why we're not together anymore. You just can't deal with your emotions in a healthy way. And that includes how you receive anything that feels foreign or uncomfortable to you. If I didn't know better, I'd say there were traits of pathological deviance in your psychological profile. You need help. You really do."

When she stopped, Jacobs realized that half the patrons in the bar were staring in silence at the three of them. And staring directly at her, dumbfounded, were Ressler and Sid.

You could hear a pin drop.

Shrinking in her seat, she was about to apologize when the bar exploded in cheers and laughter and jibes like, '*what a shame— for the beer, I mean! Wasted on that asshole.*' And '*looks like that's the only golden shower you'll be getting' tonight, Doug!*'

)(

"I deserved it," Ressler admitted before Jacobs could apologize. Which is exactly what she'd started to do once he returned from the bathroom and the jibes of the bar crowd had fallen off, the clusters of patrons returning to whatever they were doing prior to the spectacle. "You know I hate this gruesome shit as much as you both do." He gave Sid a playful punch on the shoulder as he sat down. "Well, maybe not as much as you, big fella. But I do hate it. So I cope by acting the class clown. And I apologize."

It was the first time Siobhan could remember him being so frank and vulnerable. In public, at least. She'd seen plenty of glimpses of it in private. One time, he'd even broken down in tears as she'd held him. That was after the discovery of a twelve-year-old girl who had been raped and murdered and left in four different trash cans around the city. But she'd never seen him so honest and mature in front of anyone else before.

"And I'm sorry," she replied. "Not for pouring it on you, but for wasting your beer." She winked and a bashful smile crept onto her face as she leaned into Sid and wrapped her arm around his. Like the father figure he was to her, he patted her hand and gave her a closed-lip smile.

"So, can we get back to our case?" Ressler asked.

"Yes, please," said Siobhan.

Sid looked at his watch. "I've got ten minutes. Then I'm out. If not, I'm gonna come home to face a Mrs. Younger that won't be all too happy with me. And as much as I love you two, I love that big hunka burnin' love a damn sight more."

"Okay let's jam this out and decide what's next," Siobhan directed. "The person who called in Sheila McCabe's murder corroborated that he was leaving something at the scene, which checks out. Then he gave our switchboard operator the Gemini moniker. So, it's clear that the caller and killer are one in the same. Now, how do we corroborate that he's also the same person who mailed the wordsearch to the media? If we can link Sheila's killer to that puzzle, then we definitely have a serial killer on our hands. So…any idea how to connect those dots?"

"In the wordsearch, he gave us today's date as his next kill date, Ressler offered.

"True," Jacobs returned. "But, as Sid said, anyone and everyone in the Bay area had the chance to see that puzzle last week. And today's date was written right there. So, that's not proof. A copycat would've seen it the same as anyone else. What other ideas do we have?"

"Alright, but the caller knew about the Halloween card we were gonna find. He called himself the Gemini, which is how the card is signed. He also knew about Hannah's severed finger, which no other member of public would've known. So that places him at both Sheila McCabe's house tonight and the phone booth and abandoned convertible at Mount Diablo in August."

Sid Younger concurred. "That's right, and he said he was responsible for taking Rosalie Sherwood in June. No reason to lie about that."

Siobhan flipped through her notes, pulling out the 8x10 photo of the wordsearch, and laid it side-by-side with the smaller Polaroid of the Halloween card. She palmed them both to the center of the table for all three of them to cross-reference.

"Wait!" Sid Younger held up one hand as he scanned the wordsearch and Halloween card upside-down. "You know, I didn't see it before. But looking at them both like this makes a difference somehow. He stubbed his meaty fingertip at the top right of the puzzle, three lines down. "Look...what's this?"

Ressler twisted in his seat to see what his partner was seeing. "You mean that number three? There are a couple of them. Why is that important?"

But Siobhan Jacobs saw it, too. "Oh my God. Sid, you're right." She tapped her manicured nail upon three characters: **E31**

With her other hand she tapped the front of the Halloween card, specifically the skeleton's hand making the OK sign. In it was handwritten: **E3:1**

"Goddamn," is all Doug Ressler could muster.

"Not only are they the same," Sid proclaimed, "but I know what it means. It's a bible chapter and verse. The Old Testament, if I'm correct. There are at least five that start with the letter 'E,' but I'd bet my hat on it being Ecclesiastes, chapter three, verse one."

"Sid, that's amazing!" Siobhan applauded. "How did I not see it? Can you remember how that verse goes?"

Although directed at Sid Younger, Jacobs was looking at them both when she asked. Ressler chuckled, waving away the very idea that he would have even the first clue about a verse in the Old Testament. But Sid leaned back and stared at the ceiling, his lips silently moving while he ran through the lessons of his Baptist upbringing.

"Okay, I got it! Do either of you two like The Byrds?"

"What the fuck's some folk pop group gotta do with the price of tea in China?" As short-lived as the pint he was drinking, Ressler's beer-soaked humility was eclipsed by his usual sardonic style as he tapped the empty glass and signaled J.B. for another.

"Because they had a huge hit song just a couple years ago called 'Turn! Turn! Turn!' Remember? It's basically E3:1 put to music. It goes: 'There's a season for everything, and for every purpose under Heaven. A time to be born, a time to die; a time to plant, a time to reap; a time to heal...*and a time to kill.*'"

)(

"That's more than enough to connect our guy tonight with the wordsearch," Siobhan acknowledged. "But I do have one more thing—a *big* thing—to share. When I came back here, it wasn't just to prove that we have a serial killer on our hands."

That label still sounded odd to Siobhan's ears instead of 'multiple murderer.' But it sure did roll off the tongue a lot easier.

She now spoke directly to Doug. "I suddenly remembered the time you came home and told me about a woman who had come to see you at the precinct that day. It was sometime a couple months ago? You said she claimed to have some information about another missing girl."

It took Ressler a moment. "You mean Lyndsey Roe, the little

girl who went missing from Panhandle Park?"

"Yes! I'm glad you remember."

How could he not? The six year old had been abducted in the middle of the day on a sunny Sunday in the park, and this nutjob claims she's a psychic and has info about what happened.

"How's that linked to this? It's way out of our guy's M.O."

"I agree. But the lady who came to see you? She's very connected to our case now."

"The crackpot…?""

"The psychic, yes," Siobhan rebuked.

Ressler made a *pfffft* sound. "Those whackjobs some crawling outta the woodwork when word gets out about cases like these. Especially when the victim's a woman or a child."

"Well, my love, it's not really about whether you believe that woman has the gift of second sight or not." She turned to Sid, her open backhand covering her mouth as if it would prevent Ressler from hearing what she was about to tell Sid: "Though I personally think she does."

Sid Younger nodded vigorously. "Mmmm-hmmm. Me too. I remember the one you're talking about. Pretty gal. Single mom with a kid at home, I think. I took over the interview after Ressler threw a hissy fit."

"So, what about it?" Ressler's frustration had begun to rear its ugly head. He remembered the ale in the lap—and took a deep breath. "Sorry. Please go on, Siobhan."

"You told me that psychic's name was—"

"That crackpot's name," Ressler corrected her.

'—That *psychic's* name was Cassandra."

Ressler shrugged. "So what."

"Seriously? C'mon, Ressler. Cassandra…*Cassie*."

Sudden realization dawned. "You're not gonna tell me her last name is Kennedy…"

Siobhan Jacobs lifted her hands, palms upturned. A 'there you have it' gesture. Sid's eyes grew wide as he pressed back from the table in astonishment.

"That's what I said her name was...?" Doug Ressler seemed genuinely flummoxed. "Are you sure about that?"

"I'm certain," Siobhan professed. "I remember it because of her last name. You don't often hear it outside of the news, or the front page of those gossip rags at the grocery store checkout." She became solemn, absentmindedly twirling the stem of her empty wine glass between her fingers. "The psychic—the woman and mother—who came to see you was called Cassandra Kennedy. And now, for some reason, she's gotten herself caught in the crosshairs of our killer."

29

)(

WAKING TO THE stomach-churning scent of stagnant blood, Cassie stirred upon the dirt floor as the metal gate to their block of cells slammed shut. The echo of its jarring clang overlapped the sound of the man fastening its padlock, the chains that bound it jangling as he yanked twice to ensure it was secure.

She counted the sound of his footsteps until they could no longer be heard, the steady cadence of his stride as certain as the clicks of a metronome. After thirteen they faded away. But it took an additional count of eighteen more silent beats until a faint and faraway thud of another door found its way to Cassie's ears.

Thirty-one steps in total.

With an average three feet per step for an adult male, that made it a hundred feet—and at least three locked doors—between herself and freedom.

But what lay beyond?

According to Rosalie, he came and went at all hours of the day and night, his visits erratic and unscheduled. Sometimes with the body of his latest victim dragging behind him. Which meant it was highly unlikely they were anywhere near the city.

They could scream all they wanted: it wasn't going to achieve much. Other than tearing at Cassie's already raw throat, that is.

"Rose," she whispered. "You there?" Although still sore and swollen, adding a depth to her voice that made it much more husky than her natural timbre, the pain in Cassie's throat had subsided to the point where speaking softly was again possible.

She waited in silence, listening for the telltale sounds of Rose stirring in her cell, but heard none.

"Rose?"

Nothing.

"*Rose.*"

Silence.

"*Rose!*"

"I'm here," she answered in a voice weaker than before. "You scared me. For a minute there, I thought you were him."

Cassie massaged her throat. "My throat is hoarse. It's sore, but at least I can talk. Barely. How about you, hun, are you okay?"

Two cells away, Rose nodded in the dark. Then shrugged. "I don't know. I need food. He hasn't brought me any since you showed up. And I'm hungry."

"I just heard him leave, Rose. What does that mean...will he be back with food and water?"

"When did you hear him leave?"

"Just now. You didn't hear the gate slam?"

Rosie shook her head though there was no one to see it. "No. Are you sure?"

"Yes, I even counted his steps. Wherever we are, whatever this place is, it's big. At least a good hundred feet to the outside world. Maybe more. That's why every single sound echoes in here. There must be some kind of big, empty chamber just beyond these fucking pens we're in."

"I must be really out of it," Rose admitted, "because the last thing I heard was him dragging in that new lady after you passed out again."

Now Cassie's heart quickened, and she pulled herself closer to the wooden slats of her cell door.

"Wait, there's another woman here? *Hello*—" Cassie called out as she beat her palms upon the door. "Hello! Can you hear me?"

"No, she can't. She was already dead when he dragged her here." Rosalie swallowed, feeling her chest tighten. "Cassie...*oh my God*...I think he used some kind of saw to—" Rose retched, thick, viscoid mucous foaming in the back of her throat "—to cut her up into pieces." She coughed, a dry, choking sound.

"You sound really bad, Rose. We need to get him to give you some water." *And me too*, Cassie thought as she propped herself against her cell door, feeling weak and unsteady on her feet. "But you know what, Rose? Fuck this victim mentality bullshit. What we really need is to just get ourselves the hell out of here...before he picks one of us for his next."

"How? *I've tried*..." Rose's voice trailed away until it was so quiet that it was barely audible. More than the effects of dehydration, what Cassie was witnessing was the active deterioration of the young woman's hope—a survival conviction that had kept her alive for all these months on her own.

"Together, Rose. That's how."

To this, Rosalie did not respond.

"Hey," Cassie said with a dramatic smile to brighten her tone, an old trick she'd learned from a friend in the radio biz, "tell me a little more about yourself, hun. You said you've only just turned twenty, is that right?"

A sound of shuffling from Rose's cell, but no audible reply.

"So you can't be married, like the rest of us?"

The shuffling stopped.

"Twenty-one. I just turned twenty-one. And actually, I am. Well,

I kinda am."

"I'm sorry, that's right. You said you're old enough to drink now." Cassie chuckled. "Legally, I mean."

Now Rose half-laughed-half-coughed. "Yeah. I was wondering how—" (another choking splutter) "—how I was gonna explain to my dad that I already know I like Scotch and hate tequila."

"Scotch? Me too! There's not many of us gals around that do. So that's pretty groovy that we have that in common."

Rose tried to answer but broke into another dry, hacking fit.

"And what do you mean when you say that you are, 'well kinda'? Are you talking about marriage already, at your age?"

Rose composed herself with several deep breaths before answering. "I was married. Well, I am. Widowed, now. Robert and I got hitched when we were both nineteen. His number came up for a tour of duty in Vietnam. So we decided to elope. I wanted him to have the absolute best reason to make it back home, y'know? A wife waiting for him...maybe the prospect of a kid or two...somewhere down the line."

It was a thought that tore at her heart, and Cassie didn't have to ask what happened.

Rose told her anyway.

"He was killed a little over sixteen months ago in a battle near Bong Son in south Vietnam."

"Rose, I'm *so* sorry. I can't imagine losing your husband at just twenty-one years old."

"Twenty." As she spoke, Rose's fingers ran over a pendant around her neck. "In fact, it's *why* I'm here. It was the anniversary of his death, and I was beside myself. Inconsolable. I don't even know how, but next thing I know I was wandering around Mount Diablo park. I don't even remember the hour-long drive it takes to get there. All I can see, even to this day, is getting out of my car and just walking. Aimlessly pacing around the plateau in a daze, just before the summit. Do you know it?"

Cassie admitted that she did not.

"Well, it's quite beautiful. You can see four counties from up there. At least, that's what the sign says. All I know is that I saw trees and hills until it all became a beautiful green blur in the distance. Funny, isn't it? How real life isn't cordoned off into neat little boundaries like it is on maps, its ownership arbitrarily dished out for this governmental body or that one."

She fumbled with her necklace again, the ball chain jangling.

"That's what got Robert killed. A fucking boundary line on a map. In a fucking leach-infested rice paddy, all the way across the world. Now they're still there: the Vietcong, I mean. But he's all gone. How is that right?"

Rosalie lifted the pendant and kissed it. This time, its tiny metallic jingle caught Cassie's attention.

"Rosie, hun? What's that sound I keep hearing?"

"Oh, that's Robert's dog tags. Well, one of them, at least." She lifted the small rectangular tag and read it out loud: "'Sherwood, Robert A. 7953378420. B pos. Protestant.' That's his whole life, stamped into a little rectangle of metal."

Name, Department of Defense number, blood type and religion. No mention of his wife. No mention of his life yet unlived. Just the basic facts.

Again, Cassie apologized. Like most, she found the idea of the entire fucking war unfathomable. As Rosie had said, young American men were being mowed down in their tens of thousands...for nothing more important than an imaginary line on a map. If it was for a better reason than that, the government hadn't done a very good job of saying so. What was worse was the fact that nearly five thousand of those casualties—nearly ten percent—were from California alone. No other state in the union even came close, save New York. And even their losses were twenty-five percent fewer than California's. And every single one of those men had mothers, fathers, sisters, brothers, friends, wives, sometimes even children, all of whose lives were forever changed by the loss of someone they loved; someone who made their lives better. Someone who they would never see again, hear from again or hold again in their arms.

All for a line on a map.

It was beyond unimaginable. For Cassie, it was utter insanity.

"I'm so sorry, Rosalie. I can't even begin to imagine what you're going through. And I can't express how much I wish you didn't have to."

"It was the worst thing to ever happen to me. I truly don't know how long I wandered around that plateau before I finally realized I was up there all on my own. I hadn't told anyone where I was going because I didn't know myself. And now it was starting to get dark. So, I was more than a little relieved when I saw a man signaling me from the trail, just a little ways below me."

"A man? Weren't you worried?"

"Like I said, my first instinct was relief that I wasn't all on my own up there. I mean, I couldn't even remember where I'd parked my car. And if I'm honest, I was starting to panic. Besides, this guy was wearing a sling around his right arm, and he had a nice face. *A friendly face, y'know?* Handsome, in a non-threatening kinda way. And he wasn't all that much bigger than me. So, I figured he was harmless."

"But he wasn't."

A little sound issued from Rosie's throat, a noise like disappointment. "He told me he had a flat tire and was having trouble changing it. He had a spare, but you know, with his arm in a cast and all. He said if I wouldn't mind helping him, he'd drive us around until we found where I left my car. The way I figured it, if I didn't help him, we were both stuck. If I did, we could both get the hell out of there and I wouldn't have to wander some mountaintop all alone in the dark. So I did. Help him, I mean."

"Only his arm wasn't really hurt, was it," Cassie guessed, a statement more than it was a question.

"No. I guess it wasn't. I bent down to look at the tire, but just like his arm, there was nothing wrong with it. Before my mind was able to register that, he yanked his left arm out of that sling. He had a cloth bunched up in his left hand. It smelled kinda sweet, and he covered my nose and mouth with it while he wrapped his right arm around me. Even though he wasn't very big, I was surprised, y'know? I didn't do anything to stop it. The next thing I know, I'm waking up here, on this dirt floor." Rose fiddled with the dog tag some more. "So in a way, I guess Robert and I both died that day."

"Except you're still here," Cassie assured her as Robert's dog tag rattled like a tiny windchime around his widow's neck. "Rosie? Have you ever played any sports?"

Surprised by the question, Rosie balked. "Sports? Why?"

"Because, we're getting out of here. Do you think if you reached through the bars just right you'd be able to toss me Robert's dog tag without us dropping it…?"

30

) (

THE ADDRESS CASSIE gave Detective Sid Younger during her July interview did not exist. At first, Sid thought he might have written it down incorrectly, perhaps a simple typo or transposed numbers. But there was no record of a Cassandra Kennedy in any governmental database.

First port of call was the office of the Property Appraiser of San Francisco County, where Sid struck out. Still, drawing a blank was better than drawing the short straw as Doug Ressler had. Sid's partner was now spending the better part of his morning at the county offices of the California Department of Motor Vehicles.

The place where dreams go to die, Ressler ensured he didn't have to be there a second longer than necessary. A flash of his badge and a little sweep of his blazer to reveal just a hint of his firearm, and all the pimply teens, freaks, flower-child hippies and octogenarians kindly sidled from the line.

Still, he came up empty.

"You don't think that chick has anything to do with these murders, do you...?" Back at his desk, Ressler chewed on a #2 pencil, a once-a-day replacement for a cigarette per Sid's incessant nagging. Similarly, Sid was grazing through a Ceasar salad, a once-a-week replacement for his usual corned beef on rye, per Doug's constant cajoling about his weight.

"Siobhan said her team found semen in the blood samples they took from Sheila McCabe's carpet. So unless this Cassie chick's got a dick, I don't think so."

Ressler grimaced. "Can you imagine getting off so hard on doing the sick shit this fucker does, that you can't help but stroke it? Right there, right then, all over the corpse of the woman whose throat you just cut?"

Sid stopped chewing, put down his bowl, and swallowed hard. He wiped creamy dressing from the corner of his mouth. "Thanks for that, Doug. C'mon, man. I'm eating here."

"Aaaah, toughen up, you big fat wuss."

Sid whipped him the finger and grabbed his bottle of RC Cola. "I'm gonna pull her interview file again. Maybe there's something I missed when she came in claiming to have info on the Roes' disappearance."

And there was.

It was small. A long shot.

But it was something.

)(

THURSDAY / OCT 16

"Where exactly is this café?" Ressler was donning his blazer over his shoulder holster and already heading for the stairs, car keys in hand.

"Haight-Ashbury. A place called Brewster's, I think. It's the only one I can find that matches what she said."

"Hippy-Fucking-Central," Ressler declared, unimpressed. "Of

course the weirdo who thinks she's psychic would be from the Haight. How did you establish this was the place?"

Sid had found it in a simple five-word note he'd scribbled in the margin of Cassie's interview report:

FRIEND PATTY CAFÉ HAIGHT ASH

It was an addendum he'd made to Cassie's comment about a friend who had come over for morning coffee before she opened the café she owned. Ms. Kennedy had then revealed that she'd lost track of the remainder of that day. It was later that night that she'd experienced what she was certain was a prophetic vision about Veronica Roe and her daughter Lyndsey; another woman called Janice Wynn; plus an unidentified man. That dreamlike—

nightmarish

—vision ended with them all in some kind of dungeon or dark holding cell.

Below this part of the interview notes, in his own bastardized version of shorthand, Sid had scribbled one last notation: that the psychic had slept most of the following day away, failing to even see her daughter, Isabella, off to kindergarten.

) (

Brewster's was busier than they'd expected it to be on a Thursday morning. One minute, the café owner was pulling cappuccinos from a fire engine red espresso machine; the next, fresh-roasting imported green coffee beans in a small-batch roaster. All the while she was explaining every move to her new part-time assistant, a young man by the name of Joseph who was eager and polite and, if he worked out, could alleviate some of Patty's overly-hectic schedule.

Exhibiting an atypical level of patience, Doug Ressler said

nothing as the café owner and her new protégé bustled back and forth behind the counter. It didn't hurt that she'd plied them with bottomless coffees and warm chocolate croissants as they waited.

"Alright, sorry about that." Patty Brewster grabbed her smokes and beckoned the detectives to follow her to the small table she always set aside for her breaks. "Is this about Cassie?"

"So you do know her," Sid confirmed as Doug Ressler grunted, speaking over his partner:

"What makes you say that, Ms. Brewster?"

"Yes, of course I know her," Patty said to Sid. To Ressler she answered: "I reported it last Sunday. An officer came out but told me there was nothing he could do—officially, at least—until she'd been gone for at least forty-eight hours." Patty took another drag and spoke without exhaling, her words thin and wispy. "It didn't help that it was the same cop that came last time."

She released the smoke, and it billowed toward the ceiling as Ressler and Sid stared at one another in disbelief.

"She's missing?" Doug Ressler sat upright, leaning in, and Patty's breath caught in her throat. She coughed, and a small puff of off-white expelled with it.

"What do you mean, 'she's missing?' Why are you here, if not for that?" Patty's expression fell, instantly alarmed. "God, please don't tell me she's been hurt…or worse—"

"She's fine," Sid Younger replied, "as far as we know. But we have reason to believe she might be in need of our help. Do you have any idea where Ms. Kennedy might have gone?"

Patty shook her head.

Doug Ressler straightened in his seat, squaring up to the café owner. "Why did you say, 'this time,' Ms. Brewster?"

"*Miss* Brewster, please. I've never been married. Single and proud of it. Patty is fine, detective."

"Right. Patty. Why, 'this time'?"

Patty stubbed out the remainder of her cigarette without

finishing it. A thin thread of smoke spiraled up and away as she appeared to withdraw from the moment, disappearing to a place somewhere deep within herself.

No, not a place within, Ressler mentally corrected himself, countering his initial interpretation. *She's gone back to a different moment in time. They've had a falling out of sorts. Maybe an argument? And in her mind, this chick's in that moment right now.*

"Something happened," Patty admitted, and Detective Doug Ressler settled back into his chair, his arms crossed.

What a shame Siobhan isn't here, he thought, and a smug look crossed his countenance thinking how proud the psychiatrist would be proud of his psychological assessment. There was a reason she was the head of Criminal Forensics—Jacobs was the best at interpreting human behavior. Period. She could sniff out motives behind actions and predict a perp's next move better than anyone. It's also one of the reasons they couldn't make their budding relationship work: she was always one step ahead of Ressler's bullshit.

And his frail male ego knew it.

"What happened?" Flicking through the pages of his memo pad, Sid absently clicked his pen with his thumb. The ballpoint tip extended, retracted, extended, retracted…until Patty's side-eye became fixated on the action. "Sorry. Anyway, tell me what happened—"

"—She had another vision. A really bad one. For a client, right here in the café."

Patty lit another cigarette, her hands trembling just enough for Doug Ressler to notice, while most others would not. "But I'm not sure how much I should really tell you." She took a long puff and the exhale danced along the ceiling in a smoke ring. She eyed both detectives with an air of suspicion.

In response, Sid closed his notebook, clicked his pen shut and laid it alongside the tablet in a neatly parallel line. "Miss Brewster,

I understand how you feel. And I assure you, we're all here for the same reason: to assure your friend's safety. So, how about this—everything from here out will be off the record." He showed his palms in the universal sign of surrender, then laid them on the tabletop, lacing his fingers as if in prayer.

Doug Ressler slumped back in his seat but said nothing.

Looking from one to the other, Patty took another puff and signaled Joseph behind the coffee bar for another latte. She asked the detectives if they would care for another, but both politely declined. "Alright, here goes. Off the record, Cassie was doing work here for a short while. It was my idea, actually. She's got a gift, y'know? She sees things the rest of us can't."

"We're not the IRS," Ressler informed her, deadpan and losing interest fast. "We don't care if you and your friend had a side-hustle for cash. Just tell me what's got you spooked."

Now Patty's defenses kicked in, her response as curt as the detective's was churlish. "I'm not *spooked*. And I don't appreciate the inference that we were cheating the tax man."

Even though they were.

In her left hand, her cigarette noticeably shook, enough that it caught Sid's eye. Patty followed his gaze and realized it herself, instantly depositing the cigarette in the ashtray and steadying her wrist with her other hand.

"Okay, look. A woman came here, wanting information about her missing daughter—" She proceeded to tell them about Meredith Harper; about the awful vision Cassie had of Meredith's daughter, Hannah Wilson; about the Deep Purple album. All of it.

"And she had this was all before there was any news about Hannah Wilson's murder…?" Sid had asked the question of Patty, but was eyeing Doug Ressler. Ressler knew exactly what his partner was thinking: we gotta confirm this album thing with Morris Miller over in Contra Costa County, whose case it was.

"A couple days before the news coverage, yes."

"And did she see the perpetrator?" Ressler asked.

"At first, the man Cassie saw was faceless. You ever see those mannequins in the fashion department down at the Emporium department store?" She looked both men up and down, realizing that fashion wasn't their strong suit. "Okay, maybe you haven't. But it was like those: just this plain white featureless face. But the second time she had the vision, she thought she might have recognized who he was."

"The perp," Ressler confirmed more than asked.

"Yes." Patty's hands had begun trembling to the point that Patty could barely pick up the steaming mug Joseph had quietly set upon the table. Patty no longer tried to hide it. She took a careful sip, sucked in her top lip, then chewed on the bottom. "And this is off the record. Officially, right? All of it?"

"All of it," Ressler assured her and softened his stance. He leaned in and covered Patty Brewster's shaking hands with his own. They were big and warm, and despite the man's irascible nature, to Patty, his touch felt like safety.

"I don't know why, 'cause she hadn't seen him for something like sixteen years, but Cassie thought the man who killed Hannah Wilson was her brother, Solomon."

) (

Patty relayed the heartrending backstory Cassie had shared about her and her brothers losing her parents, then being taken in by their aunt and uncle. And the terrible, terrible things those people—*those monsters*—had inflicted upon Cassie and her brothers, none of whom could have been more than ten years old at the time. She described how she and Cassie had gotten drunk (despite their conversation being off the record, she left out the part about getting high) and talked the whole thing out until Cassie's identification of Solomon seemed more likely to be a case of repressed guilt than one of Cassie actually seeing her brother.

"In fact, we pretty much convinced ourselves that the entire vision she had was a mixture of childhood guilt, a longing to see her brothers again, and stress over her breakup with Bill."

"Bill?" Sid Younger asked.

"Her husband, yes. Well, not exactly husband. Not legally, anyway. But they were as good as married."

Without breaking eye contact, Sid scribbled the name *William Kennedy* in his journal next to *Solomon Albrighton*, among others, making a mental note to do a search on both men later.

Patty explained that after the breakup Cassie was having a terrifying recurring nightmare about a faceless man who would break into her apartment and attack her.

"She told me about it just before she started offering readings here," Patty explained. "The breakup with Bill has been harder than she admits. Even though she's never said it, I know she's been worried about money. And she was spending way too much time on her own, just her and Bella—"

"—Her five-year-old," Sid repeated, recalling the name from his interview notes, and Patty narrowed her eyes.

To her, it seemed such an odd way to describe Isabella. Still, she nodded, confirming it.

"Anyway, she'd started having that awful nightmare more and more frequently. And it was becoming too...*lifelike*. So, when Cassie then had a vision of Hannah, it only reinforced her belief that her own nightmare was also a prophecy of something bad that was going to happen to *her*. As you can imagine, when we figured out that the Hannah thing was more a product of Cassie's own mind than a supernatural divination, that realization made us both feel a whole lot better." Patty paused, ensuring she had their full attention. "Until the local news came on, that is..."

"Because then you both knew that what Cassie saw did really happen," Sid deduced out loud, a conclusion for his own benefit as much as any other reason.

"And yet she didn't come to us to report it," Doug Ressler quipped, shaking his head in disdain. "Why the hell not?"

"Would you?" Patty fired back without hesitation. "After the way you treated her the first time?"

Doug Ressler decided to pull no punches. "You mean the time she read a newspaper headline or watched the TV news, then came to us claiming some kind of psychic insight about Mrs. Roe and her daughter Lyndsey? Is *that* the first time you mean?"

"I don't care if she heard it from a little bird sitting on her shoulder à la *Mary Poppins*. After telling her she was a nutjob, why the hell would she ever come back again?"

Doug Ressler conceded the point but found it odd that the café owner and Cassie had had some sort of falling out after the Hannah Wilson vision. "So, what about you? Why did you and Cassie stop talking? 'Cause it sounds like it was right after that."

"It was. That was the last time I saw her. We went from daily visits, sometimes several per day, to nothing at all. For what, the past two months now? It hasn't been for lack of trying."

But you could've tried harder, a voice inside her castigated and Patty's eyes began to glisten.

Sid leaned in, addressing her in a soft, pastoral voice. "You haven't seen your friend for the last time, Miss Brewster. I'm certain of that. But we are going to need your help." He opened his palms and Patty instinctively placed her hands in his, tears beginning to well in the corners of her eyes. "I'm going to share something with you, Patty. Something that may be hard to hear. But it's really important that you trust me. Can you do that?"

Patty slowly pulled her hands from Sid's and wiped her eyes, nodding. "Yes."

"Is there someplace we can go that's a little quieter? I'd like to show you something."

"There's my office right there, in the back room?" She pointed toward the beaded curtain, behind which was a small space barely separated from the café's dining space.

"Anywhere else?" Ressler asked, unsure if what he knew Sid was proposing was the right way to approach this, but willing to give anything a shot right about now. "Do you live nearby, Miss Brewster?"

Blowing her nose, Patty nodded. "I own this building. My flat is right above us."

) (

They were met at the top of the stairs by a small ivory-colored dog with a face so dark and flat it appeared to be almost pushed-in. Its eyes were adorably oversized, to the point of being Disney-esque, and they sparkled with joy as its whole body wriggled with excitement, a long, silken tail curled over its back and wagging enthusiastically.

Sid bent down with a pained grunt and gave it a cuddle.

Ressler walked straight past, but the dog turned and followed him, weaving in and out of his stride.

"Guess I'm chopped liver, then," Sid exclaimed as he rose from his kneeling stance with an inadvertent groan.

"If you were chopped liver," Ressler argued, "He'd still be all over you, my friend."

"She," Patty corrected him. "She's a girl, not a boy."

The dog gave her a soft, gentle bark, followed by a contented sigh as she jumped into Patty's arms. "She's a little lion with a joyful spirit, for sure."

Doug said nothing, staring past them as Sid laid his attaché case on the kitchen counter and retrieved a photo from a folder stuffed with notes. Ressler's stare was cold, unblinking. A silent *'are you sure we should do this'* kind of look.

Beyond Patty's peripheral vision, Sid mouthed the words for

Doug to just let him do his thing. He was shaking his head in frustration until Ressler surrendered and Patty turned Sid's way to see what it was that she was missing.

"Miss Brewster, I'm going to show you a photograph, and I want you to tell me if it means anything to you."

Sidling onto the edge of a kitchen stool, Patty tentatively agreed as she mentally prepared herself for something less than pleasant.

She wasn't wrong.

On the counter in front of her Sid placed the photo of a crudely crafted Halloween card. In a dramatic but simple move he'd perfected over the years, he rotated it slowly until it was correctly facing her. "Do you recognize this by chance, Miss Brewster?"

Patty scanned the photo without touching it, pinning her hands beneath her legs. Emblazoned across the top were the words, 'From your secret pal.' At the bottom left was a rhyme which began, "I feel it in my bones…' Although it appeared to have been drawn by a child, something about the image oozed a dark, negative vibe. Patty grimaced, a sour taste rising in her mouth. She averted her eyes, back to Detective Younger.

"No. Should I?"

Now Sid laid a second photo atop the first. This one showed the inside of the card and Patty gasped the instant she saw it.

"What is this? Why does it have Cassie's name in it…?"

"We found it this past Monday—" Sid began to answer but Ressler steamrolled over him.

"—It was left for us at a murder scene. A woman by the name of Sheila McCabe was stabbed to death in her home as her young daughter slept in the next room. This card was left by her killer."

Patty froze, every muscle tensing. Despite her heart instantly jumping to nearly double its previous rate, her face paled as if bloodless.

"This—" She began to speak but her mouth had gone dry. A

blank, faraway stare had frozen upon her face as Sid Younger opened and closed cupboards until he found where she kept the glasses. She took only a sip of the water he poured, enough to wet her lips. "This card...*with Cassie's name in it*...was left by a killer at a murder scene?"

"I'm afraid so," Sid confirmed. "Which is why we would like to find her. And quickly."

Patty nodded her head, numb and a little dazed.

"When Ms. Kennedy came to us in July—when she claimed to have had a vision about Veronica Roe and her daughter—the address she gave us was fake," Ressler stated dispassionately.

Patty Brewster just stared at him as if he'd just recited a passage in Latin. Or perhaps sprouted a second head.

"What my partner's trying to say," Sid intervened, "is that we don't have the correct address on file. It could be a clerical error as easily as anything. That's why we came to you, Miss Brewster. Cassie had mentioned both you and the café when she and I spoke, and we're hoping you wouldn't mind showing us where she lives?"

) (

Joe on the second floor buzzed them in. Peering from behind his door cracked open, he studied the detectives as they accompanied Patty to the third floor.

"Did you touch this handle?" Sid asked as he stood before the entry to Cassie's apartment. Standing slightly ajar in its splintered frame, the strike plate had been torn from the jamb and now lay feet away where the living room transitioned to a small kitchenette.

Patty didn't know how to answer that question. "I—um—well, yes, of course. I come here all the time."

"But not in the last two months," Ressler qualified.

"No, that's right."

"Any old prints would be long gone, given that Cassie would've touched that handle every day. The question is, did you touch it Sunday when you came over to check on her?"

Patty stared off into the memory, her tongue playing over her lips as she went back over the scene in her mind. "I—uh—no, I don't think I did."

"You don't *think*, or you *didn't*?" Ressler insisted.

"I was scared for her. And Bella was crying inside. So I pounded on the door and remember it just opening. I didn't have to use the handle, the lock was already busted. I just pushed it open like this."

She reached between the two men and pressed the center of the door. With a grating creak it swung slowly open, exposing them to the ammonia smell of old urine and vomit. All three squinted and flinched away. Sid covered his nose and mouth with the crook of his elbow, peering cautiously over the sleeve of his blazer as he took the lead and entered.

The apartment was alive with flies.

Hundreds of them. Maybe thousands. They swarmed around stale vomit and a half-dozen mounds of feces, a sound like an unfettered electrical current thrumming through their ears.

Ressler shook his head in disbelief. Following Sid's lead, he buried his nose in his jacket sleeve.

"You told the officer about this when you called Sunday?" Sid's question was so muffled it was barely audible above the droning buzz.

"I—don't know…it wasn't like this." Patty tried not to retch.

"The door wasn't busted?" This from Ressler.

"No. Uh—I mean…yes, it was. The place smelled like pee. But I don't remember feces. Or vomit." The smell as she strode deeper into the apartment only worsened and she he hacked and dry-spat, swatting at flies that divebombed her face to light upon her mouth and eyes. "I don't recall if I told the officer about the door."

Sid seemed unconcerned whether she did or didn't. He threw

open the windows in the bay that overlooked the park. A gentle breeze ushered in fresh air and a dozen flies or more departed. Ressler and Patty joined him, and together they opened every window in every room until the stench was sufficiently diluted that they could breathe without the sensation of their lungs burning. More flies buzzed away. Only a diehard few hundred remained and they mostly left the three of them in peace, favoring instead the random piles of shit and vomit which they regurgitated with their own bile before sucking it back up into their straw-like mouths.

"There's nothing here." Ressler swatted a pair of flies from his hair. "Unless Siobhan's team can find something."

"Well, we need prints anyway. That doorknob, for a start." Sid side-stepped a pile of vomit en route to the phone perched on a table at the end of the couch, and a cloud of flies jittered in unison. "I'll make the call."

"Wait. What about this?" Dangling comically by its ankle in Patty Brewster's left hand was a paper cutout of a skeleton.

Doug Ressler approached her, never taking his eyes off the floor as he navigated around piles that seemed to move as if alive.

"New shoes," he muttered to explain the fastidiousness as he slapped a fly from his face. "That's not your friend's?"

"No way," Patty answered. "Me? I adore Halloween. But Cassie hated—" She cut herself short, an abrupt change of expression upon realizing that she'd just referred to her friend in the past tense. She cleared her throat and wet her lips. "—Cassie *hates* Halloween. Now that she's told me about what happened in her childhood, I can understand why. After what she went through— losing her parents, the abuse, being locked in a closet like they were—she's had more than enough horror for a lifetime."

"Put it down," Ressler demanded, his voice as monotone as it was authoritarian, something you'd expect from a bomb disposal expert if you just picked up a live grenade. "Slowly and carefully.

I need to mark where you just touched it."

She laid it on the counter with the greatest care and Ressler ensured that Sid corroborated that her left thumb and forefinger had gripped the cutout by the skeleton's right foot and ankle.

"Did you touch it anywhere else?"

"I'm sorry. I—"

Ressler gestured for her to stop talking. "Just tell me if you touched it anywhere else."

"No, just the ankle. It was lying here. Under her mail."

"We're gonna need that dusted, and the mail, too. Not just the doorknob."

"I'm on it." Sid was already dialing the police HQ in Mission Bay. "Siobhan Jacobs, please. This is detective Sidney Younger. I'm at a live crime scene."

It was only a matter of moments before Jacobs picked up. *"You found her...?"* she asked, praying for a positive response.

"Afraid not. But we were right about the café. Doug and I are with Miss Brewster as we speak. I'm actually calling you from Cassie Kennedy's apartment. I'm afraid we have a live crime scene, and we need your folks down here."

Siobhan was silent as she took a moment to process this. *"Okay, sure. Yeah, of course, I mean. What's the address?"*

Sid covered the mouthpiece with the palm of his hand as he asked Patty for the house number. To Jacobs he then repeated: "One-twenty-two, Lyon Street." When Siobhan did not respond, he stated it again. "You get that?"

"You're shitting me, right?"

"What's the matter?"

"Sid, is her apartment on the third floor? It was a statement more than a question.

"Yes, but how did y—"

"God-DAMN-it. He told us, Sid... in the puzzle. Christ! It was there all along. One-two-two, in the lower left corner. Followed by a three."

Sid held the phone to his chest as he waggled his finger toward his attaché case, which Ressler brought to him. He snatched the photo of the wordsearch from the case folder, and there it was, at the bottom. And just above it was the letter **L**. Running diagonally down to the right were an **I, O**, and **N**.

LION.

"It's misspelled, but that's because he's playing us. He knows damn well how to spell it. Just like he knows how to spell the name of the newspaper and—" Siobhan Jacobs voice cracked *"—he fucking handed it to us, Sid. 122, apartment 3, Lyon Street. It's. Right. Goddamned. There. How did I miss it?"*

The phone line crinkled in Sid's ear, a static like the scrunching of tissue paper when you're keen to open a gift.

"We all missed it Siobhan. We *all* missed it. Let's just get your guys out here and see if we can make up for lost time." Covering the mouthpiece, he turned his back on Patricia Brewster. In a near-whisper he added: "And Siobhan? Given the rest of the crime scene, I gotta say, things aren't looking too hopeful down here."

) (

"They're on their way," Sid told them as he hung up the phone, unconsciously rubbing his face as if it would wipe away his emotional fatigue. "There's not a lot more we can do until we see what the forensic guys come up with. Unless, Miss Brewster, you can think of anything else that might help us find your friend?"

Patty shook her head. Her eyes weary. She asked Doug Ressler if it was okay that she light a cigarette and he gave her a nod, pulling his own pack of Marlboros from his jacket's inner pocket. But with her hand visibly trembling, Patty struggled to get the flame to take, so Ressler snapped open his Zippo and lit it for her.

"See, he's not as much of an ass as he first seems," Sid confided, giving her a wink.

"That's right," Ressler declared and lit his Marlboro. "Usually I'm much *more* of one." His expression was wooden, and Patty averted her eyes. Then a sly half-smile crept onto his face; his voice softened. "We *are* going to find her, Miss Brewster."

It was the first time Sid could recall Ressler actually making a promise of that kind. Not only did he never do it, he'd chastised Sid for making that very mistake in the early days of their partnership, all those years ago. *Your mouth's writing checks your actions might not be able to honor*, he'd told his new partner when Sid had said much the same thing on what was only their third case together at the time. *Sometimes, despite our best efforts, it just doesn't work out that way. Then you've only set them up for even greater heartbreak.* And he was right: that had been a case of a missing child, and when the result wasn't what Sid claimed it would be, Ressler had Sid go it alone when it came time to breaking the news to the boy's parents. Looking that young couple in the eye and telling them that their three-year-old son was never coming home was the hardest thing Sid had ever done.

And he never made the mistake again.

Now he shot Doug a look, but Ressler only looked away.

"What else can I do to help make that true?" Patty asked, her trembling hands slowly steadying.

"Anything at all," Ressler advised. "It doesn't matter how silly or unimportant it might seem. If it comes to mind, just lay it on us. We'd rather more than we need than not enough."

) (

"She gets blackouts sometimes. Loses track of hours. Sometimes days. The first time I called you was right after she had the vision about Hannah Wilson. She asked me to stay with Bella for the night because she needed to check something for herself. She said it would verify to her if the vision was true. Of course, I said yes.

But then she ended up not coming back home for three days."

"Where was she?" Sid asked. "Did she tell you?"

Patty paused, making sure she relayed it correctly. "First, she said she had this inexplicable pull to go to the Presidio. That was the last she remembered until she found herself walking home."

"Walking? Cassie doesn't own a car?"

"She does." Patty moved to the Bay window, leapfrogging over a pile of dried feces squirming with translucent wings, and looked to the street below. "Hey! I don't see it! That's good news, right?" She spun around, and for the first time in the past hour, a semblance of hope was alight in her eyes. "If it's not here, doesn't that mean she probably drove off somewhere, and maybe this isn't some kind of abduction?"

It was a fair point, and as Sid busied himself with scribbling notes in his pad, Ressler chewed over the idea.

"It could be." He didn't have the heart to share the possibility that Cassie's abductor could just as easily have forced her into the car. "What kind of car is it, Miss Brewster?"

"A bug, you know, a VW Beetle."

"Color?" Sid asked, his pen poised.

"Tan, I think? She was never much of a clean freak or motor head, so it really was just something she used to scoot around town. Maybe it was a kind of dirty off-white? I'm not a hundred percent sure."

"Ahhh, I know the color you're talking about. Volkswagen calls it Toga White. To me it's always looked like the color of an old T-shirt that's been worn too much and is now more grey than it is white. I think your description is better. 'Dirty white' definitely nails it."

Sid had barely finished his sentence before Ressler was pressing Patty for more details. "You said she walked home?"

"From where? If you can remember, it could give us a place to start looking."

"I do, because it was crazy. Cassie told me she walked all the way home from Oakland."

Sid stopped writing and peered overtop his notepad. "Oakland? To Haight-Ashbury? Christ, that's a good fifteen miles. And she'd have to cross the Oakland Bay bridge by foot. And you say this was—" Sid checked his notes "—August?"

"That's correct, yes."

"Fifteen miles, over one of the busiest bridges—which has no pedestrian option, by the way—in blistering August heat? Why?"

"I think she left the bug at the Presidio, maybe?"

It didn't add up, and Ressler's eyes narrowed into a skeptical squint as he wrestled with the pieces of an incomplete puzzle. "Then how would she have gotten to Oakland in the first place...and why not make her way home by the same method?"

Patty shrugged. "I wondered the same thing. But when she came home that Sunday it was clear she'd walked it. Her feet were filthy, her shoes visibly worn from when I saw them just days before. And her car was missing., Next thing I know, it's parked back on the street again, just outside the building." Patty pointed to the spot Cassie normally gravitated to. "Right there."

Sid joined her at the window and craned to see the street below. There was an empty spot, three down from the building's front door. "How did she get it back, do you know?"

"I think maybe she called you guys, and one of your uniformed officers found it parked over at the Presidio?"

"Well," Ressler interjected, "we can check that, for sure. And the whole time she was away, Isabella was staying with you?"

"That's right. Well, I stayed with her. Here. In the apartment."

"I know she's only five, but I think maybe we should talk to her," Sid suggested, and Doug Ressler agreed. "She might be able to help us more than you'd think. You know what they say—out of the mouths of babes."

In response, Patty let out a nervous titter. But neither detective cracked a smile.

"Oh, you're not joking," she realized out loud.

"No. If it's alright with you, we'd love to meet with her. ASAP." Sid closed his notebook and tilted his head in the direction of the doorway. "How about this—you and I go get Bella while Detective Ressler waits for the Forensics team. Would that be okay?"

"Ummm...sure?" Furrows of confusion wrinkled Patty's brow, her eyes narrowing as she tried to grasp exactly what they were asking. "But I really don't see how Bella can help us. Not to mention, you've already met her, Detective. In my flat, just now."

Already heading for the door, Sid stopped in his tracks. His gaze sharpened, an expression of concentrated confusion. "Am I missing something? We met no one at your place but you, Miss Brewster."

"Yes, you did, actually" Patty insisted, bringing her hands together to express a small shape in the air roughly the size of a loaf of bread. "Isabella is Cassie's little Pekingese mix, Detective. Who did *you* think Bella was...?"

31

)(

ROSALIE SHERWOOD UNCLASPED her husband's dog tag from around her neck and bundled it into her fist. She held it tight to her bosom, her eyes wet. It felt hard for her to catch her breath. "It's all I have left of him."

Cassie understood her reticence. But she also understood that time was running out. "And you'll still have it, Rose. I promise you. On my life."

Never a truer word spoken, Cassie quipped to herself. *Because if this doesn't work, we're both going to die.*

"Softball," Rose revealed, answering Cassie's previous question. "I played softball in high school. Varsity. We went to State my senior year."

At last, the odds were tilting in their favor.

"That's fantastic, Rose. This should be a cakewalk for you, then. All we have to do is coordinate with one another audibly, so I know when you're going to toss it."

"I don't know, I mean—what if I miss…or what if you drop it? It's all I have left of my Bobby. And if the man sees it, he'll do something awful. To both of us. I've survived this long. I don't wan—"

"—I promise you, Rose, I won't drop it. I'm a good catch. Did I tell you I grew up with three brothers? And boys show you how to do stuff. Like play catch…and how to pick a lock. I can get us out of here, Rose. If I have those dog tags."

Silence.

A light jingle of the tag against its metal beaded chain.

The sound of Rosie's uncertain breaths.

"H-How…do you think we should do this?"

"You'll need to reach out of the bars in your door as far as you can. Then swing it in small circles, kind of like the way you'd wind up to a pitch in softball, only sideways. And I'll catch it."

"But you can't see it. How will you know when I throw it, or where it is so you don't miss it?"

"It's pitch black in here anyway, hun. I wouldn't see it even if we were facing each other. We'll count to three together. Okay? And when you release it, I'll be ready to grab it." Cassie extended both arms through the bars of her door, flexing her fingers in the air. "How far apart do you think we are?"

"I'm pretty sure we're two apart. There's one cell, the bad one, between us."

Cassie pulled her arms back in and felt for each wall in the dark. She touch the wall to her left by merely leaning that way. The same with her right. "My cell can't be more than five feet wide, if that. How big is yours?"

"Same," Rose replied. "I think. I'm not real tall, but I can almost touch both walls with my arms extended out to my sides."

"Is your door in the center of your cell, like mine?"

"Yes."

"So, if the pen between us is the same width, that means you're about eleven feet from me."

"Eleven?"

"Yes, we're each two-and-a-half feet from the edge of our pens, the one between us probably five feet wide. And let's say six inches for each wall. So, two walls between us makes another foot. So that's eleven, total. Do you agree?"

Rose did not reply.

"Rosie, I need us to agree on this. If it goes wrong, I want to know that we both agreed on everything."

"You just said it wasn't going to go bad. You promised. Now you're trying to cover your ass if it doesn't?"

"I just want us on the same page. How far is it from the pitcher's mound to home base in softball?"

"Forty-three feet."

"Okay, so this is a quarter of that. And you aren't going to throw it fast. Or hard. Just put a nice, gentle spin on it so that it's going around in a circle. That way it'll wrap itself around my hand. Does that make sense?"

Rose agreed that it did, but a lingering reluctance in her voice belied her words.

"Listen, hun. Have you ever tied a pair of sneakers together and tossed them over a phone wire?"

Rose hadn't.

"Well, again, when you grow up as the only girl in a family of boys, that's the kind of stupid stuff you learn. When you toss those sneakers, all that has to happen is for one of them to hit the wire. Once it does, the other one will wrap around it, since both shoes are tied together. Then they both end up whipping round and round that wire until there's no more shoelace left. *Et voila*, you've secured those suckers in a way that they're *never* coming undone. Not without someone getting up there with a ladder to unravel them. This is the same. The spin you put on that chain will make it wrap around my hand. You see? So, I don't even have to catch it, really. I just have to make contact with it. You—and physics—will do the rest."

That made sense to Rose. And as much as she didn't want to relinquish the only memento she had left of her beloved Robert, the alternative was worse.

Way worse.

She didn't have to ask what Robert would do. She already knew. When he received his draft notice in the mail her first thought was to get him to Canada. *Screw the government,* she'd said. *What do we owe them? Certainly not your life, Robert.*

And he'd thought about it. Genuinely thought about it. But in the end, he knew that if he didn't report to his induction center, they'd only choose another lottery number in his stead. And Robert couldn't imagine a life where someone else paid the price for his cowardice. So he went, and paid it himself.

The ultimate price.

If he were here right now, Rosie knew what he'd do. Without a shadow of doubt. Hell, he'd have already done it by now instead of dicking around, debating it in his head.

Rose gripped the chain and tag in her right hand and thrust her arm through the bars.

"Okay, let's do this."

"Do you need more time, Ro—"

"—No! Just do it. I'm gonna count to three, and then release."

"Release on three? Or after?" With both arms extended through the wood bars in her door, Cassie again flexed her fingers and wrists. It was so dark that she couldn't see them moving.

"Three, and then I'll release. Ready?"

Cassie breathed deeply. As did Rose. Together they exhaled in unison, and Cassie could hear the racing of her own pulse as it cycled through her ears.

"I'm ready."

"One," Rose counted and began to swing the chain clockwise. "Two." *Ten feet,* she told herself. *No. Wait. She said* eleven *feet.*

The chain spun a little faster, a modest *whoosh* of air playing upon her cheeks as Rosalie pressed her face to the door, looking in the direction of Cassie to achieve the correct follow-through.

"Three!" she announced and released the chain from her grip.

Spinning through the air, the jangling windchime sound grew as it came toward Cassie as if in slow motion. She splayed her fingers wide on both hands, creating as large a net as possible.

The air current kissed Cassie's wrist.

She felt the chain brush her left hand...

I've got it!

...and fast as a trap she clamped her fingers shut.

They closed on nothing but air.

The chain spun a full cycle around her wrist, a small tinny sound of metal upon metal passing before her in the dark as the tag spun past.

With a cry, Cassie snapped her right fist closed...

...and the chain snagged around her thumb.

"I've got it!" she screamed as the tag spun like that archetypal sneaker on that childhood overhead wire—

—but then spun free.

It ricocheted off the outside of the door with a clap, shooting toward the floor at an angle.

With her left hand she caught the tiniest loop of the tag's chain before it plummeted from reach.

Squeezing as tightly as possible, Cassie held on for dear life.

Literally.

She exhaled deeply, a sigh escaping her lips as relief flooded her senses, leaving her light-headed.

"I have it Rose..." she announced, the confirmation so quiet it was barely audible. *"...I have it."*

With the care of a surgeon she pulled her arm back through the bars, reminded of all the times she'd beaten her ham-fisted brothers at the electric board game, *Operation*, avoiding that infernal, nerve-shredding buzzer.

Shaking as a flood of adrenaline coursed through her system, she dropped to her knees in the dirt. Between her thumbs and forefingers, she gripped the dog tag of Robert Sherwood, feeling his name and blood type stamped in relief upon the metal.

And Cassie Kennedy sobbed.

Two cells away, Rosalie Sherwood also wept in relief.

She might actually be home soon...

) (

Bending the dog tag back and forth, it took most of the night for Cassie to rive it lengthwise. By the time it snapped in two, her thumbs were raw and bleeding. Come daybreak, the dried blood, now darkened to a near-black, had caked in the crevices of the stamped metal which served as the perfunctory summary of Robert Sherwood's life.

Two cells down, the voice of Robert's widow, twenty-one-year-old Rosalie, kept her company as Cassie fashioned the metal into thin pieces. Staying awake to share random stories of her late husband, Rose would sporadically prompt Cassie to ensure she was still awake.

"How's it coming over there?"

"It's taking a while, Rose." Raw, weeping lesions on her thumbs and the knuckles of her forefingers sang with pain. She blew on her left hand. Shook it. But this did nothing to lessen the pain. If not for the lack of a flame, she would have believed you had you told her that you were holding a Zippo lighter to her skin. "I have to take breaks. It gets too slippery with my blood. I hafta snap it just right, or I won't be able to use it."

Snap it.

Robert's dog tag.

The only keepsake Rose owned which had been with her husband when he died. Now it was being destroyed at the hand of an unseen stranger who the widow not only had to trust with her most prized possession, but with her life.

Feeling as though she wanted to throw up, Rose shook off the emotion by conjuring another image instead.

"Did I tell you about the time Bobby found a snapping turtle in the middle of the road?" The question was rhetorical, with Rose not waiting for an answer. "It was hot that day. *Really* hot. And somehow that turtle had gotten himself upside down. Its legs were barely moving—I think it was exhausted from trying to right itself but getting nowhere. Honestly? I think it was close to dying. So Bobby stops smack in the middle of the road, makes me get out, and leaves both doors wide open. Well, you can imagine, no one could drive past us in either direction. We have ourselves a nice long driveway through the trees, but that road before the turn is busy. So, before we know it, there are like six cars lined up, waiting to get past us. Bobby didn't care. He wasn't about to let that thing get run over, or worse, die slowly from the heat. So he picks that thing up and carries him through the woods, a good hundred yards to the lake. At first it was trying to bite him, and who could blame it? But Bobby held it with his elbows bent far out in a way that it couldn't. The funny thing is, it stopped trying after a minute or two. He said it could tell that he was trying to help it, not hurt it. And when Bobby slid that poor thing gently into our lake, he said it dived under for a second but then popped back up and looked at him. I swear, he said it just looked at him. He thinks it was the turtle's way of saying thank you.

"Well, by the time he gets back to the road, there are at least twenty cars lined up and honking to get by. I don't have my license yet and couldn't drive a stick shift, so I had to just smile and look silly all that time. But it was worth it, knowin' that it saved that turtle's life." For a moment, Rose was back on that road as the love of her life appear through the line of trees, a smile from ear to ear gracing his face. "He wouldn't even let a turtle die. But then he goes to Vietnam to shoot at people and be shot at. Go figure…"

Rose's voice trailed away and was quiet after that. As the first light of morning dispelled the darkness, numerous spears of heat shining through the wood slats of their doors, she silently cried.

In her own cell, Cassie inched her way to a dark corner unaffected by the light. With her pulse throbbing inside her blisters, she closed her eyes and succumbed to a sleep plagued by another vision she did not welcome…

)(

Trembling upon the dirt floor and pulling herself into a tight ball. She heard the bombs, smelled the gunpowder, witnessed a lush green jungle in a faraway place. Steadily, her heartrate climbed, her pulse cycling through her ears until it became a steady, rhythmic thrum.

She was alone, at first. Wading through a marshy tract ahead of a dense outcropping of palms and tropical trees. It could have been beautiful, had it not been terrifying. In her hands an automatic rifle jittered in her grip from muscles which now tensed beyond her control. Despite the searing heat and humidity of a sauna, she shivered with cold.

"*Bobby?*" it was a whisper-shout that would be heard no more than a few feet away.

When she received no response, Cassie inched forward, her boots sucking into the mud with every step. A *thwuckkk* sound marked her progress…and her location.

Something moving caught her eye, in the tree line to her two o'clock, and Cassie dropped into the swampy water. Holding her breath, she listened.

A rat swam by her foot, chirping as it leapt to a mound. It swiped its paws over its face to dry its whiskers, defecated in the mud, then scurried off through the reeds, their stalks swishing.

The silence returned. That tense, deadly silence. Once offering a respite from her worries, now it would forever be the harbinger of a fate so horrific you'd wish you'd never been born.

She lifted her chin from the murky water and peered through the tufts of rice, her pupils dilated and vision sharp.

Whatever the movement had been, it was either gone or more patient than she.

Pressing from the water in a one-handed pushup, she supported herself on the stock of her rifle, its butt planted in the mud. With one deep breath she rose to her knees, tucking the mud-encrusted rifle stock against her shoulder. She now slid her right foot beneath her and forward, planting her boot in the mud so that her leg was bent ninety-degrees at the knee. Resting her right elbow upon it, she held her index finger against the trigger, her breaths reduced to short, shallow wheezes. Eyeing down the length of the barrel, she swept the gunsight along the tree line.

Slowly. Oh-so-slowly. First right. Then left.

But she saw nothing.

No humanoid shapes. No motion.

"*Bobby*," she called out once more, this time the hushed shout was a little louder.

Again holding her breath, she waited, listening.

Only the gently swaying stalks of rice answered as the easy whisper of a breeze snaked through them.

Now rising with the guarded slowness of a sloth, she dared to stand. The action was barely noticeable. More than a minute passed before she was supporting her weight on both feet and trudging forward.

"Bobby..." This time, the soldier's name was spoken, not whispered. No one answered her. In the trees, nothing moved. She swallowed. Cleared her throat. Stood fully erect. "Bobby!"

Then came a sound—faint and garbled.

Cassie swung sharply to her left, her finger poised on the

trigger and ready to send a hell storm of 5.56mm rounds to her ten o'clock. With her heart pounding in her chest, she raked her M16 back and forth, expecting the thud of 7.62 x 39mm rounds into her torso.

But none came.

Instead, Cassie heard the muffled sound of choking.

At her feet, the stagnant brown of the rice paddy swirled with something dark and oily: a film that seemed to float atop the water's surface. It grew as the muted choking erupted into a coughing, guttural gasp.

Lying with his face half-buried in the mud was the mangled body of Private Robert M. Sherwood. His right leg had been torn in two just above the knee, the splintered femur poking through the mass of shredded muscle and skin where the inch-long AK-47 rounds had blown through it. His combat jacket was in tatters up and down his right side, the frayed edges seared. A twisting mass was pouring from it like molasses, and it took Cassie a moment to realize it was Robert's intestinal tract oozing from his body into the water where it bobbed along the surface.

She dropped to her knees and grabbed his hand. Though one eye was upon her, it was impossible to tell if Robert could actually see her. He tried to speak, but only thick clots of blood gurgled from his mouth. He coughed, and his throat cleared just enough to utter the name *Rose*.

"Rose?"

His one eye above the water line jittered in the direction of the sound of Cassie's voice. It blinked once for yes.

"Don't you worry about your girl. You'll be outta here and bangin' her brains out in 'Frisco before you know it. Lucky bastard. That's what you are, my friend."

Robert Sherwood's mouth twisted into the semblance of a smile, but his one eye blinked twice. He gripped Cassie's hand even harder, and she said nothing, only squeezing it in return.

Slowly, his eye closed—opened—closed again.

Trembled open.

"Hey," Cassie said in a hushed, soothing voice. "She'll be alright. I promise. I'll make sure she is."

Robert Sherwood blinked very slowly, just once, then gasped. His eye remained open as the last bit of air from his lungs released in a faint but steady sigh, a runnel of blood trickling from his gaping mouth.

Just beyond the trees, a line of fire strafed the ridge and Cassie ducked for cover. Exploding in a trail of billowing black and red clouds, moments later she was assaulted by the perverse and unmistakable odor of napalm—a combination of gasoline and laundry detergent—as the incendiary gel devoured a tract of jungle from one plateau to the next.

On the horizon, a wave of Hueys skimmed the treetops, a dozen-plus legs dangling from each side of the choppers' open bellies as mounted M60 machine guns scanned the ground.

Already growing tepid in hers, Cassie released Robert's hand and tore the soldier's dog tags from his neck. Rising onto unsteady feet, she blundered through the mud and water, flailing and waving frantically to be seen as a dozen choppers cantered to the ground. One-by-one, they took off just as quickly with their bellies full of battle-worn soldiers.

Stumbling into the makeshift Landing Zone just as the last of the helicopters was preparing to take flight, Cassie was torn from the dreamlike vision by a series of terror-stricken screams…

32

)(

BELLA IS CASSIE'S Pekingese dog? Are you sure?" Fascinated, Siobhan Jacobs was trying to process how this fit into everything else. Somewhere in the back of her mind a tiny bell had begun to ring. Where it was, and what it meant, she did not yet know. But that bell invariably meant she was getting close to a breakthrough. "Is it possible you got it wrong?"

Perched on the corner of his desk with his arms crossed over his chest, Sid Younger shook his head.

"No way. Not only is it in my notes, but I *remember* it. When she reported seeing the disappearance of little Lyndsey Roe in a vision, she told me how important it was for her to help because she also had a daughter. A five-year-old. Here, look…" Sid tossed his interview notes to Jacobs and there it was, plain as day. "It took me awhile to get her trust back after the whole Ressler debacle. I really had to take the softly-softly approach to get her to just open up a little. Honestly? I'm surprised she was willing to talk to me at all after the way Doug berated her. Maybe she thought she legally had to, or something. I dunno. But I assure you,

Cassandra Kennedy told me she had a daughter."

"So, why lie?"

"She's a nutjob," Ressler answered Jacobs. "That's why. Just like I called it, back in July."

"I don't buy it," Siobhan disagreed.

"Nope. Neither do I." Sid slid from the corner of his desk and began combing through his files, digging through a pile of papers. "But something isn't right." He grabbed the Gemini Halloween card in its clear protective evidence bag and studied it, squinting, pulling it far away, then so close his nose all but touched it.

"*Something* isn't right, Sid? Just *some*thing? Brother, there's not *one damn thing* that's right about this case." Ressler sidled up to him and snatched the evidence bag from his hand. "I mean, just look at this shit. A hand-drawn motherfuckin' Halloween card. Is this for real?"

"He's an angry, psychotic narcissist," Siobhan Jacobs admitted. "A thrill seeker. He wants us to know he's smarter than us. And leaving clues like the wordsearch, and that card you're holding, not only massages his own ego but makes it more exciting."

"The thrill of the chase," Sid reflected out loud as he studied the card in Ressler's hands.

"Yes," Siobhan confirmed. "As for the childish manner with which he goes about achieving those goals, like I've noted before, the chances are high that we're dealing with a man who's suffered intense physical, emotional or even sexual abuse as a child. Most likely prolonged abuse over a long period of time. And when that happens, the natural development of our social coping mechanisms is disrupted. They might even fragment, dissociating from a reality they can no longer bear. As a result, two things may happen: First, the individual could display an increased risk of violence. Second, a small part of the psyche could remain rooted in the maturity level of the age at which the child suffered such abuse. In the worst possible cases, where fragmentation comes into play, an individual's emotional development may simply cease altogether. In that case, although incredibly rare, they will create alter egos to deal with an unbearable reality."

"So, we're dealing with an angry little boy in a grown man's body, throwing temper tantrums," Ressler quipped.

"In a manner of speaking," Jacobs answered. "Grossly oversimplified, but if that makes it easier for you to deal with this, then yes. That's kind of correct."

"I get all that," Sid acknowledged. "But we're still missing something. In the wordsearch, he not only gave us a deadline, but the actual address of Sheila McCabe."

Siobhan shrank in her seat, unable to hold Sid's gaze. Her eyes darted to the floor, the walls, anywhere but his face as the weight of that failure pressed down upon her like an anvil atop her chest. That one missed clue would forever be a silent rebuke that would humble her more than she would ever let on.

She swallowed hard, her mouth dry as cotton, believing that Sheila McCabe's little girl would still have a mother if only she'd spotted the clue in time.

She reached for her glass of water on Sid's desk and in her haste, spilled some.

"Alright, Sid," Doug Ressler reprimanded, spotting the flutter in Siobhan's hands. He tossed the Halloween card on Sid's desk. "We *all* missed that clue. It's not her fault."

"But he's right, Doug. I *shouldn't* have missed it."

"And I shouldn't be jacking off to Penthouse centerfolds. But hey, none of us is perfect. You're gonna make more mistakes. I'm gonna keep on getting my rocks off. What can I say? Welcome to being human, Jacobs."

Sid rolled his eyes. But Siobhan laughed, almost spitting out her water. A tiny drop fell from one nostril as she choked it back and swallowed.

"Alright, kiddies. Let's not hang out in the wading pool but dive into the deep end. What are we missing *this time?* That's all I'm trying to say." Sid patted Siobhan's knee, shooting an awkward smile her way. "If this guy's an immature narcissist who thinks we're all dumb as a box of rocks—*and* he gets off on the thrill that we could catch him any moment—then there has to be something we aren't seeing. Either in this card or back in the wordsearch."

"I agree with you, Sid." Jacobs patted the back of his hand which was on her knee and stood to loom over both pieces of evidence. "These are sexually motivated crimes. Not only does he get off on them emotionally, but he literally gets off on them physically, as evidenced by the semen we found mixed with the blood in Sheila McCabe's living room. He's not going to stop until we stop him. And it's only gonna escalate—either in frequency or brutality, or both."

Her eyes set upon the phrase **HELP ME** running diagonally down the left bottom quadrant of the wordsearch. And then the word **HELP**, which appeared twice more, each interconnected and adjacent to the plea, **STOP ME**.

"He needs us to be close. Otherwise, it loses its intensity." She turned to Ressler. "I'm not being funny here Doug, but when you masturbate, how often do you do it to the same centerfold?"

Taken aback by the bluntness of the question, Douglas Ressler actually blushed.

"Are you serious?"

"I am. *Please.* Be honest. The life of Cassie Kennedy could depend on it."

Slightly embarrassed, and suddenly more timid than either Siobhan or Sid had ever seen him, Doug sheepishly admitted: "I don't know. A couple times, maybe?"

"Then what," Jacobs pressed. "What do you do the next time?"

"Find something else—another spread, most likely?"

"And why? Honestly."

Growing pinker by the minute, Doug Ressler literally shrank

into himself. "It loses its luster, I guess? Can we please stop talking about this now?"

"You brought it up, big fella," Sid scoffed. But Siobhan Jacobs wasn't laughing.

"That's right," she said, talking aloud to herself more than she was talking to either detective. "You don't find it quite as enticing anymore. You need something fresh, exciting, so that it feels as good as you need it to. Our perp is the same, don'tcha see?" She tapped the wordsearch sealed in plastic. "Sid is one-hundred percent right—there has to be a clue in here somewhere; something to reveal where his next kill is…and when. Otherwise, it's just not gonna get his rocks off the way he needs it to."

She tilted her head. First one way, then the other.

"What's this?"

Siobhan traced her nail under a word in the puzzle.

Planting his palms on the desk, Sid leaned down to see what she was drawing their attention to. "Wolf? Yeah, we saw that last week. before the McCabe murder. Remember?"

"Oh, I remember," she assured him. "But spell it out backwards for me now."

"F-L-O-W. Like, 'go with the flow,' maybe?"

Siobhan shook her head and tapped two more letters after that. "Now read it again, Sid, including these two."

"F-L-O-W-E-R."

Jacobs nodded. "When you see it the way you naturally would, it reads 'Wolf.' Look at it through a different lens, however, and it reads 'Flower.' Talk about opposites: Big and scary with an inclination towards violence one way; soft and fragile, even beautiful, the other."

Now the words were jumping of the page at her as if they'd been typed in a different color ink.

"Oh, God." She ran her fingertip along the line immediately above this. Then again at the very top. "Jesus Christ. Guys, I think

I might know who our guy is…"

) (

"Just spit it out for Christ's sake!" It was the third time in as many days that Ressler had badgered Jacobs about her off-the-cuff remark. This time, he all but demanded an answer.

"No, Doug. I told you, it's only a hunch. And if I'm wrong—and I could very well be—that error could get Cassie Kennedy killed. I've already failed Sheila McCabe. Believe you me. I'm not gonna let you corner me and we end up failing Cassie as well."

"But if you're actually right?"

"Then we're one step—one big step—closer to drawing this Hell to a close. But don't you think we should be focusing on where *Cassie* might be? What if she's still alive, Ressler? It's been a week now since she went missing…"

"Sid's working on that. My job is to find this piece of shit who took her and put him away. You could help—"

"—And if I'm speaking out of turn, it would not only be *un*helpful, it could actually hinder our case by steering us in the wrong direction and wasting more time, a resource we have precious little of right now." Jacobs was shaking her head in frustration, closing off her stance.

Defensive body language: Activated.

"God! I wish I hadn't just blurted it out like that. I'm sorry. Genuinely. Okay? It was unprofessional of me to say anything before I had the information to back it up. But please, let me work this out. If I find anything at all to back up my theory, even the slightest, of course I'll share it with you and Sid immediately."

Unconsciously mirroring her guarded manner, now Ressler crossed his arms over his chest. Realizing her own affectation reflected in his, Siobhan relaxed her posture and shook out her vexation with a deep, cleansing breath.

"Look, Doug. We're on the same team. One thing that can help me narrow down whether my idea is right or wrong is knowing what you learned about Solomon Albrighton. According to Patricia Brewster, that's the name of Cassie's brother, correct?"

"One of them, apparently. And we're still working on that. It takes time."

Siobhan eased her sullen frown into a hint of a smile. "I know it does. Are the Pennsylvania State Police offering any assistance?"

"The Cambria County Sheriff's Department. And yes. They assure me they have no record of a Solomon Albrighton having been incarcerated."

"But according to Patricia, Cassie admitted that her brother had attacked their uncle, who was molesting them… He went to juvie. So there'd have to be a record. Even if it were publicly expunged."

"Not this time, there isn't," Sid interjected. "If it's even true. Miss Brewster could have heard it wrong. Maybe his name, or the fact that he even went to juvie. Or…it could all be a figment of someone's imagination."

"Like Cassie's husband, the elusive William Kennedy," Ressler divulged. "We've spoken with NASA as well as Mr. Kennedy's employer, International-something-or-other in San José. And neither one has a record of a Bill or William Kennedy. According to them both, he's a ghost."

) (

"Take a look at this," Sid hollered to Jacobs and Ressler, hunched over the Halloween card on his desk and studying it so intently that he barely blinked. "I want you to focus on how he signed his alias: Gemini." He waited until both Siobhan and Ressler were peeking over his shoulder before he slowly rotated the card ninety degrees clockwise. "Now tell me what you see."

"Wait, does that letter 'M' look right to you?" Siobhan Jacobs tilted her head, paused, then twisted her neck to revert to the original perspective. Viewed this way, as they had been doing since they first discovered the card, it appeared to be a rounded-off 'M.' Now she untwisted and viewed it at Sid's rotated angle. No longer a letter, it became an unmistakable number 3.

"Do you see it, too? G-E-3-I-N-I," Sid spelled. He pulled the copy of the wordsearch next to it, tapping the center of it. "Now look here." Typed backwards, starting at the seventh letter from the right, was the same. "E31 is everywhere. We already spotted it up here in the wordsearch. Then it appears in the hand of the skeleton here." He slid the Halloween card across the desk. "And now we spot it in his very name, on both the card and the wordsearch."

"We already went over this, Sid." Ressler was unconcerned with going over the same old ground, keen to move forward, not backward.

"Yes, we did. But other than the creepy reference to 'a time to kill,' what purpose does it have? It *has* to have more meaning than that. This guy's too clever. So I think we should change the way we're approaching this case."

"Which is…?" Ressler asked.

"We've been spending all our time focusing on the question of *who* and getting nowhere fast. I figure if we focus on the *where* and *when*, the *who* will automatically follow. Those clues have to be here somewhere. If there's any chance of finding Cassie Kennedy before he adds her to his list of victims, I figure this tactic is our best shot."

Ressler wasn't so sure. As far as he was concerned, it was likely that the chick's head was already pickling in a jar on the psycho's mantlepiece somewhere.

But Siobhan Jacobs had to agree with Sid.

"We know he needs to give us all the answers in order to feel more powerful than we—to prove his intellectual superiority because we can't figure out who he is, even when he puts it right in front of our faces. So yeah, let's focus on the *where* and *when* instead."

"That's why I looked into this wordsearch some more," Sid told them as he circled his finger around a jumble of letters in the lower righthand corner. "I took it home and shared it with Mrs. Younger last night. That hunka burnin' love of mine adores puzzles. So, she gets all the credit for what I'm about to show you. 'Cause I think she's found the *when*."

He tapped a letter 'H' on the second row from the bottom of the wordsearch, five letters from the right. Then traced his finger slowly up. The letters 'A' and 'L' were above it. Now he moved his finger up one row but over to the right—a diagonal move—which revealed another 'L.' Then up another row and again back to the left, a second diagonal to a letter 'O.' Up again to a 'W,' an 'E' and another 'E.' Then immediately right to an 'N.'

"*Halloween*," he read out loud and pointed to the calendar on the wall behind his desk. "Today's the twenty-seventh. Halloween is this Friday. Coincidence?"

"No such thing with this guy," Siobhan Jacobs answered. On the outside, the psychiatrist appeared calm, if somewhat pensive. On the inside, her heart was racing, her fingertips starting to feel numb. All she could think of was the way she'd failed Sheila McCabe. And now here she was again, another déjà vu moment, with only four days to stop him from butchering Cassie Kennedy. She forced a polite smile, doing her best to shake it off. "He places a high value on meanings and interpretations in these cryptics he leaves behind for us. Numbers are powerful. There's no mistake that the chapter and verse he quoted is 3:1, the same date as Halloween. Tell Mrs. Younger she did a great job."

"She'll be thrilled to hear it."

"Hey, man," Ressler chided. "All those Sundays you wanted to go out and do something but all she wanted was to spend the day in her housecoat poring over the *Ledger's* puzzle page? Well, you'll never be able to say a word about it again. Enjoy doing nothing every Sunday for the rest of your life."

Sid smirked. Shrugged. "If it helps us find Cassie before this psycho guts her like a fish, I guess it's worth the next few hundred Sundays."

Siobhan slid her arm around his shoulder and patted him on the back. "Awww, Sid. You're one of the good ones, y'know?" She gave him a peck on his temple and ruffled his hair.

Sid blushed but smiled, secretly loving it.

"Well, there's more," he added as he straightened his necktie as if the act would erase the warm fuzzies and restore his professional persona. "We still have to find the *where*. So, knowing it has to be in these clues somewhere, I took the liberty of speaking to Morris Miller over at Costa Contra County, and he mailed me a copy of one of the photos they took of Hannah Wilson's convertible at Mount Diablo. I want you to look at the Halloween card, particularly how our guy writes the two letter 'I's in the name Gemini. Then I want you to look at this picture of the convertible's trunk."

Jacobs raised on her toes and craned to see around Ressler who was already examining the photo and card.

They both saw it, almost instantly.

Painted across the trunk in Hannah's blood were two slightly curved lines that looked like back-to-back parentheses in the wrong order. When placed next to the signature in the Halloween card, the resemblance to the way the Gemini wrote both letter 'I's was unmistakable.

"They sure as shit look the same to me," Ressler agreed. "Jacobs? What do you think?"

The head of Forensics stared at the photo, then the card. Then the photo once more, all the while nodding. "Sid, when did we say that car was found?"

Detective Younger flipped the photo over and looked on the back. Typed across a sticker printed with the insignia of the sheriff's department was:

AUGUST 23, 1969

"Two months ago, almost to the day."

Ressler stepped back. "Okay, but why scrawl two weird parentheses across the trunk?"

"They're not parentheses, Doug," Jacobs responded. "Those two curved lines are the astrological sign for Gemini. In ancient Babylonian culture they were gods known as the Great Twins, or Divine Twins. Pollux and Castor. Their Babylonian names mean 'the mighty king' and 'he who has risen from the underworld.'"

She exhaled uneasily, her nerves aflutter.

"He's been telling us he was responsible for Hannah's murder all along. That zodiac sign is his calling card. He took credit for killing Hannah long before we ever heard the name Gemini."

Her eyes skated from the Halloween card to the convertible to the wordsearch and back. They settled on the front of the card and the cutout paper skeleton with E3:1 in its right hand. The clue had already revealed an unsettling line about a "killing season" drawn from a biblical verse, along with a potential deadline hidden within the numbers. But with the clue surfacing repeatedly in everything linked to the case—especially now that it was embedded in the killer's actual alias—Jacobs couldn't shake the feeling that its full meaning had yet to be uncovered.

"Sid, you're the most versed on biblical studies. Do you happen to know who is attributed to authoring Ecclesiastes 3:1?"

"That would be King Solomon of Israel."

"Solomon!" Ressler repeated without hesitation. "Goddamn. Didn't Brewster, the chick who owns the café, say that was the name of one of Cassie's brothers?"

Digging through his notes, Sid concurred. "Another one called Joey apparently died as a child. The third, she said Cassie referred to only by his nickname: 'Catcher.'"

"I remember. Some bullshit about J.D. Salinger. Hey Siobhan, is it possible that either Solomon or this Catcher guy are Cassie Kennedy's twins?"

Deep in thought as she studied the documents spread across Sid's desk, the question went unheard as Siobhan's thoughts spun in a manic flurry of options and connectivity.

...Gemini; twins; young vulnerable wives; Solomon; Halloween; Ecclesiastes; Catcher; J.D. Salinger; Holden Caulfield, Salinger's unreliable narrator who abhors phoniness, and the duplicity he shuns being exhibited in his own nature...

"Except Solomon Albrighton doesn't seem to exist," Sid answered in her stead. "According to the Cambria County Sheriff over in western Pennsylvania, anyway. Not a juvie record to be found. No priors. Not even a birth certificate."

"Fine, then Solomon's a figment of someone's imagination. Forget about him." Ressler perched on the corner of the desk, crumpled his paper cup of coffee and tossed it across the room, landing a three-pointer in the wastebasket. "So we focus on this Catcher guy. But how do we find the cat, when all we have is a nickname?" The question was rhetorical, immediately answered by himself. "The only way is to study the hard facts. Like the prints we took at Kennedy's apartment."

Sid, like Jacobs, had become lost in a maze of thoughts.

Ressler glanced from one of his partners to the other. Waited. When neither replied, he roused Jacobs by nudging her with his foot. "Hey. I said, what's the word on those prints from Cassie's apartment?"

FOLLOWING PAGE:
Crime scene photo of
Hannah Wilson's Ford Galaxie
convertible, courtesy of the evidence
archives locker of the Contra Costa
County Sherriff's Department.

[Federal Bureau of Investigations
Case File 10-63; Document 10-63-4]

33

)(

THE SCREAMS CAME without pause, one on the heels of the other. So piercing were they in Cassie's ears, she expected to open her eyes to find that she and Rosie were somehow together in the same cell.

With the macabre image of Rose's husband still lingering in her mind, Cassie staggered to the door and clung to the bars as she pressed her face between. The intense stench of rot turned her stomach, rising in waves from the dirt corridor mottled with thick pools of congealed blood.

Two cells down, she could see that the door was wide open.

So *he* had to be in there with her.

No! No, no, no, no, no!

"Stop it!" Cassie shouted through the bars at the top of her lungs, desperate to be heard above Rose's screams. "Leave her alone! YOU HAVE TO STOP!"

But Rose's screams persisted.

"SOLOMON! I SAID STOP!"

A tearing sound.

Low, muffled growls; an indecent, almost bestial moan.

Then, as her brother overpowered the young widow, a shriek so agonizing Cassie had to clamp her hands over her ears.

God no, God no, God no!

A wave of adrenaline flooded over her, and Cassie found herself once again on the verge of drowning in the self-induced panic she had suffered so many times before. But those had been the result of dreams; visions; premonitions; hallucinations.

This time, it was really happening.

No no no nonononono!

What could she do—?

God, please help me!

Their plan had been simple: Cassie would split Robert's dog tag in two and use the pieces as a tensioner and rake to pick the padlock on her door. Her brothers had shown her how to do this with paper clips when she was young, and she had taken to it like a natural. Not only did she exhibit the necessary agility, her young, slight fingers had also been impressively sensitive to the process.

"Could give the Artful Dodger a run for his money, you could," her youngest brother, Catcher, had applauded in a cringeworthy Cockney accent. His class had been reading Dickens' *Oliver Twist* at the time and, unsurprisingly, Catcher had connected with the story on an intimate level. "Fagin should be so lucky to have a plucky lil' mite like you in his gang. Orphans, pickpockets and thieves, the lot o' ya!"

But that had been a lifetime ago. Her older fingers were less nimble now. The basic principle of the pick remained the same, however: hold light tension on the cylinder while raking a second piece of metal along the inner length of the keyway. If you did it just right, the top pins would tumble upward, the lock would snap open, and she and Rose would be one step closer to freedom.

But the two pieces she'd been fashioning from the dog tag weren't finished. She'd snapped it lengthwise, so each piece was narrow enough to fit the lock's keyway. But she'd only started to file them smooth by rubbing them against the brick and stone walls. Still coarse and uneven, they just weren't ready yet.

They were going to have to be.

In blistered and swollen fingers that felt as thick as they were unresponsive, Cassie snatched the pieces from the dirt. The one still attached to the ball chain necklace would've been the perfect tensioner with a little more time. But that was a luxury they no longer had. Solomon had come in the night.

And Rose's petrified screams were escalating to something beyond human.

With her heart jackhammering in her chest, Cassie bent the end of the chained piece to ninety-degrees, thrust her arms through the bars and fumbled for the lock. With the padlock lifted from the clasp, she jabbed the tensioner at the keyway's opening. Stretching to the extent of her reach, the makeshift tool's rough edges snagged against the outside of the barrel. Not only would it not slide in, she also nearly lost her grip and dropped it. Had it not been for the chain still attached to her wrist, it would have fallen to the ground and skittered across the corridor, forever beyond her reach...along with their one chance of escape.

Straining at this untenable angle, she tried again and again. But the metal sliver was just too rough, too uneven, and it refused to slide into the lock.

Realizing it was impossible to both maneuver her fingers and watch them at the same time, Cassie turned her head to the side. Staring away from the padlock into the void of the chamber beyond the first metal gate, she freed up an extra inch of reach.

Quivering like tissue paper streamers in a breeze, her fingers groped and plodded as she now worked blind, fumbling at the keyway. As numbing pins and needles had begun to crawl down her arms, the bent end of the tensioner suddenly slid into place.

Before it could slide back, she yanked on the chain around her wrist and the tensioner rotated toward her just a hair, enough to keep the upper pins from locking. Inserting the second piece of the dog tag into the keyway, Cassie held her breath and focused on the feeling in her fingertips as she slowly pulled the rake toward her, back again, then toward her once more.

At the top of the padlock's barrel a single pin tumbled upward. It was announced by a tiny click she felt rather than heard. With the tensioner still pulled taut, the pin held securely in place.

One down, five to go…

Reverberating from wall to wall, Rose's broken screams plateaued to a single, bloodcurdling cry. With tears streaming down her cheeks and shaking to the point of losing control, Cassie forced herself to pretend they did not exist as she continued to rake back and forth.

Two more pins clicked into place.

…c'mon, c'mon, c'mon…

Then another.

…two more to go…

She exhaled and took another deep breath, holding it as the ripe metallic stench filled her lungs.

One more pin popped upward.

…last one now…

She angled the end of rake toward the floor and the tip pressed against the final pin. With a minuscule pop as glorious as any sound she'd ever heard, the final pin rose up from the keyway.

Glorious sound, her inner voice repeated, realizing she had heard the pin lift away, not just felt it.

She heard it because Rose's screams had stopped.

One sharp twist of the chain and the tensioner turned, popping the padlock open. Wrenching it from its hasp, she tossed the lock to the ground. Putting all her weight against the hefty door, Cassie pushed it open with a strained heave and toppled into the hallway…

34

)(

THE PRINTS ON the handle, the one at the building's ground floor entrance, were unusable," Siobhan reported. "Too many people going in and out. But the door to Cassie's third-floor apartment? Only one print."

"A single print? I don't buy it," Ressler contradicted. "She lived there. There would be prints all over."

Jacobs waggled her finger. "My apologies. Many prints. One profile," she corrected. "The same with the stack of mail on the counter. And the paper skeleton cutout Miss Brewster found in the kitchen. All the same profile."

"Do we have a match?" Sid was flipping through his notes, hoping something would jump out at him. So far, nothing did.

"They've been on it almost two weeks. Nothing matches any of our ink cards from previous violent crimes. There are still a few left to compare, some outliers, but it's not looking good. What about Contra Costa County?" Siobhan asked. "Did they manage to pull any prints from Hannah Wilson's convertible? Or the payphone box at the scene? If so, we could make a comparison."

"I called Morris the minute Sid and me got back from Lyon Street," Ressler divulged. "He said there were prints, alright. But with the downpour they were having that night, nothing could be lifted. They're in the same boat as we are with our West Summerdale scene. A lot of mess, but nothing usable."

"So, we have our '*when*'—Halloween—just four days from now. But no prints means no name." Jacobs was pacing, staring at her feet as she summarized to herself out loud. "Which means we still have no '*who*.' And that means no home address, no workplace, and no way to narrow down the '*where*.'"

Still, she found it impossible to shake the feeling they were missing something. The answer had to be there, waiting for them to find. They may not have a name or a face, but they had behaviors, and that was Siobhan's forte. Considering everything she now knew about their guy, the likelihood that he'd left out the clues that proved his intellectual superiority was about the same as him simply walking into the station and turning himself in.

Which is to say, not very.

...Salinger...duplicity...Catcher in the Rye...

Siobhan leapt back from the table, her eyes wide. "Jesus Christ, his name is Holden!"

Staring in astonishment, Sid and Doug watched as she began pacing back and forth in tight rebounding passes before them.

"The main character in *Catcher in the Rye* is Holden Caulfield. He's a deeply disillusioned young man who finds adulthood, and pretty much the entire world, full of phonies. Cassie told her friend that her youngest brother was nicknamed Catcher, after J.D. Salinger's novel. That's because her brother's name is Holden, Holden Albrighton!" Her eyes were alight with excitement. "Just like Salinger's main character, the only world Holden has ever known has been one of pain and suffering and hypocritical two-faced phonies. Don't you see? Two faces—twins—just like Janus, the Roman god with two opposite faces. That's why he's taken the name Gemini."

With her heart pounding like a piston, Jacobs dialed her office.

"We need to get our prints verified by the Cambria County Sheriff's Department back in Pennsylvania," she told Sid as the phone rang in her ear. "If I'm right, they'll be a match for a Holden Albrighton. Sid, Do you think there's any chance their office has a tele-facsimile machine like ours?"

)(

3:42 PM / THURSDAY / OCT 30

Slack jawed and staring at the phone's handset as if he'd never seen one before, Sid called out to Ressler. His partner was at the coffee machine, engaged in an animated debate over the 49ers' 24-21 win over the Baltimore Colts the previous Sunday.

"Jesus, Nancy. Keep your skirt on," Doug moaned as he tossed the paper cup and propped himself against Sid Younger's desk. "What's so fucking urgent?"

"I just got off the phone with the Sheriff's Department over in western Pennsylvania, that's what. Christ, Ressler. It's a match. Siobhan was right."

He plunged down the phone's switchhook buttons, tapped them a few times, then listened for a tone before dialing Jacobs' office in the county building. Waiting for the connection never seemed so slow as each of the seven digits in her number clicked like little bones each time the dial spun back to its set point.

"You were right," he blurted out when Siobhan picked up, before she'd even finished saying hello. "No tele-facsimile at their end, so I had a copy of the prints airmailed."

A moment's pause as Jacobs replied, something which Doug Ressler could not hear.

"Yes. A full match. Holden Albrighton," Sid relayed to Siobhan as he looked at Ressler. "He blinded his uncle with a coat hanger in 1953 and was remanded to juvenile detention at the age of nine. He was released in '62 when he reached eighteen. No details of his whereabouts for the next five years. But in the spring of '67 his number came up in the draft and he was conscripted to the Army to serve his twelve in Vietnam. Holden was one of the lucky ones: he made it back home. But are you sitting? 'Cause I don't think you're gonna be ready for this…" Sid held the handset slightly away from his face to speak to both Ressler standing at his desk and Siobhan over the phone "…Holden Albrighton served in the First Cavalry. The same platoon as a young man by the name of Robert Sherwood."

Across the phone line, above the gentle hiss and static, Siobhan Jacobs audibly gasped then confirmed: "Sherwood, as in Rosalie Sherwood, the Gemini's first victim taken from Mount Diablo back in June."

"The same. Private Robert Sherwood was Rosalie's husband."

"Was?"

"Robert Sherwood was killed in action in Bong Son. One year to the day before Rosalie was taken."

As the line softly crackled, Jacobs withdrew to that place within herself where the rest of the questions yet unanswered jockeyed for her attention.

…Gemini…twins…Holden…Vietnam…Ecclesiastes 3:1…a dog named Bella who Cassie spoke of as if it were her daughter…

in Siobhan Jacobs' mind a spark ignited, and she hung up without saying a word.

)(

8:07 PM / THURSDAY / OCT 30

Bursting into their office, Jacobs' feet barely touched the floor as she bounded to Sid and Ressler's desks, dropping a receipt between them. It wafted slowly down to cover the file Ressler was studying.

"What's this?"

"I visited the Property Appraiser's office today. That piece of paper is the record of ownership of Cassie Kennedy's building on Lyon Street."

Sid snagged the paper from Ressler's desk and read it aloud: "Albrighton, Holden. Recorded deed registered July 8, 1968. It's why you had no record of a Cassie Kennedy in the city," Siobhan reminded them. "It's her brother's place."

"Cassie's brother owns the whole fucking building?" Ressler shook his head. "This is making no sense to me now."

"Did it ever?" Sid sniped, a forced chuckle masking the frustration he could no longer contain. "Because it sure as shit hasn't to me. Seven years chasing some of the sickest cats in this city, and this one takes the cake." He glanced at the industrial wall clock hanging cockeyed above the coffee machine, his eyes heavy with concern. Then at his own wristwatch. "Less than four hours before that woman's blood is on our hands. And I couldn't feel more useless right now."

The hum of the office was the only sound as this reality set in. They knew the *when*. They knew the *who*. But Cassie's fate depended upon them deciphering the *where* before hers became just the latest name in a growing list of the Gemini's sadistic kills.

The head of forensics dragged a chair from a nearby desk and sat alongside Sid, a black and white two-tone Mary Jane manically tapping the air. She swiped the folder Ressler was studying and began rifling through it. "We're missing something. Jesus. We have his name now, why can't we figure out where he took Cassie? He's smart, but he's also a creature of habit. He's got his ritual down pat by now, so you know it's gonna be where he takes all his victims. And we know for a fact that Sheila McCabe was deceased when he dragged her from her home. Which means wherever he goes, it needs to be close enough that he can get to it with relative ease, but far enough from the populous that he isn't seen carrying or dragging a body behind him."

Sid chewed on his lower lip as Doug Ressler stood and turned his back on them both, staring at the oversized map pinned to the wall with the location of each of the victims' homes and kill sites marked in red.

The farthest point north was Sausalito; the farthest south was also the farthest west—West Summerdale Street, near Clarendon Heights. Twenty-five miles away, as the crow flies. The farthest east was Mount Diablo, a good fifty miles away.

"Where he takes them could be anywhere. I mean, Christ. If we draw a triangle," Ressler rapped his knuckles on the map, "the center is over here, east of Oakland. Just look at the square miles of wilderness, mountains and wasteland." He began naming a random few while marking each with another knuckle-rap. "Lafeyette Reservoir. Sibley Volcanic Preserve. Redwoods Park. Rheem Valley. Any of them would be a match for what you're proposing, Siobhan, and—"

"—And they would all require a vehicle," she deduced as Ressler placed a finger to the tip of his nose.

Without saying a word, his partner snatched his leather-bound journal from his desk and flipped frantically until he found their interview with Cassie's friend two weeks earlier, café owner Patricia Brewster. With a thick black grease pencil in fingers that had begun to shake, he made three fat circles around a notation he'd jotted down about Cassie's car. He tossed the journal to Doug and Ressler read the passage aloud:

"VW Bug. Dirty white. Toga—that part is in parentheses and has a question mark next to it. What gives, Sidney? You don't trust your partner on car finishes?" He shook his head in mock disdain and continued reading. "The Presidio. Walked from Oakland.

Parks in front of the building."

Sid was already on the phone to Reagan, the staff sergeant, and reeling off the details he needed checked before Ressler had taken a breath. Within moments, a beat cop by the name of Repak was standing at attention before them.

"At ease, patrolman," Sid told him as he pumped two open palms in his direction. "This isn't the army. I'm looking for details about a—"

"—A Volkswagen Beetle, Toga white. Yes, sir," Repak beat him to it. "It was abandoned near the southern end of the Golden Gate. Lemme see…" Repak rifled through his report log. "…Yes, I remember now. Late on Sunday night, August the twenty-sixth, into the early hours of Monday morning the twenty-seventh. It's registered to a person by the name of—"

"—Holden Albrighton," Siobhan preempted, and Officer Repak blushed as she held his gaze.

"Um, yes ma'am. That's correct. A gentleman by the name of Holden Albrighton is the car's registered owner. The vehicle was collected the following day at our impound lot across the road."

"You said it was located the twenty-sixth of August?"

"Yes, ma'am."

"That lines up with the weekend Patricia Brewster claimed Cassie went missing the first time," Sid noted.

"And the same weekend Morris Miller got an anonymous call that led him to Hannah Wilson's decapitated body in the trunk of her Ford Galaxie convertible," Ressler threw into the mix.

"Is there a problem, sirs? Uh—ma'am—um, sirs?" Fidgeting with his report log, Repak's voice had grown timid as he stood among two of the department's most senior detectives and the head of the county's forensics.

Smiling as her bright green eyes held his, Siobhan Jacobs put him at ease. "No, Officer Repak. You've been very thorough. And helpful. Thank you."

"Anything else, ma'am? Sirs?"

Sid shook his head; Ressler had already turned his back and was again studying the wall map. In particular, the Presidio area.

Gazing over his shoulders at the same, Siobhan considered a sea of possibilities as she viewed the vast, mostly green area that made up the Golden Gate's southern tip. A mix of parks, beaches, woodland—and a sporadic few small, sparsely inhabited and winding roads—the Presidio was unlike the majority of the rest of San Francisco which was comprised of dense city blocks packed with businesses and residential buildings.

At once her eyes widened.

Leaping from her seat, she called out just before Repak disappeared around the corner. Waving him back, she bristled with anticipation as Sid and Doug looked on with curiosity.

"You said someone came to collect the car that same Monday?"

"Um, yes ma'am."

"By a woman? In her twenties…going by the name of Cassie Kennedy?"

Repak flipped through his report log. "Uh, no…ma'am. By a gentleman. It says here, the car's owner."

Douglas Ressler slammed his fist into the wall map. "Are you goddamn kidding me right now? He was *here*? In our fucking *station*?"

Tensing and confused, Repak's confirmation was barely a whisper. "Mr. Holden Albrighton picked up the car. Yes, sir."

Siobhan stepped between Repak and Ressler, drawing the young officer's attention solely upon her.

"You're not in trouble. We're just under the gun here, so to speak. Repak—" she eased closer, near enough that he could smell her perfume, and softened her stance "—do you happen to have a record of exactly where the VW was found at the Presidio?"

Nodding, his breaths uneven, Repak fumbled through the log, dropped it, picked it back up and shuffled through it once more.

He began to speak, stuttered. Cleared his throat.

"Yes, ma'am. It was located in the east parking lot off Merchant Road. First row, third space. We always document that so we—"

"Merchant Road," Sid interrupted. "That's over by the old military batteries. The artillery emplacements that used to be part of Fort Scott."

"Yes, sir," Repak confirmed. "That particular parking lot is a stone's throw from Battery Boutelle."

Doug Ressler froze. "Emplacements?"

"You've seen them," Sid assured. "Big concrete bunkers. Built into the cliffs overlooking Golden Gate Beach and Fort Point Rock. Those badass guns were designed to fire a sixty-pound shell seven miles or—" Sid cut himself short and jumped to his feet, his eyes wide. "Holy *shit*. Bunkers. Built into the cliff. Could it—?"

Now Siobhan Jacobs' voice fluttered, adrenaline coursing to every muscle until she felt incapable of standing still. "Repak, are you telling me that Holden Albrighton's VW was found next to Battery Boutelle…off Merchant Road…in the *east* parking lot…"

"Yes, ma'am?" he said, the importance lost on him.

"*Third* space… Row *one*?"

Puzzled, Repak merely nodded.

"East parking lot, space three, row one. East, three, one—" Her eyes grew wet as she jostled in place, barely able to contain herself and shifting her weight from one foot to the other. She unconsciously shook out her hands, her tingling skin flushing with goosebumps. "—E31."

35

)(

S MEARED WITH SHEILA McCabe's desiccated blood, Cassie pushed herself up from the ground and hobbled to her feet, shaking and gagging as the rancid scent of sweaty pennies filled her nose. She swiped the back of her hand across her mouth and the earthen taste of Sheila's moldering blood permeated her tastebuds.

"Solomon!"

Her brother's name echoed hollow through the chamber. It faded into silence as Cassie crept forward, hyper-aware of the silence as her feet softly scuffed through the bloodstained dirt. With the chain of Robert Sherwood's dog tag still bound around her wrist, she inched past the cell to her immediate left—

the bad one, Rosie had called it

—where the door had been left ajar. Burying her nose and mouth in the crook of her elbow, she stifled her gag reflex as droning flies swarmed over butchered remains strewn throughout the six-by-four pen like the offcuts of an abattoir. Most were mutilated beyond recognition. But in one corner, a single human eye—clouded, colorless, and partially collapsed—stared at her with a milky white pupil. The eyelids around it were intact, but had shriveled so that their lashes appeared extraordinarily long. In another corner, a matted scalp caked with gelatinous clots lay upon a pile of what appeared to be human jaws, teeth and ears. Scattered all around a butcher's block table lay the torn and mangled scraps of feet, arms and legs whose bones poked from their raw, meaty ends. No longer resembling flesh, these were covered with a blanket of small white grains that appeared to be rice.

Except some of the rice was twitching.

Not rice, she realized, swallowing down the bile that rose to burn her esophagus and choke off her breath. *Fly eggs. Thousands of them. Small, squirming spawn preparing to hatch.*

Myriads already had, and the maggots that slid from their sheathes were hungrily burrowing into the rotting human meat upon which they fed.

Draped across the wall shared by Rose's cell, a rope of entrails had been hung. Coiled around the wrists of a dozen or more women's hands, they were a grotesque human garland. Perhaps most disturbing was the fact that each bore a wedding band on its third dainty finger: some modest and thin, others wide and glimmering faintly as the dying shafts of shifting light played one last time upon their precious metals and stones.

Now the bile in her throat resurfaced and yellow-green liquid spotted the dirt as Cassie held her knees. Still crouching and catching her breath, she spat and wiped the acid taste from her lips as her pulse throbbed fast and heavy in her ears.

For how long she stayed that way, she could not say.

It was the faint moan that roused her, so soft it was almost a sigh. Coming to her through the intermittent patches of light which alternately irradiated then darkened the block of eight cells, its quietness was more haunting than any of the curdling screams which had come before it.

"Rose?" Cassie whispered...then waited. When Rosalie did not respond, she crept closer. Like the cell between them, Rose's door was also unlocked and open.

"Rose..."

A gurgling sound. A low, guttural hiss like the air escaping a punctured tire.

"Rosie."

Cassie's heartbeat galloped at such a pace and ferocity that it was painful, every manic beat a heavyweight boxer's jab to her ribcage. Except, from the inside out.

"Rose, hun. It worked. I'm out..." She swallowed back her fear and asked the one question she wasn't sure she really wanted the answer to: "...Where is he?"

When Rosalie did not reply, Cassie took one final step toward her fellow captive's door—

) (

9:39 PM / THURSDAY / OCT 30

"Jesus H. Christ, you gotta be shittin' me." A skeptical Doug Ressler repeatedly shook his head in response to Siobhan's theory about the mental condition of Holden Albrighton. Still, he floored the accelerator, the rear tires of his Ford Custom 500 squealing as they laid down smoky black lines across the asphalt. He reached out his window and planted the magnetic cherry on its roof as the car fishtailed into traffic, the reflector spinning within the red light so that it pulsed brightly against the dusky buildings.

Sid Younger tightened and buckled his seatbelt, bracing himself as they tore through their second red light. After sliding across the rear bench seat and slamming into the driver's side door panel, Siobhan Jacobs did the same. Her only brace was the driver's seat in front of her, and she grabbed onto it, her knees pressing into the seatback. They punched into the small of Ressler's back, and he elbowed them away with his right arm.

"No way that's for real," he shouted at the rearview mirror, the comment directed at Jacobs behind him. "Fugue state? What the fuck does that even mean?"

"I've heard of it," Sid shouted over the whine of the siren, coming to Jacobs' defense. "Haven't you seen that crazy film starring Joanne Woodward? It was based on a book written by two psychologists."

"Corbett Thigpen and Hervey Cleckley," Siobhan interjected. "And yes, Sid is correct. It's a very real disorder."

"It's bullshit, is what it is." Ressler swung the steering wheel sharply to the right, cutting across traffic onto Van Ness Avenue. Both Sid and Siobhan were pitched to the left. Neither complained: the analog clock set into the dash of Ressler's Ford now read 9:43.

Two hours and seventeen minutes, Sid noted but said nothing. He didn't have to. The others were all too aware.

"At the conference I told you about earlier, the one where the FBI shared their research on Ed Gein and others? One of the medical keynote speakers was a psychiatrist by the name of Cornelia Wilbur." Siobhan leaned forward, speaking loudly to be heard above the wail of the siren. "Dr. Wilbur's a highly respected psychoanalyst. She shared her account of treating a patient with a severe variant of this same diagnosis for eleven years. All the way up to '65. The reality is, Doug, that you may not like hearing about stuff like this. But it doesn't matter if you feel comfortable around it. It's out there. It's fact. And it's documented."

"And if you're wrong?"

Jacobs didn't want to think about that. Her conclusion was the only one that made any sense. And the only one that fit all the clues the Gemini had left. She took in a shaky, uneven breath.

"With only two hours until midnight, I pray for Cassie Kennedy's sake that I'm not."

) (

The wail from Rose's cell was so haunting, the first—the only—instinct Cassie had was to run; to just get out of here. Save herself, find some help, then come back with police and ambulances and flashing lights and men in uniforms who would protect them.

With panic burning in her chest like a red hot poker, she turned back from Rose's door. Behind her, the chain-link gate to the block of eight cells was ajar, its padlock lying on the ground, its shackle open. She could just bolt through the barrier, slam the gate shut, lock it, and sprint across the chamber. Solomon had the key, but it might just buy her enough of a head start to get away.

Thirty-one steps in total, she reminded herself. *Only a hundred feet across the antechamber, then a third and final door to freedom.*

But if that last barrier was locked it didn't matter how much of a head start she had: Solomon would be on her in seconds, and with nowhere left for her to run. On the other hand, the chain-link gate was unlocked. So, wasn't there a chance he'd left the last gateway unsecured too?

Stay and help Rose...or go save herself, but come back with real help.

It was a literal life-or-death roll of the dice.

As adrenaline lit up every nerve in her body like Fourth of July sparklers, Cassie took one slow, silent step toward the gate.

Waited.

Took another step. Touched the gate. Slinked her fingers through the diamond pattern of chain links.

Holding her breath, she pulled it slowly toward her.

Softly...*softly*...it opened wider.

One more pull, and she would be able to squeeze through. Then it was a mad sprint through the pitch black chamber, hoping she didn't come undone before she reached the final portal.

She coaxed the gate toward her one last time—

—and it creaked.

A shrill, unmistakable *skrrrreeee*, it pierced the silence and Cassie's breath caught in her throat. In an instant, a flurry of options whirled through her mind. But she found herself incapable of acting upon a single one. Instead, her body went stiff as a board, her fingers gripping the gate's chain links so tightly that her nails were turning purple.

Holding her breath and praying she heard nothing in response, Cassie listened past her pounding pulse for any indication of movement. And for a handful of desperate moments, that prayer was actually answered.

But then they came: the slow, heavy footsteps behind her.

With her eyes squeezed shut and her heart clapping like hail on a tin roof, Cassie forced herself to turn and look.

Saturated with blood and scraps of clinging, sinewy tissue, Solomon Albrighton stepped from Rose's cell. Filling the narrow corridor with his massive frame, in a hand as big as a catcher's mitt Solomon slowly traced the blade of a military knife through the air in repeating, almost hypnotic figure eights. With each turn of the blade a series of viciously serrated teeth played across the scant light from Rose's cell as he stepped slowly toward Cassie, his expression somehow crazed and devoid of emotion at once…

) (

10:17 PM / THURSDAY / OCT 30

With siren blaring, Ressler peeled off the Presidio Parkway and fishtailed left, roaring through the tunnel beneath Shoreline

Highway. Filling the underpass with sound, the small block V8 drowned out the blare of the siren, and Ressler flicked it off before they emerged onto Cranston. He let off the accelerator, and the growl of the engine dropped to a soothing purr as they coasted onto Merchant Road.

"Alright, easy now." Sid yanked the plug from the cigarette lighter and the revolving cherry light on the roof went dark. "The east parking lot is just up here, on the right."

With the heel of his left hand, Ressler depressed a switch on the dash and the headlights momentarily brightened, then faded away. Gliding through the dark, the Ford Custom 500 drifted into the parking lot, empty save three cars.

One of them was an off-white VW Beetle. Unassuming and devoid of occupants, it sat in the first space of the third row. Just as it had when Repak had sent the department's tow truck two months earlier.

Ressler pulled up behind it and cut the engine, blocking the VW in as Sid lowered his readers from his forehead. Squinting in the dark, he compared Repak's report to the VW's license plate.

"Numbers match." He exhaled—a long, slow breath to steady his jangling nerves. "That's our guy."

In the back seat, Siobhan Jacobs felt a charge like an electric current run through her, every muscle tensing and aching to be out of the Ford. Suddenly frantic, she unbuckled her safety belt and popped the door, lurching from the car and into the cool night breeze that kissed her face as she doubled over, hyperventilating.

"You okay?" Doug Ressler kept his voice to his whisper as he placed his hand gently upon her back. "Breathe into your cupped hands. The carbon dioxide will offset the excess oxygen and replenish the CO_2 that's being pulled from your bloodstream."

She did as instructed, and the lightheadedness slowly waned until she was capable of standing upright without feeling woozy.

"Sounded like you actually cared, for a minute there," she joked, but the jibe came off with more bitter resentment than humor.

Ressler ignored it and unholstered his revolver.

Sid double-checked his flashlight by shielding its lens with one hand while clicking it on and off.

Together, the three stood at the edge of the parking lot, looking over the embankment to the abandoned military battery twenty feet below and the shimmering lights of the Golden Gate peeking in and out of the fog. From somewhere in the cold disquiet, the low, mournful moan of a foghorn sounded.

"Which one?" Ressler asked, shifting his gaze slowly from right to left at a number of emplacements. "There are more than I expected."

Pointing to their left, Sid showed them the shadowy outline of Battery Boutelle. "But this one?" he whispered, indicating a complex arrangement of geometric shapes at the bottom of a ravine immediately in front of them. "That's Battery Marcus Miller. The third of three gun batteries, in fact."

Ressler and Siobhan both followed his hand as it swept slowly toward the bridge, the silhouettes of various shapes meandering into the darkness. In the glowing, fog-diffracted corona of the bridge's lights, the bunker all but disappeared.

"There are four batteries here. To the north of Marcus Miller you have Battery Cranston. To the south of Boutelle, you have Godfrey. He's gotta be down there, somewhere. In one of them. And hopefully, so is Cassie Kennedy."

"If he's there, then she's there," Siobhan assured him, shivering as the silence and cold, damp air conspired to amplify her trepidation. "And if he's alive, then she is."

"Well," Ressler deduced as he peered down into the shallow gorge below, "if you're carrying or dragging a body, which one of these bunkers would *you* choose? Ever lift a hundred-fifty pounds? It ain't easy. I, for one, would be heading for that nearest one, right down there." A pointer dog on the scent of a kill, his left arm was outstretched, his right at his side with his fingers wrapped around the grip of his revolver as he began shuffling down the hill.

Sid took up the trail behind him, determined that Siobhan Jacobs stay back despite her insistence that she come with them. "Keep close to the car. If we spot anything at all, I'll call for backup before we go in."

In moments, they were nothing but shadows in the darkness as they skulked through the brush to the bunker.

Folding her arms across her chest and hugging away the cold, Siobhan stood alone in the creeping mist at the edge of the parking lot. Catching the weak glow from the blinking bridge lights, the hands of her silver Cartier revealed it was 10:32 PM...

)(

Solomon took a slow, lumbering step toward Cassie and his sister froze, her breath sucked from her lungs.

He was naked, painted from head to toe with Rose's blood. It matted his hair and reeked of wet copper. His penis was stiff and erect, smeared with feces and gelatinous strips.

In Rose's cell, all was quiet.

"No! No no no no no nonooo!" The realization snapped Cassie from her fear paralysis, and she cried out for her fellow captive, leaping past Solomon towards Rose's cell door. "ROSIE, RUN! PLEASE! GET OUT OF H—"

A hand to her throat stopped her, Solomon's fingers easily wrapping around her neck. Like a dog sprinting unaware to the end of its chain, Cassie's head snapped back. She lost her footing. Began to tumble. Feet airborne.

With Solomon's fist clamped to her throat, she dangled in the air like a rag doll, her brother's grip choking off her breath—

What had once been a natural creek bed in front of the bunker was now a dusty, serpentine path. Worn smooth by endless tourists' footsteps, it had become as hard as a dedicated pathway. At its haphazard edges were faded candy wrappers, soda cans and potato chip bags blown by the wind and ensnared in the brush from countless junior high field trips.

At first glance, it appeared perfectly ordinary.

But a swath of loose, freshly disturbed soil cut perpendicularly across it. Barely noticeable unless you were looking for it, it started at the bottom of the hill they'd just descended and disappeared beneath a scraggly patch of brush. Pulled into place with deceptive care, the arrangement was just a little too perfect to be natural.

Gesturing for Sid to join him, Ressler shone his flashlight into the brake. Together they moved the branches and thorny vines aside, careful not to make a sound. Beneath it, Ressler's flashlight shone on the truth: footprints, drag marks, signs that someone had been hauling something—or someone—towards the entrance that lay concealed just beyond.

Crisscrossed with braces of rusted iron, two heavy wooden doors secured an archway set into the oxidized and graffiti-covered concrete. Set into the hillside as Sid had described, the doors guarded what appeared to be a vast subterranean passage. A massive metal latch arm had been lifted from its receiver, the heavy duty padlock hanging from it with the shackle open.

Above and to each side was more brush and overgrown vegetation that had achieved throughout the decades what no enemy force had been able: to not only invade but overcome the Marcus Miller bunker.

"Munitions store," Sid stated beneath his breath and swept his flashlight left to right. In the haze of incoming fog the beam refracted in all directions off the airborne water molecules, causing it to diffuse like a lamp.

"How big?" Ressler's light remained focused on the doors.

"It probably runs all the way beneath these three batteries. Could easily be a hundred feet or more. It could be one big chamber, or there might be cordoned off sections. I've never been in one—as you can see, the public is forbidden for safety reasons."

"So, we have no way of knowing what we'll find when we get in there. For all we know, he could be just the other side of that door…"

Sid shrugged. "Could be. How do you wanna play this?"

But Ressler had already twisted the hefty iron ring handle and was tugging the door open…

) (

Constricting her throat, Solomon's fingers gouged deep into her trachea. A fish out of water, Cassie gasped for breath. Kicking and clawing, she swayed in her brother's grip with her feet inches above the blood-soaked floor.

four-one-thousand

Small purple dots began to appear across her cheeks, the blood vessels in her left eye bursting as a steady, high-pitched squall filled her ears.

nine-one-thousand

The muscles in her face began to droop as the rings of hyaline cartilage protecting her windpipe began to depress and separate in her neck. Spots appeared before her eyes, everything beginning to go foggy.

fifteen-one-thousand

Cassie's bladder gave way and her panties darkened, a viscous, dark yellow spray of urine spritzing her thighs and running down her bare legs.

Staring into her eyes with an expression of stone-cold apathy, Solomon squeezed even harder. Swollen and dark red, almost purple, Cassie's tongue lolled over her bottom lip when somewhere across the vast antechamber—

thirty-one steps, a hundred feet, her mind autonomously recited by rote

—came the muted scraping of a heavy door.

Now a faint kiss of air, cool and moist, wafted through the subterranean concourse. With it came the salty, fermented scent of the sea cutting through the bitter, metallic stink of festering blood. And for a split second, Solomon loosened his grip.

Disoriented and unable to feel her own limbs, Cassie struck at her brother's face with the sliver of Robert Sherwood's dog tag bound to her wrist. Still crudely bent at ninety degrees, the jagged, razor sharp sliver of metal skewered his right eye.

Howling and swatting at his face, Solomon released his grip upon Cassie's throat.

Crumpling to the floor with the dog tag's silver ball chain still wrapped around her wrist, Cassie twisted the chain and tugged. The bent portion embedded deep in his eye pulled out.

Solomon's eye came with it.

Extracted from its socket, it hung by the optical nerve against his cheek as the clear, jelly-like vitreous fluid inside streamed out and the eye's global shape collapsed.

Solomon shrieked, an animalistic yowl, and struck wildly at the air. A battery of punches came fast and furious as Cassie curled into a ball on her knees and attempted to block the strikes with her arms covering her head.

A sickening crack told her the radius bone in her left forearm had just snapped in two. Even before the pain charged up it like a bolt of lightning to lodge in her skull.

With her arm sloughing grotesquely to the side, Solomon continued to pummel her until Cassie slumped face-down in the dirt.

He slammed the back of her head again and again with the heel of both hands, and with each agonizing blow her face struck the ground harder, sending blinding white spikes of light into her skull. The sour, moldering taste of earth and blood filled her mouth.

Then he was upon her, wild-eyed and crouching as he pinned her prone body beneath him.

Spinning out of control, the colors of Cassie's world began to blur to dirty grey as her breaths came fast and shallow. At her side, loose and twisted to an impossible angle, her left arm lay like a useless accessory in the dirt and dried blood. Splayed wide open, her fingers clenched and unclenched, twitching as she wavered in and out of consciousness.

On her third finger, the wedding band she had never taken off, even after the separation from Bill, glimmered in the soft glow emanating from Rose's cell.

And Solomon grew erect…

)(

A nerve-shredding howl, so guttural it was bestial, shattered the silence. Bouncing from wall to wall, it reverberated throughout the munitions' chamber and both Sid and Ressler dropped defensively to one knee.

Bracing their firearms across their non-dominant forearms, each gripped a flashlight in their left hand like a knife about to be plunged into a watermelon. Aiming them in the direction of the sound, two beams of light swept across the chamber, two weak, overlapping circles barely able to illuminate the distant wall.

The beam from Sid's flashlight began to judder.

"Jesus Christ, Ressler." Had it not been pitch-black inside the underground chamber, the whites of his eyes would have been visible all the way around his soft brown irises. "We know he's here now. I say we call it in for backup. Stand guard in front of the entrance outside. He'll have nowhere to go."

Ressler slowly scanned the chamber from left to right, never taking his eyes off the feeble beam of light.

He said nothing.

"Seriously, Doug. We don't know this layout. But he does. He has the upper hand. Shit, I can barely see a dozen feet in front of me. You can't either."

Ressler squinted; lowered his gaze to think. His flashlight's barely visible halo bobbed lazily about the far wall, a hundred feet away if it were a foot.

He shook his head.

"I can see enough. You go on. You told Jacobs you would do that anyway. Use the radio in the 500 and call it in. I'll stay here so he can't get by me. You just make sure Jacobs is safe till they get h—"

"*I am,*" Siobhan whispered from behind and both men spun on a dime, revolvers aimed, fingers on the triggers. Jacobs gasped and stumbled backward, palms in the air. "*It's me, it's me!*"

Ressler let out the breath he was holding and grabbed Jacobs by the forearm. "Get the hell out of here."

But Siobhan yanked her arm from his grip and stepped back. "We were right about the location. I know I'm right about his condition, too. There's every chance Holden won't even know where he is, let alone what's happening. And if Cassie's still alive in there? You're gonna need me to talk him down. If you don't want any more lives lost."

"I could give a shit about this psychofuck's life."

Siobhan pursed her lips. Breathed in through her nose. The exhalation was a gentle hiss that susurrated through the chamber. "I know you don't Doug," she whispered. "But I do. And we *all* want Cassie to be alright. Holden needs help."

"Help? We were at the same crime scene on Summerdale, right? Remember Sheila McCabe's blood across the ceiling? Her left hand severed from her wrist while she was still alive? Then all but decapitating her as her baby girl slept in the next room?" Douglas Ressler's brows knitted together, his forehead creasing in a series of deep furrows. "He needs a bullet to the brain, is what he needs."

Jacobs sighed, stiffening. She stepped closer. "Then do it for Cassie. Think how terrified she has to be."

"If she's still alive," Ressler retaliated.

"She's alive, at least until midnight. He's playing the 'who's smarter' game. And there's no satisfaction in beating us if he has to cheat to do it." She shook her head in the dark. "He needs to prove his superiority, and not killing Cassie until the thirty-first is part of his rules. Remember, he's ex-First Cavalry. To him, those are his rules of engagement."

Sid shook his head from side to side, sucking in air.

Ressler hooked Jacobs around the waist and pulled her near to his back. "You'll stay behind us then."

"At all times," Sid Younger added. "Are we being clear?"

"Yes. I'll stay behind you. Both of you." She offered Sid a compliant smile, but it went unseen. As did the subtle shiver that twitched her hands. She clasped them together, lacing her fingers together and pulling them in to her abdomen. It did little to assuage her nerves humming with raw, unabated fear. When another scream reverberated through the underground passage, they pulsed like a live wire.

This time the wail was a woman's, a howl saturated in pain. And the hairs on the arms of all three of them stood at attention as the cry morphed into a terror-stricken plea.

"Hold onto my jacket," Ressler demanded and guided Siobhan's hand to the tail of his blazer. He began trotting, then running, toward the sound of the woman's screams, his flashlight bobbing and his gun drawn—

)(

"SOLOMON NOOOOO!"

Dragging his sister to Rose's cell, he pinned her to the ground and tore off her panties. Cassie's cry choked off in her throat as he leveraged his weight by pressing her face into the earth.

Cassie's mouth filled with dirt.

Paralyzed with pain and heaving for breath, she was incapable of stopping him as Solomon entered her. With her eyes squeezed shut, she soundlessly wailed as he began rocking back and forth, driving her face deeper into the dirt with every thrust.

Now he grabbed her left hand and raised it to his line of sight. A white-hot bolt of pain shot through her body as the broken bones inside her arm twisted, slicing through tendons and burrowing into muscle.

Hanging from a hook in the ceiling, the yellow light of a utility work lamp reflected in a hundred tiny prisms from Cassie's wedding band. This fueled Solomon's excitement, and he rocked back and forth with building intensity.

Coughing the dirt from her throat in a visible plume, Cassie's explosive scream came back to her in diminishing iterations.

Her left eye shot open.

Lifeless and staring back at her from the dirt were the bright green eyes of twenty-one-year-old Rosalie Sherwood.

Rose's head had been sawn from her neck.

As had her left hand.

Adorning the third finger of Robert Sherwood's widow was the simple gold wedding band he'd saved months to afford. Wiped clean of the blood which stained the rest of Rosie's fingers and palm, it too shimmered in the yellow light.

Rosalie's torso had been cleaved from her pubis to her breasts, her innards torn out like a frog pinned to a board in ninth-grade biology.

The serrated blade used to dismantle Rosalie lay on the ground next to her defiled corpse, its fierce teeth snarled with clods of Rosalie's fresh, pink flesh.

Sluggish and dark, the immense pool of her blood flowed like syrup across the dirt floor. With every second its thick surface rippled, spreading wider and closer as it crept toward Cassie's face. A muted sheen reflected the faint, shielded work bulb overhead, making the pool look almost alive as it swelled. In it, Cassie saw the mirrored image of her brother bucking back and forth atop her.

Except the reflection of the person pinned beneath Solomon was not herself, but someone she had not seen since childhood.

Joey?

It couldn't be. Her eldest brother had died that night so long ago, his last moments lived in the lightless, feces-riddled confines of a cramped farmhouse pantry where their aunt had kept him like some inanimate pleasure toy for the monster. Joey had suffered the unimaginable violations, again and again, so Cassie and Holden could be free. And when suffering was no longer enough to keep the monster at bay, he died that night to save them. Just as Solomon had done what he had to do in order to protect them.

Only now Solomon was atop her—

atop Joey

—inside her as she—

he

—lay in the offal of a young woman whose only transgression was to trust a stranger in need, while she herself was drowning in a quagmire of bleak, impossible grief.

Cassie stared at the impossible reflection in Rose's blood, watching Joey's features undulate as the pool continued to spread and her own body was violently rocked.

This is a dream, she assured herself. *One of my awful visions. A product of my own tortured mind.*

Back and forth she rocked as Solomon's thrusts grew faster, harder.

I'm not here. I'm at home. With my beautiful Bella Luna by my side. We're snacking on popcorn and watching an old black and white movie. Maybe one of the Abbott and Costello films. Bella always did like those. Her favorite was the one where they meet the Wolfman.

Now Joey smiled at her.

Tell me more, he said from the rippling puddle of red, and insisted she focus on him as Solomon neared climax. *She sounds so lovely. Your whole life sounds lovely. I can't wait to be part of it.*

"But you can't," Cassie told him, and Joey's smile deflated. "You're not real."

How can you say such a thing? I've always been real. As a child I suffered every day at the hands of that monster to spare you. I stayed in that closet—that dark, rancid closet with its piss and shit and absence of light—as my eyes weakened and my muscles atrophied, and my tummy ached from hunger. I did all of these things to protect you. Just as I will protect you now.

"But you haven't protected me—"

Oh but I have. And I am. Look. Look at your reflection. Who do you see, sister? Is it your own beautiful face, or is it mine? Just as I have always done, I have stepped into the light to keep you from the pain you cannot bear.

Cassie did not hear the shouts of the detectives as Douglas Ressler aimed his revolver and readied his finger on the trigger. She did not see the black man at his side, screaming at her and jostling as his flashlight shone bright in her left eye. Or the pretty ginger-haired woman crouching behind them with tears streaming down her cheeks.

"—get up! Show me your hands! Slowly! Holden Albrighton, I said show me your hands or I'll shoot!" Doug Ressler tracked forward, a steady sidestep where one foot left the ground only after the other was firmly planted. In his outstretched arms, his service revolver was cocked, the trigger taut. Its sights were lined up upon the head of the man crouched upon the floor, naked and clotted in the blood of the woman whose mangled body littered the makeshift jail cell. Dangling at the man's side and bent at a grotesque angle, his left arm was broken nearly in two.

He was gyrating and masturbating with the other.

There was no one else there.

"Holden Albrighton! You're under arrest for murder! Place your hands behind your back!" With his whole body alight, adrenaline sparking from every nerve like live wires, Sid Younger approached from the left as Ressler did so from the right. For now, Sid ignored the evidence of the slaughter the man had perpetrated, his eyes blind to the horror. Later that night, however, as he would lie in the arms of his hunka-hunka burnin' love—Mrs. Younger—they would see it all, too clearly. And they would see it for the rest of Sid's life. But in this moment, he only saw the options ahead that could cause him or his partners harm, and he took every precaution to prevent every one. "I said put your hands behind your back!"

Holden Albrighton did not comply. Pumping himself faster and faster as he neared climax, he stared only at the left hand dangling at his side: the long, manicured fingers and the petite wedding band made of gold.

In the darkening pool of Rosalie Sherwood's blood, the face was now Solomon's. It was cruel and perverse and tainted with the kind of vile malignance which can only be born from an innocent suffering the most unadulterated atrocities at the hands of a monstrous soul.

Still, Solomon climaxed, spotting the fetid puddle of blood with his semen. Lurching to his feet, he snatched the military-issue M3 trench knife in his right hand as the detectives shouted and backed away.

With his left arm dangling at his side and his extracted right eye punctured and swaying from its nerve, he lumbered toward them amidst a hail of shouts and obvoluted commands. His knife sliced back and forth through the air before him in sharp, resolute sweeps.

Doug Ressler, now backed up to the chain link gate, shouted only twice more for Solomon to stop.

His finger twitched upon the trigger.

And he began to pu—

"WAIT!" Above the din and booming male voices bouncing from wall to empty wall, the pitch of Siobhan Jacobs' cut like a hot knife through butter as she leapt between Solomon and both detectives. "RESSLER, WAIT!"

Swearing and seizing a fistful of Siobhan's jacket, Ressler snapped the barrel of his pistol toward the ceiling. But Jacobs tugged away, taking another slow, careful step toward the killer.

...Gemini...two faces...states of dissociative fugue...the monster in the farmhouse closet...E3:1...

Every clue, every cry for help the Gemini had left for them swirled through Siobhan's mind in a whirlwind of realization.

...Vietnam...abuse and violence and trauma...a dog Cassie now loved and protected as if a child...

Siobhan slowly extended her hand, raising her palm and splaying her fingers to accept the killer's. "Take my hand."

And Solomon stopped in his tracks.

"...Cassie...?" Siobhan's voice was caring, protective. *Real.* Her fingers waggled lightly as she reached toward the killer. "You're safe now, honey. Take my hand. Tell Solomon to put down the knife."

Holden Albrighton tilted his head to one side, his extracted right eye sweeping across his cheek like a macabre pendulum.

Behind Jacobs, Ressler and Younger spread wide, each at an

oblique angle and ready to fire. In her periphery, Siobhan felt their revolvers leveled squarely at Holden, and her racing pulse filled her ears. Still, she took one final step forward, hiding the trembling that vibrated through her fingers as she gestured for the killer to take her hand.

"I know you're in there. Your name is Cassie Kennedy. You're married to Bill Kennedy. He works at Nasa. Remember? And even though you're separated, you still love each other. Your friend is Patty Brewster, at the café where you sometimes do tarot readings. And you have a beautiful five year old daughter, Isabella. She's home and waiting for you." Siobhan dared to inch closer. "You're safe now, Cassie. We've found you. The bad man is gone."

Blocking out the sight of Rosalie Sherwood's butchered remains and Holden Albrighton's jarring wounds, Jacobs channeled her thoughts to Sunday mornings in the park with her favorite book, and all the things in life that made her want to smile— including Douglas Ressler—and her expression softened.

"Will you let me take you to your daughter now, Cassie?"

Devoid of expression, Holden dropped the knife.

It clattered to the floor as he dropped to his knees and burst into an unfettered sob. Reaching for Siobhan as a child might, in the voice of a ten-year-old he begged her not to hurt them.

As he did this, his expression changed so profoundly that his facial features all but physically transformed before Siobhan Jacob's eyes. Once again, he was Cassandra Kennedy, unassuming psychic plagued by recurring dreams of the most barbarous and sadistic crimes.

Only, those visions were not dreams.

And they were not the product of any psychic ability.

They were memories.

Reaching for the sickening lump that hung upon her right cheek, Cassie's left arm refused to move. Sagging at her side and stretching the skin from within, the tip of her fractured radius bone threatened to burst through her wrist at the slightest jolt.

Confused, terrified, and in the most excruciating pain, Cassie's screams rose to an ear-splitting howl when she realized the thing which dangled upon her cheek was the mangled remnant of her own right eye.

Having no comprehension of how such a savage injury could have occurred only served to fuel her consuming panic, and her screams continued until her voice gave out.

For Cassie Kennedy had no awareness that she and Joey and Solomon were in fact all one and the same person.

And that person's name was Holden Albrighton.

36

)(

SIX MONTHS LATER / MAY 7, 1970
San Quentin State Prison

WHO AM I speaking with right now?" Across from Holden Albrighton, in a stark white room with no distractions, Siobhan Jacobs sat quietly, her fingers gently interlaced and resting in her lap. Her voice was soft and reserved, as delicate as the gesture that illustrated a modesty and natural, quiet contemplation that was as remote from threatening as possible

Although his broken arm had long ago healed, it remained thin and visibly weakened. Over his right eye, Holden wore a fabric patch. Unfocused and dreamlike, his left stared through her. But then it twitched, the reflex becoming a slow, heavy blinking. He touched his forehead, a pout drawing down the corners of his mouth. "Such a headache. Again." Now he grinned, lifting his chin and beaming. His voice lightened, the pitch rising to a natural feminine timbre. "It's Cassie, silly," the psychic chuckled unpretentiously. "You feeling okay, doc?"

"I'm wonderful, Cassie. Thank you for asking." Still fascinated each time they spoke, Siobhan studied the man sitting before her, absorbed by the natural way in which he morphed from one personality into another. "Is Holden still with us, Cassie?"

Cassie shifted in her chair. A sense of discomfort flashed across her face, mirrored in her body language. In a moment it was gone, and she again relaxed into her chair, preening her pragmatic grey prison blouse before resting her elbows on the table between them. With an unspoken look she asked if doing so was permitted, and Jacobs consented.

"I haven't seen my brother Holden since before he went to war." She did not make eye contact with the psychiatrist. "I miss him. I wish I could see him."

Siobhan Jacobs put down her pen and closed her leatherbound folder. "You don't recall seeing Holden yesterday?"

Shifting in her seat, Cassie Kennedy crossed her legs and inattentively tapped her toe in the air. "You sure you're feeling alright, Dr. Jacobs?" She forced a smile, behind which there was no emotion. "I was joking when I asked you that a moment ago. But now I'm really starting to think you're imagining things."

Siobhan nodded, an unspoken *ahhh* crossing her lips.

"What about Joey, your eldest brother? We haven't talked about him in a while. Would you like to share something about him? It would be nice to get to know him better."

Cassie stared at her hands resting upon the table, her fingers squeezing one another as they laced in and out. "Joey died when I was nine."

"Yes, I'm sorry. You've shared that with me before and it's heartbreaking."

"I did?"

Jacobs nodded. "How did he die? Do you feel strong enough to share that with me today?"

"He died saving us from the Monster." Cassie rubbed her left forearm, gliding her slim fingers over its smooth skin. "Feels weird, still. After all those weeks in that cast."

"I can imagine." Siobhan said nothing more, offering instead an easy, supportive smile.

"It's funny. Not funny-ha-ha but funny-odd," Cassie told her. "I actually can't remember how he died that night. All I know is that he did." After several minutes of silence, Cassie cleared her throat. "He stayed in that closet, so we didn't have to. Did I tell you that?"

Siobhan said that she had.

"And every night the Monster came. He did terrible, terrible things to my brother, Dr. Jacobs. Just awful." In her left eye, moisture began to shine under the harsh overhead fluorescent tube. Cassie rubbed it with the heel of her hand, then instinctively began to do the same to her right before remembering that it was no longer there. "Now that's true love, isn't it? Suffering such inhumanity, so that we wouldn't have to."

"Who's the 'we' in that statement, Cassie?"

"Me and Solomon and—" Cassie hesitated, swallowing hard as if forcing down the truth "—and our baby brother, Holden. It all started with him, you know. The late night visits to his room when everyone was asleep. But Joey heard. And he tried to stop it."

"What happened then?"

"We knew our aunt would never allow it to happen again. Except she did. She ignored it, pretending it wasn't happening at all. Eventually, we just accepted that she either wouldn't—or couldn't—help us."

"But that's not all she did, or did not do. Isn't that right?"

Now a tear formed lazily behind Cassie's eyelid and rolled thick and slow down her cheek. She shook her head back and forth, and when Dr. Jacobs offered her a tissue she accepted it, wiping away the salt-laden track. "No, that's right. Before long she actually began to help the Monster do the things it did. And if we did not cooperate, or cried or made any sound at all, she punished us. None of the boys ever said why she would do such an awful thing, and they hated her for it. But as a woman myself, I understood. In my own way, at least. Even back then."

"And what was that, Cassie? Why do you think she helped your uncle hurt you?"

"Because she was scared. Every now and then I could hear them through the walls. My bedroom was next to theirs in that old farmhouse, you see. And sometimes I heard her voice and it sounded sad. A little frantic. Like maybe she wanted him not to do it anymore. But then I'd hear the slap and the sound of her falling and the soft cries from low to the ground as he stormed away."

"So you think she was protecting herself."

Cassie shrugged.

"I think so?" She became contemplative. "I'm a mother myself, you know. Did I tell you? Isabella is her name. I call her my little Bella Luna because she lights up the darkness like the moon."

At this Siobhan Jacobs genuinely smiled. "Yes, you did tell me. And it's a lovely story."

"I miss her. My Bella. Do you think I can see her soon?"

"If we can make some more progress, I'll try to make that happen."

Suddenly skittish, anxiety contorting her features, Cassie leaned forward and blurted out: "Where is she? Do you know where she is? Oh my God, is she okay? I really should be going now. I'm quite sure she needs me."

Cassie began to stand but Jacobs asked her to please remain seated.

"She's fine. Bella is with your best friend, Patricia. From the café. Do you remember?"

Relief washed over Cassie's face. Tidying her skirt and carefully folding the pleats beneath her, she sat back down.

"You know, Solomon saved us too. Joey took the beatings and the things I can't bear to think about. But Solomon was the one who finally got us out of that hell."

"When he attacked your uncle, you mean—?"

"When he did what he had to, to protect us from the Monster."

"Do you recall what happened next?"

Cassie's fingers clenched, so tightly that small pricks of blood appeared in the palm of her hand. She shuffled in her seat. Cleared her throat. Now she locked onto Siobhan's eyes and did not let go.

"Cassie doesn't want to talk about that. She's gone to sleep now," Holden said in an entirely different voice.

"Is this Holden I'm speaking to now?" Jacobs stiffened in her chair, just enough to be noticed, and the man across from her sneered. He traced a curved line in the dust on the table.

"This is Solomon, you stupid Irish cunt." He eyed her up and down, a thirst evident in the unsettling stare. He wetted his lips when his gaze was drawn to the ring on Jacobs' left hand. "Married now, are we, Dr. Jacobs? What a wonderful surprise. To that arsehole of a detective, no doubt." For a moment Solomon's voice mimicked a light brogue.

"*Lieutenant* Ressler, yes. But you already know that. You've known it for months now." Siobhan swallowed back the unease that began to build in her chest, stemming the tide of panic that would drown her if she allowed it to. "I'm not comfortable with this conversation, Solomon. I'd like to speak to Holden now."

Solomon slammed his fists against the table and with the meat of his right hand, dragged a second curved line through the thin film of dust—

two backwards parentheses

—and smirked. "That's not going to happen, doc. I'll do anything to protect my baby brother. We all would, in our own way. But you already know that, don't you."

He casually rose from his seat and violently slammed his hands into the table's edge. It slid across the floor with a juddering squeal and struck Siobhan Jacobs' right shin.

Her shriek was soundless as she recoiled, protecting her face with her arms as Holden lunged for her. But the prison guards were upon him and driving him to his knees before the pain in her leg had even begun to register.

)(

"Still the same?" Douglas Ressler was carefully applying a balm to the abrasion across his wife's shin as she sprawled across him on the sofa that evening.

"We make a little more progress every day. But it may be too little, too late. Tomorrow, I have to decide if I'm going to sign him off as competent...or not. A man's life is literally in my hands."

Ressler pursed his lips, shaking his head without realizing it. "He's taken plenty of lives. More than we probably even know. There were a dozen left hands draped across that fucking dungeon wall. We've only identified half of the victims. I'm willing to bet there are at least a dozen more we don't even know about."

Cold disquiet suddenly settled over the room and Siobhan found herself trying not to cry.

"That may be the case, Doug. *But I haven't. I haven't killed anyone.* This matters to me."

She laid her index finger across her cheek, careful not to smudge her eyeliner as she blotted away the tear forming there.

Her husband apologized as Scott McKenzie's easy, folksy voice serenaded them with his song, 'San Francisco.' They both said nothing, only listening and allowing the singer's sentiments of hope and love to wash over them. When it was over and KFRC went to a commercial, Ressler finally spoke again.

"I still don't get it, though. Not really."

"What don't you get?"

"Multiple personalities. Alters. Host personality. It just sounds like so much science fiction."

There was no animosity in the statement, this time a genuine expression of his lack of understanding.

"I wish it *were* science fiction. It would be a better world if every child were allowed to just grow up without having to learn how to survive such vicious and depraved abuses."

"So he *was* abused, then. That much is true?"

"Absolutely. Every record from his therapist at the juvenile home where Solomon—sorry, Holden—was detained confirms it. That poor boy was raped, over and over, by a pedophile uncle whose attacks were assisted by Holden's own aunt."

Ressler glowered, sickened by the thought of it. He couldn't begin to imagine a child having to suffer such assaults. "So there never were any siblings, is that right?"

"Only in Holden's mind, baby. To him, they are very real. When children go through intense recurring trauma, some may develop MPD—Multiple Personality Disorder—as a last-ditch way to cope with such painful experiences. We don't know why some do and some don't. But when it happens, that fragmentation of their personalities enables them to separate from the emotional pain and navigate through life without the constant reminders of what they've endured. It's a form of compartmentalization, just as your mind does when you go to work and have to leave your personal worries behind. MPD is the same, only at a much more extreme level. The various personalities they create are known as 'alters,' and each is created by the host—in this case, Holden—to serve a very specific purpose in helping the victim deal with what happened to him as a little boy."

"So, he's not a crossdresser, then…" Never one to holster his thoughts, Ressler was trying his best to wrap his mind around the fact that for extended periods of time, Holden was living as a woman, rather than a man.

"No, babe. Cassie was a safe place for him. She still is." Siobhan pulled her leg from his lap and sat up, becoming rigid as a sober look darkened her face. "But would it matter to you if he was? A crossdresser, I mean? Would you have treated him differently?"

"Of course not. Listen, I'm just trying to understand it."

"The early fifties weren't like today, Doug. Hell, just recently we saw young people from all around the world descend upon Panhandle Park to expand their collective consciousness through mind-altering hallucinogens. To experiment with living communally. And, in a nutshell, turning their back on the nuclear family and white-picket-fence social norms as they expressed their sexuality through free love. It's a different world now to the one we grew up in twenty, even just ten, years ago."

Siobhan sipped her wine, turning the stem of her glass between her fingers.

"For a little boy in the fifties being raped by a man, it's understandable that his mind dissociated from what was happening to him. Because to a young Holden, only girls had sex with boys. Cassie is the product of that belief set. It has nothing to do with his sexuality or gender."

"But why keep playing the role of Cassie?" Ressler asked her. "Even into adulthood."

"Well, for a start, it's not a role he's playing, babe. He has no more control over any of his fragmented personalities than you have over Sid, for example. Once the alternative identity serves its purpose, it recedes into the background and allows another to come into the light, so to speak. With Cassie, her protective, maternal nature was a source of comfort to Holden. It's easier for him to live his life as her than it is to live as any of his other identities. You have to understand, to Holden, he *is* Cassie. He *is* Solomon. And—"

"—And he is Joey. So why claim that Joey died?"

"Joey had fulfilled the purpose for which he was created. He was always going to die. Look at it this way, if Holden's life were a movie, Joey would be the expendable secondary character. Once Holden's psyche decided that exposing his little sister—as he sees the Cassie identity—to such abuse didn't sit right with him, his mind created Joey to take the abuse instead. When the rapes ended, as they would eventually have to, Joey simply ended with them. No Joey, no abused child. No child abuse, no lingering emotional pain. At least not to the degree it would haunt him if Holden himself had to deal with the memories of the abuse directly."

"So," Ressler summarized, "if each personality or alter has a purpose, that would make Solomon the personified version of Holden's toughness. The heavy, so to speak, who came in to do the dirty work. In this case, finally taking out the piece of shit uncle who was raping him."

"Yes. Solomon is unthinking, unafraid and unmerciful. Cassie, a.k.a. Holden, has described Solomon to me as a large, physically imposing man who towers above her and has fists the size of catcher's mitts. Think about that for a minute. To the Cassie identity, that is reality. Even though Solomon—and Cassie—are both actually Holden, who is himself a rather slight man with more refined features than many. Hence the reason Cassie did not cause a stir when she walked down the street: she's actually a very pretty girl."

Ressler appeared faraway in thought, trying to imagine this through the eyes of Cassie as his wife was explaining it.

"So, to her, Solomon is a giant. Larger than life."

"Yes, because he had to be. Solomon is essentially a beast whose role was to eradicate those responsible for Holden's pain. But as Holden's aunt is no longer part of the equation, Solomon still hunts for her in the guise of women who he believes are her."

Suddenly, and for the first real time, Ressler understood why his wife was in such turmoil over her responsibility in determining Holden's mental competency.

How do you sentence a man to death when he has no idea that a part of him—a part he can't control—has even done anything wrong?

They discussed the duality of Holden serving as both prey and predator at once, and how each of the five personalities were mutually unaware of the others.

"To each of them, they were, and remain, the only one. Cassie believes she is Cassie. Solomon believes he is Solomon. There's simply no other option. And Holden only steps into the light when the world around him feels safe enough to do so. It's why Cassie describes him as her youngest brother—the one they all wanted to protect when they were 'kids.' Because Holden is the most valued…and also the most vulnerable."

"I get that," Ressler acknowledged, "but how is that a mutually unaware situation, if Cassie knows about Holden?"

"Because she does not see herself as a fragment of him. To Cassie, Holden is as real as you or me. She has conversations with him. She has memories of him. The same with Solomon. And Joey. When Cassie was in that bunker, she truly believed she was locked in there. You saw for yourself the evidence that she picked a lock with pieces of Robert Sherwood's dog tag, even though the padlock was never actually shackled to the door latch. She truly believed, and felt, herself being raped by Solomon. It's how she managed to do what you or I would find inconceivable: spearing her own eye and extracting it. To Cassie, she was fending off an attacker. The eye she punctured was Solomon's, not hers."

Ressler trembled all over in disgust, finding himself squinting at the very thought of it. He shook off the image by taking his wife's hand in his own.

"Gotcha. But five personalities?" Counting on her fingers, he gently kissed them, one at a time, then gingerly folded them toward her palm. "Cassie, Solomon, Joey and Holden makes four." He held Siobhan's thumb standing proud above her palm and kissed it, too. "So where's the fifth?"

"Janice Wynn." Siobhan answered and kissed his hand in return. "She came later, but still served a purpose."

"Which was…?"

"Cassie is a good soul. She'd never hurt a fly. Holden, too, even though he was a soldier in Vietnam. Killing there was his duty. A matter of survival. But put him back in everyday society and he's as conscientious as we are. He loved Hannah Wilson. But Solomon would not allow that. It was Solomon who arrived at Hannah's door that day. Not Holden, as Hannah expected. And when she freaked out, Solomon struck."

"Because Solomon is charmless and couldn't lure someone if he tried. From what you're saying, he's one step from an animal."

Siobhan placed her fingertip to her nose. "Correct. So, enter Janice Wynn. Not as put together or as pretty as Cassie Kennedy, admittedly, but certainly charming enough to convince a child to come with her." She waggled her empty wine glass and Ressler took it to the kitchen for a refill.

"So Cassie Kennedy was never a psychic," he shouted over his shoulder. "Her visions were dissociated memories of Solomon's and Janice's actions. It's why she knew so many details about the Roes, and about Hannah Wilson's attack at her Sausalito home."

In Ressler's mind he saw the missing poster for little Lyndsey Roe with her ivory dress and a matching bow in her hair, and his stomach tightened.

He served his new bride her fresh glass of chardonnay—*oaky, not buttery*—and forced the conversation to pivot.

"Whaddya say we hit the sack soon?" He winked at her, a comical, overexaggerated gesture. "And I'm not talking about going to sleep. Nudge-nudge, wink-wink."

He narrated the gestures as he performed them and Siobhan giggled, patting him on the backside as he turned for the bedroom.

"Tempting. Very tempting." She winked back with equally exaggerated hokeyness. "But I have my final session with Holden tomorrow. And I really need to be alert. You understand, right?"

"Of course. My part in it is pretty much over. In many ways, yours has only just begun." He blew her a kiss and said goodnight before disappearing down the hallway.

Alone in the living room, Siobhan waited until he turned out the light in their room at the end of the hall before she buried her head in her hands and cried.

) (

"Oh my, don't you just look spectacular this morning!" Holden beamed with delight as Siobhan Jacobs joined him in the interview room. Only it wasn't his voice. Nor was it Cassie's or Solomon's. "Loving this look with your hair! You must give me the name of your stylist."

With his ankles bound together by heavy shackles and handcuffs locked to his wrists, the metal clinked and jangled with every slight movement.

"I'll be sure to do that." Slightly perplexed, Siobhan pointed toward the bindings. "This is new."

"I guess that's what happens when you slam a table into your head shrink's legs."

"Mmmmm, I see." She waited to find if Holden had anything else to say about the matter. When he didn't, Siobhan shuffled through her notes, familiarizing herself with where they had left off the day before. "Holden, today is a very important day. Do you know what a competency analysis is?"

Studying his nails, Holden shook his head.

"No, darlin'. Why?"

He placed his palms flat upon the table and looked up to hold Siobhan's gaze. A single eye, dark and devoid of emotion, drilled into the psychiatrist's.

"And I'm afraid you have me mistaken for someone else, dear.

My name is Janice, not Holden." Lowering her gaze, Janice went back to examining her nails, *tsking* at the state of them. "I really must get to that mani-pedi appointment, so if you could hurry it along?"

"Oh," Siobhan said in feigned surprise. "I am *so* sorry. I guess I do have you mistaken." She pointed to her own right eye, tapping her cheekbone just below it. "You don't often see eyepatches. I guess that threw me."

"This ol' thing?" Janice Wynn sneered as she lifted the black fabric patch and leaned forward to display the sinewy hole where Holden's bright blue eye had once been. "Catfight. Looks worse than it is. But you should see the other gal."

"And who would that be, Janice?"

"That Cassie chick. She really got the shit end of the stick, lemme tell ya."

Pretending to rifle through her papers, Siobhan spoke without looking up, her nerves firing off warning shots. For the first time since their interviews had begun, the head of Forensics had to force herself to concentrate to keep her voice from cracking.

"Oh yes? How so?"

Janice leaned ominously forward, a single, cold steel-blue eye locking onto Siobhan's. Janice's lips curled slightly. Not into a smile, but into something humorless; dark and threatening. Each of her slow breaths amplified the sensation of menace, making Siobhan feel small and powerless in Janice's suffocating presence.

"Because the bitch is dead," Janice Wynn sneered. "No use for her anymore. Much like you, you big sloppy C-U-Next-Tuesday." Now Janice leaned back in her seat, threw back her head and guffawed. "There's no one else here now, but me. So I don't really care about what day it is. I don't care about your interview. I don't care about your analysis. And I sure as shit don't give a rat's ass about any cocksucking thing that comes out of your Mick whore of a mouth."

It was an extreme response. More than extreme. And Siobhan bristled. Still, something felt off. She'd been introduced to Janice just once before. And while that interview had been brief, Janice had presented herself in a way that was somewhat socially awkward, yet charming. It was a perfect overlay for the role she fulfilled as the lure for children like little Lyndsey Roe. She hadn't come across as disagreeable in any way in that meeting, let alone caustic. Not even a bit.

This Janice seemed more like Solomon.

Or maybe it was an act.

"Janice. I would like to speak with Holden. Can you ask him to come into the light, please?"

Slapping the table, Janice laughed loud and hard. "Now why would I do that? Because you want to analyze him some more? See if he's fit to be strapped into that great green monster in the basement so he can suck on hydrogen cyanide until every cell in his body dies a slow, excruciating death by suffocation? He's quite fine where he is, thank you. The shadows suit him."

"Because I have something for him, that's why. Something I think he'll like." Siobhan sat forward, bolstered by the eagerness which slept across her interviewee's face. "Or should I say, I have some*one* for him."

She signaled to the armed guards just beyond the interview room and they unlocked the door. While never taking their eyes off their prisoner at the table, they held the door open as a woman stepped tentatively through, something small and uneasy fidgeting beneath a blanket.

Playing it cool, Janice sat upright, her expression little more than detached disinterest. She crossed her arms and adopted an air of aloofness. But she did not take her eye off the door.

Siobhan, on the other hand, studied Janice's face intently as she made their introduction.

"Janice, I'd like to introduce you to Ms. Patricia Brewster."

And there it was—the slightest twitch in Janice's left eye. While the rest of her stature remained staunchly unresponsive, that eye had just belied the pretense.

"I believe you know one another? Patricia, this is Janice Wynn. Janice, this is Patricia Brewster."

Janice smirked and tightened her arms over her chest as much as the handcuffs would allow. "No idea who this bitch is."

At the sound of her voice, the thing beneath the blanket in Patricia's arms began to squirm.

"You sure?" Siobhan asked. "I seem to think you not only know one another, but are friends. Close friends."

"Best friends," Patricia interjected, her voice shaking. Wet and jittering every which way, her eyes focused on everything and anything but the person who had once been her Cassie.

Patricia Brewster sidled next to Siobhan, standing at what felt a safer angle behind the psychiatrist's chair.

"See?" Siobhan confirmed. "Best friends. She recognizes you."

"She's full of shit, is what she is. And a disgusting lesbo," Janice denounced, her sour face twisting into a snarl. "I can tell by the smell of her nasty poontang. It reeks all the way over here." Janice wrinkled her nose then spat, a ball of gelatinous mucous splatting onto the table.

And the writhing blanket in Patricia's arms jiggled free.

"Oh, and this little gal," Siobhan declared, "is Isabella."

Flailing free of Patricia's arms, Bella leapt onto the table. Slipping and sliding, her little paws scurried across its surface, her entire body wriggling back and forth as she erupted into a series of ecstatic barks.

She leapt into Janice's arms and licked every inch of her face.

Janice did nothing.

But the recognition was evident.

To Siobhan Jacobs, it was unmistakable. "That has to feel amazing, doesn't it, Cassie? To not only see, but actually feel, your

Bella Luna in your arms once more?"

Janice pushed the dog away, a hard but calculated swipe so that it would flit across the table but not slide off. Instantly, Bella was pawing for purchase to scrabble back to her mommy.

This time Janice swiped at her harder, and Bella yelped and flew off the table.

Siobhan caught her before she hit the floor, and immediately called the guards to take the dog away to safety.

"That seemed a bit extreme, don'tcha think, Janice? I mean, who doesn't like dogs? You're locked away in here for six months already, with a lifetime of isolation lying ahead of you, and you don't enjoy the affection from a little pup who clearly misses you? Feels a bit...*odd*. Some might even say, *contrived*."

Jacobs gestured for Patricia Brewster to take a seat in the chair she'd just vacated, but the café owner remained standing. Her face had blanched, her expression troubled and tense, and Siobhan was certain she could see the pulse of Cassie's friend throbbing in her neck.

Janice had no reply, but the sternness in her face had softened.

"Janice, I'm going to share something with you," Siobhan said. "And I want you to be honest with me. Can you do that?"

Sticking to her position, Janice merely tilted her head.

Siobhan shrugged. "Fine. I'll take your silence as consensus. So here it is, in a nutshell. If I deem you competent today, Holden, you're going to trial. You'll be found guilty, we both already know this, and, like you said, you'll go to the gas chamber."

Janice's eye—Holden's eye—did not blink.

"Or," Siobhan countered, "you come clean with me. Admit everything. And I write up a report that says you're incapable of understanding the consequences of your actions, so we can get you the help you need. It may not be the life you—or Cassie— thought you would have. But you'll be alive. And you'll be in a Federal medical institution with some limited freedoms and choices, instead of waiting in San Quentin for your life to end."

Siobhan perched on the edge of the table, her body language open and vulnerable.

"The FBI have approached me. They want to help you."

Janice/Holden laughed. "And why would they do that, exactly?"

"Because they want to study you. They're launching a program to better understand people like you. They help you; you help them. *Quid pro quo.* It's ready when you are. The only catch is that you wouldn't be in California. The therapy is at an institution back east. A highly respected facility called Barrow Moor."

In response to this, Holden's good eye flitted to Patricia, then back to Jacobs, looking less and less like Janice and more like the handsome, compassionate face of the man Hannah Wilson had fallen in love with.

"She can come visit you, yes," Siobhan assured. "And even your sweet little Bella Luna. All you have to do is say the word."

Jacobs allowed the silence to consume them as Janice all but disappeared and Holden shrank in his seat, his cuffed wrists jangling as he nervously tapped the tabletop.

In the corner, stock-still, Patricia Brewster did everything in her power not to break down into a flood of tears.

"Tell her, Cass," she implored, though the person she spoke to now looked very little like the friend she so loved. "Tell her you want help. I understand it now. All of it. It's not your fault. That was someone else who did all of those horrible things, not you. Not my Cassie."

And Holden Albrighton broke into tears.

)(

When he composed himself, the voice was now Cassie's; the expressions were Cassie's; even the features of Holden's face had changed just enough that they had become Cassie Kennedy's

"I'm *so* sorry for what I put you through," Cassie told Patty. "How could you ever even begin to forgive me?"

She held out her cuffed hands and spread them apart, beckoning an embrace, and Patty Brewster sprung toward her, arms wide as tears glistened on her cheeks.

Siobhan Jacobs grabbed her by the elbow and pulled her back, restraining her from reaching across the desk.

But Patty twisted away.

She stumbled around the desk and threw her arms around her friend. "I've missed you, Cass," Patty whispered in her friend's ear. "God, I've missed you. Bella misses you. How did any of this ever happen?"

Twitching and lifting her cuffed hands to her head, Cassie pulled back just enough to look her friend in the eye. She rubbed her temple, squinting.

"These damn headaches…" She grimaced, a pitiable pout drooping the corners of her mouth; shook her head as if fending off a stubborn, lingering sleepiness. "I miss you, too, Pat."

Not Patricia. Not Patty. Not Trish… but Pat.

And Patty pulled away.

Or tried to.

But Cassie's voice had grown heavy; masculine. Her single eye had followed suit. No longer soft and remorseful, it was the dagger-sharp eye of the identity claiming to be Janice Wynn.

Everything from this point on occurred as if in slow motion:

Siobhan twisted toward the door, her ginger hair sweeping around her in a flowing arc.

Wide-eyed, the guard on the other side lunged for the handle.

From somewhere down the corridor, Bella began barking.

And Holden Albrighton captured Patty Brewster in a perilous embrace by sweeping his cuffed hands over her head and pulling her to him in one seamlessly executed move.

"*Don't worry, Trish,*" he whispered in Patty's ear, his voice steady and calm. *"I really did love you when I was Cassie. But Solomon will never let me go. I knew he was in me, all along. If I had been brave enough, I would've stopped him. This is the only way left."*

With a violent heave, he tossed Patty to the side. Ensuring the guard had a clear shot—and with no one left between them—Holden rushed the door.

) (

Cassie never took her eyes off Patty.

Not even when the bullet tore through her chest.

"Take care of my precious Bella Luna," she bade her friend as she stepped into the light where Holden was waiting for her, his arms open wide.

And Janice receded into the darkness.

Where Solomon, too, was waiting...

∞

DID YOU ENJOY THE STORY?

Your positive feedback is especially valuable for independent authors like me! It helps the books you love reach more readers like you who will enjoy them, too! So, I'd be honored if you'd take a moment to post a rating with a brief comment about your experience on Amazon, Goodreads, or your favorite book site. Thank you for your support!

JOIN MY INNER SANCTUM

Receive personal updates pre-release offers, free book swag and more before anyone else! Sign up for free at

AGMOCK.COM

STRIKE UP A CONVERSATION

Instagram • Facebook • Twitter • YouTube

@AGMOCKAUTHOR

** WARNING: SPOILERS! **

REFRAIN FROM READING UNTIL YOU HAVE FINISHED THE BOOK

WHEN I FIRST had the idea to write *Now is the Time of Monsters*, I had no idea the toll it would take on my own emotional and psychological wellbeing. "This will be fun," I told myself as I dove into the research, starting with a week-long trip to San Francisco where I walked mile upon city mile, rode the cable cars and trolleys, chatted with locals and tourists alike, and genuinely just got a feel for the real vibe and history of this colorful town.

As a method writer, I immerse myself into the world of my story and characters on a very personal level. In many ways, I *am* my characters. So, portraying the mental struggles of Cassie Kennedy, our primary protagonist, became *my* struggles—on a very real level. Add to this the inherent challenges of writing a character who is not only believable but intriguing...without giving away the fact that she is both the protagonist and antagonist at once...and I had myself a recipe for emotional turmoil on a daily basis for over nine months.

For the story to feel as legitimate as possible, I'm proud to have engaged in more research for this book than any other project to date. These efforts included studies on Dissociation, the contemporary history of San Francisco (in particular, Haight-Ashbury and the youth counter-culture movement of the 60s) and extensive research into serial killers from Ed Gein to Charles Manson, Edmund Kemper, Ted Bundy, John Wayne Gacy, Jeffrey Dahmer, the Zodiac, and others. Much of the Gemini in *Now is the Time of Monsters* is an amalgam of them all.

Armed with a new understanding of Cassie's unique disorder, along with an enhanced knowledge of the history and *modus operandi* of some of America's most notorious killers, I then dove into the FBI's publication, 'Serial Murder: Multi-Disciplinary Perspectives for Investigators' issued by the Behavioral Analysis Unit-2 of the National Center for the Analysis of Violent Crime, Critical Incident Response Group. I hope the result is a character and story that are both credible enough to be real.

It's very important to note that this is not about gender or sexual identity. Dissociative Identity Disorder (known as Multiple Personality Disorder in the 1960s) is the fragmentation of one's identity in order to cope with extreme trauma. It most commonly occurs from intense and repeated abuse as a child, and may include both genders, as each alter identity created serves a critical role in the child's coping mechanisms. These may follow the child into adulthood...sometimes being integral to their entire lives. It is also important to clarify that an individual who suffers from varying degrees of dissociative states is in no way more disposed or less disposed to violent behavior. Like all of us, some may have the propensity to be. (Though oversimplistic, the phrase 'hurt people hurt people' is a sad reality for many caught in a cycle of generational abuse.)

Please keep in mind that despite the extensive research as well as having many factual aspects woven into the storyline, this is a work of fiction—a 'what if' proposition to intrigue and entertain.

If it also helps raise awareness and/or talking points centered around the sensitive and important issue of mental health, then I am honored to have catalyzed such important conversations.

For a free **Readers Discussion / Book Club Guide**, the true crime facts I combined into this story, acknowledgments, research list and a free Spotify playlist to get you into a groovy '60s mood, visit AGMock.com/Readers-Guides or scan the QR CODE.

SCAN FOR GUIDES

A.G. MOCK *is an award-winning thriller & suspense*
writer whose career spans both the UK and the US.
He currently lives in rural South Carolina with his
incredibly patient wife, two peculiarly challenging
but adorable rescue dogs, and at least one brazen
ghost who likes to clatter about in the upstairs rooms
and occasionally fill the house with a distinctive
scent of warm leather, vanilla and tobacco.
His wife and dogs he treasures wildly...
...the ghost he can leave or take.
NOW IS THE TIME OF MONSTERS *is his fourth novel.*

EpochThrillers.com
AGMock.com

Made in United States
North Haven, CT
13 December 2024